Praise for Thomas Mallon's

TWO MOONS

"Mallon has a fabulous eye for the people at the edge of the historical picture. . . . The poisonous Washington atmosphere of hateful Reconstruction politics, tinged by the specter of malaria, practically seeps from the pages of the book. . . . *Two Moons* is a novel about a quaint kind of homegrown ambition and optimism that is uniquely American. You could call Thomas Mallon either a dreamy scholar or a scholarly dreamer. Either way, his fiction is as lucent as moonlight."
— *The Washington Post*

"[A] playful, bittersweet, nearly perfect novel. . . . The book's blend of brainy repartee, soulful poignancy and literary game-playing calls to mind the work of Tom Stoppard. . . . Droll, probing and heartbreaking. . . . Keeping one eye on the cosmos and another on its characters' dreaming and scheming, the book does justice to the charms, struggles and inconsequence of human affairs in its own or any other era."
— *Chicago Tribune*

"Mallon spreads, like a tapestry, a defining historical moment. He then illuminates it through the lives of its minor players, both real and imagined. . . . *Two Moons* is rich in texture and atmosphere."
— *Star Tribune* (Minneapolis)

THOMAS MALLON

Two Moons

Thomas Mallon is the author of eight novels, including *Water-gate*, *Henry and Clara*, *Dewey Defeats Truman*, and *Fellow Travelers*, and seven works of nonfiction. He is a frequent contributor to *The New Yorker* and *The New York Times Book Review*, among other publications.

www.thomasmallon.com

TWO MOONS

a novel

THOMAS MALLON

Vintage Books

A Division of Random House LLC

New York

FIRST VINTAGE BOOKS EDITION, FEBRUARY 2015

Copyright © 2000 by Thomas Mallon

All rights reserved. Published in the United States by Vintage Books,
a division of Random House LLC, New York, and distributed in Canada by
Random House of Canada Limited, Toronto, Penguin Random House
companies. Originally published in hardcover in the United States by
Pantheon Books, a division of Random House LLC, New York, in 2000.

Vintage and colophon are registered trademarks of Random House LLC.

The Library of Congress has cataloged the Pantheon edition as follows:
Mallon, Thomas.
Two moons / Thomas Mallon.
p.   cm.
I. Title.
PS3563.A43157   T96 2000   813'.54—dc21 99-34235

Vintage Books Trade Paperback ISBN: 978-1-101-87252-9
eBook ISBN: 978-1-101-87254-3

Book design by Fearn Cutler de Vicq
Author photograph © William Bodenschatz

Printed in the United States of America
10 9 8 7 6 5 4 3 2 1

For Andrea Barrett

In the present state of our terrestrial system immortal bodies cannot exist. Had immortality been intended for man on earth, Infinite Wisdom would have adopted another plan . . .

—*Celestial Scenery; or, The Wonders of the Planetary System Displayed,* 1839

Open thy lattice, Love,
Listen to me,
In the voyage of life,
Love our pilot will be.
He'll sit at the helm
Wherever we rove,
And steer by the lodestar
He kindled above.

—*Stephen Foster*

TWO MOONS

ONE

The black ball rose up the flagpole. Spotting it from two blocks east, Cynthia May allowed herself to slow down. The hoisting of the canvas sphere, as big across as a wagon wheel, meant that ten minutes remained until noon, when Potomac ferry captains and fat boarding-house mistresses all over northwest Washington would watch it drop and reset their clocks, and she would be due inside the Naval Observatory for her appointment.

She crossed E Street at the corner of Virginia, taking off her hat as she went. March 8th, and already so hot that, after twenty blocks of walking, she'd sweated through the skimpy silk lining beneath the straw. With the hat in one hand and her book in the other, she had no hand free to hold her nose against the stink coming up from the water filling half the street. She wondered why the whole swamp that was Foggy Bottom didn't sink, once and for all, into the river; and why the steps of the young man who'd been following her at a constant distance these past few blocks now seemed farther away. Had he been slowed by the smell, or by the thin streak of gray he'd no doubt noticed in her hair as soon as she took off her bonnet?

She turned around to smile, to show him the thirty-five years on the face atop her still-slim frame and, God only knew how, still-fast carriage. The boy looked startled, but appreciative, as if pleased to be fooled by such a handsome woman, however much she might be past eligibility for his serious attention.

She stepped onto the Observatory grounds, this supposed park without a bench to be found. Lifting her skirts and drawing them tight, she hoped to minimize the grass stains they were bound to acquire from the patch of shaded lawn she picked to sit on, a dozen feet from some clerks eating an early lunch. "You filthy thing," she hissed, smacking the mosquito on her bare wrist. *"Die."* She closed her eyes, determined, before the interview, to compose herself against the unnatural heat of this city; even now, a quarter century after leaving New Hampshire as a ten-year-old girl, she would not accept it. It was *winter.*

Her eyes still shut, she soundlessly recited five trigonometric formulae. Her numbers were fine; fixed and reliable, as she knew they would be. It was her appearance that was shaking her confidence, the spinsterish agitation her face might betray. *Perhaps a bit hysterical,* she could picture the examiners noting at the bottom of her paper, until they realized she was not a spinster but a widow, and their amusement turned to something worse, a depressed sort of pity that would make them decide how, all things being equal (or not) among the candidates, they'd really be better off having some bumptious young man about.

Even before noon arrived, she had worked her anticipated resentments into a grudge that felt actual, even long-standing. Rising to her feet, briskly enough to startle the nearby diners, she strode toward the building's east wing and into the Chronometer Room, where in a voice more loud than was necessary she greeted a young man bent over his desk.

"I am Cynthia May," she said. "I have an appointment with Professor Newcomb."

Mrs. John May, she was about to add, in case the fellow mistook what she'd told him for two Christian names, like Mary Jane, as people often did. But he just held up his left hand, like a policeman, indicating she should come no closer and say no more. With his other hand he tapped a telegraph key. A second later, up above, she heard a light thump.

"Time ball," he said, grinning broadly as he beckoned her forward with the same hand he'd used to halt her. "My one tap makes it fall, and gives Western Union their signal. So they can set all their clocks."

Surprised that the boy's keystroke should connect her to people far from the local ferry captains and boardinghouse mistresses, to cities not seething with faction and heat, she let her own face relax into a smile. More quietly than before, she said: "Mrs. John May, for—"

"If it's Professor Newcomb you want, you don't want me," said the boy. "But the truth is you don't want him either, not just yet. If you're here about the computer's job, you're wanted first in Davis's office." He crooked his finger and drew a path on the air. "He likes to look 'em over."

Who could "he" be? Admiral Charles Davis had died three weeks ago. Cynthia knew so from both the *Evening Star* and Fanny Christian's most recent gentleman caller, a young ensign whose presence one evening at the boarders' table had been a rare concession from Mrs. O'Toole. Approaching the admiral's office, she could see that she was right: Charles H. Davis was now no more than his portrait, which hung outside the door, draped in black, the late subject's walrus mustache and rectangular flaps of hair quite immobile and unwelcoming.

Inside, she took her place on a bench between the two other applicants. Standing beside a desk, a much younger man, with the same flaps of hair and mustache, looked her up and down quite neutrally, not pausing in his drone of instructions to a slim, balding clerk whose nameplate identifed him as Mr. Harrison. "Tell Professor Baird at the Smithsonian that he may bring his party of ladies here to look through the Great Equatorial *if* he gives us plenty of advance warning, *if* the night they pick turns out to be clear, and *if* they get here *early*."

"Yes, Commander Davis," said the clerk.

"The *son*," whispered the job-seeker at Cynthia's right. "A lieutenant commander. Also Charles H. He was attached here when the old man was carried off. They've made him officer-in-charge until the new superintendent comes on."

Cynthia watched the younger Davis brush away a length of hair that hung in limp contrast to the stiff wisp of gold braid sparkling his uniform.

"Professor Newcomb will be along any moment," Mr. Harrison said to Cynthia, repeating the explanation he must already have given the others, his soft tone an apology for the lieutenant commander's preoccupation.

"*Then,*" said Davis, still standing over his clerk, "you can tell Mr. Morrison that the narrative of the polar expedition is *not* yet ready for issue, and when you're done with that you can write Mr. Watson up in Oswego and tell him that the report he requests of the 1874 Transit of Venus is not yet published. That's right," he said, looking over to the applicants, as if to warn them of the Observatory's chronically short appropriations, "eighteen hundred and seventy-*four.*" And with that he marched back from Mr. Harrison's desk to his own.

The young officer was clearly overwhelmed, whether with mourning or his temporary responsibilities, Cynthia could not tell. Whichever the case, her sympathies lay more naturally with the hard-worked Mr. Harrison, who was already into his ink bottle, turning the lieutenant commander's complaints into correspondence. His labors would go more quickly with a Remington, she thought, though the acquisition of one here anytime soon had to be unlikely, given how everything else seemed behind schedule. The Interior Department, where she worked, had just purchased a half dozen of the machines—the first cause of her presence here today. When she'd heard that the reward for mastering the Remington's use and listening to its sixfold clatter in the clerks' room would be only fifty cents more a day, she had decided to act upon a piece of information picked up from Fanny Christian's gentleman caller.

"They're hiring another computer to work with the stargazers," he'd said in mocking awe of the scientists whose perimeter he sometimes paraded along. "Some of those fellows have domes bigger than the one on the building," he'd added, provoking such laughter that Cynthia had been able to slip away from the table without excusing herself. For the past eight nights, she had sat in her room working with *The Principles of Trigonometry,* an almost forgotten prize-book she had carried away from Miss Wilton's School for Young Ladies in Laconia, and brought with her to all the places, comfortable and shabby, that she had called home for the past twenty years. Always good with numbers—"freakishly so," Miss Wilton had said—she had made it her business to find out what the Observatory position entailed. She decided that, with a week of cramming, she just might escape her desk at Interior. Instead of becoming a typewriter, she would make herself a computer.

Despite the lieutenant commander's hints of institutional poverty, the Observatory job paid a dollar a day more than the one she had, an amount no doubt equally compelling to the two aspirants she sat between, a dismayingly pretty girl, probably no more than twenty-five, and a plump young man whose finger-poppings seemed louder to her nervous ears than the clatter of the Remingtons she was truant from today. She'd sent a note around to her department early in the morning, claiming to be ill. As it was, three days after President Hayes's swearing-in, the new Secretary's men would be too busy looking for the money the old Secretary's men had stolen to notice the absence of one female copyist.

"If you would fill these out," Mr. Harrison said, handing the applicants writing boards with forms headed PERSONAL INFORMATION.

All right, then: *May, Cynthia.* Not like Mary Jane. She wrote her name in the Spencerian hand she'd struggled to master twenty years ago, and which Remington would soon kill off just as surely as if he'd blasted it with one of his revolvers. DATE AND PLACE OF BIRTH: *April 10, 1842, Laconia, New Hampshire.* Where it would still, quite sensibly, *be* winter, and Mr. Harrison and the put-upon lieutenant commander would be warming their hands at the same open stove, and getting a bit friendlier for it. She looked left, into the lap of her distaff competition. Even worse than she'd feared: *b. 1855.* Oh, honestly.

PRESENT ADDRESS: The first word looked more like a command than an adjective, an order to embarrass herself into admitting that 203 F Street, Mrs. O'Toole's peeling green lodging house, was her only remaining perch in the world. LENGTH OF STAY AT PRESENT ADDRESS: Having to put down "7 months," the seven long months since she'd left the *last* lodging house (nearly as bad as the current one) seemed an affront, and so she wrote down *24 years,* the amount of time she had lived, one way or another, in the District of Columbia, ever since her father, Frederick Lawrence, the bank manager in Laconia, had hitched his family's then-prosperous wagon to the little shooting star that was Franklin Pierce.

Fred Lawrence's usefulness to the curly-haired lawyer during a state constitutional convention in 1850 had earned him a summons to Washington at the start of 1853, to work under old Mr. Guthrie in the Treasury. Cynthia could still recall that man's Kentucky accent and wide-brimmed hat from the one visit she and her eleven-year-old twin brother had been permitted to make to the department early in Mr. Pierce's single, unsatisfactory term, during which the bank in Laconia failed, leaving her father to decide, even as Mr. Buchanan came in and the country began seriously to shatter, that Washington would now be a better place to sustain his family. Within five years, his bad judgment and the rebellion had reduced him to little more than a scrivener, who moved his family from one set of rooms to another, each smaller than the last. Frederick Lawrence, in his soft, pious voice, would remind them that they were hardly starving, though he ceased to use that word when information came, in the summer of 1864, that Frederick Lawrence, Jr., had in fact starved to death, at Andersonville.

NAME OF WIFE, the form requested. Mr. Harrison's courteous inked carat—"or husband"—prompted Cynthia to write *Sgt. John May, dec. 1863, Chickamauga.* Married less than three months before that battle, she had brought her child into the world six months later. There was even a place for Sally on the form. A box marked CHILDREN, a small clerkly grave for *daughter, d. 1870, diphtheria.* Two years after Cynthia's father; five months before her mother.

For the last six years there had been no mouth to feed but her own, at the hotel restaurants and boardinghouse tables along F Street. From one rented room to the next, she carried with her what few pictures, books, and spoons she could stand to look at or afford not to sell.

Johnstown, Pennsylvania: so that's where the chubby knuckle-cracker next to her had come from. Go home, Mr.—what is it?—Gilworth. Go home and leave this job to me.

Could they *please* get on with the test itself? Having completed the sheet of personal questions, she put down her writing board and opened up her book, surprised, once she did, by the absence from the page of cosines and tangents. So accustomed had she become to seeing *The Principles of Trigonometry* open at her pillow and plate that she only now remembered how Hawthorne's *Life of Franklin Pierce* was the book she had carried with her this morning, determined to sell it for whatever it would fetch. She no longer had any desire to possess this nearly last family heirloom, a campaign tract signed by both author and subject; the symbol of her father's wrong turn. Whether or not she came home with this new job, she would come back with money for a new dress, something with no collar and plenty of color, something she could not wear to the Interior Department in the daily pursuit of Mrs. O'Toole's rent and her own weekly bag of oranges, which were cheaper than the doctor or tonic she'd require without them.

Where was the celebrated Professor Newcomb, inventor of the clock-drive on the Observatory's biggest telescope? Mr. Harrison had promised, the other day when she'd come to inquire about the position, that the great man would administer the examination himself, and the young man who had just entered the room and begun exchanging words with Lieutenant Commander Davis could surely not be he. So pretty and slender, scarcely older, she guessed, than "b. 1855." But the little roll of papers in his hand did look as if they might be examinations. He was tapping the baton they made against his cheek. Looked at all together, the blush of his brow and the blankness of the paper and the color of his eyes made a sort of red, white, and blue bunting, the banner at a summer picnic or—on second thought, against the black mourning of his hair—the flag upon a coffin. He was approaching them now; the slightly crooked teeth in his emergent grin making him look even younger, less a preoccupied intellect than a fellow of feeling and mischief.

"This is Professor Allison," explained Mr. Harrison, who had come out from behind his desk to make the introductions. "He will conduct the examination in the library."

They were led off single file, clear to the west wing, all the time listening to the young astronomer's Carolina accent. "Professor Newcomb couldn't make it, I'm afraid. He's been called away to a meeting. I don't know where or with whom. Perhaps the head of the Royal Society, or the empress of Brazil. I'm to be your poor substitute." He gave a humorous bow, his frock coat, Cynthia noted, nipping attractively into the slim waist. "You can take your places and get started," he said, pointing to some desks beneath shelves holding hundreds of ledgers. "It's all fairly clear on the page. But if anything is not, I shall be wandering in and out, and you can grab my arm and ask your questions." With that he was gone, leaving them with one another and the printed exam books.

She did have questions, the ones she often wished to pose to merry young men on the streets and to women like "b. 1855": What is it like to have missed the war, to have scampered through those years as a child, and to be living today in the here and now, not walking through an eternal aftermath? What must it be like to hear politicians speak of "reconstruction" as a civic task, duly planned and just completed, instead of a word for what would never come to your own inner dwelling, whose wooden beams remained split and strewn by the tempest?

The following exercises are to determine with what degree of accuracy and rapidity you can use the tables of logarithms. Since no mistake must be made in your work it is necessary that, after writing down each logarithm, you read it off from your paper, look back in the table, get the corresponding number, and see if it agrees with that given on the paper. You must proceed in reverse order in taking out numbers corresponding to logarithms. Write neatly and carefully and write your name on each sheet of paper.

"B. 1855" would have no trouble following the neatness injunction. Her examination and logarithms book were perfectly aligned on her desk; the extra pencil she'd brought lay perpendicular to both. Not a strand of her upswept hair dangled from her small straw hat.

Exercise in 5-Place Logarithms. From the following values of log cot α find α (to the nearest tenth of a minute), and then log sin α, log cos α, log β cos α and β cos α. log β = 0.10909. The algebraic signs in the first column are those of the cotangents themselves.

Cynthia's last look around before beginning revealed a now fretful Mr. Gilworth of Johnstown, Pa. Could he really be finding this exercise so difficult? She set about filling in the table, sprinkling the numbers like raisins into a cupcake tin. It was more soothing than sewing, and less of a strain on the eye.

log cot α-	α	log sin α	log cos α	log β- cos α	β cos α
+0.99102	5° 49.7'	9.00672	9.99775	0.10684	+1.27891
+9.82162	56° 27.0'	9.92086	9.74247	9.85156	+0.71048

Her columns grew longer, and if she squinted at them, the confetti of inkings began to resemble a skyful of stars. She had time to let her mind wander. The Magi's search for Bethlehem; the music of Milton's crystal spheres; the prognostications of the D Street astrologer in whose parlor Cynthia had lately spent a dollar she could not afford: they could all be reduced to these numbers. There was actually no need to squint and pretend that the digits were the stars. They were, by themselves, wildly alive, fact and symbol of the vast, cool distances in which one located the light of different worlds.

She knew, from some long-ago visits here with her father and mother—a free weeknight amusement—that the Transit Circle, through which the men see stars cross the meridian, lay just beyond the walls of this room. The astronomers look up and watch the stars come in and out of their line of sight, and as the night wears on and the men grow tired—she is sure of this, so strongly has she imagined it—they have to feel it is not the axis of the earth, but the stars themselves that move. *Parallax*—she had recited the definition several times while she lay in bed studying this week—"the apparent change in the position of an object caused by a change in the viewing position of the observer." What a comforting delusion, what an exaltation, when the object is a star, and the "viewing position" this Earth no God would choose for the center of His universe.

As her columns lengthened and she went on to problems no. 2 and 3, she heard schoolchildren shuffling through the hall outside. Elsewhere pieces of equipment were being wheeled and crated. Here in the library the astronomers came and went in quiet, disputatious pairs—the older ones wearing full beards, the younger just muttonchops or a mustache—to fetch down a volume and settle a point. And yet, all this activity was only preparation or postscript. This was a theater, and what counted could not happen until night fell.

Mr. Gilworth was left-handed, and he attracted Cynthia's attention when his numerical jottings, so much slower than her own, gave way to a fast cursive movement. Added to the distressed expression on his face, it could mean only one thing: he had thrown in the towel and was writing a note to the examiner, like the wretched pupil he had no doubt always been back in Johnstown, Pennsylvania. A moment later, on his feet and trying to salvage some dignity, he put a small sour grape into her ear. "You know the dead admiral?" he whispered. "The elder Davis? Don't believe what you read in the *Star*. It was malaria that killed him. And you know where he got it." He pointed straight down, meaning "right here," though nothing could feel more salubrious than the unaccountably cool confines of this hushed library. "Take care of yourself," he said.

She gave him the smallest of smiles as he retreated, leaving his half-done exam on the farthermost desk. If he didn't go home to Pennsylvania, she decided, Mr. Gilworth had a great future. He was in a city that would always require men who can change what they want on an expedient dime.

She was finished, and hoping they'd notice how she'd done the whole thing in ink, without one cross-out. Should she open Hawthorne's life of Pierce? Or would that be too showy a way of idling out the time remaining, during which "b. 1855," she could see, was still slowly, and in pencil, proceeding with what she wagered was only problem no. 2.

They are going to pick me. A week from now, instead of trudging up the stone steps of the Patent Building and into the Interior Department, I shall be coming here each morning to calculate the men's infinite gazings upon the night before. Yes, Professor Allison—he had come back into the room for the first time—you are going to pick me.

Right now he stood over "b. 1855," looking at her paper—without interest, Cynthia judged; not displeased, but certainly not impressed, either. She looked back down at her own work. No, whatever the girl was still doing, it wasn't going to be good enough; not as good as what she herself had already accomplished without a flaw. And would accomplish every day, just as perfectly, in dresses more colorful than the ones on the hook back in her room. Surely, their eyes having been fixed on the stars all night, the navy men here, come daylight, would not mind a rustling of bright fabric, however old its female wearer.

He approached, reentering her field of vision, crossing *her* meridian, the polished centermost floorboard in front of her desk. He looked at her paper, upside down, his head bowed low over it, to compensate for his vantage point. And when he raised his head, his face, flushed and smiling, rose up like the sun.

"Cynthia May," he said, pointing to the name she had obediently inscribed upon each sheet.

"Yes," she replied, looking into his eyes. "Like Mary Jane."

•   •   •

"I'll cut your tongue out!" cried Mary Costello. She scooped up Ra, the yellow tabby who had his paw in the cream and looked as if he might splash a drop or two on her silk wrapper or—worse yet, sweet Jaysus!—the chart she was preparing for the man himself. "Away with you, now," she murmured, kissing the old cat and placing him in a patch of sun on the windowsill above her hand-painted sign: "Madam Costello, Disciple of Mlle. Lenormand, Paris. PLANET READER." It was a big day here at the corner of Third and D Streets. "Mustn't make a mess," she cautioned Ra, making her way back to the consulting table. "Not with our magnificent Scorpion coming."

The senator, as he'd told her on his single previous visit, had a birthdate of October 30, 1829, seven days into his Sun sign, which, according to Master Gabriel's *Gospel of the Stars,* open next to the teapot, made him and those similarly born "full of courage and anger and much given to flattery. Many promises will they make and little will they perform. After the serpent's fashion they will beguile those who trust them and with smiling faces will lure their enemies to destruction."

"Well!" laughed Mary Costello. "We can't go telling him *that,* can we, pussums?" Unworried by Master Gabriel's dire trumpetings, she poured herself another cup of tea. The sky, thank heavens, held as many explanations as it did stars. Whatever the Sun failed to yield, the moon could supply; what the monthly cycles would deny you, the hourly ones might provide. Born at noon, or close to it, the senator could safely be promised measures of fame and prosperity even greater than those he already enjoyed.

Did she have time to peruse one of Master Gabriel's competitors before he arrived? She consulted the clock on the mantelpiece. It always ran behind, and for a moment she wished she might live nearer the river, close enough to see the ball drop at noon. Clients had a right to expect a certain *precision,* and a clock such as hers, unable to keep up with Earth's movement through the heavens, must surely fail to inspire confidence. She draped a scarf over it, hiding the face if not the ticking, and went back to her books and her chart-in-progress. Her predictions for the senator's absent wife, home in Utica, and for his mistress in her mansion above the city, were phrased so politely they would sound more like inquiries after the health of family members than nuggets of celestial information designed to manage his movements between the women.

"I shall never keep all the politics in my head, ain't that so, Ra?" If the senator did become a real client, she would have to take the *Star* regularly, not buy it every third or fourth day and put it into the canary's cage half-read. She had trouble enough keeping straight what she actually knew of the sun, moon, and stars; how would she manage the long list of the senator's enemies and concerns?

Well, this wouldn't be the first load Mary Costello had hoisted in her forty-seven years; and she was a much quicker study of earthly mortals than the spheres that swirled around them. Ten minutes after he'd pulled her doorbell on Sunday night, a complete surprise, she had a pretty good idea as to why the senator had come to seek her out. He was, he'd told her, responsible for the President due to be enthroned the following morning. Having more or less created the commission that settled the mad, disputed election in favor of Governor Hayes, he stood as the Prime Mover, the hand that had flung the Sun into position. And yet, she could tell that this knowledge had left him, maybe for the first time in his life, afraid and resentful. Having failed to become the Sun himself (what he really craved), and newly aware of those seeking to banish him where no light shone at all, the senator had reached a secret crisis in his fortunes and confidence. So he had come to her in the night, looking over his well-muscled shoulder, dressed in his magnificent clothes and face and voice, this gorgeous brute requiring whatever reassurance she could call down from the stars.

She looked around for her turban—not a piece of professional paraphernalia, just something she used to hide her thinning hair. "Now, don't I look *lovely*, pussums?" She laughed at herself in the mirror, before taking the window seat below Ra's sill. Together they looked out onto the street, toward the people getting down from the trolley: the women, sweating in their velvet; the anxious, office-seeking men, moving between their hotels and whichever new Cabinet Secretary they'd be calling on next. She usually welcomed drop-ins, but the senator had instructed her to keep the decks clear this afternoon, and she had hung a "by appointment only" shingle beneath the placard invoking Mlle. Lenormand.

She hoped he wouldn't ask for a complete horoscope, at least not yet. Only with great difficulty—using lima beans to calculate, when she ran out of fingers—had she located the moon's position in his Sun sign. Numbers and history had never been her suit. When told, ten years ago, back in Chicago, that the twelve signs of the Zodiac matched up to the twelve tribes of Israel, she'd asked Iris Cummings just who these twelve tribes were, and how come they hadn't turned into a baker's dozen under the hot desert sun.

Looking over the windowsill and down at her sign, Mary Costello realized that these days she sometimes thought she *had* been a pupil of Mlle. Lenormand's, and that Mlle. Lenormand really was a famous Parisian planet reader instead of a name she'd found on the label inside a hat at Cooley & Wardsworth's. If the truth be told (but who had to tell it?), it was Iris Cummings who'd taught her the stars. Iris, the smallest girl at Madame Lou Harper's establishment on Monroe Street, but smart as could be; could talk about Venus and Jupiter by the hour whenever she came into the Hankinses' gambling house, where Mary Costello in those days wiped tables. Al and George had loved superstition; behind the bar, amidst the pinochle decks, there was always a pack of tarot cards, and they craved hearing little Iris go on about all the mysteries that only *seem* beyond our reckoning. Mary had started making notes, first inside her head and then on a tablet she kept in her shack one street behind Hair Trigger Block.

She'd picked up plenty, certainly enough to tell the senator that the moon in Scorpio is an evil thing, and that those born with it require quite a bundle of additional planetary influences to keep from hurting other folk. Yes, she *could* tell him that, but what she'd learned in life—more important than all she'd learned from little Iris or Master Gabriel—would make her keep her trap shut about this unattractive lunar truth. She gave people as much knowledge as they could comfortably stand, and no more.

Candles: lit or unlit? "What do you think, pussums?" Unlit, she decided. The senator sought not hocus-pocus but expertise, a heavenly species of the facts and figures his committees knotted into laws and budgets. Wearing a bracelet or two less wouldn't hurt, either. She slid one off her wrist just as the doorbell rang. Fluffing her turban, she looked out the window and saw—oh, *bejaysus!*—not the senator at all, but that tiresome girl, that tall bird of an Aries who lived a couple of streets away and had been here a week or so ago. And what for? She mocked the stars' predictions even as she sought them. Every other female who came up these steps settled for an encouraging word about a lover or a legacy, but this one couldn't make clear what she was seeking to know. Now, how to get rid of her quickly?

"The *sign*, Mrs. May. Please read the sign!" Madam Costello reached over the windowsill and tapped the "by appointment only" board.

"No," said Cynthia May. "Reading signs is *your* job. Can't you let me in for one fast question?"

A different look lay upon the younger woman's face today, nothing like the pinched and pawnbrokered aspect that had come to the door just a week ago. You'd have thought she'd found love *and* a legacy since then.

"Oh, come *in*," said Mary Costello, trying to grumble, though secretly grateful for some company to take the edge off waiting for the visitor she was beginning to fear would never show.

Cynthia bustled up the steps. "I won't even take tea," she said. "I won't even sit down."

"Darlin'," said Mary Costello. "You're practically giggling. And if you commence to, I'm sure to start giggling meself." She immediately proceeded to, prompted by her guest's improved disposition and her own habit of snatching any sign of cheer, like a stick of firewood, to keep her spirits alight.

"My question is this," said Cynthia May. "Does a person's coloration tell you anything about him? The way his hair and eyes and flesh come into harmony, like an artist's paints?"

Madam Costello looked puzzled, then disapproving. "I think you want one of the ancient humorists, dear, those that could tell you whether the look of someone's face means a lot of blood or too much bile. I could never read anyone's temper or future that way. Never thought of studyin' the phrenology, either. All that muckin' about on somebody's scalp." She affected a little shudder. "Long ago I had the chance to be a hairdresser, but I thought it a foul opportunity. Now, is this all about a feller?"

"New employment, actually," said Cynthia. "Though a gentleman figures into it. If I knew his birthdate, I'd ask you something astrological. But I don't."

"Now, didn't I tell you, seems like just the other day, you'd soon be in a new position!"

"You mentioned nothing of the kind," said Cynthia.

"Well, I should have," replied Madam Costello. "You looked as if you were needin' one. You was nothing like the blooming creature before me." She glanced over at the clock, only to see the scarf that covered it. "Now, *I'm* about to enter a new situation, too, missy. So you'll have to be off."

"A new client?"

Mary Costello laughed. "A new *patron,* let's say."

"Someone important."

"Well, yes, but I mustn't say more."

Of course, she *did* say more, and started to say it within ten seconds, because she had never really had a patron before, certainly not on the order of this one. Her excitement and her sympathy for this peculiar woman got the better of her resolve, kept these past four days, not to jinx the senator's business by discussing him with anyone but Ra. She and Mrs. May were soon sitting at the consulting table, drinking the tea she'd planned on offering the man himself. As the clock ticked away under its veil, Mary Costello tried to drown the sound, along with her gathering doubts, by pouring out her whole life's story. She chattered through her past at the same speed with which she took clients through their futures. Before Mrs. May was halfway through her cup, she knew the whole tale of Mary Costello's departure from Cobh at the height of the famine. How, her first husband already dead, she'd arrived in the New World half starved and too ugly for the gamahucher that became the lot of half the girls with the strength to walk off the ship. How she'd cooked and sold papers at three different railway stations, until she arrived at the great western terminus of Chicago, where she found herself a second husband, a pork seller who made a pile, or at least a half of one, purveying meats to the soldiers at Camp Douglas. How he died of his own new wealth, carried off by the flux that entered his fat body with the drinking water from the river, dark as gravy some days, running with all the unsalable bits beaten out of the poor animals you could hear and smell dying every hour.

From then on she'd worked in saloons, the best of them the Hankinses' gambling house, and never complained about her shack near Hair Trigger, tar and felt being a grand sight better than the thatch in Galway she could still recall. Of course, even tar and felt couldn't survive the Fire; but *she* did, spending the nights in Lincoln Park and getting her first good laugh since the flames started when the *Tribune*'s editorial— "CHEER UP"—blew past her feet. That she could read it at all was thanks to her first husband, bless his soul, who had taught her, letter by letter and word by word, before the blight took their whole green world.

He had a sister who'd ended up in Washington, and Mary had, by some miracle, through every disaster and displacement on the twenty years' journey, stayed in touch with her. It was she who got Mary here and on her feet, explaining that this city was every bit as much about the making of money as Chicago. And so, six years later, Mary sat in this parlor with her little business that did tolerably well but could surely use the munificence of a grand fellow like the senator, and—oh, why ever was she telling the girl all this?

"You left out Mlle. Lenormand," said Cynthia.

"So I did," said Madam Costello. "And much else besides." She read Mrs. May's quick expression, and could see that she understood there never was a Mlle. Lenormand; and then the two women laughed together.

"May I offer you this?" asked Cynthia. It was the *Life of Franklin Pierce,* which she extracted from her pocket and slid across the table. "It's worth ten dollars, I guarantee."

"And why would you be offerin' it?"

"Because I want you to read the planets for me. All spring and summer, whenever I want to come, though I'll take care not to arrive when your important customer is on the premises."

"Now, miss," said Mary Costello, her face falling from fear that the man was never coming around again. "Since you know there was no Mlle. Lenormand for me to be a disciple of, why would you still be wanting me to look into the stars for you?"

"Who is to say that what you know, however you know it, isn't so? Maybe whoever *did* teach you truly knew a thing or two."

"Oh, Iris Cummings knew a thing or two, that's for sure!" said Mary Costello. "All you had to see was the look on Big Jim Gunn just after he'd been with her!" Her loud laughter made Ra turn his head. "Ah, miss, I don't know," she sighed, opening up Mrs. May's book to see the signatures of subject and author. "Well, Jaysus Mary. This would be the one that was President?" She pointed to the black ink, thinking how much this might have impressed the senator if only he'd kept his word and come. In any case, ten dollars was nothing to be sneezed—

"Almighty!" cried Mary Costello, as the doorbell rang. She and

Cynthia jumped from their seats. "All right, missy, readings through the summer whenever you like, though right now you're to be off with yourself. Immediately!"

Cynthia had gone to lean out the open window and see just who was on the steps. He must be six foot three, she thought, resisting Madam Costello's tug at her waist. The single curl that fell halfway down his brow, the beard that jutted to a sharp point: both had as much gray in them as gold, enough to make her suppose that this fine-looking man—growing impatient, she could see—might be closer to fifty than forty. But for all that—"Oh, *no!*" she cried at her sudden realization. "It's *Conkling!*" She took care to whisper the identification as she spun around and looked at Madam Costello. "You slyboots."

There was no amusement, no female conspiracy, in the astrologer's expression. She wanted Mrs. May out *now,* and Mrs. May knew it. So Cynthia gathered her skirts and headed for the door, one step ahead of the lady of the house. But when she got her hand on the doorknob, she turned around to say: "He's just as one of the other boarders described him. Joan Park sat in the ladies' gallery for half his speech, the one that finally settled the election. She nearly drooled the details of his appearance to all of us at supper."

Cynthia opened the door. Roscoe Conkling—who had spent an active amatory life hoping never to be surprised by a second woman in any room where he had arranged to meet but one—drew back, though only for a moment.

He stared at her, then tipped his hat.

"I was just leaving," said Cynthia.

His entrance into the parlor prevented that. He crossed the threshold and came forward like a wave, forcing her to step backward. Madam Costello rushed to take his hat and gloves.

"What a shame," said Conkling, ignoring the astrologer to look straight at her previous client. "Are you off to meet your fortune?"

"I met it earlier this afternoon. At least that's what I hope," said

Cynthia, who began moving toward the door. "I think you'll hear the spheres playing a wonderful tune today."

"Then I can trust her to set them in the proper motion?" he asked, pointing to the planet reader.

Cynthia just smiled and took a step forward.

"Here we go, sir," said Mary Costello, urging the senator into the parlor with a sweep of her hand.

Conkling continued to stare at Cynthia. He yielded no ground, forcing the younger woman to walk around him in order to exit.

She descended the steps to the street, not daring to look back, and only after what seemed a long time did she hear the door shut.

Out on the sidewalk, just a few paces away from the house, stood a young man with thick spectacles and a waistcoat shiny from wear. "Excuse me," he asked her, with as much abruptness as apology, as if he had long since learned to be unembarrassed when accosting strangers. "The gentleman you were speaking to: that was Conkling, wasn't it?"

Alarmed by the sheer need and avidity in the man's gaunt face, Cynthia replied: "He never gave me his name."

"I know it's him," said the young man, starting a great rush of words. "I've been following him for two blocks. I need a job, you see. I've knocked on every undersecretary's door and come up with nothing. I've been waiting for some help from fate. I know that's what it takes, and I'll bet this is it. Do you know how long he'll be inside there? Do you think he'll speak to me when he comes out?"

"I've no idea," said Cynthia, in response to both questions. She wanted to calm the man, to ask him who he was and how he'd come to the District, but she couldn't make herself do it. He was too desperate a version of herself; their very kinship made her want to get away. He was the sort of person she was *ceasing* to be, and he felt like bad luck. How fortunate she felt to have her own hopes depending on the lovely Mr. Hugh Allison instead of the great "Lord Roscoe."

The young man went on talking. "I'm going to wait at the bottom of those steps." For the moment, though, he allowed himself to lean against the lamppost. Cynthia could tell he'd not had much to eat of late. "I've been here for a month and a half," he explained. "And never imagined it would be so confusing—nobody knowing which party was about to take over, nobody listening to anyone else. But everyone listens to *him*," he said, pointing to the house containing Conkling. "Isn't that so? Isn't that what they all say? If he could only steer me in the right direction, I know I'd be able to do the rest. All I need—"

The young man fell suddenly silent, dumbstruck by what he'd just noticed at the parlor window. Cynthia looked over her shoulder to see what it might be.

Framed between the musty swags of curtain, Roscoe Conkling calmly glared at the sidewalk; behind him and to the side stood the astrologer, still helplessly holding his gloves and hat.

After a few seconds, the senator raised his hand, pointed to the young man, and with a slash of his index finger indicated that he was to be off, immediately. The threadbare fellow raced across the street and out of sight, as if he'd been hit with a stick. Cynthia, sickened with inert sympathy, watched his terrified dash before looking back toward the window, where Roscoe Conkling stared at her for a few long last seconds, and then nodded twice, as if saying yes to something, for both of them.

• • •

"Tell him that I want him. Now."

Roscoe Conkling hit the punching bag with his bare fist. The stunned leather rattled its metal stanchion, and the Arlington Hotel's bellboy cried "Yes, sir!" before taking off in search of the fellow who ran errands for the residents.

Stripped to the waist, Conkling resumed his workout, refusing to take a bite of his boiled fish and spinach, or even a sip of soda water, until he had given the bag two hundred jabs. His colleagues might be over at Wormley's, bloating themselves on venison and hock, but at forty-seven, he remained as lean as when he'd entered the Senate ten years ago, and he was determined not to put on a pound or an inch in the ten years to come.

If he could stand it here that long. Ten years *already,* and no higher? It wasn't Hayes's going to the White House that bothered him so much. Better that the stolid old Buckeye, still full of holes from the war, had gotten the nomination than James G. Blaine, Conkling's chief rival for mastery of rhetoric and the Republican party, who for years had mocked his looks and strut. No, he thought, breaking the first bit of skin on his knuckles tonight, the problem wasn't even Blaine. It was Evarts, the New York lawyer just named Secretary of State. What a brazen reward it appeared! Nominating the man who'd argued and won the President's case before the Electoral Commission! A commission that Roscoe Conkling had created, to decide the disputed election and keep the Republic—already by December bristling with Democratic and Republican militias—from yet again rending itself in two.

Hayes now claimed to have intended naming Evarts all along, and he was so dully honest he was probably telling the truth. But, Conkling thought, the sweat running down him now, the scandal wasn't even in how it looked; the scandal was in what it would *mean,* to him, Roscoe Conkling, and the Republican party in the state of New York, which was only to say Roscoe Conkling twice, for he and the state party were one and the same.

Evarts and the President were over-mindful of the Democrats' anger; too sensitive to whispers about "His Fraudulency" having been set up in the Executive Mansion without truly having won the election; too embarrassed by what they were finding in (or missing from) Grant's cupboards. They had caught the nervous malady of reform and were looking for remedies: palliatives for their foes, smelling salts for themselves. They were readying bills to raise an army of "Civil Service" clerks, each full of "merit," a procession of worker ants loyal to no one but themselves. If Evarts had his way, they would soon be infesting the New York Custom House—*Roscoe Conkling's* Custom House, the great turbine of patronage through which foreign goods passed so that money and grateful labor might pour forth upon Republican candidates, all over the city and state of New York. Evarts had never cooperated, never understood; he was blind to the beauty of the machine, as gleaming and efficient as the Corliss engine, whose towers and platforms and unimaginable horsepower had sent shudders through last year's centennial crowds in Philadelphia.

If he had guessed it would be Evarts (and he should have), he would have built, he now swore to himself, an electoral commission that would have thrown the disputed prize to Tilden—yes, by God, to the Democrats who'd made the rebellion and soaked the country in blood. Now, three days after Hayes's almost furtive inauguration, there was little he could do to stop Evarts's nomination. He had tied it up in committee, but within a day or two he would have to let it out, and see whether Hayes and his new Secretary destroyed the Custom House before Roscoe Conkling could make himself—or, once more, Grant—President in 1880.

He sat down at his desk, a towel draped over his shoulders. The day was cooling off. A breeze blew into these rooms where, no matter how many politicians came calling, no cigar had ever been lit. He looked down at the neat stacks on the three sides of his blotter: his thick, gilt-edged notepaper; the pamphlet in which his commission speech had been reprinted; the encomiums from the foreign press (clipped and sent by Custom House agents who guided the papers through the port of New York). Beyond these accolades, what was his reward for all this statesmanship? *Evarts.*

Perhaps he had been wrong, four years ago, to refuse Grant's offer of the Chief Justiceship. He'd thought: he already had the Chief Justice's daughter; did he need the late Salmon P. Chase's job, too? Kate herself had argued against his filling her papa's robes. She had seen bigger things, the biggest of all, ahead for him. And back then she'd believed, so long as she possessed her children and the favors of

Roscoe Conkling, that she could endure her marriage to the drunken whelp Sprague. By now, though, Sprague's sodden tyranny had sapped her cheeks and spirit. Even when absent from it, traipsing through Europe alone in the old Chief Justice's Washington house, she was no longer the girl whose looks and temperament, during the war, had enraged Mrs. Lincoln and enchanted every man left in the District of Columbia. She had grown, if not timid, then tired, and if weariness were all that Roscoe Conkling required, he might as well bring his own wallflower, Julia, down from Utica, where all these years, for both their sakes, he'd kept her stored. Julia meant recess—not just the congressional kind, during which he saw her and their daughter, Bessie, but a recess of the spirit, too, the dullness and retraction that always came upon him when he was out of Washington and in her presence.

That Kate might be fading into a copy of Julia; that his own political fortunes might be leading him back to Oneida County instead of the Executive Mansion just blocks from here: these terrible forebodings had drawn him, twice now, to the Irishwoman's parlor at Third and D. A sense that destiny might be slipping from the War God of the Norsemen (a sobriquet he liked, though he feared it was a coinage of Blaine's) had sent him looking for some destiny he might have overlooked, a better sort than the faltering one that now loomed; something hidden in the sky behind a bank of clouds that his own keen eyesight had not managed to pierce. He had been looking at the stars for years, gazing blankly at them from a hundred porches and lawns onto which he'd gone to escape the smoke of his colleagues. The other night, unwilling to watch those men cough bits of tobacco and turtle soup into the spittoons at Wormley's, he'd stayed here, opening up the window and his Shakespeare.

He read the Bard straight through each year, not just so he might quote him, but to find himself in the pages. And on Sunday night he had found himself in Edmund, ranting with self-satisfaction in the first act of *Lear*:

This is the excellent foppery of the world, that when we are sick in fortune, often the surfeits of our own behavior, we make guilty of our disasters the sun, the moon, and stars; as if we were villains on necessity; fools by heavenly compulsion; knaves, thieves, and treachers by heavenly predominance; drunkards, liars, and adulterers by an enforced obedience of planetary influence; and all that we are evil in, by a divine thrusting on. An admirable evasion of whoremaster man, to lay his goatish disposition on the charge of a star.

It was Roscoe Conkling he'd heard in the cut and thrust of those lines. This was the voice he sent up to the galleries, to Kate Chase Sprague and the women he didn't even know; the voice with which he beat back every fool on the floor who lacked his head for figures and for consequences and for the long historical view. But it was a voice whose sudden hollowness, in all of a moment on Sunday night, he'd begun to fear. He'd felt an overpowering urge to seek its opposite, to turn its empty certainties inside out, to reverse the tide of its cheap scorn.

And so he had headed out to Trinity Episcopal at Third and C, where during the war, when it was a makeshift hospital and he a new congressman, he used to see the boys from his district bleeding through their bandages. In the years since, he had sometimes repaired there to think. But on Sunday night, a block before it, he had passed the planet reader's signboard. He had always read, and always resisted, the astrologers' notices in the *Star*. But this time he had gotten to Trinity only after he'd given in and called at the Irishwoman's; he sat in the church to consider what she'd told him. He was moving out of Mars' control toward that of Jupiter, which ruled a man in his years past fifty, bestowing on him more respect and less contention, increasing his "gravity" in a way the Irishwoman made seem literal and heavy. But, she had added, before he could cross over to the new planet's dull protection, he must first, beginning this October, pass through his forty-ninth year, one of the grand climacterics for a man, full of snares to health and fortune.

It had sounded more actuarial than astrological, but for all that, nearer the heavens than the false altitude of Capitol Hill, whose thick, overheated air he'd been choking on lately. If he were again to believe in himself, or even *be* himself, he required something new to believe in, a secret, even a ridiculous one. This winter he had experienced the first real illness of his life, a loss of vitality that had him, in January, collapsing in the Senate cloakroom after giving the two-day speech now preserved in these pamphlets on the desk. Almost an hour had passed before he roared back over the border of consciousness. He'd felt a doctor slapping alcohol onto his back and tried to throw him off. But the two senators who'd dragged him home from the chamber to his couch at the Arlington pushed him back down, and made him submit to their judgment that he was too sick to attend the evening session. Even so, the following morning he strode down the aisle, ten minutes late and sicker than anyone knew. Light-headed though he might have been, he instantly realized, from the hush accompanying his entrance, that he had carried the day—and saved the Republic as surely as the general had a dozen years before.

The whole episode was a harbinger of the dread climacteric, and he had decided he would fight it off, grab it by the throat and squeeze it, as if it were Blaine (who came to him in dreams) or even death itself. He would live again by asserting his will, by once more vanquishing something. His great act of conciliation, of statesmanship, had yielded nothing but Evarts. From now on, he would seek only victories, shunning compromise like the slow, fatiguing poison it had proved itself. He required an enemy, and he required a woman, a new one, who would first bewitch him and then surrender.

Still waiting for the errand boy, Conkling thought for the second time that day of Franklin Pierce. He would have nothing of him back in 1852. Still in his early twenties then, defending forgers one year, prosecuting slanderers the next, he'd gained his first political foothold with the Whigs, canvassing Utica against Pierce and for General Scott. Why should the Irishwoman have had that old campaign biography out? Did it signify, he wondered, her ability to reverse the disastrous course of his current planetary influence? Think of it, after all: what had proved better for him than Scott's defeat and Pierce's victory? With the Whigs past reviving, the time for the Republican party, the home of all his victories, had arrived. So who knew what disguise his current celestial blessings wore? Yes, the book was an encouraging token. Even if it wasn't what he now most wanted from Madam Costello.

"It's about time!" he shouted down the stairs, at the first sound of the hotel's dogsbody. "You'll have a dime for this and nothing more." He instructed the boy to carry an envelope with a gilt-edged note to the woman who did business at the southeast corner of Third and D. "Wait for a reply," he said, somewhat more softly, realizing it was this lad who would be bringing him what the note politely demanded of Mary Costello: the name and address of the woman he'd passed coming through her door.

•   •   •

"And then," said Commodore Sands, caught between a laugh and a wheeze, aiming his diminished voice into Hugh Allison's politely lowered ear, "he's supposed to have tapped the hull and said, 'The damned thing's hollow!'" The retired officer, both palms pressing on the tip of his cane, rocked in his chair until his long white beard shook. "'The damned thing's hollow!'"

Hugh laughed, too, even though the story of the new Navy Secretary's amazement over what floated the vessels in his charge had been making the rounds for several days; and even though he knew the old commodore's merriment would soon dissolve into quiet gloom over the service's lost luster: Thompson, the landlubbing Hoosier who had gotten Navy as a political reward, had fewer than thirty hollow hulls to keep track of.

"He can't be worse than his predecessor, sir."

"What's that?"

"I said I doubt he'll steal so much as Mr. Robeson did."

"Oh, yes, you're right about that. You're right about that, son."

Benjamin Sands patted Hugh Allison's arm, the gesture demonstrating both kindliness and his desire to leave. Three years after his retirement, he still came out to the Observatory for an occasional look through the twenty-six-inch Great Equatorial, the glory acquistion of his tenure. Tonight, however, as so often, the mists swirling over Foggy Bottom had failed to clear. The dome would not be opened up.

"Shall I take you home, sir?"

"No, no, Mr. Allison. I've got one of my sons-in-law coming to fetch me. You go about your business. I'll wait for him outside."

"Good night, sir."

"Good night, son. And mind you don't fall asleep here."

"No, sir."

"Where have you got your rooms?"

"Up in Georgetown, sir."

"A good mile away?"

"At least."

"Good, good. You need respites from all this." He twitched his nose and waggled his finger, and Hugh nodded his understanding; the old man was referring to the unhealthful air beyond the dome.

The commodore began shuffling off. "Poor Davis, eh? Poor Davis."

His younger but now dead successor had shaken with chills through much of the winter. These past few weeks Davis's son and interim replacement, now bustling into the dome, had shaken mostly with impatience, as he struggled to bring the Observatory's affairs into some sort of order. "It was old Sands," he now complained to Hugh, "who started letting you prima donnas streak around like your comets, doing whatever you please."

"You can hardly blame me," Hugh replied with a laugh the lieutenant commander failed to appreciate. "I only got here last summer."

But Davis's point was well taken. It was why the civilian astronomers had loved the old commodore; he'd understood that their enthusiasms and eurekas would not take flight if confined by navy discipline and limited to navy needs.

Tonight Hugh was supposed to train the Great Equatorial on some double stars that Pulkowa Observatory near Saint Petersburg had asked the Americans to help investigate. An old friend of his up in Cambridge was working on the problem, too, and getting more or less nowhere, something the great Professor Newcomb took pleasure in teasing Hugh about. Any minute that would start again, since Newcomb was inside the dome, too, nipping at Davis's heels, reminding the acting superintendent of another perquisite he had somehow neglected to bestow upon Simon Newcomb.

He might be the handsomest among them, thought Hugh, but Newcomb's lush brown hair, one wing of it combed out to look as if it were catching a breeze, was more appropriate to some painter working his will on the models in a Paris atelier. He was, in fact, a seducer—not of women, but of the legislators and club presidents and hostesses who then advanced Simon Newcomb's reputation for both genius and a charming ability to inspire public understanding of the arcane work performed by himself and his less glamorous colleagues.

"I'll tell you something, Allison." He had just clapped Hugh on the back. "A few years from now, you'll be able to pick up a telephone and ask your Harvard mate exactly what the weather is doing up at his end. And then, on nights when it's fine down here, and he tells you it's fine up there as well, you can let *him* look for your double stars, and *I* can have another night under the eyepiece here! What do you say?"

Hugh just smiled. He was supposed to be grateful for the teasing, grateful the man had noticed him; but if he answered Newcomb's question, he'd soon be required to blush with pleasure over the imitation of his Southern accent—affectionate, of course!—that was sure to ensue. And if he chose to tease the man back, to say that the use of "mate" betrayed Newcomb's origins (Canadian) just as surely as Hugh Allison's soft vowels did his, the response would be a stiff little smile, a signal that Mr. Allison, just six years out of Harvard College, was decidedly out of line.

So he said nothing, and walked back to the little table with the paperwork he'd brought to occupy him while waiting on the weather. That reference to the "telephone": it was exactly like Newcomb to have on his lips the very thing whose "possibilities" all the clubwomen and lecture-going clerks in town, armed with two inches' worth of knowledge from the *Star*, were buzzing about these days. They spoke, for all of ten seconds, about the latest "miracle" God had wrought, before turning to the more pressing subject of the patent wars breaking out over the instrument, and who finally stood to make the most money from it. When the Observatory was rigged with a telephone, it would surely be Newcomb's doing, and as he talked into it—to the program chairman inviting him to speak, or the *Leslie's Illustrated* editor asking him for a scientific pronouncement on the modern world aborning— he would never realize how the telephone's wires only stitched him more tightly to the earth and its noise. When Simon Newcomb spoke to audiences about the "outer planets," they widened their eyes at the vasty phrase, unaware that the eminent man's specialty made him, to Hugh Allison's way of thinking, no more than a cosmic housecat, afraid to quit the solar system's verandah for the true open spaces of the universe.

Hugh would have preferred anyone else's company in the dome tonight, even that of dour Asaph Hall, so serious and secretive in his pursuits, a man who had struggled through life while Newcomb swanned. More self-taught than schooled, Hall had had to interrupt his early career for stints at carpentry and computation, all the while encouraged by his religious, grudge-collecting wife, who still governed him as the tides did the moon. Alas, only Newcomb stood here now, Davis having scurried off to deal, even at this late hour, with one more unpaid bill and leaky pipe.

Would the new permanent superintendent, whoever he turned out to be, keep giving them the latitude the commodore had established as the norm? Bless the old man. Hugh could picture him last year, just after his own arrival, standing in line to greet Dom Pedro, the visiting emperor so hungry for American wonders. Benjamin Sands, who fifty years before had sailed along the Brazilian coast in the *Vandalia,* ended up being too shy to impart this reminiscence, since it would have meant interrupting Newcomb, who was reassuring Dom Pedro and his empress, at considerable length, that from now on he would make certain they received, back in São Paulo, each and every monograph he produced.

The paperwork before Hugh was perilously dull. If he wasn't careful, he really would fall asleep here. He ought to start back for his rooms, but the thought of lying there alone, amidst all the Moorish furniture his mother had imported at Charleston and then sent north, made him linger in the dome, taking the one-in-a-hundred chance the skies would clear and Newcomb would give the signal to open up.

He looked over at the Great Equatorial, its mouth closed, its long gullet denied the spoon-feeding of light they'd meant to bring it tonight. For all its hugeness, and all the clock-driven power that kept it moving with the objects of its attention, the telescope was oddly unassertive, a receptor, never sending forth any light of its own. Between his index finger and thumb, Hugh took one of the gold buttons on his vest and twisted it, until the metal disk caught a flare of gaslight; then he wiggled it, so that the reflection played, like a djinn eager for escape, against the highest metal in the dome. Newcomb, sensing something above him, but not quite sure where or what it was, looked quizzically at Hugh, who let go of the button and looked down at an item of work he had promised Davis to have done before morning.

If you put the three examinations side by side, there was no comparison. Poor Mr. Gilworth had taken himself out of the running, and the younger of the ladies, for all the prettiness of her hand, was clearly too slow at her calculations. So that was that. He took a sheet of stationery from the table's little drawer: "Mr. Harrison," he wrote. "Please send a note to this Cynthia May—whatever her last name is—and have her report on Monday morning."

TWO

Mrs. May, you ought to be getting home now. It's nearly six."

"I could go a bit further with this one, Professor Harkness." She pointed to the photographic plate, made in Tasmania on December 8, 1874. "It's one of yours."

"Ah, yes," said William Harkness, the trace of a Scottish infancy in his voice. He regarded his three-year-old labors. "Not a very good plate, either. None of them is." He sounded apologetic, as if the bad weather that had greeted the Transit of Venus teams that day in '74 remained his fault, and the whole expedition had been a spendthrift act.

"Not at all," said Cynthia. "The image here is quite clear, almost sharp." She pointed to a small dot of planet crossing the Sun. "And the numbers are coming fine."

The numbers were, in fact, not so fine. The trigonometric reductions that would yield Earth's distance from the Sun—once the speed of Venus's transit across the star was factored in—were, in truth, still hopelessly incomplete. Not from any flaw in Cynthia May's mathematics—Professor Harkness had more than once marveled at her exactitude and speed—but by a cluster of coefficients beyond his control. Congressional appropriations for the work had proved as unreliable as the Pacific skies three Decembers ago. Cynthia was the only computer now assigned to the 237 pictures the astronomers had managed to shoot, and there was no telling how soon they would have to shift her to something else. Realizing that this transit would not be the lustrous career-enhancer it had once appeared, Simon Newcomb, formerly much involved, had stepped discreetly out of Venus's shadow and back into the moonlight of his prior research, where he would stay until some other part of the sky disclosed an opportunity for his shooting star. Quiet Professor Harkness had been left holding the bag.

"May I walk you eastward?" he asked. "I'm about ready to leave myself."

He lived in Lafayette Square, and if she looked at the case objectively, the way Fanny Christian would, she'd be rushing to put away her papers and slide rule in order to join him. William Harkness, a bachelor turning forty, impressed her as solid and solicitous, but he wore the dullness men put on once they'd become disappointed with themselves. This ought to be a fascinating creature, thought Cynthia: what other navy man or scientific here could claim earlier careers as a newspaper reporter and army surgeon? But now, stranded on Venus, his beard going gray, Professor Harkness was a curiously routine specimen, a gentleman preoccupied by numbers, no different from the men she'd grown used to at Interior.

"Professor, I'm going to stay and finish two more calculations. Not the whole plate, I promise."

"Very well, Mrs. May. We all appreciate your zeal. But do make sure not to stay past six-thirty."

If it were up to her, she'd stay past nine, by which hour she'd have a chance to spot Hugh Allison, arriving for his night's labors. In the seven weeks she'd been here, she had seen him only twice, when some daytime errand had him calling on Mr. Harrison or the Observatory's librarian. Even then she'd merely spied him through the window of this little room they'd put her in, just beyond the one in which they kept the ships' chronometers, hundreds of them, here for adjustment and repair, ticking madly, practically begging to get up and walk, as in some fairy tale. Spending six days a week in here, she scarcely saw the other computers or the astronomers, let alone the 9.6-inch refractor and the Great Equatorial, whose nightly grindings didn't commence until she was asleep at Mrs. O'Toole's. "And where does Mr. Allison focus his attention?" she'd once asked Professor Harkness. "I don't know that he *does* focus" was the only response.

Even so, she would not lose her new optimism, her belief that this job might lead not only to more money but to some imaginative perspective from which she could regard herself as the denizen of some faraway star instead of the overheated little District of Columbia. Venus, alas, was failing to prove such an alternative home, not with Professor Harkness as its sober governor and her own attentions limited to the planet's movements on one day three years ago. Still, each evening when it came time to put away her ruler and turn down the lamp, she felt a certain pride in the accuracy of her work. She never had more than a dozen eraser shavings to sweep from her desk before walking out to the Observatory's lobby.

There, right now, beside the pier of the 9.6-inch, whose tube and lenses were concealed on the third floor under the dome, she ran into Mr. Harrison, who was putting on a pair of gloves.

"How fancy we are," she said, fingering the writer's bump on her own bare middle finger as she watched the clerk struggle into the tight gray kid. "What might be the occasion for these?"

"I'm going to meet our future," he grunted, not looking up from his efforts.

How cryptic we are, too, she thought, waving good night and stepping off into Foggy Bottom's already thickening air. The stink hit her as forcefully as ever. The only remedy was to keep moving, exactly what the stagnant pond on E Street as well as the Potomac itself—more a lake than a river by the time it reached this basin—refused to do. As her long legs scissored east at a great clip, she again congratulated herself on not wearing any face enamel, which would only be soaking in the moisture and smells and making her carry them home. Fanny

Christian was all excited about some new powders she kept on her vanity table, insisting they might soon replace paint completely, but her evangelism had little chance of converting Cynthia, who had never applied a drop of the old stuff, not even during the first year of the war, when she'd been trying to catch John May's eye.

"My racehorse," he used to call her, both to compliment and mock her stringy vigor. Sometimes she was like a cat with the evening crazies, quick-pacing the parlor to no clear purpose. Vitality was shooting out of her now. She'd felt it starting to burn hours before; by six o'clock it had become the chief reason not to join Professor Harkness on his bachelor's stroll home. She was in a mood to cover ground and count streets, to make a long tangential trek, twice the distance and with three times the turns her walk home required.

After several minutes, she was rushing through Lafayette Square, ahead of the professor, for all she knew, and then angling up Vermont Avenue, clear to Fourteenth and M, where a circle of ground had been fenced off for an equestrian statue of General Thomas, "the Rock of Chickamauga." The granite support was already in place, as yet without its horse and rider. The District's new bronze forest of wartime commemorations generally repelled her, but something in Cynthia felt denied by this empty pedestal, so like the bulky first-floor piers of the 9.6-inch and Great Equatorial. She would like to see this general, no doubt wreathed in laurels for having so famously defended his army's left flank—while John May got shot on the right one, to die on a litter during the retreat to Rossville that General Thomas had finally had to make in any case. "One must look at the numbers," she could remember a friend of her father's telling her after the battle. "Sixteen thousand Union losses; eighteen thousand Confederates, Mrs. May. A few more such victories and the Confederacy is done for." He had meant to comfort her with this thought that Chickamauga had not been such a Union defeat as it looked—even if poor Sergeant May, by dying, had failed to contribute to the encouraging ratio.

She started back down the other side of Vermont Avenue. For more than a dozen years she had been in retreat, pretending at first it was the orderly kind that John May's company had made to Rossville. In fact, she had been routed. Half of John's pension had gone to his mother, and she had borrowed so heavily against her own half, to support the three sick and unemployable souls she had left to her, that it was soon gone altogether. In the last months of her daughter's life, when her father was already dead, Cynthia and her mother and Sally had been reduced to a single room. The little girl had coughed in one bed, while Mrs. Lawrence, palsied and delusive, shook in another and Cynthia slept on a pallet between them. In the space of six months, both beds became empty. The morning after Mrs. Lawrence's funeral, perplexed and frightened by the quiet, Cynthia had walked to the washstand and stared at the old, gaunt woman she saw in John May's shaving mirror. Lacking the courage to kill herself, she had instead smashed the glass against the basin. Two days later, blinking at the sun, she emerged from the room; four weeks of searching after that, she was at a desk, paginating government reports from the Indian territories.

These last six years she had marched in a somnolent lockstep, pretending not to care if life drove her to the last ditch. Only recently, hardly daring to admit the change in direction, had she turned around and begun pushing back. Her first nights working with *The Principles of Trigonometry* had been a strictly numerical business, in which the real sum of every problem she solved was the extra dollar a day she hoped to gain by moving from Interior to the Observatory. But the astral purpose of all the numbers soon began to paint her imagination, turning it blue and silver like a night sky. The world acquired a new immensity, and made a thrilling suggestion that the stale, small circle in which she moved might feel huge and giddy if she thought of it as a speck flying through the void. Her mind soon began sliding upon the tangents she was only supposed to be measuring. Today she felt determined to get away from pictures of Venus in its endless frozen transit and find her way up from those ground-floor piers to the actual telescopes.

On Pennsylvania Avenue, she stopped at a sidewalk photo vendor to look at the oval-framed miniatures of yesterday's soldiers and today's Great Men. She flipped through the pictures of blue-coated boys—leftover images, unnamed and unclaimed, taken by camp photographers. She was hoping, as always, to spot one of John May. The odds against this were nearly infinite, but the exercise had a soothing fidelity. She had no photograph or sketch of her dead husband, and she sometimes wondered if she might one day gasp in false recognition at a picture in the bins, one that matched not the John May who had gone to war, but the mutation of his face inside her head after four thousand nights of dreaming alone.

She went through the last half-dozen soldiers in their stiff, proud mattes before moving on to the actors and statesmen, florid poses in floral frames, filling two trays of the seller's bin. She laughed at all the bought-and-paid-for senators straining to look Roman, each jowl arranged for maximum nobility. To think there were people who collected these images, while the boys to their left had lacked anyone at home to send their likenesses—let alone, when the time came, their bodies.

And, wouldn't you know it, here was the funniest one of all. She looked through the thin glass at the long straight nose and pointed beard, under which there was no hint of a jowl. The muscled shoulders and well-developed chest brimmed up against the bottle-green waistcoat, certain to have been tinted the exact shade on the subject's orders to the photographer. A single curl, a corkscrew like Hyperion's, spiraled down a marble forehead toward two eyes whose pupils seemed determined to project light instead of absorb it. "The Hon. Roscoe Conkling, Utica, New York."

It had been a month and a half since his card arrived, along with a ticket to the Senate gallery. They were still in her purse. She had carried them around with continuing annoyance at that stupid Irishwoman, who was surely responsible for their arrival. "Madam Costello" had turned out to be a panderer, no better than the trull who'd taught her planet reading back in Chicago. It angered Cynthia every time she thought of it. The ridiculous incident had put a stop to her astrological readings before they'd begun. At the very least, she ought to go take back her *Life of Franklin Pierce*.

And yet there was, she supposed, another side to the matter. It was not as if she hadn't felt flattered by the great man's absurd attention; those burning eyes of his needed spectacles. And it wasn't as if, having fallen into a new rut, like transiting Venus, she had ceased to be interested in what the other planets' movements might have to say about her future.

She stuffed Conkling's visage behind the less grandiose one of George McCrary, Secretary of War, and gave herself a choice: she could go home, or she could barge in on Madam Costello and set things to rights. If she did the latter, she would be too late for dinner at Mrs. O'Toole's table. But did she not now make $1,150 per annum? Could she not sit down, three hours hence if she so pleased, to eat a chop at any restaurant in town?

She reached back into the bin.

"How much is Conkling?" she asked the vendor.

"Twenty-five cents."

"I'll take him."

•　　•　　•

"You don't like cats," said Madam Costello.

"I *do* like cats," said Cynthia, lifting Ra from her lap and planting him on the floor. "As a species they have their uses." At Mrs. O'Toole's they kept down the mice, creatures Cynthia detested not from female fright, but for their mingy pathos, the sort of neediness she was sure people attributed to *her*, even now, when she was struggling back to something like life.

"It's me you can't abide, ain't it?" asked Madam Costello, pushing forward her lower lip.

Cynthia sighed. "No. But you must know I'm cross with you."

"How couldn't I!" the astrologer moaned, knowing she was about to be forgiven. "Seven weeks since we made our arrangement, and you haven't been back until today! I know I've done *somethin'* wrong."

"You know exactly what you did wrong," said Cynthia. She set Conkling's tinted picture on the table between them.

"What a lad!" cried Madam Costello, fingering the subject's high forehead. " 'War God of the Norsemen,' " she said, reverently.

"More like the Beau of the Post Box," said Cynthia. "Stop being coy, Madam Costello. You know it was you—"

"Call me Mary."

"—who gave him Mrs. O'Toole's address. So he could send me his ridiculous note."

"He has a lovely hand, don't he?"

Cynthia stared, daring the woman to stall her any longer.

"Yes, dearie, I told him where you was at." The astrologer played with the ribbons on her cuff as she searched for a suitable explanation. "I just thought, what with the both of you being creatures of the political life—you remember that book you brought round with you—well, I thought it only a sort of civic service to acquaint the two of you."

Cynthia laughed aloud, and after a few difficult seconds, Madam Costello couldn't help joining in. "I'm sorry. But it's the nature of me work. I *reveal* secrets. I don't keep 'em. And besides, he's safely back in Utica right now, with his wife."

"Poor Mrs. Sprague," said Cynthia.

"Oh, then you know about his lady friend?"

"Every page and barmaid on Capitol Hill knows about the two of them. You can't be much of a soothsayer if *that's* your idea of a secret."

Madam Costello looked hurt, but decided to ignore the remark. "Come summertime Mrs. Sprague can return to the arms of her husband."

"A great pleasure for them both, I'm sure." The two women again laughed together. They doubted whether Kate Chase Sprague, that fading belle who had dazzled the city fifteen years ago, would even bother quitting her late father's Washington mansion to summer at her drunken husband's Rhode Island estate.

"In any case, what does your War God want with someone besides his wife and his mistress? With *me*. He must have some compulsive attraction to the withered."

"Don't go underestimating yourself, Mrs. May. But if it's any comfort, you've got nothin' to worry about from him until June. Maybe even October, if those talkin' in the *Star* are right." Upon confirming Hayes's Cabinet, including Evarts, over Conkling's lofty abstention, Congress had decamped for home, and the President might well decide to wait a whole six months before calling it back into special session.

"You've become quite the expert in public affairs, haven't you, Mary?"

The astrologer was too delighted by this first use of her Christian name to be bothered by the sarcasm, or by Cynthia's reaching for the pile of newspaper cuttings at the far end of the table.

"I have to keep current," protested Mary Costello. "Now don't be disrupting them. They all pertain—"

"To the War God's fortunes, I see," said Cynthia, leafing through the stack. "Here's one you should have circled in red wax: 'The commission soon to be appointed by the Secretary of the Treasury to inquire into alleged irregularities in the New York Custom House, and the alleged perpetration of frauds in the importation of goods . . .' *Alleged* irregularities, indeed! The source of your War God's war chest!"

"I have to read the stars in light of current circumstance," said Madam Costello, with as much grandeur and plausibility as she could summon.

"You mean you tell him what he wants to hear," said Cynthia, as she replaced the clippings on the table.

"The stars don't just illuminate the invisible," said Madam Costello.

"They also make plainer what we can already see. And let me ask you, Mrs. May: if you harbor so many doubts, why have you come back? Surely not just to scold me."

"A good question," said Cynthia. She stood up and walked over to the parlor's small fireplace, fingering some china ornaments on its mantel and carefully choosing her words. "Because I half believe you," she said, not taking her eyes from the object in hand. Once trigonometry had brought her own attention to the stars, she had found herself tempted by astrology's mathematics. They seemed to be a gaudy grease for the heavens' machinery, something to set the spheres moving even faster. "The stars and the planets are too orderly to be without meaning. I doubt your Master Gabriel actually knows how to read that meaning, and I'm certain no Presbyterian preacher has seen into it." She paused to pick up another figurine. "But *I* want to see into it."

"It sounds as if you want me to be teachin' you the trade," said Madam Costello, who quickly corrected herself: "the art of reading the planets."

"Right now," said Cynthia, "I want you to help me see the heavens through a telescope." She walked briskly back to her chair and pulled it close to Mary Costello's. "The first thing I want you to tell me are my prospects for getting off Venus."

Within a few seconds, she had dispelled the astrologer's perplexity, explaining to her the past month and a half with Professor Harkness. She described the comings and goings of the Observatory men, the sights and sounds beyond the walls and above the ceilings. She needed to know the likelihood—and best methods—of penetrating them. Madam Costello listened intently, not even rising when the colored man from the nearby hotel arrived with the dinner pail she ordered three or four nights a week.

"Set it down in back, Charlie. Would you be wantin' to join me, Mrs. May?"

"No," said Cynthia. "And I shouldn't keep—"

"I can warm it later on the stove. Right now I want you to answer me somethin'. What happened to the young feller who figured into things the last time we spoke? The one whose coloring you was so keen on."

Pleased by the astrologer's memory, Cynthia had no hesitation responding: "I'm still not sure what he does. He doesn't advertise himself like Professor Newcomb."

The older woman got up and went over to a bureau near the front of the room. From a middle drawer she extracted a large sheet of paper, which she set down between herself and Cynthia.

"What is this?" the younger woman asked.

"The beginnings of your star chart," said Madam Costello, who pointed to a small annotation at the paper's bottom right corner. MRS. MAY, APRIL 10, 1842. "I'm an honest woman," she explained. "You gave me your book in exchange for my readings, and so I set to work, before you disappeared."

"Tell me my chances of transiting away from Venus."

Madam Costello sighed. "Well, there's all sorts of figurin' to be done. First, we need to know where the moon was when you came forth from your mammy." She took *The Gospel of the Stars* from the top of the bureau and opened it to the chart of constants on page 59. "'Divide the year of birth by 19, multiply the remainder by 11 and divide the result by 30,'" she read, trying to conceal the anxiety that this part of her job always provoked. "'To this remainder add the day of month and the constant according to the above table and divide the result by 30. The remainder will be the moon's age. To find her longitude'"—she pronounced the word with a hard "g"—"'on any date, multiply her age by 12, which will give the number of degrees that are to be added to the Sun's longitude at noon.'"

She reached behind her for some paper and a pencil, wincing as her corset pinched.

"Three hundred and forty-eight degrees," said Cynthia.

"Sweet Jaysus! How did you do that?"

"I applied the constant and did the arithmetic." Impatient with the older woman's marveling, she asked, "Now what do I do with the number? The 348."

"You add it to January 21st, when the Sun enters Aquarius. That'll give you the moon's position when you were born."

"Three hundred and forty-eight days after January 21st is January 4th."

Madam Costello crossed herself to ward off whatever spirit was serving up these instant calculations, and also because the moon in Capricorn was a celestial phenomenon she wished on no one. Stirring with awe and suspicion, she asked Cynthia: "You really done these numbers in your head? And you're really an Aries?"

Cynthia nodded.

"Most Aries have a wound on the head or a birthmark on the foot."

Cynthia invited her to come around to the back of her chair. She lifted the strands of hair that had fallen from her upsweep, and a tiny scar, a white half-moon at the base of her skull, became visible. "A falling icicle from the top of a pine tree. I was six."

Mary Costello looked down at the slim neck and shoulders until a motherly affection for this peculiar overage girl washed out all other conflicting feelings. She patted Cynthia's cheek and went back to her own seat. "You wouldn't know the feller's birthday, would you?"

"Christmas Eve, 1849." Before Madam Costello could attribute this knowledge to further infernal gifts, Cynthia added: "The day I started work I saw Mr. Harrison, the clerk, flip past it in his file, when he was inserting my own card."

"This young man needs you," said Madam Costello, suddenly.

Cynthia gave her a hard look, doubting the older woman could know such a thing without doing her own laborious mathematics.

"But you'll be needing him," said Madam Costello, whose eyes were closed and who seemed to be operating on instinct.

"How can that be?" asked Cynthia, disappointed. As a prediction, this mutual need sounded rather vague.

But Madam Costello was quite definite in her elaboration. "I mean you'll be needing *him*," she said, pointing to Roscoe Conkling's glass-covered picture. "October 30th, 1829. The moon still in Aquarius."

·   ·   ·

Three pillows on the bed—giant puffed worlds of purple, red, and saffron—supported Hugh Allison's head and feet. The great lampshades and ottomans among which he slept, like a sultan with no seraglio, came as a slight shock whenever he arrived home from the smooth brick and tubing of the dome. The pieces his mother had sent were so comically heavy that his bedroom looked ready to sink through the floor below—a dangerous prospect quite opposite from that imparted by the japonaiserie Mrs. Allison had shipped to Harvard Yard in 1867. That assemblage of items had been so light he sometimes thought his plastered room would detach itself from Grays Hall and float away. There his furnishings became the source of some teasing more witty than Simon Newcomb's, but his Southernness had hardly set him apart. Simple chronology united him with his classmates, and set *all* of them apart from the recent Union dead, whose profuse, still-new ghosts turned each lecture hall and dining room into a grim basilica. Born on Christmas Eve 1849, Hugh had joined a civilian regiment of younger brothers, all of them born too late to go. They felt themselves blessed, but derelict, too, as detached from any clear destiny as Mrs. Allison's translucent Japanese birds.

He had stayed on for graduate study and spent several years after that at Harvard's Observatory, arriving here last year as the centennial faded and the election campaign grew white-hot. Newly resident in the District of Columbia, he'd found himself once more a noncombatant, ineligible to vote and, thanks to the commodore, subject to a less military sort of discipline than that preferred by Professor Pickering in Cambridge. Even so, no amount of freedom seemed likely to afford him the opportunity to do the only real work he hoped to accomplish, out far beyond this last double star he'd been investigating.

Although the windows were open, he felt flushed with heat and impatience while trying to answer a letter from his mother. Across his legs lay another of her gifts, a breakfast tray inlaid with a mosaic quotation from the *Rubaiyat;* atop that sat Hugh's thus-far blank piece of writing paper. Mrs. Allison's letter of April 11, lost between a pillow and the silk-covered comforter, expressed relief over the just-commenced withdrawal of federal troops from South Carolina, but so casually that a reader might have thought she was referring to some forty-eight-hour episode instead of a twelve-year occupation. This was her manner, a disproportion universally regarded as charming, even if it also caused, as it did in the incident she reported two paragraphs below, the merciless excoriation of a local shopkeeper who lacked the proper shade of green ribbon.

Mrs. Allison's husband, a shy lawyer more interested in gambling than the courthouse, deferred to her in all things that didn't directly involve cards or horses or dice. Hugh, while growing up, had often tearfully taken the side of some housemaid or cook who'd displeased her. These days he paid attention only to the airier portions of her long epistolary monologues, replying with a light breeze of his own. "Yes, Mother," he began writing. "I had read that the troops were leaving. See what miracles Rutherfraud B. has performed? The other day he spoke to the deaf-mutes at their college here, after viewing marvels of botany and rhetoric they had managed without their full five senses. The *Star,* alas, makes no mention of his having delivered any of them from silence with a clap on the ears."

Deciding to forgo his waistcoat for a venture outside his lodgings, he sealed the letter and tucked it behind his belt. The jade clock showed three-quarters past seven, time for him to go dine somewhere along High Street on his way down to Foggy Bottom.

A street or two from his rooms, not far from an oyster house that looked suitable, he passed the offices of the American Tract Society, where a plainly dressed sidewalk solicitor invited him to put money into any of three boxes: one for the destitute; another for the missions;

and the last for a special collection of "$2,000 to print a life of Christ in the language of Japan."

The undauntedness of this last scheme—its humble reaching through space and time to connect two points—appealed to Hugh's feelings, which these days tended to quicken only when a nerve connecting them to his intellectual occupations was tripped. The hand-painted sign of this gentle tractarian proved just such a stimulus; Hugh reached into his trousers pocket and extracted a half-dollar, which he tossed into the third container.

"God bless you, sir," said the man behind the money box.

"And God love you," Hugh replied, with a smile, having recovered his merriment and faithlessness.

Walking away, a tract in his right hand, he pondered the collector's evident belief in the usefulness of his work, and the certainty with which he had no doubt accepted his post on the pavement. Hugh himself had spent the past few weeks irritated by the pointless task he had been given to perform by the overworked and temporary Lieutenant Commander Davis. Pulled from the double-star investigation he'd been making without much enthusiasm, he was now chasing, all on his own, one fitfully visible comet, plotting its course for a report that would be filed to the Observatory's credit, something the Navy's budget-makers could tally, like a sortie performed or a sinking accomplished. Hugh feared for Commodore Sands's old free rein; if the elder Davis's permanent replacement arrived with a taste for quantifiable results, Hugh Allison might never find himself acting as anything but a small supply ship for the fanfared voyages of Simon Newcomb.

Who besides himself might be under the dome tonight? And what sort of sky would greet him once he crossed New Hampshire Avenue? Would the fog be low enough for them to open up, to begin the night's work by listening to the grind of the retracting metal, terrible groans produced by the unequal settling of the different walls that separated the Observatory's rivalrous precincts?

With the institution's lateral arrangements so rickety, how, Hugh wondered, walking south into thicker air, could he construct the ladder he imagined raising into the galaxy?

"Why, Mrs. Hall!" he cried, greeting the astronomer's wife. Two doors from the oyster house, she was unexpectedly in front of him, carrying a bolt of cotton cloth. "You must have woven that yourself," he teased his Georgetown neighbor, "to have acquired it at this hour!"

"No, Mr. Allison. The dry goods man agreed to stay open late the other day when I placed my order. I told him this would be the only time I could come for it myself. I didn't trust any of my boys to see that the shopkeeper had secured the right variety."

Even in the weak streetlight, he could see dark circles around her eyes. Her nose was long and she was far too thin, but her mouth, Hugh noticed, was an oddly voluptuous Cupid's bow.

"And I'll wager Mr. Hall was unavailable to help," he said. "Already under the dome?"

"Oh, yes," said Mrs. Hall, checking the sky. "The weather's not good, but I make sure he doesn't get discouraged. I always get him out the door."

"Indeed," said Hugh, who like every other man at the Observatory knew the story of how Mrs. Hall had years ago taken it upon herself to write the letter that persuaded Captain Gilliss to give Asaph his due by promoting him to professor.

"Mr. Allison, you went to Harvard, didn't you?"

"I did," Hugh answered. "They indulged me for four years at the College, and then another four and a half at the Observatory. A scandal, really."

At the latter he had bounced from one project to another—measuring the mass of Io, peering into the Mare Imbrium dust, finding another star in the Omega Centauri cluster. He had worked well—some said brilliantly—when he worked at all, but over time he'd become occupied by the musings he couldn't share with his Cambridge colleagues. "A year or so ago they told me it would be an excellent idea to apply for the post that had opened up here. You'd be amazed at how solicitous they were of my professional fortunes." He soothed Mrs. Hall's embarrassment by laughing. "I understood the message. And so here I am."

"My eldest son is now in Cambridge," she said. "Preparing for the College's entrance examinations."

"I've still got a few books that he could use. Cook's lectures on chemistry, Wayne's *Apology* for Plato. Would you like me to send them up to him? I can assure you they never suffered from overuse."

Mrs. Hall nodded. "That would be very kind of you. I don't like Cambridge, Mr. Allison. I want my young Asaph to succeed there, but I shall never like the city or the College. Mr. Hall and I were there before the war. We had lodgings on North Avenue, and he did computations until they finally began to regard him with some seriousness." She looked at Hugh with a sort of severe affection; if she could not approve his own lack of ambition, she seemed to like him the better for his having experienced Harvard's disenchantment. "We were mocked for living on bread and milk, but we persisted, and when we left there for here we had three hundred dollars in the bank."

"I'm afraid I had a very easy time of it—my mother sent money whenever she sent a lamp or a cabinet. I'm sure your boy will make more of life there than I did, Mrs. Hall. I can't say I was a very serious undergraduate."

"They always thought me *too* serious in Cambridge," she replied. "I suffer from headaches and they called me morbid."

"I'll tell you a secret, Mrs. Hall." He smiled as he lowered his head and whispered. "I'm morbid, too."

"A merry man like yourself? Mr. Hall says you're always larking about."

Hugh laughed. "*That* should worry me, I suppose."

"But it doesn't. So then where is your morbidity, Mr. Allison?"

"I think a lot about death, Mrs. Hall. I want to cheat him."

She appeared startled by the remark.

"I don't think of him as my enemy," said Hugh. "Just my competitor."

"There is only one way to cheat death, Mr. Allison. And that's why I'm relieved to see you carrying that." She pointed to the tract in his right hand.

"Oh," said Hugh, laughing now. "I'm afraid I was only trying to be polite. That's why I took it from the fellow back there."

"You disappoint me. Mr. Hall lacked religion when I first came to know him. But when we lived in Ohio, early in our marriage, I succeeded in securing his acceptance of Christianity. Too few of the men at the Observatory profess their faith seriously, I'm afraid, even while they go about investigating God's domain."

"Then I suppose you're saying I should read this."

Mrs. Hall's full lips couldn't help turning upward into a smile.

"God wants to come into your heart, Mr. Allison."

"Can't I go to Him instead?"

Her expression withheld judgment on the nature of his question; she waited for some explanation.

"He made us in His image, did He not, Mrs. Hall? What if we completed the job by giving our images an eternal life, equal to His?"

"Are you speaking of a spiritual quest, or an astronomical one?"

"I don't know," said Hugh, before he added, with a laugh, "but please don't tell Mr. Hall, in any case. He'll think I've larked straight over the edge. As it is, I suppose *you* think I'm blaspheming."

"If this is to be your work, Mr. Allison, you should pursue it against all discouragement from anyone."

Her mind—he could tell from the hard, set look on her face—was not in the religious empyrean where she spent half her time, but back upon her ambitions for her son, and the slights so long inflicted by astronomers upon Asaph Hall and herself.

"You're right, Mrs. Hall. Here's to faith in unlikely schemes." He raised an imaginary glass. "Now, before I have my oysters, I'm going to go back and contribute another half-dollar toward that Japanese New Testament!"

•　　　•　　　•

Harry O'Toole, the landlady's gaunt son, sat under the engraving of a mournful dog that dominated the boarders' parlor on F Street.

"Four hundred and seventy-six thousand, two hundred and six dollars and six cents from Internal Revenue," he said, "and four hundred and eighty-six thousand, four hundred and ninety-one dollars and eighty-one cents from Customs."

Joan Park, the Treasury clerk who had asked him to read the daily balances from the front page of the newspaper, nodded seriously, as if the figures were her personal responsibility. Certain that her Pitman squiggles required as much brain power as Mrs. May's logarithms, she sped up her embroidery needle to contrast with Cynthia's idle grip on a teacup.

Cynthia was sure that her absence from the supper table had been the boarders' postprandial topic of conversation until a few moments ago, when she finally arrived to join them for the tea and cookies Mrs. O'Toole made Harry set out nightly—"a little lagniappe" was how she liked to put it, her conversation having reclaimed another of its Southernisms. Like many of the old secesh landladies in the District, she'd lately thrown off an obsolete caution before her Yankee transients.

"Anything else of interest, Mr. O'Toole?" asked Joan Park.

Harry scanned the *Star*. "More about the new 'merit system' over at Interior." He looked over the newspaper at Cynthia to say, with admiration or sarcasm she couldn't tell, "I'm sure Mrs. May would be distinguishing herself if she hadn't changed places."

"Veterans will still get preference, 'merit' or no merit," said Louis Manley, who had bought his way out of the war and was, at thirty-six, unhappy with his position in the Bureau of Engraving.

Fanny Christian and Dan Farricker, the two lodgers who worked outside the government, ignored the federal talk and concentrated on the checkerboard between them. Dan, who sold pianos at Decker Bros., was the closest thing Mrs. O'Toole's house had to a blade, though at thirty-one and with thinning hair, he was, even viewed objectively, beneath the twenty-two-year-old Fanny's marital ambitions.

Good company is all he was, after she came home from her work at Palmer's hat shop. Cynthia regarded the two of them over by the tea wagon, knowing they were waiting for Harry O'Toole to go to bed so that Dan might break out a deck of cards and Fanny take off the shoes that had pinched her feet all day in Palmer's showroom.

Cynthia's eyes were sharp enough to read the fine print of Harry's paper three feet away, and she found herself wondering what stories Mary Costello would be clipping tonight. How honest *was* the woman? The astrologer had been square enough to start that chart in exchange for the book, but Cynthia now suspected she'd passed on the volume to Conkling as a sort of *bona fides,* evidence that he'd gone to a politically minded necromancer, without telling him she'd acquired it ten minutes before.

The sound of the 9:00 bell came through the parlor window. It was still, after all these years, calling the slaves home. Cynthia pictured Professor Harkness pouring himself a glass of warm milk over in Lafayette Square, where all would be even more placid than in this parlor. She glanced at the legs of the table near Harry, their wooden claws clenched, as if in anticipation—but of what? The sight annoyed her, made her wish the carvings would relax and send the table with its lamp crashing to the carpet. Her mind went back to the Observatory, wanting to know how far the mist was rising against the dome, whether it was high enough to stop the night's work or just rustling around the building's base like the dry ice she had seen once or twice on the stage at the National. If the sky was clear, the place would soon be springing to life, with Hugh Allison going about his business.

Otherwise, he'd be home in Georgetown. She had spied his address in Mr. Harrison's card file, right beside his birthday, and had copied it onto the back of Conkling's gallery pass. Looking at the parlor's clock, a minute behind the slaves' bell, she tried willing Harry and Mr. Manley and Joan to retire. Once they were gone, she could sneak back out, past Fanny and Dan, who would be just enough absorbed in each other not to notice.

The Irishwoman had helped make her bold. She was still embarrassed to have called on the planet reader, but wondered whether the first sight of Mr. Allison would have excited her like destiny itself had she not already begun thinking of what prophecy, as well as consolation, might lie in the stars. She did not want to lose her new resolve; she did not want to resume her retreat. Tonight she would split off from this latest bedraggled parlor regiment, and with the stars' light to guide her, she would double back toward the battle of life.

●   ●   ●

"Here to join your gang?" asked Captain Piggonan.

"Surely no one's come out besides myself," replied Hugh Allison, who had seen how high the mist was two blocks before reaching the gate. "Well, aside from Asaph Hall," he drawled. "But he's a Puritan. I'm just an optimist."

The captain's muttonchops drooped. Hugh began to sense there was something he didn't know.

"Actually, you'll find quite a crowd," Piggonan confessed awkwardly. "They're all in the library."

Hugh gave him a puzzled look and set off. As soon as he entered the room, the half-dozen astronomers he found amidst the books and desks ceased what appeared to have been general conversation. They nodded their greetings and split up into murmuring clusters, the dispersal revealing a table set with cakes and whiskey and a coffee urn.

Hugh wondered whether he should seek an explanation from Mr. Hall, who had lately been observing a giant white spot on Saturn, as well as the satellites of Uranus and Neptune, objects too indistinct and far away to be of much interest to astronomers lately concentrating on the two inner planets in their transits across the Sun. A moon circling Mars would be another matter, of course. With the exception of Hugh Allison, no scientist here was indifferent to the planet's proximity and myth, or to the way it traveled alone, like a bursting shell that never quite landed.

Yes, he would ask Hall. But the dour Yankee had just put his nose into a book, making use of whatever time remained until this unexplained little party got under way.

"What's going on?" Hugh instead asked Simon Newcomb, who was brushing past him.

"No waistcoat?" was the only reply he got.

Old Professor Yarnall then? He'd been here for a quarter century and was said to be finishing the great star catalogue he had been working on all those years. But Lieutenant Sturdy, recently assigned the task of helping him complete it, was leading the old gentleman to the coffee urn. Would he have to ask Professor Eastman, the man to whom he had reported since being ordered to chase the comet? Eastman was in charge of the 9.6-inch and the Meteorology Department— the Observatory's dullest realm, to which Hugh dreaded being someday assigned. If they ended up wanting weather from him, he might as well be outside with the watchmen, who even tonight would be checking the dry and wet solar thermometers and reading the barometric pressure.

"Henry," asked Hugh, finally approaching Eastman's assistant. "What the devil is afloat?"

Henry Martyn Paul was just four years out of Dartmouth. A big, genial fellow, at least six-two, he was engaged to a minister's daughter and sang in a choral society. A few inches below his deep-set eyes, the bars of a mustache hung like the tassels on Hugh's Arabian draperies, and looked almost too heavy for even his big face to support.

"Admiral Rodgers," he explained.

"Ah," said Hugh, finally realizing what the social commotion was about. "The new, if unyoung, broom. But he wasn't expected until next week."

"I know," said Mr. Paul. "But he's on the scene. I think they've got him over at the Willard now having dinner. Mr. Harrison was told this afternoon to assemble a greeting party." Embarrassed that this should all be news to Hugh Allison, he added: "They really just scared up whoever was on hand."

THOMAS MALLON

"Yes, I suppose I'm *not* handy," said Hugh, giving the room a bemused scan.

Henry Paul declared, "I can't say it's a job I'd want to be starting at sixty-four years of age."

"I heard that," said Simon Newcomb, who had stopped at a nearby desk to inscribe one of his monographs for the incoming superintendent. Young David Todd, who boarded with the Newcombs, often minding the children and reading to the astronomer's wife, held the book open to its front flyleaf and blotted his mentor's signature while Newcomb held forth. "Do you really think this place will faze a man who's surveyed the North Pacific and the Sandwich Islands, fought the Seminoles and raised the first Stars and Stripes on the recaptured soil of South Carolina?"

He didn't wait for Hugh Allison to answer this custom-made jibe. He was off to another shelf, searching for more inscribable tokens of his accomplishment.

"I thought Rodgers was coming from the Boston Navy Yard," Hugh said to Henry Paul.

"That's a while back. Mare Island out in California was his last post. They say he ran the place honestly, too. Under Robeson!"

"Well," said Hugh. "We'll see how he likes working for Thompson."

"'The damned thing's hollow!'" said Mr. Paul, repeating the by-now famous words of the new Navy secretary, and blushing with the realization that he'd just sworn. "Maybe the admiral will come up with some more money for *our* part of the service, too. You know, there's talk of a couple of new ships, what with the Turks and Russians going to war."

"All I want from Rodgers," said Hugh, "is to get away from the 9.6-inch and this damned comet."

Eastman shot him a glance.

"God, I'm hot," Hugh complained, a bit less vocally, to Henry Paul. "Do you think Headmistress Newcomb will let me pour some soda water?"

As soon as he reached the tray of bottles, Mr. Harrison came rushing into the library with Professor Harkness and Commodore Sands, who had evidently been the new superintendent's dining partners at the Willard.

"Gentlemen!" the clerk called out, as he attempted to peel off his gray gloves. "I have the honor to present—"

Captain Piggonan and Lieutenant Sturdy, the two Navy men amidst the civilian astronomers, snapped off salutes.

"Rear Admiral John Rodg—"

The new chief officer waved off the clerk. "You all know who I am, and I'm pleased to see you." With white tufts of hair and a puffy, clean-shaven face, Rodgers looked more like an old Federalist than a modern man, thought Hugh. The admiral's dress belt girdled a large circumference of waistline, and his wattles shook when he talked. Still, he moved toward the center of the room with a quick step.

"I didn't expect such a company of welcomers. But I didn't expect such an approach, either." Rodgers's facial expression showed severe disapproval of the muck he'd met with outside the Observatory grounds. "At my last post, the roads washed out each spring. In the summer, a single mulecart raised a tornado of dust above them. We were given half the money we required to improve them. *But we improved them.*" Unsure whether this was a scolding or a pledge or a mere report, the company of scientists remained silent, until Newcomb, attended by David Todd, strode over to the admiral, shook his hand and began piloting him through the half dozen introductions that would lead to the refreshments.

Hugh watched as Rodgers made each astronomer's acquaintance. He had something clipped but, it seemed, particular to say to every one of them, and he got the last word of each exchange.

"Now you, young man," he finally said to Hugh himself. "You can't afford a coat?"

"I hadn't anticipated a chill. Or such distinguished company."

"Discover another comet," said Rodgers. "*Then* you can come in without a coat."

With that he was off to a spot under the portrait of Captain James

Gilliss, the Observatory's wartime superintendent. He motioned for Professor Harkness.

"What happened to him?" asked Rodgers, pointing up at the portrait.

"Captain Gilliss served here from 18—"

"How did he end up?"

Harkness appeared to hesitate, as if struggling to avoid some indelicacy.

"Toward the end of his tenure, he was increasingly unwell, complaining of, primarily, or first—"

"You mean malaria," said Rodgers. He turned and looked at them as if they were all mad, their heads too high in the clouds to notice the mire that anchored their instruments.

"Mr. Harrison!" he called. "I shall be in at eight o'clock tomorrow morning. I shall want two bottles of quinine on my desk. And at that time you can tell me"—he was already halfway to the door—"what *his* secret is." He pointed back toward Professor Yarnall, easily the senior man in age and service.

Without having touched a single cake or drop of coffee, Rodgers was gone. Professor Harkness, after raising his palms in a gesture of perplexed apology to his colleagues, followed him out.

Asaph Hall, still holding the book he'd been consulting, and eager to remove himself from this sudden vexation, asked Hugh Allison: "Do you think viewing conditions may have cleared?"

Hugh swallowed the last of his soda water. "I daresay the dome has blown off."

•   •   •

In fact, the view was no better than before. The fog and temperature had both risen. A few minutes after Rodgers's exit, Hugh strode across the grounds, removing his collar and stuffing it into his waistband, where the letter to his mother still hung, limp with humidity.

Looking toward the main gate, he noticed a female form in a dark-colored dress. She was watching the admiral go off in his carriage, and taking care, it seemed, not be be observed. A closer approach revealed the figure to be, of all people, the new computer.

"It's nearly eleven o'clock," said Hugh, coming up to her from behind.

"I know," she said, turning around.

"What are you doing here, Miss, Cynthia May, is it? I'm afraid I can't remember the rest of your name."

"Just Cynthia May. Mrs. May," she said, regretting her coquettish-ness the month before. But as she looked at Hugh Allison's face in the available moonlight, she more than ever understood what had made her lie, and she had to force herself to blow away the deception: "Mrs. John May. I am a widow. Please walk with me," she urged. "I don't want Professor Harkness to know that I've returned."

"You've still not explained what you're doing here." He said it with no hint of rebuke, only curiosity, as if inexplicable behavior, including his own, were a familiar part of his experience.

"I came to see you. I intended to go to your lodgings in High Street, but when I started out the night looked clearer than it is now, so I headed here instead. I thought you might have come out to observe. And I see that I was right."

"You know where I live," said Hugh.

"Yes," she said, evenly, while struggling to read his expression. Was she only wishing it to register pleasure, or was that really there?

"And what is *your* address?"

"Number 203 on F Street."

"You walked here from there? For the second time today?"

"Yes."

"And you intended to walk all the way up High Street? Tell me what for." He was *not* angry. He was intrigued; she was certain.

"I want to know what it is you do here."

"Comets. Apparently for some time to come."

Her eyes brightened. "I'm stuck in Tasmania. It's been December 8, 1874, from the moment I arrived here."

"Ah, the Transit of Venus. Tell me, Mrs. May, do you know what a comet really is?"

"I can scarcely imagine, but I'm sure it's something wonderful."

He pointed to the mud at their feet, a suspension of ashes and newsprint and even a horseshoe. "I suspect a comet is the most awful collection of debris. It may look like that gas lamp over there, but that's just the light it takes from the Sun."

"Even the Earth steals its light," said Cynthia.

"Yes," he sighed. "It does."

She could not understand his disapproval of something so elementary, but it didn't matter. The important thing was that he hadn't jumped back at the thought of her waiting for him in the dark.

"Let me work with you on the comets," she said, before she could lose her nerve. "I'll speed you up and get you the more quickly on to something else. I'm the fastest computer here. I'm faster than any computer you knew in Cambridge."

He pointed to Rodgers's departing carriage. "You needn't worry any more about Harkness. He just went off with the new commander. Now we must find *you* a carriage, so you don't have to take that walk for a fourth time in one day. If we can't, I'll walk you home myself."

"It's quite all right," said Cynthia. "I walk as fast as I calculate."

"It's far too late. You'll get knocked down at a crossing before the horse sees you."

She pulled the white collar from his waistband, delighted to feel it still soaked with the sweat of his neck. She fastened it around her upper left arm. "There," she said. "It will steal the moonlight. And the drivers will notice me." She adjusted her hat and set off. "Professor Allison, you need me."

THREE

H ow long should the batter pudding steam?"

"Three-quarters of an hour, Maureen."

They couldn't lower their damned voices? Conkling got up from the chair in his study to shut the door, rather more loudly than he might have. The rasp of the cook, the refined birdsong of his wife: he *would* not endure any more of those female noises floating up the stairwell and disturbing his peace.

Pudding, no less. Since the old cook's death he'd been hoping for lighter fare, but that late mass of starched Irishwoman had left her daughter and recipe book to carry on in her place. With the Special Session definitely put off until October, he was stranded here in Utica to fatten and fume in the dainty world of the Seymours. When he had married Julia twenty-two years ago, he did not calculate—no one could have—the extent to which he would become the enemy, a sort of caged, snorting bully, in his own house. No one could have foreseen that his brother-in-law, the delicate Horatio, would become the state's Democratic governor in the middle of the war, or that Horatio's Copperhead colleagues would rob Roscoe Conkling of the congressional seat he'd won just before it. Things became even worse in '68, by which time Conkling had fought his way back and up into the Senate. As he made himself ready to campaign for Grant, who should become the general's Democratic opponent but Horatio. There was never any doubt that Grant would beat him, or that Conkling would work on the general's behalf, but all the gentle, sporting brother-in-law jokes had sickened him; the quadrennial mortal combat he loved was tamed into the sack race at a family picnic.

And what a family. Inside this house in Rutger Park, the atmosphere always swayed with the vapors. When Grant's partisans, nine years before, had hinted at a drop of madness running through the Seymour clan, Conkling had almost choked on the denials that gallantry obliged him to issue. The charge was probably the truest thrown by either side. How long had it been after their marriage—six months? a year?—before he decided that Julia's once-attractive delicacy was something weaker than mere feminine frailty?

He had made certain, from then on, to save himself, to keep his vitality undrained by all that was needy and flailing and unsoothable within her. Tonight, after the pudding and the whining, but before the tears, he would decamp to Bagg's Hotel downtown, as had long been his custom, for a few nights at a time, during these long stretches when the congressional calendar forced him home. He had spent last weekend in New York, at the Fifth Avenue Hotel, and though both the planet reader and political instinct counseled lying low just now, it was all he could do to keep from grabbing the straps of his valise and summoning a ride to the railway station.

He made himself sit still, even with the women's voices leaking in under the heavy oak door. He reached for the first newspaper on a stack that gave the lie to his oft-repeated declaration that he read only the *Herald*. He read *everything*, even Curtis's unending attacks on him in *Harper's*, because they got his blood up after too long a bath in the stagnant Seymour waters. He needed his enemies sharp and uncrushed, so that he could do the crushing. And if one believed the papers—which he did not, at least not enough to desist from this new hidden vice of consulting the stars—his enemies were harder and more jagged than ever.

The Custom House hearings were on every other page. Hayes had insisted on sending the smug, pince-nezed reformers to Hanover Street and dragging all the party's best lieutenants before the investigative commission's amused stenographers—all in the name of a new snivel service. At the head of the commission Hayes had even put John Jay, that Union Leaguer suffering the perpetual dread he'd never get to be Chief Justice like his grandfather.

What really lay at the heart of all this was Hayes's hatred for Roscoe Conkling, the kind of hatred one can only muster toward somebody one owes everything. His Fraudulency despised the foot-soldiery of the Custom House for failing to carry New York for him, and he hated Conkling for being the one who, at the last possible moment, he had needed to make him President.

Oh, to have the general, instead of this trimmer, back in the Mansion! By god, if things kept going the way they were, they would *put* the general back.

"Mr. John O'Brien, United States Weigher for the Twelfth District," reported the *Times, "was not aware that his assistant weighers and laborers drew money on the pay-rolls while acting as officers of election; he had no body-servant who drew pay from the Government, and did not know any one who had; he could not advantageously reduce his force."*

Well, good for Mr. John O'Brien. But dozens of others would have to testify before it was over, and who knew whether they would all hold up, especially the ones forced to talk behind closed doors. Chet Arthur, Collector of the Port of New York, was trying his best to keep the whole stew from boiling over, but so far his best hadn't been very good. Sherman had let him help pick the investigators, but given the aggression they were displaying, one had to ask if Arthur—that loyal, perfumed popinjay whose job paid more than Hayes's own—shouldn't stick to picking the best wines and wallpapers off the latest boat to come in from LeHavre.

There was no telling how far this would go. Three years ago they had lost the moiety system, a trinity that Conkling had relied on more than the one above the stars. One-half for the United States Government; one-quarter for the officers who opened the crate and found the violation; and one-quarter for the informer who had suggested they open it. By this method, even Julia's imported china had fed three people before it ever got to Utica.

He himself had never taken much, had always stuffed the party's pockets fatter than his own, because the party *was* the country. It had saved the Union, while Copperheads like his brother-in-law would have gently waved the traitors good-bye. To this day, every time anyone accused Roscoe Conkling of waving the bloody shirt, he became only more determined to grind their faces into the stains.

"My dear Chet," he started writing to Arthur:

> I want your concessions to be strategic, and less numerous than your obstructions. Both can be made in the same tone of sweet reason. When the commission calls for a better class of men to work the Custom House, ones untainted by "politics," I want you to tell them that better men will only follow better pay. When the commissioners cry for reductions in the force, tell them in a firm voice that the inevitable effect of such "reform" will be foreign goods slipping through without a duty being paid, because they have evaded the notice of the remaining inspectors' overworked eyes. Make these bolts of untaxed cloth sound like Hessians; ask Mr. Jay if he would really let our shores be vulnerable to such invasion. I count on you to strike a noble pose throughout. Do not let them utter "politics" as an insult.

He had nothing to be ashamed of. He had brought the Electoral Commission into being, given the country a means of resolving the deadlocked election. And as that group did its unappetizing work, he had stayed away, let others do the deal-making at Wormley's, where amidst the stench of tobacco and whiskey and the sauces thick as mud, Evarts and company had lifted the lash off the back of the South for the last few votes needed to make President a man who, when all was said and done, not one of them truly wanted.

Now they cried "Reform!" as if reform were something that might stir the heart. "Mr. Conkling is a passionate man," his colleagues liked to say, encoding a curse in the compliment. They meant that Mr. Conkling had too *much* passion, was too impatient with the lace of figures and amendments and courtesies in which they loved to tangle themselves like parlor pussycats. A year and a half ago, when Bruce, the Mississippi Negro, raised his hand to take the oath, they sat behind their newspapers, trying to hide their dismay: when they'd cried abolition, they hadn't quite meant for it to come to *this*. So who strode across the floor to shake Bruce's black hand? Roscoe Conkling, whose tongue and gaze they now had one more reason to fear.

"Papa." A soft voice, the only female one he loved hearing in this house, followed an even softer knock.

"Come in, my darling."

His daughter, Bessie, whose full beauty had arrived with her twentieth birthday, stood before him.

"Pale blue is most assuredly your color, my dear." He gently took her hand. "*One* of your colors."

Bessie looked at the carpet; her father's ability to assess the female form was too well known—here in this house, especially—for her to encourage its display.

"You were muttering," she said.

"Ah," apologized Conkling. "The newspaper." It had long been his unconscious habit to read the most agitating stories aloud, taking the parts of both villain and hero if the journal supplied sufficient dialogue.

"Are you upset?" she asked.

"No, my darling. And you mustn't be either. This little spring shower over the Custom House will blow away. It's mere foolishness."

"Oh, I hope we've not declared ourselves opposed to foolishness altogether!" She smiled at him. "I've had less than my share of it lately."

He looked at her, questioningly.

"I should so like to have been in New York on Tuesday."

"I see," said her father, letting go of her hand. "I'm sorry, Bessie. It would not have been a good idea."

"I do hear it was rather grand," she persisted, determined to risk teasing him.

"I didn't pay the reports of it much attention." The reports of how Hayes had been in New York; unveiled a statue in Central Park; dined with the Chamber of Commerce at Delmonico's; stayed at the Fifth Avenue Hotel—arriving just two hours after Roscoe Conkling had checked out from his weekend stay. If the general were still in office, it would have been Conkling on the President's right at Delmonico's, a seat no doubt occupied the other night by Evarts.

"They say the crush at Governor Morgan's mansion was enormous," said Bessie, trying to retract her father from whatever angry reverie he'd just entered. "The lines of police had trouble holding back the crowds on Fifth Avenue. Even a pair of Russian dukes put in an appearance."

Conkling sighed. "And you should love to have been there, darling?" He looked up at her with fondness, even a hint of apology.

"Of *course*," she declared, swatting his boldly patterned waistcoat. Instead of joining her in laughter, her father's face darkened.

"I suppose you should like to have been there with Walter."

"Papa, *don't*."

Now that he had broached the subject of Walter Oakman—Bessie's new suitor, whom Conkling thought not half good enough—the two of them knew the rest of this conversation was hopeless. The tide of Conkling's rage was sweeping in. His wit and kindness would remain hidden, like beach glass, until it washed out.

"It was better not to have been there, Bessie. Lines of police! To hold back a crowd turning out for one of nature's born followers. I'll tell you something about police lines, Bessie. You're too young to remember." He reached into the bottom left-hand drawer of his massive desk, extracting a stiff, yellowing paper dated January 1, 1863.

"'Head Quarters, Washington, D. C.,'" he read. "'Guards will pass the Hon. Roscoe Conkling and Family within the lines of the Defences of Washington, By Command of Maj. Gen. Heintzelman.'" He paused for a moment. "You were just a little girl. Perhaps you *do* remember that last trip?"

"I remember, Papa."

"And then we had to come back here for two long years."

"Thanks to Uncle Copperhead."

This remark did make the two of them laugh together, over the long-ago time when Bessie Conkling, who listened so closely to her father's words, thought that was her Uncle Horatio's real name.

"Yes, Bessie," her father said, once again grave. "Those were the greatest of days. And when you hear these stories about me and Mr. Arthur and the rest of my friends, remember what party we've given all our service to."

That his worst opponents were these days *inside* that same party was a point Bessie understood to be not worth making. In their desertion of the general, and their coinage of "Grantism" as a slur, her father's enemies had deserted the party and thereby the country, and from the way he saw it, their very senses. She just nodded.

"I do wish it had been possible for you to be in New York," he said with as much gentleness as he could muster. "I can still see you floating past the flowers at Nellie Grant's wedding, outshining every other bridesmaid." Three years on, the East Room nuptials of the President's daughter could still make Conkling vibrate with emotion.

Fearing a detour into the maudlin, Bessie risked a piece of gossip. "Have you heard that Mr. Evarts is begging Mrs. Hayes to break her rule and at least serve spirits to the diplomats?"

"I hope she stands her ground," said Conkling, resisting the raillery she'd hoped for. Fired up by his own temperance and his hatred of Evarts, he added: "I suspect there's a good deal more about her that I would admire. She's an educated woman, and I've always found that . . ." He let his voice trail off. He knew his daughter would find it unseemly for him to name even what mental qualities he found attractive in a woman; it had been too painfully long since she'd heard him admire *any* quality manifested by her mother, whom she loved as much as she did him.

"But I have no wish to know more of Mrs. Hayes," Conkling briskly concluded. "Not if it means having to see more of her husband."

"Well, perhaps I shall develop a taste for drink. That way I won't be disappointed to miss any more presidential occasions." Bessie leaned down to kiss her father's forehead, at a spot just to the right of his famous curl. "Will you be joining us for dinner tonight?"

"Yes, I shall be here."

She smiled, and rustled out of the room.

Her gaiety; her sly charm. He hated to see them squandered on Walter Oakman, or to be crushed by his own moods. But he *was* his moods, and it was her sort of spirit, that kind of cleverness, that he required. One could not, alas, fully receive it from a daughter, and these days he could not even snatch it from Kate, not since her return from Europe last fall, with the gloom settled permanently upon her. With her son at school in Germany, mementoes of her father were her only distraction. She must have auctioned off a thousand of his possessions in '75, and still the Edgewood mansion was smothered under the old Chief Justice's spirit and things.

On those occasions when they still met, Conkling's physical ardor could be greater than before. The early, thrilling sensation of plundering Sprague's treasure had subsided, replaced by the excitement of complete command. If she had aged, he—despite the winter's illness and self-doubt—could stoke himself into a vitality that burned more urgently than ever. But he needed a woman whose time was approaching, not passing away.

This one who had refused his invitation to the gallery, just before the session ended. How he loved her for that! Whatever he'd surmised from that single exchange outside the planet reader's rooms, he had been right. He always knew for sure, always made up his mind at the first flashing sight of them. "Your War God's war chest!" It amused him even now to think of the remark, along with all the other information the Irish necromancer had passed on in her last two letters, since the woman had begun calling there again. By now he could even name her fellow lodgers, and he knew all about her wizardry with numbers. He would make her drink, make her rattle off tables and equations as she lay pinned, naked, under his arms. How much more exciting the struggles of a woman with a brain than the surrender of those doxies, their wills as soft as their too-ample bosoms, in the back rooms of Wormley's and the Willard. No, if he were to walk into Mrs. O'Toole's parlor tonight, it would be straight to Cynthia May that he'd make his beeline, shocking the pretty young bitch who worked in the hat shop.

Not to be back until autumn! Could he lay such a long flirtatious siege in the months that intervened? He had put that to the planet reader in his last letter, and gotten her reply two days ago: "As the war god, Mars, you travel alone, without a moon. But if you become Jupiter, and hurl your thunderbolts to protect the state, she may yet be in your orbit." It was nonsense, perhaps, but he needed it; he needed a great deal more, and soon, if he weren't to swell up and die here in Utica.

Perhaps it was Neptune, not Jupiter, that he should become, at least between now and the fall. The general had set sail yesterday on his trip around the world, a two-year trek that would lead him through the Pyramids and Peking and over every other point on the globe. By the end of it he would reach his real destination, home, where Americans would realize at last how much they missed him.

Maybe he should do a brief version of the same, just as far as Paris and Piccadilly, and only long enough for Hayes's crowd to realize— once the Indian wars turned out to be not quite over, and the dollar not so sound, and the South not so pliant as they'd hoped—how they needed Roscoe Conkling and all the troops he could still command.

A sudden realization brought his fist down onto the desk. If he

went abroad, he would have to ask Evarts for a passport and letters of
introduction to anyone worth seeing. What could be more galling!

And yet—looked at another way—what could be more delightful?
Let Hayes and Co. wonder what he was up to, whose counsel he was
keeping and supplying. It was a grand idea.

He heard himself laughing—not, he hoped, loudly enough to bring
Bessie back. He now had much to do in here. He had to write Evarts
and then the steamship line, and before he wrote either, he had a
longer, more delicious letter to write. He unstoppered a bottle of violet
ink and let his pen suck up the stream of it that he would discharge to
Mrs. Cynthia May at 203 F Street.

•   •   •

"From the Greek, *kometes*," said Hugh. "A 'long-haired star.'"

Cynthia had never worn stays, but she wished for them now, thinking they might disguise her trembling. "That's a foolish name for
something so beautiful," she replied. "And aren't comets always
omens?" She was aware of his hands on her ankles, steadying her on
the second step of the short wooden ladder leading to the telescope's
eyepiece.

"It's icy green," she reported. "Just like my dress. And just like the
aurora. Which *I* have actually *seen*." Over supper in a tavern on Fifteenth Street, she had tried to inflame his interest with tales of meteor
showers and other sky phenomena visible to a child of New Hampshire.

"All right, Mrs. May. Come down now. There are no omens up
there."

"I don't want to come down," she said. "I'm tired of numerical representations. I want to see the real thing."

"The eye's image is itself just a representation."

"Oh, rubbish. This *is* real, and I don't care about perihelions and
the rest of it tonight." Their task was to measure how far Comet No. 2

of 1877, discovered on April 6th by Dr. Winnecke of Bonn, had moved in the two days since Hugh Allison had last observed it through the 9.6-inch refractor. Several times during the past three weeks, he had gone to Cynthia's desk in the morning to give her the times and coordinates he had noted the night before, so that she might help calculate the comet's distance from the Sun. One or two more fixes of the already-fading object and their work together would be finished— unless Hugh was also assigned to track D'Arrest's comet, whose return, after six and a half years, was expected any week. At supper, that prospect had given him and Cynthia the chance to speak of where they had been during the fall of 1870, the time of its last visit. Hugh Allison had been entering his last year at Harvard College, while Cynthia May was starting work at the Interior Department, six months after Sally's death and one month after her mother's, her once-mad grief having hardened into something cold, suddenly, like a gas changing straight into a solid.

This afternoon he had proposed bringing her back to the dome to join him in the night's observations. He'd said that getting her reductions on the spot would be a way for him to speed this dull project to completion; but they both knew the invitation had really resulted from her weeks of entreating to have a look at the body whose travels she was helping to map. So he had bought her supper, the two of them talking of their pasts until the sky became its blackest. Just before ten o'clock, he had sneaked her by Captain Piggonan and up to the telescope.

He tickled her ankles. "Now."

"All right," she said, laughing. "I'm coming down." She leaned into the eyepiece for one last glimpse of Herr Winnecke's comet (their calculations had indicated it would never be back) and to consider, for a second or two, that her own eye now pressed against the instrument through which Abraham Lincoln, a month after Gettysburg, had looked at the moon and Arcturus. It would be another opportunity for him to proclaim indifference to all matters political and historical. It would also feel like a betrayal of John May, whose last letters from Tennessee, with their mentions of Father Abraham, were the source of her own grudging fondness for Lincoln.

He offered his hand, helping her down to the linoleum patterned like a carpet at the foot of the stepladder. The modern flooring was one of the few features Admiral Rodgers had found to approve of in his whirlwind first month, during which he had personally gone to New York to order equipment and periodicals; loudly complained to the Board of Health about the state of the streets beyond the Observatory's front gates; and begun preparations for assembling the parties who would go west next year to witness the transit of Mercury and a full solar eclipse. Mr. Harrison complained to Cynthia that he had to ice his hand some nights, so relentless was the admiral's appetite for correspondence and clerical reorganization of all kinds. Rodgers's zeal for on-site improvements did not, however, lessen his already firm conviction that the whole institution should be torn down and rebuilt somewhere less occluded and disease-ridden.

Cynthia took a seat at the little desk near the globe, while Hugh climbed back up to the refractor to find the comet for himself and call down its coordinates. Segmenting it through the filar micrometer's wire, he turned it into one point of a plane triangle with Earth and the Sun, and then instructed Mrs. May to digitize it into one more piece of information about the known world.

By the curved wall of the dome she worked the numbers. Looking at the swift movement of her writing hand, she thought of Charles Bogue, the murdered pencil seller whose killers, according to the *Star,* had just been convicted in court. Did his humble life mean more, or less, when contemplated against the heavenly immensity she had just seen? Was he not exalted, and leveled, to the same degree of mystery, wondrous and infinitesimal, as a Ulysses Grant? She was conscious of a new peacefulness within herself, a swelling of what she'd begun to feel with *The Principles of Trigonometry.* The Earth seemed nothing more than a streetcar doing a wide endless loop of the celestial city.

John May, in his hasty grave in Tennessee, and Sally, inside her mean box in the Presbyterians' cemetery, were actually *sitting with her*, fellow passengers, just across some narrow aisle separating life and death. They were all on the same wheeled mote, ineffably whirling with Herr Winnecke's comet.

"They'll kill us if they find us," said Hugh.

She looked up in alarm. "You promised no one else would be here until eleven-thirty at least."

"I hope so," said Hugh, drawing out the words in dire mockery, but not taking his eye from the telescope.

She regarded the small of his back and his thighs. "There's a piece of gossip I didn't tell you over supper."

"And what's that, Mrs. May?"

"I heard Professor Harkness talking with Mr. Eastman. About Professor Newcomb. It seems he isn't getting what he wants. He thought that Admiral Rodgers would instantly recognize how he ought to be running things here, and now he knows that he's miscalculated."

"He should have gone to Harvard two years ago," said Hugh. "When he had the chance. But no. 'If Harvard needs my services, surely the government needs them more.' That's actually what he said. Pompous ass." Hugh shifted his head and looked at the comet with his other eye.

"What a scandal that you should quarrel amongst yourselves," she said. "How *can* you, with infinity in front of your faces like a balloon? I want another look."

He turned around but did not step off the ladder, just smiled down at Cynthia and began reciting, with theatrical self-amusement: "'O, not in wrath but lovingly, / In beauty pure and high, / Bright shines the stranger visitant, / A glory in our sky.'"

"What is that?"

"Mrs. Hall's verse about Donati's comet. It hangs on one of the walls downstairs. The comet came through in fifty-eight, seven years after D'Arrest's. And it's said to have been much more spectacular. My father took me to see it through a telescope in Charleston when I was eight."

"'Said to have been'?" Cynthia mocked. "Of course, Master Allison couldn't be swept away by such ephemera, not even at eight years old."

"Not even at eight years old," he said, still smiling.

"You shouldn't make sport of the Halls," she scolded.

"I don't," said Hugh. "I admire them far more than the Newcombs of the world. Glum old Asaph had to eke out his living doing more mathematical calculations than even you could stomach. But he kept at his work, with Angeline saying her fanatic's prayers behind him, and the two of them climbed into the sky one humble rung at a time." He stepped down the ladder and said, "Let me look at your numbers."

She knew he was leaving out the story of Mr. Hall's years here during the war, when he shyly managed to do his astronomy after days spent helping the wounded on the battlefields outside the District. Did Mr. Allison think that was just another humble rung?

"Irritatingly perfect," he said, looking down her columns.

She laughed and ran to the stepladder, determined to claim another look at the comet as her reward. But before she reached the second step, the two of them heard voices from the adjoining second-floor room. Hugh put a finger to his lips and pointed to the door near the steam pipe. "This instant," he whispered, and in no more time than that the two of them were standing out on the roof with their backs against the walls of the dome, lest whoever entered it spy them through the door's small panes of glass.

Cynthia's heart pounded. She wanted him to take her hand, but he was standing on the other side of the door, flush with its hinges, while she stood inches from the knob. If she looked sideways she could see his face, observe the calm smile that rested on it. With her naked eye she tried to find the comet in the sky, so that she might wish on it, implore its Maker not to let everything new in her life come crashing down—not like this, as if she were in some farce at the National. But she could not see the moving speck of light, so she stood still and looked at the treetops as voices came out the tiny open window.

Admiral Rodgers was the louder of the two men speaking. "What's all this?" he asked.

"Mr. Allison's notes, I believe" was the reply—from Asaph Hall, by the sound of him.

"Allison. Is he solid?"

"I shouldn't know what to say," responded the admiral's companion.

"He doesn't much like whatever he's given to do," said Rodgers. "I suppose he wants a project of his own. But I haven't heard him propose one."

"One's heart must be in one's work" was all Professor Hall would say.

"And your heart," said Rodgers. "Is it really in, or on, that white spot on Saturn? You've been measuring it through sixty rotations, they tell me."

Asaph Hall made no response.

"Does that spot constitute your real ambitions, your dreams?"

"Oh, I couldn't say."

The admiral laughed. The two of them were very near the door now; Cynthia could hear Hall nervously spinning the globe.

"I haven't yet decided just how far to let you all roam," said Rodgers. "On your own, that is." There was a pause, during which Cynthia imagined him staring at the astronomer. "Are the most powerful dreams the silent ones, perhaps?" By now the admiral didn't seem to expect an answer. Cynthia and Hugh heard him go on to declare: "I'd say the dome itself is in better shape than the roof. The timber out there is rotting."

The roof's two inhabitants looked at each other, aware that the moment of maximum peril had arrived. But then, from inside, they heard a loud, resigned sigh, and footsteps beginning to move away from the door. "Well, Professor Hall," said Rodgers. "Keep walking with me. I learn a bit more each time I pace the building with one of you. But don't do all the chattering."

Cynthia, shaking badly, heard the two men exit the dome on the other side. The sound of Rodgers's laughter preceded that of a closing door.

"My heart won't stop racing," she said.

"Come here," Hugh offered, gently moving her to the widow's walk. "There's no need to whisper now." They looked down into the rising mist at the three watchmen going about their meteorological measurements. Rodgers had lately gotten them deputized as District of Columbia policemen. Along with everything else, he was determined to halt nighttime vandalism on the Observatory's grounds.

"Where is it?" asked Cynthia.

"Our comet?"

"Yes."

"On the other side. But you couldn't see it without the telescope."

"Where did it come from?"

"Sidereal origin," Hugh explained, with no great interest. "A chunk of matter belched from one of the stars. At great speed, I'll grant you that." He waited a moment before turning to look directly into her eyes. "I, too, don't want to 'calculate' everything, Mrs. May. I didn't come here to do a catalogue like Professor Yarnall. Believe me, I have no wish to turn the heavens into Montgomery Ward."

"Why *are* you here?"

He wasn't going to answer. He had anticipated her question before finishing his own remark; he was already gesturing toward the door that would take them back inside the dome.

She tried to keep him out on the roof, beside her, by pointing down to the dark grounds below. "It's hard to believe that even now we're moving back toward the Sun, rushing our face into its light."

His own face betrayed no reaction to this banality, still the most advanced astronomical small talk she could make.

"Isn't it strange, as well," she added, "that this should be the last place in the city that the sunshine hits? The Capitol catches it first, and then I suppose the Church of the Ascension, and only then does it leak down to Foggy Bottom."

"Stop thinking of what comes *to* us," he said, with unexpected sharpness. "Such as the Sun's light. Such as the comet. Start thinking of the light that might come *from* us. At the same 185,200 miles per second. If Monsieur Foucault was right when he measured it in Paris."

He looked at her—pleased, she thought, to see her trying to attach this huge number to whatever cryptic possibility he was suggesting. His face, lit more from within than by the moon, or the bit of gaslight still shining out through the windowpanes, seemed flushed with kindness; engaged, at least for a moment, by her presence and gaze. But looking at him was like looking at the comet. For a second she could see the full, hale nucleus; then just the vague shimmer it threw off as it flew.

• • •

A week later, on Friday, the 25th of May, Cynthia sat in the kitchen behind Madam Costello's parlor. Between the two women sat a tureen of turkey soup brought over by Charlie from the hotel. It was barely past six, still light out, as Mary Costello watched Mrs. May's troubled brow.

"We should do the day of the week that you were born," said the astrologer. "I can get out the constants for that."

"'A child that's born on the Sabbath day is fair and wise and good and gay.' *Very* occasionally."

Madam Costello shook her head. "There's much more to be learned than that."

"I've lost interest," said Cynthia.

"In the stars?"

"In your representations of them. Your charts are the same as theirs. Zodiacs or perihelions—I can't care for any of that now."

"Because you looked through their telescopes? Well, that's what you *wanted,* ain't it? Why the sour face?"

Cynthia began the full story of Friday night, offering its details with pride, though at every sign of Madam Costello's enthusiasm she indicated caution, by way of a raised finger or pursed lips. This was, she would have her know, a *sad* story, with a disappointing or at least inconclusive finish. "There's some odd enterprise he keeps hinting at, some peculiar vision that keeps him apart from the other men. He's a changeling, Mary, a boy who's been snatched into some nighttime world, maybe by one of your leprechauns. He's silly with what he sees, but lonely with it, too. There are moments when I feel he's on the verge of wanting to impart this vision to *me.*" She paused to shake her head with self-disgust. "How I flatter myself."

When she ended her account, a considerable silence ensued, while Madam Costello, in her most concentrated manner, set about finding the salient point:

"He held your ankles, dearie."

Cynthia made a disgusted sound. "And probably got cut for his trouble. He hasn't come to see me since. I don't know whether he'll be using me again, don't know what they'll have him work on next, let alone what he'd *like* to work on. I'm back doing the Transit of Venus, at least until the money runs out and they put me on something else. Meanwhile, I'm trying not to fall asleep in front of Professor Harkness."

The planet reader was at a loss for something to say.

"And the worst of it is, he'll be having his hands around a much younger pair of ankles tonight." Cynthia paused to lower her spoon. "Can you do voodoo on her?"

"Whom is it we might be talkin' about?" asked Madam Costello, trying to convey both gentility and the faintest hint that some kind of offensive action might be possible.

"The younger—what else?—sister of a colleague's fiancée. I hear he's taking her to a supper at Commodore Sands's house. You'd like the old commodore. They all say he looks like Merlin."

"Dearie, it's not all the same: voodoo, magic, planet reading."

Cynthia sulked, worrying a not-quite-cooked piece of carrot in her mouth. Mary Costello looked at her, deciding it was just as well that Mrs. May had lost her interest in astrology. She wouldn't have to do any more readings for the girl's half-hearted reception, and she wouldn't have to witness any more of her satanic arithmetic. She could, as a lover of romance and a good cry, just dispense some maternal affection toward her.

"How is your War God?" asked Cynthia, after biting through another carrot.

"Oh, suffering through more talk of 'gross abuses' in the weighers' department. Honest me, why don't these government fellers spend their efforts investigatin' things like all this bad vinegar being sold in Chicago? It's carryin' folks off as surely as the river water took me husband."

Mary Costello didn't much care about the vinegar, which she'd learned of only from the *Star*, the same place she followed the weighers' testimony. She was just trying to postpone the evening's work. She had to translate the paper's latest on the Custom House hearings into planetary movement and advice, and transcribe the latest tidbits of Mrs. May's conversation—all for the great man up in Utica. She would report the girl's adventure with the telescope, yes. But should she mention the beau at her ankles?

Looking across the table at Cynthia, whose expression might help her decide, she discovered the girl's eyes to be brimming with tears.

The astrologer quickly rose from her seat and came around the table. She took the soup spoon from Cynthia's hand and lay the girl's head upon her breast, encouraging her to sob.

"Oh, Mary, it was wonderful."

Stroking the poor thing's hair, Madam Costello quietly offered a suggestion. "Darlin', I have a henna so pale it's more yellow than red. What do you say we rinse some into you?"

· · ·

Commodore Sands's dining room had no bell pull for summoning a servant, but the old gentleman accomplished that device's purpose by tugging on the tip of his long beard to signal the unmarried daughter who acted as his hostess. Two quick tugs indicated it was time to separate the men and women around the big Eastlake table.

The ladies' expulsion could not come soon enough for Hugh Allison, whose companion for the evening, from the moment he'd picked her up in the carriage, had never relinquished her lapdog. Hugh wished that the dog, part of a recent unaccountable craze, might somehow swallow a broken glass before going on to ingest Miss Ellen Gray. The animal was the girl's whole conversation. Whatever the table discussed, an eclipse or an Indian massacre, reminded her "exactly of Buster" and some piece of the dog's naughtiness that she would go on to recount. Hugh could not believe this flibbertigibbet was a minister's daughter, just as she, he was sure, could not believe a man with such good looks and beguiling eyes could be paying her so little attention.

As soon as Miss Gray and Buster had been banished with the rest of the women to the front parlor, Sands led the men upstairs to the library and passed around cigars. Hugh and Miss Gray's future brother-in-law, Henry Paul, lit theirs with a certain sense of humor, puffing like riverboat gamblers instead of gentlemen who'd grown into this after-dinner pleasure. The commodore turned to Professor Harkness, the only middle-aged man in the room, and said: "I'm glad to have these young people around. It does me good."

Harkness looked toward Hugh and Henry Paul, and nodded his agreement, with restrained enthusiasm; he might have reminded the commodore that he was chronologically closer to the young people than to their kindly old host.

"I got the idea for this evening at the big wedding," said Sands, referring to the nuptials of Admiral Porter's daughter, two weeks ago at Epiphany Church. The retired superintendent had spent most of his time taking appreciative notice of the young couple there, instead of, like so many others, straining to be noticed by the assemblage of Navy brass or Mrs. Rutherford B. Hayes herself.

"Now Rodgers may not be young, but he's a man of the future," said the commodore to Harkness.

"That he is," said the professor.

"I heard him fuming the other afternoon," said Henry Paul, "about the cost of dragging all that marble to the Capitol for the big Navy monument. 'Another damned sarcophagus,'" Paul grunted, in pretty fair imitation of the observatory's new chief. "Said he'd rather have a functioning service than a memorial to vanished glory."

"I don't know how they got the marble over the pavements," said Harkness. "Wood or concrete, half of what's in the District crumbles as soon as it's laid."

"We *do* have too many monuments," said Sands, softly. "This proposal of Sheridan's to bring back Custer's body. *It's* a sort of monument. Dangerous, and silly. We're always better left where we fall. Bury a man at sea and the ship sails right on." He seemed afraid of slipping into his own sad daydream; the other men noticed his effort to raise his voice and sit up straighter. "Now, will he be letting you do what you want?"

The question, addressed more or less to them all, concerned Rodgers.

"I hope so, sir," said Harkness, normally not much more of a conversationalist than Asaph Hall. He knew the commodore's unrestrictive regime remained a great point of pride to the old man. "I can still remember the first annual report issued during your tenure, how it gave us individual credit for our accomplishments."

"And your mistakes," said Sands, laughing. "But it *was* better to have names put to feats, instead of just claiming them all for 'the Observatory,' as if the building itself got up each night to do the work." He turned to Hugh Allison. "Mr. Eastman called on me the other day. He says you've been looking at a new comet."

"Yes, sir, but she's already beginning to disappear."

"'She?'" asked Harkness, as if it weren't perfectly routine for the men to refer to celestial bodies as their naval counterparts referred to ships. All at once Hugh realized that Captain Piggonan had, in fact, seen Mrs. May the other night; and had said something that found its way to Harkness and who knew how many others.

"Will 'she' be back?" asked Harkness.

"I don't believe she will, Professor." He paused, knowing he could keep himself as calm as he had on the roof last Friday. "The trajectory I've been seeing doesn't indicate periodicity. Mr. Eastman does, however, expect D'Arrest's comet to be back in about a month, its fourth visit since '51."

The commodore, who couldn't resist the lure of his own past, said, "How I still remember those meteors way back in '33. Not that that shower we watched together was anything negligible; right, Mr. Harkness? How long ago was that? Four years? Five?"

"Ten, sir. November of '67."

"Ten!" cried Sands, clearly distressed.

Hugh tried to distract him. "Herr Winnecke's comet is nothing so spectacular as either of those showers, I'm sure, Commodore."

"Oh?" said Sands. "A small light?"

"Yes," said Hugh. "A kindly light, though not one that will lead anyone much anywhere."

"Not on a par with what this French fellow may soon give us!" said Henry Paul. The journals had been full of the latest electric light experiments. "But unless he succeeds in turning it down, it won't do much good for anybody."

Hugh could not let this go unchallenged. "What's wrong with a great big light, a powerful blaze?" he asked. "Why confine it to a parlor?"

Harkness was about to extol the sort of useful, modest light in the commodore's library, which electricity might allow into the room even more efficiently than the gas jets did, when Buster came tearing over the threshold, yelping without letup.

"Henry, if you was creatin' a dog," said Hugh, in the drawl he used only for sarcasm, "would you make up a mastiff or"—he pointed to the creature at Mr. Harkness's trouser cuff—"*that* thing?"

Ellen Gray had rushed into the room just in time to hear the question, and she looked hurt. Her future brother-in-law hid his laughter behind his left hand, while Hugh removed Buster from Professor Harkness's pants. Not used to such a firm grip, the animal immediately ceased barking.

"Allison," said Henry Paul. "Think of a whole city, every single house shining with its own electric lights, tens of thousands of them."

"We'd have even more trouble seeing than we do now," said Harkness, imagining the astronomers done out of their nights.

"But think of how much work everyone else would accomplish," offered Henry Paul.

"I don't know," murmured the commodore. "I'd miss blowing out my lamp."

With the hand not encircling Buster, Hugh extracted his pocket watch. "May I see you home, Miss Gray?"

Annoyed that the conversation hadn't been transformed by her arrival, and unable to think of Buster's analogical relationship to whatever they *were* talking about, she shook her head.

"Then I'm sure Mr. Paul and your sister will manage to get you there." He deposited Buster, who instantly resumed yelling, into her delicate hands.

"Commodore," said Hugh. "My thanks for a very pleasant evening. Gentlemen, please convey my compliments to the rest of the ladies."

While getting his hat in the vestibule downstairs, Hugh could overhear Sands, who he knew liked him, ask the remaining guests: "He's not terribly Southern, is he?"

Harkness answered: "When it comes to laissez-faire, Commodore, he may be the exception who proves your rule. The boy needs military discipline, never mind scientific direction."

Before he could hear this last remark, Hugh was gone, into the night, on foot and sick with a vision.

His mind went back seven years, to the spring of 1870, when Willie Dietrich, a glum little pansy who lived in the same Harvard house and was terribly sweet on him, asked if he might paint his portrait. He'd sat for him half a dozen times. The canvas that resulted was to say the least flattering, though less distinguished by the subject's smoldering beauty than a kind of absurd serenity. To look at the painting, one might think young Mr. Allison knew all about the future and considered every one of its coming manifestations perfectly acceptable. Hugh had let Dietrich keep the portrait for himself and had never seen it since leaving Cambridge.

Some weeks after the picture was finished, Hugh and another friend, on slightly drunken impulse, had dropped into a Brattle Street studio to be photographed. They sat motionless for several minutes, the backs of their heads in metal posing clamps, and thought no more of the adventure once they were back out on the street. After a week, they nearly forgot to claim their pictures—and to pay the bill. But once he did pick up his order, Hugh sat on the steps of Grays Hall, holding the photograph a foot in front of him, and realizing how different its subject was from Willie Dietrich's Hugh Allison. The young man in the photograph was no less idealized—the art practiced on Brattle Street having its conventions, too—but *this* Hugh Allison seemed to know so much less about the future than his painted version. It had nothing to do with the expression, or with any intention on the part of photographer or subject. It had to do with the way the young man in the photograph had existed for only the few minutes of his exposure, not a half-dozen sittings over several weeks, each prolonged by whatever excuse Dietrich's ardor could invent. The man in the photograph had existed only at two-thirty in the afternoon of June 2, 1870, and he owed his continuing visibility not to someone's paint box but to his own reflected light—what had come off his face and burned its way through the photographer's lens, finally settling on the glass plate. It was an act of total assertion, the perpetuation of himself *by* himself.

Now, *think,* Hugh had told himself in 1870: if that light were to travel not a fraction of a fraction of a second to reach the glass eye that was looking for it, but a thousand years or more, a trillion times a tril-

lion miles, then the face reflecting it would remain alive for the unimaginable length of the journey.

The day he'd called for the photograph had been the first of a
Commencement weekend, when the Yard was full of whatever boys
remained from the Class of 1820, old men now, wisps of white hair flying over their stooped shoulders. As he held his own picture, their
catastrophe struck him full in the face, in a way the Recent Glorious
Dead's never had. No amount of manly nostalgia, with which the
weekend was replete, could mask the sheer cruelty and meaningless-
ness of the old men's lives, or his own. As night snuffed the spring day,
he had gone walking, the photograph in his pocket, through Mount
Auburn cemetery, whose gravestones were awash in moonlight and the
merry airs drifting over from the old men's parties.

The picture had been with him ever since, between the leaves of a
notebook.

•   •   •

"Oh, *you!*" cried Fanny Christian. She and Dan Farricker were
having a tug of war with his new silver-tipped cane, while Louis Manley explained to Harry O'Toole how some dismissed employees from
the Bureau of Engraving had gone directly to the Executive Mansion to
plead their case.

"You mean the 'White House,' don't you?" asked Joan Park, mocking the name that had lately caught on. She'd been a clerk for ten years
now, accumulating the useless pride of the old-timer against the late-
comer, a capital she would pile up for another thirty years.

Cynthia listened to them all and watched the clock and thought
about how much more illuminating the conversation at Commodore
Sands's was bound to be.

"Over at Interior," said Louis Manley, "your former bailiwick, Mrs.
May, one candidate for a clerkship submitted his application to Secretary Schurz in four different languages." He waited vainly for some sign

of astonishment or disgust from Cynthia. "That's not 'merit,'" he declared. "That's showing-off."

Mr. Manley was more than usually worried these days. The Freedmen's Bureau would soon close for good, sending out another rush of displaced employees to compete for his own post. When he mentioned this for the third time tonight, Mrs. O'Toole, who had entered the parlor with another pot of tea, just smiled. In recent days, Mr. Alexander Stephens, the Confederacy's vice president, had argued a case before the Supreme Court, and the son of John Tyler—the one American President she revered, for his subsequent service to the South—had applied for a position with the Pension Bureau. Oh, there would be talk, the usual business about rewarding the sons of secession, but Mr. Tyler would get the job, and the complainers would go back to their whispers about what really alarmed them: the appointment of dusky Mr. Douglass as the District of Columbia's marshal.

Cynthia glimpsed the landlady's satisfied expression and imagined the sort of inner recital provoking it. She could keep quiet no longer. "Mr. Manley," she said, "don't forget the competition from the freedmen themselves. The Treasury Department's just appointed a colored messenger." Mrs. O'Toole shot her an annoyed glance. "And a colored clerk," Cynthia concluded.

"Oh, Mrs. May," said the landlady. "I hadn't noticed you. Forgive me, but these days we're never quite sure *when* you'll make it home. But here you are. And, oh, here's a piece of mail I've been keeping safe for you."

Had the witch steamed it open? Cynthia took the envelope that Mrs. O'Toole withdrew from her pocket. A quick look revealed no return address, not even her last old aunt's in New Hampshire. The half-dozen faces in the parlor waited for her to open the letter, but she had no intention of satisfying anyone's curiosity but her own. She wished them all good night and walked upstairs to her room.

Undoing her hair, she forced herself to look into the mirror. Would Mary Costello's henna be such a bad idea? Yes, it would. She would feel even more like an old lady making a fool of herself over a boy. D'Arrest's comet could make its whole round of the solar system in the space of years lying between herself and Hugh Allison. She had no wish to get a better look at the web of lines nature had begun spinning around her eyes, but Mrs. O'Toole kept the gas lamps stoppered so low that she had no choice but to light an extra candle if she wanted to read her letter. The candle would be on her bill with everything else at the end of the month.

What if, through her own folly, she soon couldn't pay it at all? The other morning Mr. Harrison had *said* something—humorous, she thought, though she couldn't remember his exact words—and Professor Harkness had *looked* at her, oddly, she'd begun to believe. Once again, she tried to reassure herself: Admiral Rodgers could not possibly have seen her and Hugh. The superintendent had never stopped talking that night. And if Professor Hall had somehow glimpsed their shadows, he would never say a word. She had to be imagining things; but her lack of caution that night now made her wonder if she hadn't been a fool in more ways than one.

Utica, New York? Written last Friday, May 18th. Oh, dear God!

My dear Mrs. May,

Our mutual friend Madam Costello tells me that your fascinating work on the Transit of Venus threatens to remain incomplete due to a lack of sufficient appropriations. I should hate to see you straining your eyes for naught, so I have taken it upon myself to write to Secretary Thompson to see if we can't come up with some additional monies for this most worthy project—and your most remarkable skills. I wouldn't want them, or you, wasted behind the counter in a hat shop. I should so enjoy hearing from you before I set out on some travels. In hot haste,

Roscoe Conkling

There it was, her own prattle, right down to Fanny Christian, coming back to her in the wavering candlelight. This Irishwoman, who not two hours ago had cradled her head and dried her tears, was simply unbelievable—though not anything so absurd as the attentions of this lawmaking satyr. That she could sustain his interest on the basis of a moment's encounter, while losing Hugh Allison's as soon as night turned back into day! There must be a half-dozen girls getting these purple-inked notes with every post. Yes, *girls;* but a stringy widow who had entered the second half of her biblical round?

Where was his photograph? She had to look at it, to marvel that such a lack of discretion could proceed from such a powerful presence. Was it in the top drawer? No. She hadn't even bothered to bring it home from Madam Costello's after putting it on the table a month ago—when they were supposedly clearing the air! Well, it didn't matter. She didn't need the picture to figure out Conkling's behavior. There was no risk to it at all, not when he could simply pulverize anyone who attempted to make trouble or scandal. *What, after all, is this letter?* she could imagine him thundering at some caster of aspersions. *Nothing but the sort of attention one might pay a constituent. A bit of largesse across state lines!*

She blew out the candle, and the fine webs around her eyes disappeared, leaving her, in the dimmer light, what she knew she had once been, and what the purple letter allowed her to admit, silently and in the dark: *beautiful. I was beautiful.*

As soon as she said it, she felt ashamed, and afraid. The letter had disturbed her already raw nerves. She rose and went to the window, knowing she would not be able to see Herr Winnecke's comet, but also knowing, for certain now, that it *was* an omen. Of what she still could not guess.

FOUR

Lieutenant Sturdy and Professor Eastman were sick. The officer's temperature had passed 105 degrees, and his teeth were chattering like a steam-driven loom. Before day's end, he would likely be up, if not around, complaining only of headache to the ensign bringing him quinine, and waiting for the moment, three days or so later, when he would collapse into the disease's second phase—the one Professor Eastman now suffered through.

Out on the Potomac this Saturday morning, nothing hinted of the miasma. Here at the edge of the Observatory grounds, only a distant shimmer of late spring heat interfered with the sight of some single sculls and four-oared shells practicing for Monday's regatta, when local crews would fight for a cup against the Nassau Club of New York.

Henry Paul and Hugh Allison, on their way to the riverbank, discussed "the sister-in-law," Miss Gray.

"She calls you Hugh Callous-Man," said Henry.

"On the basis of that one evening?"

"Well, no. I'm afraid I've told her you're accustomed to disappointing the sex. That there have been lots of crushed ladies, and so she shouldn't take it to heart. According to our brethren who remember you from Cambridge, I'm even telling her the truth."

"Is that what they say?" asked Hugh, scanning the bank for the single female they'd come to fetch. "I suppose they're right. Nothing stirred the young ladies of Brattle Street like the chance to gaze into my sad eyes, moist with what they were sure was my homeland's defeat. You can imagine, Henry, how shattering the war must have been for a fifteen-year-old it never deprived of so much as his dessert." He laughed. "I *tried* to tell them, but they wouldn't listen."

"My Augusta has another girl in mind for you."

"Thank her all the same, but no. I'm so bored with bouncing curls at the pianoforte, I may become a Miss Nancy. Ah, look, there she is."

"Mrs. May!" called Henry Paul. Cynthia, who had taken a respite from her desk to watch the practice, turned around. "We've come to find you. Or at least Mr. Allison has. I just tagged along."

"We've been talking about young ladies," said Hugh. "I suppose the banks will be crowded with them a couple of days from now."

"A disagreeable thought," said Cynthia.

"But a lovely sight," said Mr. Paul. "What do you suppose they'll be wearing?"

"Lace mitts," said Cynthia. "A little marabou near the buttons. I pick up a great deal of useless information from one of my fellow lodgers."

"And what shall *you* have on?" asked Henry Paul.

"I shan't be out here. But I'm wearing darker colors these days."

"Why is that?" asked Hugh.

"I worry that I've been too conspicuous for my own good."

Neither man said anything. A few moments later all three of them had their attention seized by a rower who'd caught a crab with his oar and was shouting his disgust.

"Don't worry," said Hugh. "He may capsize, but he can't sink. The river's got more salt in it than the Dead Sea." He pointed to a deforested stretch on the Virginia side, but Cynthia missed whatever point he was making. Her eyes had returned to the sight that had distracted her from the oarsmen even before Hugh and Mr. Paul came along: the wharf, down past Long Bridge, from which both John May and her brother had left Washington, never to return.

"I hate to break up our riparian party," said Hugh, "but I did come to retrieve you, Mrs. May."

As they walked back to the Observatory, it was Mr. Paul who offered her his arm. While she walked between them, both men managed to talk right past her. They were chewing on the latest pieces of gossip to come over from Annapolis: a measles outbreak at the academy; two new practice ships that had been commissioned; some experiments a Mr. Michelson—who'd piqued the interest of Simon Newcomb—was beginning to do with the speed of light.

"The exact velocity isn't important," said Hugh. "The implications of great speed are what count."

"Not important?" asked Mr. Paul. "What use can imprecision be?"

She could tell that Mr. Allison didn't wish to engage his colleague too particularly on this subject. He let her presence shelter him from such conversation. "Well, Mrs. May would object to *any* lack of exactness, I'm sure."

For the past two weeks Mrs. May had been toiling over the numbers for somebody's monograph on the nebula of Orion. She'd been feeling worried and more than a little ignored, and she wasn't going to serve Hugh Allison as some comic totem of fastidiousness.

"How is Mr. Eastman?" she asked.

"Not terribly well," said Mr. Paul.

"The *miasma*," she said impatiently. "You talk of imprecision? I'm amazed by the vagueness with which all you scientifics discuss whatever keeps laying waste to you."

"It's bacteria," said Hugh, with a clipped confidence that should settle the point. "An airborne bacillus, the cause of most every disease you can name. This one lives in the mists."

And that stopped any more discussion until the three of them arrived at Mr. Harrison's office, where nine-year-old Angelo Hall, already out of school for the summer, was being handed the *North*

American Review and a bag of lemons, with instructions to bring these items and everyone's good wishes to Professor Eastman, the Hall family's neighbor on Gay Street.

"There's *A*saph, *S*am, *A*ngelo, and *P*ercival," Hugh whispered to Cynthia, hitting the first letter of each name. "If Mrs. Hall weren't past delivering him, you can bet they'd still be praying for a Herbert."

"Run along, then," said Mr. Harrison to the boy, before turning to Hugh and Henry Paul. "Now, I hope you two also want to make yourselves useful."

"We three, actually," said Hugh.

"My apologies, Mrs. May," said the clerk. "It's been a troublesome two days."

"I'm to have Mrs. May, starting Tuesday, for five mornings," said Hugh.

"Yes," said Harrison. "Professors Harkness and Eastman have already told me."

"Oh," said Hugh. "Then it's all taken care of."

"Except, of course," said Cynthia, "for the small matter of telling me what I shall be doing."

"She *is* wonderfully precise," said Hugh. "Didn't I tell you, Mr. Paul?"

Cynthia made a stern face, and Henry Paul thought it best to go sharpen a pencil over Mr. Harrison's wastebasket.

Hugh explained: "It's D'Arrest's comet, Mrs. May. She's arrived, all too punctually, like a maiden aunt. And now she's got to be entertained. I'll sit up with her nights, if you'll speed the calculations along each morning. Once we've discerned her current curve, I'll treat you to a supper to celebrate what will be, by then, her predictable departure."

Too surprised to give him the insult he deserved, she only nodded and said, "Then even *you* must admit that this one is an omen. Of grilled swordfish and Madeira. I won't forget." She walked over to Mr. Harrison's desk to complete her time sheet for the week that was ending, and lost her pleased feeling when out of the corner of her eye she noticed Henry Paul giving Hugh what appeared to be solemn advice. She strained to catch the last words of it—"especially now, with the gases"—and understood that Hugh had just been warned not to dare think of again bringing her here at night.

•   •   •

Three hours later, on another river, Roscoe Conkling crossed the deck of the chartered steam ferry *John H. Starin* and entered its dining room. The ship would soon embark from West Twenty-fourth Street for the short trip across the Hudson to Hoboken, New Jersey, where the senator would transfer to the vessel taking him to England. Out of deference to Conkling's famous self-discipline in food and drink—and because the dozen passengers had already taken a very ample luncheon at the Custom House—the ferry's table groaned under the barest minimum of champagne and hock and sweets.

Those making this brief *bon voyage* voyage included the Collector, Mr. Arthur, whose kid gloves and velvet collar befitted the nation's highest-paid federal employee, and Alonzo Cornell, the Custom House's stone-faced second-in-command, who also found time to serve as chairman of the New York State Republican committee. George Sharpe, the Surveyor, popped a champagne cork as the whistle blew and the *Starin* pulled out from the dock.

The senator was expected to make a toast, and he did not disappoint: "Had your purpose been to add to my regret at leaving these shores, and to the pangs of this parting, you could hardly have chosen a more effective method. Your unexpected presence and exceeding kindness make it harder to say good-bye even for a brief season." In fact, the only thing making him sorry to go was the chance that another week at home might yet bring a reply from Mrs. May. "Nevertheless your farewell gives me immense gratification, and will be treasured with grateful remembrance wherever I may wander and whatever skies bend above." With a gentle motion of his hands Conkling stifled the cries of "Hear, hear!" and promised he would not allow his remarks to lengthen into something they "might expect from Mr. Evarts," whose grandiloquence was as well established as his enmity toward all of them. "But, gentlemen, I do wish to say something else." Here he lowered his voice to stop their laughter and excite the surge of fear he always could. "One of the most pleasant among the incidents which I anticipate in my journey abroad will be to thank the English people for England's reception of General Grant."

As soon as this line brought them to their feet huzzahing, Conkling sat down. The English had gone mad with adoration for the touring ex-President, forgetting how a dozen years before he'd put an end to the rebels for whom they'd displayed such sympathy. If they now insisted on swooning for the general wherever he went, through the streets of Liverpool or the halls of Oxford, that was fine with Roscoe Conkling, whose identification with Grant could only be perfected by traveling in his wake. He had timed his own departure perfectly. With the first reports of the Jay Commission's investigations into the Custom House being cheered in the press, Hayes was bound to act before many more days passed. The President would at last declare an open war on the machine, and Roscoe Conkling's absence would rattle those expected to carry it out.

"Now tell me, Senator. Just when will you be back?"

"The second week in August," Conkling confided to Cornell, who'd chartered today's ferry from an old associate with whom he'd once run a steamship line upstate. Huge and impassive, Cornell might lack the elegance of Chester Arthur, but Conkling admired his very coarseness, the way he'd thumbed his nose at his book-loving father and gone off to work as a telegraph boy. Ezra Cornell may have founded Western Union and his university, but his boy had made a *real* ascent, not this charade of starting at the bottom that Bessie's young man was intent on acting out.

Still, it worried Conkling that Cornell's brutish face was one of those the public fixed to the Custom House. Between Cornell and

Arthur, his dandyish opposite, there was little the average man could look at and find sympathetic, and with all the sworn evidence about "bones" and "hatchets" and other duns filling the newspapers, the machine's men had begun to sound like the thieves in Fagin's den. Testimony that the term "general aptitude" really concerned an applicant's political know-how had provoked what Conkling regarded as the most detestable sound in the world: the laughter of one's enemies.

He watched the sidewheel paddles of the other ferries and felt glad for this chartered steamer, which had allowed him to avoid the farm wagons and the newsboys at the docks of the commercial boats. Only the chance to see the ladies returning from their shopping could have made public conveyance worthwhile, and it was too early in the day for that.

But the expense and show of this departure! The newspapers were sure to tut-tut about such extravagance during the fourth year of an economic slump. They had blanched at the uncountable millions the Custom House had taken in during the last twelve months, and crooned with pleasure over the way Mr. Hayes, that Cincinnatus out of Cincinnati, set such a wonderful example by paying for his own servants in the Executive Mansion—these days less a seat of power than a needlepointed sampler, the whole fraudulent "First Family" gathered around the piano as the Interior Secretary picked out psalms and the Vice President, that detestable Wheeler, sang the bass notes.

The men were talking about it even now. George Sharpe, already drunk, shouted "Where are the oranges?"—the same question parched dignitaries were said to whisper at Hayes's teetotaling hearth, knowing that at least one steward would be good enough to soak the citrus slices in whiskey.

"Don't worry, Roscoe," shouted Arthur, tapping him on the back. "When you return, we'll let *your* trunk stay on the dock beyond forty-eight hours." A roar of laughter greeted the Collector's reference to the latest Treasury regulation, designed to limit the time that incoming goods might be coveted and pawed by the machine's men. It was one more niggling preview of reform, and along with it Secretary Sherman had also just ordered that hearings on the Philadelphia customs operations be modeled on what had been done in New York. If Conkling was right, the ultimate plan to bring them all down had been hatched at last Tuesday's meeting of the Cabinet.

"Conkling," whispered Cornell, as grave as the others were raucous. "I cannot take the number of men down twenty percent. And that's what Sherman's going to ask."

"Let Arthur take it down by eight. Not a percent, not a man further. And make sure the lot he fires includes at least one of Sherman's friends. Send him a signal."

"But how am I going to assess the ones who remain?" worried Cornell. Surveyor Sharpe's testimony on the "voluntary" nature of all political contributions at the Custom House had gone down as risibly as "general aptitude."

Conkling looked at Cornell without answering. Smart as he is, the senator thought, he doesn't see what's coming. He doesn't understand that he and Sharpe and Arthur aren't going to be reined in; they're going to be sent packing. When Hayes did what Conkling expected him to, the machine's men would have no choice. They would have to strike directly at the President, strangle his administration on the floor of Congress, or it would be the end of them.

"There's the *Mosel*!" cried Chet Arthur, brushing a crumb from his scented whiskers and saluting the ship that would transport their chieftain across the Atlantic.

Conkling remained seated until the last possible moment, thinking how, when the final battle was joined, he would require a woman as surely as Booth had needed a horse.

• • •

On Friday, June 22, Cynthia had the afternoon free to navigate the noisy aisles of Washington's Center Market. Looking up toward the grand ceiling of the young Gothic structure, she thought of the shabby old Baghdad that had once filled half of Lafayette Square, and where as a girl she had gone to buy groceries before meeting her father at the edge of the Treasury's lawn.

Madam Costello, walking the aisles with her, knew no other market from her time in the capital, and had remarked coming in that with more great brick piles like this, the fire would have gone easier on Chicago.

"Look, look, look," she now ordered, tugging Cynthia toward a table of scarves. "This gold one'd be like a royal sash with your new locks."

"I don't think so," said Cynthia, checking the pin in the borrowed turban that covered her newly hennaed hair. "Oh, *why* did I give in and let you do this?"

"Because he's bein' so encouraging," said the astrologer. "You've got your new comet and your supper and your new hair. Pin him down about the supper, dearie."

"I have," said Cynthia. "He said a week from tomorrow."

The two women embarked on a long promenade past household furnishings. Cynthia regarded the tables full of pillow slips and wash-basins and all the other things she had never had to purchase during her years in lodgings; they made her feel estranged from the normal world. Did Mrs. O'Toole, obliged to buy such things in great multi-ples, feel even more peculiar? She hoped so.

"Get me out of here," said Madam Costello, "or I'll burn an even bigger hole in me pocket. Did you see that paste jewelry, round the bend and five miles back? You'd swear it was the best opal, wouldn't you? The birthstone for October."

"I know all about your Scorpio," said Cynthia, looking down at the much-shorter woman and noticing the thinness of the hair that had lent out its turban. For more than three weeks, since the arrival of Conk-ling's letter, she had been unable to summon any real anger toward her. The scoldings and sarcasm were no more than a light comedy between them. She ought to hate the Irishwoman's treachery, but her new fears only left her admiring a certain shamelessness she needed more of herself. She now reasoned: what harm could Conkling actually do? He was a comet of highly doubtful periodicity: another appearance, even in the mails, was most unlikely. By now—sailing after Grant, the newspapers said—he would have turned his attentions elsewhere.

She could not, alas, turn her own attentions from the odd and beautiful Mr. Allison. In fact, she worried that her old cheese-paring caution would reassert itself, and that Hugh would begin to look only like danger instead of new life. If she wanted to maintain the boldness of her approach to him, she needed Madam Costello, this fairy-tale crone, to keep her nerve from burning low.

"All right," she said, pushing the older woman out into the sunshine over Indiana Avenue. "You were going to tell me more about Capricorns."

"Well," said Madam Costello, shifting her ragged reticule from one hand to the other. "They're often associated with sin."

"That makes no sense," said Cynthia. "Christ Himself was a Capricorn."

"*Is*," said Madam Costello, crossing herself. "But Christ is a very new soul. Go back further. Think of the scapegoat, dearie. And think of this, too: why was the Christ baby put into the manger with the goat?"

"I haven't the least idea."

"To conquer sin and death."

Cynthia scowled. "So Capricorns are associated with *both* redemption *and* sin."

"Yes."

"This is why I always lose you, Mary. You see that, surely?" She took an orange from her dress pocket and began peeling it. "All right, keep going."

"Funny thing is, for all these associations, they ain't generally very spiritual, your Capricorns."

"Well, he does seem more interested in how the heavens function than in who made them."

"They're not terrible hard workers, either. They ain't the men to hew the wood and draw the water."

"He's not the busiest bee at the Observatory, I'll grant you that. But he can't help it. This comet bores him. When he gives me its position each morning—"

"Nor are they the most favored lot. In the body, I mean. They can be awful plain, and narrow in the chest."

"*That* is rubbish," said Cynthia, throwing the orange rind into the street. "He could not be more scrumptious. The chest maybe *is* on the narrow side, but I'd rather look at him than at one of these trencher-men exploding all the buttons on their vests."

Mary Costello, ignoring the rebuke, searched her brain for anything else she could recall about Capricorns without her books in front of her.

"Coal," she said. "The Capricorns govern coal."

Cynthia offered no response to this piece of information, and the planet reader had no idea of its significance herself. She just nudged the younger woman with her elbow and said, "We'll get you to squeeze him into a diamond, eh?"

Around the corner, on Seventh Street, some larger than usual typography sprang up from the newsman's stack of the *Evening Star*: EXECUTIVE ORDER ISSUED. Madam Costello fetched two cents from her bag. "Will you read it to me, dearie? Nice and slow? You won't trip over some of these words the way I do."

In fact, the news on which Mary Costello would now have to put the best astrological face was all too plain: "No assessments for political purposes, on officers or subordinates, should be allowed. No useless officer or employee should be retained. No officer should be required, or permitted to take part in the management of political organizations, caucuses, conventions, or election campaigns."

Cynthia, done reciting, looked down at the Irishwoman, who was twisting the reticule's string much too tightly around her finger.

"Surely you don't have to worry about this right now," said Cyn-

thia, as soothingly as she was capable of saying anything. "He'll probably be home by the time your letter could ever find him."

"The cable, dearie," said Madam Costello, lifting her eyes from the
planks of the sidewalk. "The big wire under the ocean. The office boy
has instructions to send him something from me every third day."

•   •   •

At 6:00 P.M. on Monday night, June 25, Admiral Rodgers came
into the central dome and stood at the pier of the 9.6-inch refractor.

"I've been looking for you," he said to Hugh Allison.

"Sir," said Hugh, who had dozed off. "I had D'Arrest's comet well
in sight last night. I'll be looking again—"

"You'll get your best view after midnight. Don't spend the hours
until then in here."

"How is Mr. Eastman, Admiral?"

"Listless. Aching. But past any delirium. If the initial fever had
been half a degree higher, we'd have lost him. You appear a bit listless
yourself, Mr. Allison."

"I hope not, sir." He also hoped the charts on the table where he sat
concealed the copy of the *Atlantic* he'd been reading.

"Do any of you," asked Rodgers, "ever look at the Sun?"

"It's never been a specialty here, sir."

"The head of the Army Signal Corps wants us to observe the Sun's
spots and what he calls its 'protruberances.' Something different from
the spots, I gather."

"We'd need better spectrographic equipment," said Hugh.

Rodgers removed a chip of peeled paint from the telescope's pier.
"He has a good mind," said the admiral. "I like his company." General
Meigs, the Army's chief of staff, was Rodgers's brother-in-law, and the
admiral easily socialized across service lines. "More stimulating than
the Ancient Mariner, certainly."

"And who might that be, sir?" asked Hugh, as if he didn't know the nickname for Hayes's Navy Secretary. He noticed a smile as Rodgers worked off another couple of paint chips with his thumb, revealing the pier's antebellum color.

"The other day," said the admiral, "he remarked on how some ensigns had just 'won their spurs.'"

Hugh's laughter had barely escaped his lungs before Rodgers snapped: "And how do you plan on earning yours?"

The admiral did not seem to expect an immediate answer; if he had startled Mr. Allison with the question, that appeared to be enough for the moment. "I'm thinking about holding monthly meetings of the entire staff. As things stand, *I* talk to all of *you,* but you don't talk amongst yourselves, except in your little cliques. For instance, I'll hear from a third party that Mr. Harkness doubts Mr. Newcomb's accuracy, but Mr. Newcomb never hears of it at all. Let us air these things."

"It's too bad the air itself is one of our difficulties," said Hugh.

Rodgers, peeling away at another brick, allowed the change of subject. "I'm determined to connect this place to the sewer. The Board of Health are quite uninterested in our drainage problems, but there is no reason we can't run a pipe from the Twenty-third Street gate to the corner of Twenty-second and Virginia." His middle finger finished the second brick and moved on to a third. "And then there's the boiler." He flicked some dust from his hand and turned to face the younger man. "It would require thirty thousand dollars to repair everything on this site. A hundred thousand might allow us to start a new building somewhere else. What do you think we ought to do, Mr. Allison?"

Hugh straightened the charts on his table. "I'm sure you'll make the right decision, sir."

"You think so?" said Rodgers. "All right, suppose I choose to try to get us out of here altogether. Where am I going to find the money?"

Hugh looked the admiral in the eye, but said nothing.

"The Ancient Mariner wants to separate us from the Navy, and do you know what, Mr. Allison? He may be right. It makes about as much sense for the Navy to be measuring distant stars as it does for sailors to be wearing spurs. We've long since known all we need to about navigating by the heavens, and I daresay the Navy doesn't need you doctors of philosophy to keeps its chronometers in working order. Tell me what you think."

"About putting a civilian in charge?"

"Yes."

"Whoever it was would tilt the rest of us toward his own interests."

"You may be right," said Rodgers. "Mr. Newcomb would have all of you scurrying in his moonlight. Then you'd rebel, and he'd have to hang you like the Molly Maguires." The admiral shifted the papers he was carrying from his left hand to the one that had been peeling paint. "Even so, I'm not sure, Mr. Allison. Most of you say you're happy having me about, but you may just be buttering my parsnips. Newcomb and Holden admit they would prefer somcone with a necktie giving the orders, but they may be buttering their *own* parsnips. I will tell you one thing."

"Yes, sir?"

"If I'm going to get us out of here, you're all going to have to do spectacular work. Things that get the place into the newspapers. The sort of things that will send Mr. Newcomb's clubwomen into a frenzy of admiration. It's as plain as this, Mr. Allison: you must rise to higher heights, if I'm to move you to higher ground."

Hugh nodded.

"My new astronomical acquaintances up in Cambridge say you may be the best man to have trained there since the rebellion."

"I doubt that."

"So do I, but I'm prepared to entertain the thought. They also say that you're unsound. I don't care if they're right about that, not if they're right about the other part. But Eastman and the rest tell me you've not proposed any substantial projects of your own here. Why is that?"

"Sir," said Hugh, "is it true that you'll be serving on the lighthouse board?"

Rodgers said nothing for a moment. "I've not decided. If I say yes,

I'll get to make a summer cruise of the New England coast, while they test their new illuminating devices. You've answered my question with a question, Mr. Allison. Unless you've given me an indirect answer? Well," said the admiral, deciding not to press the point, "this may be a start. Still, I won't wait long before I make you give me something definite, something bold enough to get attention, and not too bold to preclude results."

"I think I understand, sir."

"Look at this," said Rodgers, handing him the top sheet from the papers he carried. "Captain Gilliss's death certificate."

Hugh read aloud what the naval surgeon had attested to a dozen years ago, how Captain Gilliss "'departed this life on the 9th day of February, in the year 1865, and that he died of serous apoplexy. He had been stationed at the Naval Observatory for some years, a locality noted for its insalubrity. During the last summer and fall he was frequently attacked with intermittent and, on one occasion remittent fever, which left him in a weak condition; this, combined with excessive mental labor incident to his position no doubt caused his death in the line of duty.'"

Hugh handed the paper back to Gilliss's fourth successor.

"One of *my* projects," said Rodgers. "Putting together evidence of what's gone on here for thirty years. What good it will do when I state my case is anyone's guess, Mr. Allison. My own is that the Congress's pity will be insufficient to move us away from here. Their pride—in something this national astrolabe has *achieved*—could well be another matter. So get cracking, Mr. Allison. Don't give *me* apoplexy."

"Yes, sir," said Hugh.

The admiral was already on his way out, but he stopped at the doorway to turn around and ask: "Your question about the lighthouse board: *was* it meant as some sort of clue to your intentions? I'm thinking of Quincy Adams's expression for this place: a 'lighthouse of the sky.' Are you ready to find some great ship, some great astral body that's been sailing undetected?"

A formidable, intelligent man, thought the young astronomer. And as to the last point, *exactly* wrong.

But what answer could he give him? How could he say that *he* was the astral body he wanted *others,* far distant, to detect, if only as scattered spangles of light? He would appear more mad than foolish. And so, with the admiral, as with so many others now, he ended up appearing evasive, or ethereal, or without wanting to, rude. If he "larked about," as Mr. Hall said, it was partly so his cap and bells might distract them from questioning him seriously.

He could only smile and let Rodgers depart.

•   •   •

At 8:00 that same evening, Cynthia May sat in her room with Charles Reade's latest novel. Through the closed door she could hear Dan Farricker, accompanied by Fanny Christian on the piano, singing "I'll Take You Home Again, Kathleen." She failed to detect the rapping of the front knocker, but did notice the sudden cessation of music that followed, along with some unusually animated sounds from Mrs. O'Toole.

She cracked her door to listen.

"Charleston, you say!" the landlady was exclaiming. "But you really didn't need to. I'm from Columbia myself."

The softer, though jaunty, reply came up the stairs: "I should have known."

It can't be. She went to the landing.

"This is Miss Christian," said the landlady. "And here are Miss Park, Mr. Farricker, Mr. Manley. My son, Harry, I'm afraid, is indisposed."

"I seem to have interrupted your entertainment," said the visitor. "Miss Christian's sheet music appears frozen in mid-turn."

She would kill Fanny; if the girl said one word to him, she would kill her.

"You must join in the merriment," ordered Mrs. O'Toole. "It's such a pleasure to have visitors after the season has ended."

Oh, Jehoshaphat, the *season,* thought Cynthia, rolling her eyes and further sharpening her ears.

"Mrs. May?" the new arrival gently reminded the landlady.

"Oh, yes," sighed Mrs. O'Toole, bowing to duty. "Let me get her for you."

Cynthia darted back from her door and waited for a knock. Her disgust at having to share him with this parched little world, at his having to endure even a moment of its moth-eaten conversation, outweighed her surprise and pride. She calmly fastened a comb to her hair.

"Mrs. May! A caller."

"I shall be right down."

She waited until the landlady's footsteps retreated to the parlor. Then she pinched her cheeks, put away Charles Reade, and picked up the biography of Galileo that she'd borrowed from the Observatory's library. She went down the stairs with an index finger between two pages of the book, as if marking her place.

"Tell me this, Mr. Allison," Louis Manley was saying as she reached the parlor. "Mr. Hayes now claims that the Negro will get a fair share of offices in the South once the Custom House investigation is over. Do you think that is possible? Will your people stand for it?"

Hugh nodded at her.

"I don't know about my daddy," he said. "My mother is sure to treat any colored revenue clerk as poorly as she would any white one."

Mrs. O'Toole laughed.

"Mr. Allison," said Cynthia.

"Mrs. May," he replied, with a slight bow and much more emphatic smile. The parlor's population paid keen attention. "Late as it is, might I take you for a walk?"

"Oh, won't you stay, Mr. Allison?" cried Mrs. O'Toole. "I'll bring out my son's stereograph. We have the most wonderful pictures of Venice."

"I'm afraid I already spend too much time looking through lenses, my dear lady, and I've several hours of that in front of me before the night is over. Another time, I hope. Perhaps you'll even have some pictures of Columbia."

Mrs. O'Toole glistened for a moment, then turned a drier eye on her boarder.

"Shall we, Mrs. May?" said Hugh, offering his arm. "You may actually need a wrap, despite summer's arrival."

"Then I'll get one," said Cynthia, putting down her book and heading toward the hall.

"You'll forget where you are," said Joan Park, crisply, pointing to the now-closed Galileo volume.

"I should *love* to forget where I am," said Cynthia.

Out on F Street, she closed her eyes for a few seconds and sighed. "I feel like her," she said, pointing to the Goddess of Liberty atop the Capitol. "Set free, from all of *them*."

"You have terrible manners," said Hugh. "Worse than mine on some occasions."

"I don't know how you can bear sharing so much as a home state with that woman."

"If she let her voice relax into its natural origins, she'd sound like a moonshiner out of Pickens County. Poor Mrs. May, having to put up with her." He gave a parting glance to the Capitol and declaimed, "Ah, yes, there it is, the summit of our ambitions."

"I remember the years before they put on the top of the dome. It looked like a morning-mush bowl."

She walked with Hugh down F Street, her eyes detouring into the alleys filled with shacks and crippled veterans and Negro children carrying buckets to the cisterns.

"I hate it here," she told him. "People talk about all the roads they've paved and all the trees they've planted and how they've backfilled the canal, but it's as awful as ever."

"Do you hate it *just* here? Or do you hate it everywhere?"

"What a question."

"It's a serious question."

It *was* a serious question, he thought. He knew her woes by now. She had parcelled them out to him over the last weeks—the husband, the little girl, the small humiliations and great fears of her poverty. He also knew, or sensed, that she wanted to transcend them. But before he exposed his own heart's desire—made a burden and a gift of it to her— he needed to know that her hopes were more than weak ones whose failure would allow her to cherish her injuries even more.

"Of course I like other places," Cynthia answered. "Such as I've seen them."

"Yes, your home in the northern latitudes, with its aurora-green ceiling."

"Yes. It's lovely."

"Then why don't you go back to it?" he asked.

"Because if I did, I should have to teach school or else freeze to death."

"You don't like children?"

"I can't bear them in the aggregate," Cynthia answered. "I liked my daughter."

No, he thought; she cannot help herself.

But then, as if she did not want to grandstand with her grief, he heard her voice hoist itself into a lighter, silvery register. "If *I* had the chance, I'd go back to Charleston, to that house you described with the cypress library and the delft-tiled fireplaces."

"And the constantly shifting furniture. My daddy would come home from the courthouse never knowing if he'd walk in on Louis XIV or Genghis Khan."

She relaxed a bit and leaned into him, and they walked in silence until they came in sight of the Treasury. She was about to tell him of her own father, but could wait no longer to ask the night's obvious question. "Why did you come? It can't be to buy me my dinner. I've already eaten Mrs. O'Toole's parsnips."

"Ah, parsnips," he said. "The symbolical vegetable of the day."

"Please don't talk in riddles. Don't make me think you came out just to exasperate me."

He gave her hand a reassuring pat. They continued on to the War Department, past the southern edge of Lafayette Square. Would he now propel her down New York Avenue and toward the Observatory? She could not let him. She could not risk it.

"Look at *that* one," he said, pointing to Washington's Monument, which lately another committee was struggling to get completed more than twenty years after the funds had run out. "They may have covered your mush bowl, but there's a saltcellar without its cap. This way," he said, turning her northwest, toward Pennsylvania Avenue.

"Where are we going?"

"To Georgetown. My rooms, I suppose. It's still too early to spot the comet."

She stopped, and withdrew her arm from his. "If I'm to be a fallen woman, it's going to require more enthusiasm than 'I suppose.'"

He laughed, and took back her arm. "I'd wager you don't like lap-dogs either, Mrs. May."

"I don't like dogs of any kind, but you're talking in riddles again." She couldn't stand the feeling that their real conversation was always hiding from them, flowing like the old Tiber Creek lately channeled underground. "Tell me plainly why you came for me, or I won't go any farther."

She could feel the muscles in his arm tense and then, as if given permission, suddenly relax. "I need someone to talk to, Cynthia."

She said nothing, just tried to imagine what these words had cost him, tried to imagine the grass and the road collapsing beneath them, plunging them into the subterranean creek, where they might float, at last truly speaking to each other.

"All right, then," she finally declared. "Your rooms."

The wordlessness that persisted between them, along the many blocks to their destination on High Street, bothered her less than the fringed Moorish world he ushered her into once they arrived. Whatever he'd said of his mother hadn't quite prepared her for this. "Did your father ever come home to *these* things?"

"No. Mother wouldn't have liked the suggestion of dancing girls in his presence. Look," he said, picking up a sort of medallion from the mantel. "From her Chinese period. It's malaria. The fellow with the hammer stands for the headache, and the boy with the cookstove is fever."

Cynthia took the disk and moved it closer to the lamp, trying to see what the third figure carried. "The bucket of water?"

"I'm not certain. Chills, I should think. I'm planning on giving the thing to John Eastman once he's completely himself again."

She sat down between an orange pillow and a mauve one. "You don't have many books for a Harvard man."

"Only the essentials."

"And what are these drawings?" Tacked to the wall were several sketches, in which a blank triangle was formed between shaded squares that appeared to be, on closer inspection, a pattern of treetops:

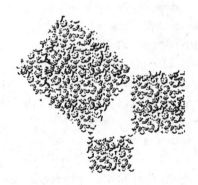

"A friend of mine found drawings just like these in Gauss's notebooks. Carl Friedrich Gauss. My friend resketched them for me and sent the stuff over from Germany. He's there in Göttingen helping to edit Gauss's writings. The trees are meant to be an actual forest. The shapes would be created by cutting great paths, hundreds of miles long, between them."

"To what end?" asked Cynthia.

"So that the shapes would be visible from great distances."

He noted her perplexity, and waited a moment before saying, in a whisper he couldn't help making theatrical: "Not from down here, Cynthia. From up above and far beyond. To whomever might be watching us."

With his lips parted in an expectant smile, and his eyes wide with excitement, he looked at her. She knew what he now expected her to ask—*who was this marvelous man, Gauss?*—but she could only pose a question she felt more to the point: "This sort of thing interests you?"

His expression collapsed, and he let his body follow, into a chair behind the table. He sighed, loudly: "I'm afraid it's *all* that interests me."

"I'm sure I'm being thick-skulled, but it sounds like Jules Verne. You mean *creatures* up above and beyond?"

"Yes."

"I don't believe there are such creatures." He still looked disappointed, so she searched for some sort of lighthearted consolation. "And if there were," she suggested, "they might be the sort who carry lapdogs. Wouldn't that be awful?"

"I'm not especially interested in the *creatures*." He came out from behind the desk, his voice reanimated. "I'm interested in the way light can carry *us,* forever, at 185,000 miles per second, more or less."

She now remembered how he and Mr. Paul had talked of Michelson, the young man over in Annapolis, but more strongly she recalled his own voice on the roof that night: *Stop thinking of what comes to us. Start thinking of the light that might come from us.* She quoted the lines to him.

"Exactly," he responded.

"Exactly? You're giving me riddles again. Really, what does all this have to do with astronomy?"

"Nothing, really." He laughed, and let himself collapse again, this time onto the same sofa where she sat. Only the immense mauve pillow, which he now compacted with a soft blow from his fist, rested between them. "The admiral had me on the carpet tonight. He's determined to get some work out of me at last." He pulled off his right boot and moaned, in comic agony: "What am I going to *do*?"

"You sound like some pupil about to be expelled. And put your boot back on."

"I just might *be* expelled. They're not forever going to be satisfied having me chase other men's comets. Nor, incidentally, are they going to let *you* chase Mr. D'Arrest's much longer. When I left the place a couple of hours ago, I saw Harrison and Harkness scratching their heads in wonder. It seems the Navy has just disbursed a pot of money to be used, quite specifically, to complete the Transit of Venus work. The two of them have no idea who squeezed it out of the Ancient Mariner, but it was surely someone powerful."

Her hand shook. Conkling's visage, the one she knew from that photograph in the street-seller's bin, seemed to dance in the gaslight. She reached up to her comb, hoping the gesture would steady her fingers and disguise the agitation that had to be visible on her face.

"What have you *done*?" Hugh cried, tossing the mauve pillow onto the floor.

"I've done nothing!"

"Yes, you have! Your hair. Bring it closer to the lamp." He swung himself around to the other side of her, throwing the orange pillow on top of the mauve. He pulled her against him, taking her head between his hands, so it was just inches from the tasseled lampshade. "It's awful," he pronounced, loosening the comb and spilling her upsweep onto her shoulders and down her back. "Promise you'll restore it to the way it was. Promise," he said, gathering up a great handful of her tinted tresses and rubbing his face into them.

She drew back, waiting for him to open his eyes, and once he did, she looked into his face, hating its youth and thick lashes and unhurt beauty. She hit it, once, with a closed fist, as hard as she could, bringing tears not to his eyes but her own, as she gave herself final permission to love him.

FIVE

Roscoe Conkling was not in Paris. "Mr. Arthur Chester" was, however, registered at a small hotel in the Place Dauphine, his room adjoining that of Mrs. Kate Chase Sprague. On July 13, as noon approached, the incognito senator sat outdoors at a café three floors below the improvised suite and took a second cup of coffee from the proprietor, who was fixing some tricolor decorations to his awning in preparation for tomorrow's Bastille Day festivities.

Waiting for Kate to come down, Conkling found himself more occupied by the just-past American Fourth of July than its continental equivalent. The English papers, which he'd bought while strolling on the other side of the river, made prominent mention of Senator Blaine's holiday oration. Conkling's sworn enemy, responsible for his most enraging nickname, had attacked the President's soft Southern policy, and warned against using recent army raids into Mexico—supposedly made in hot pursuit of bandits—as an excuse to grab territory that could then be turned into another Southern state.

What pleasure was there in having his old enemy attack his new one? If anyone were to convulse the Republican party that held all three of them, it should be Conkling himself. And yet, since docking at Southampton on the 27th, he had been wondering whether he really had the strength and stomach for combat. England had failed to excite

him: Richard III's palace was now a coffee house, and Pitt's monument
in Westminster Abbey had turned out to be a paltry thing, hardly a fit
tribute to that prescient sound-money politician. He had written to
Bessie that nothing in the shops couldn't be found less dear and better
made right at home. Even his dinner with Grant had somehow left him
more drained than nourished; the whole table of flatterers at the
Grosvenor Hotel had been less inclined to push the general back into
the electoral wars than just to sit and bask in his autumnal aura.

Conkling stared at his reflection in the silver coffee spoon, aware of
the gray flecks in his once-blazing hair, conscious that his complexion
no longer carried its old apoplectic glow. He *had* to stir his blood back
up, had to fight off the climacteric he could feel advancing ever nearer.
It would arrive, according to the Irishwoman, on October 30, his forty-
eighth birthday. How would he meet it with a sharp edge of vitality?

The cables from his man in Washington carried a note of panic.
Fright, not economy, seemed to account for all the missing verbs and
prepositions: PRESIDENT EVERY INTENTION ENFORCING ORDER. Cornell
had already been told either to quit his party post or leave the Custom
House. If he resisted, the sledgehammer would soon start smashing
the machine's inner gears. The Jay Commission had chosen to release
its second report, another torrent of abuse, on July 4th. In little more
than a week, a third report would follow with yet more appalling tales
of malfeasance in Conkling's kingdom, which he now summoned into
a mental picture: the seven hundred miles of shoreline and riverbank,
from Montauk to Albany, a magnet for eighty thousand dockings a year
and all the skimmed tribute that ran through the counting house on
Hanover Street. He pictured his chieftains back at home crying for
their leader, clamoring for his return or at least his signals. But he had
so far replied to neither his aide nor astrologer.

Was his silence really strategy, as he claimed to himself? Was it
really because his absence might unsettle the opposition that he sat
here, so far from the battle, waiting for Kate to choose from her trunk-
ful of aging millinery? Or was he, without being able to admit it, truly

hors de combat, lacking the stamina for war? Perhaps his slack feelings were attributable just to time away from his punching bag and dumb-bells; or maybe the climacteric had stolen a march on the calendar and already infiltrated his spirit.

He looked up at a carriage rolling over the paving stones. The horses pulling it were fine specimens, both as beautiful as the bay that, forty years ago, had kicked at him and broken his jaw. When Kate finally came down, they would go off to the afternoon races at Auteuil. She would keep her face under a hatbrim and out of the sun, and he would find himself more solicitous than passionate. He had not, in truth, wanted to see her here. She had made the arrangements herself, interrupting her own summer trip to Germany, and he had felt unable to refuse her. To show the same indifference to his mistress as his wife would be not only cruel but perhaps the surest sign of the climacteric's early arrival.

Kate tired him. Her faded looks and hats; her exhausted relief simply to be away from the drunken Sprague: they all went to make this rendezvous feel less like a plunge into passion than some careful lower-ing into a mineral bath. The two of them would probably fall asleep in the grandstand between races; last night he had noticed that the dear thing now even snored. The other day, up in the Place Vendôme, standing before the obelisk to Napoleon's conquests, he'd watched her fall into a daydream. He had stared at her instead of the monument, and wondered if she were thinking of Sprague—not the inebriate brute he'd become, but the rich, dashing war governor who long ago had marched his thousand volunteers from Rhode Island to Washing-ton, and slept with them in the streets of the capital until the rebel threat receded. She lived too much in the past; he must not let her make *him* tarry there more than he already did.

After their visit to the obelisk, he had ended up buying her a tiny clock in a shop off the plaza. Back at Edgewood, he knew, she would tell anyone who saw it that the purchase had been made not this sum-mer by Senator Conkling, but long ago, by her father, the Chief Justice. The lie would be meant to keep the real story from finding its way into the gossip writings of "Miss Grundy" and "Olivia," but its deeper, unacknowledged purpose would be the pleasure it afforded Kate herself, who even now—beyond mother, wife, or lover—preferred thinking of herself as a daughter.

MONEY DISBURSED VENUS. His aide's first cable had carried this postscript, and since its receipt, Conkling's mind had returned to Mrs. May several times a day. He understood from the planet reader that this woman, for all her sorrow, lived for the future, that she hated the past and its new false glamour, and longed to rise whole worlds above it and the present. She was fighting her way toward some kind of new life, and he yearned, on the basis of his single encounter and the astrologer's stream of reports, to have her provoke a revitalization in him as well. SHE IS BLOOMING WITH YOUR BOUNTY, his aide had cabled, here relaying not only the Irishwoman's every word, but adding on the "g" she would no doubt have dropped. As soon as he was home, Conkling looked forward to truly making the woman's acquaintance, to hearing from her *own* lips the misadventures of her fellow boarders and the scientifics for whom she toiled.

The astrologer's other reports, on the stars' relation to political events, were harder to interpret, and would probably be so even if the cables permitted a full amplification. But he did not like her apparent new concentration upon Hayes as a Libra, "the same as Adam himself," pure and primordial and carrying the scales of justice in his sign. Had Conkling come forth a week earlier from his own mother's womb, that would have been he. Instead, the charts said he represented the crash of Adam's eagle aspirations to the desert floor, and their foul reincarnation as the scorpion. Months ago the Irishwoman had explained all this with her cunning tact, and he'd thought he had accepted it, but her recent emphasis on Hayes—the suggestion that the President might, or even should, prevail—could not fail to trouble him. It was shameful enough to have a weakness for all this fortune-telling (a vice he had so far kept hidden better than his colleagues concealed their own propensities for drink and gambling), but it seemed intolerable that the celestial tidings should bring him further anxiety instead of solace.

And yet, there was this last bit, perhaps garbled on its five-thousand-mile journey under the ocean: the planet reader's response to his own news of having dined with the general, a Taurus, who was, she replied, the HIGHEST EMANATION OF EARTHLY TRIGON, AND CONSTELLATION OF PLANET VENUS. Her last letters to Utica had contained much about what she called "triplicities," and here was another, though the Greek word sounded like Mrs. May's trigonometry.

And what, by God, if that were the point, thought Conkling, putting down his coffee cup in a double surge of excitement and embarrassment. This might be *it,* even if it had taken the Irishwoman's mumbo-jumbo to lift the veil. The trigon *was* the trigonometry that Mrs. May applied to her transiting Venus, and the real triplicity of the high-flying Taurus could only be *the third term,* the political grail locked inside a jar of prohibitive tradition. A jar that could be broken. He sat for a second, his eyes closed, gloriously heartened, feeling the first, vital surge putting the second, guilty one to rout—just as *he* would go home to rout Hayes and all machine's foes, restoring Grant and the stalwart saviors of the Union to their central place in the political firmament. He would *not* live in the past; he would re-create it as the future.

"Monsieur patron! La papeterie, s'il vous plaît."

"Oui, monsieur," said the owner, stepping off his ladder to fetch the American gentleman his stationery.

My dear Mrs. May, wrote Conkling, at a delightful, rediscovered speed. *My climb to the top of Sacré-Coeur the other night, thrilling though it may have been, took me not a millionth the distance you travel each day to Venus without ever leaving your desk. I am delighted that the Secretary's supplement has reinvigorated your work. I, too, feel marvelously revitalized and ready to make my return home, after which, following a brief period in Utica, I look forward to coming to Washington.*

May I count on you to show me a bit of the Observatory, that I might see firsthand the good use to which you're putting Mr. Thompson's funds? Au revoir, madame. ROSCOE CONKLING

His signature looked, once more, as bold as the cables' capital letters. With one hand he stuffed the dispatches into his waistcoat, and with the other he handed the proprietor the letter to post.

"Mr. Chester," said a female voice coming up from behind.

He stood and turned to greet Kate, whose eyes, under the broad brim of her flowered bonnet, looked lovely but still half-dead. He must not fall into them.

"My dear," he said, plucking a paper flower from the newly tricolored struts of the awning. "Shall we celebrate Monsieur Lafayette a day early?"

"A fine idea," said Kate, who took his arm and resisted mentioning that it was Friday the thirteenth.

•   •   •

"I'm accustomed to seeing Mr. Todd," said the clerk, referring to Simon Newcomb's assistant, who often took the Observatory's data to and from the Government Printing Office.

"He's on vacation in New Jersey," said Hugh. "We all just had a penny postcard from Toms River. Mrs. May and I thought we would check on our own work today."

"Let me get the proofs," said the clerk, who nodded with some surprise at Cynthia. He retrieved the long galleys of numerical columns pertaining to D'Arrest's comet, then sent her and Hugh to an iron-topped table where they could go over them.

It was tedious work. Cynthia read each set of coordinates digit by digit and decimal by decimal; Hugh replied either by saying "correct" or holding up a finger while he checked the handwritten sheets from which the printers had worked. Easily bored, he would often interrupt their labor to start chatting or fuss with his pipe. At one point he crinkled his nose against the almost overpowering smell of ink, to which Cynthia seemed immune.

"It only bothers *me* with memories," she said. "Of my first job, at the Treasury—in the middle of the war, after John May went away. A friend of my father's knew how badly off we were, and more importantly, knew General Spinner and Mr. Chase himself. So I was hired and given a pair of shears, with which I sliced sheets of greenbacks from morning 'til night, until they realized I was expecting Sally. In my day, Mr. Allison, I let a million dollars slip through my hands."

He returned her smile and went back to saying "correct" or raising his finger. The way they worked the proofs matched the regulated manner of their now frequent conversations about the war. He would let her rattle off the sorrows she had locked up for a dozen years, gently nodding or saying yes or prompting her with a question when her embarrassment threatened to dry up whatever story she needed to tell. When he felt she had had enough for a while, he would jest her back into the present—as he did now, retracting the two of them from D'Arrest's orbit by pointing out two chattering idlers behind the counter. "*Their* speech still seems free." He had in mind the Public Printer's recent, much-noticed jeremiad against reform and the way it had begun "to interfere with the rights of citizenship." Hugh expected her to grin, but she responded by saying "longitude of perihelion" as sternly as she could. He rolled his eyes and resumed concentrating.

It had been three and a half weeks since he'd taken her in his arms—and then walked her home. She had not let him make love to her, and since then he had not pressed the case. Except for one night when he'd felt unwell, they had seen each other every second or third evening. He would walk her home—the two of them holding hands once they'd crossed Virginia Avenue—or to the chop house near Madam Costello's. Inside the restaurant, he would diagram with a wax pencil over the fine print of a newspaper, teaching her the rudiments of astronomy and urging her to talk of her past, as if that were simply another place—which his drawings somehow suggested it was. With each conversation they drew a bit closer. She felt herself becoming his, as imperceptibly as her hair was returning to its real color. She thought of herself as Venus—the planet, not the goddess—cautiously transiting the Sun until she was wholly, safely circled by his golden aura.

During the day, she calculated Venus's actual transit, advancing the long three-year project with funds the Observatory's men, on the basis of quite unscientific guessing, had decided were the result of "Mr. Harkness's admirer," a politically influential woman who'd been much taken with him, some months ago, when Professor Newcomb brought his associate to an evening meeting of the Washington Scientific Society.

Lately, Hugh himself had done little but write letters, at Admiral Rodgers's direction, to astronomers across the country and throughout Europe who might join the observation parties being organized for next year's transit of Mercury and full solar eclipse. He was expected to sit down with the admiral on the 30th, a week from Monday—a potential showdown that worried Cynthia and about which neither of them spoke, not even when Hugh's collegial gossip and mimicry presented a natural opportunity to discuss Rodgers's ways and expectations. They had also talked no more of Gauss's fantastical drawings. Hugh feared, she thought, her disapproval of such an outlandish preoccupation; and disapprove of it she did.

Once they'd returned the corrected sheets to the Printing Office clerk, the two of them walked south on Eighth Street toward Pennsylvania Avenue. The noontime summer dust flew up from bare patches of the road where pavement laid by Boss Shepherd, the District's modernizing governor, had failed to take. Hugh pointed toward Ninth Street and a house on the south side of E. "That's Marini's lair." He and Henry Paul sometimes went to the bachelors' cotillions run by this Italian dancing master. No less than Sir Edward and Lady Thornton, the British ambassador and his wife, had been to these gay affairs.

"And you're really going to take me there?" asked Cynthia.

"I am going to take you there. But we can't wait until the season begins for some amusement. Let's make a little excursion soon. The *Mary Washington* goes down the river a couple of evenings a week. We can get tickets right at the wharf."

"We can pick a night when it's cool," said Cynthia. "Below, say, eighty-five degrees." She pushed up the sleeves of her dress. "Honestly. Even Sitting Bull has gone up to Canada for the summer."

"Do you want to make a day trip somewhere north instead?"

"No. That would require the railroad, and by the time you keep your promise the trains aren't likely to be running."

"My darling Cynthia, have you *ever* been able to take yes for an answer?"

"No," she answered. "But you know I'm right. There, look! Proof of it!" She pointed to the already familiar sight of Albert, Mr. Hayes's Negro driver, who kept one hand on the horses' reins and used the other to hold a giant black parasol over his own head. "See? His boss is still in the District." With the railroad strike beginning to spread, and at least one governor requiring federal troops to deal with rioters, the President had so far gone no farther than the Soldiers' Home for relief from the summer's heat.

"As I've said," Hugh sighed, "you're a natural scientist. You've got deductive powers to supplement your mathematical ones."

"You remember the million dollars I said once passed through my hands?"

"Yes?"

"It was really one million three hundred and forty-eight thousand, six hundred and fifty. I was bored wielding the scissors, so I kept count."

He laughed for the next several steps, while she considered how wrong he was about her mind. Whatever its peculiar gifts, her brain was an almost entirely emotional organ. Her never taking yes for an answer arose not from any scientific skepticism, but only out of the nervous uncertainties she feared would never leave her.

"You know, I'm not for reform," she said, suddenly. "The 'civil service' variety. I'm right with the Public Printer on that."

"You?" asked Hugh. "The most meritorious of them all? You'd have Hayes's job if the world worked fairly."

"But it doesn't work fairly. And the old, corrupt ways left some elbow room for human kindness. They could always take on a genteel widow who'd fallen into want, or somebody's brother-in-law who drank and could barely read but had three children at home. That sort of unfairness kept some people from falling off the earth."

He knew her fears. He'd inferred them from peculiar things that bubbled up in her conversation, things she knew because she thought she ought to know them, or just couldn't get them out of her mind: the way profanity might get you a five-dollar fine from an out-of-sorts policeman; or default on a twenty-dollar bond get you tethered to a chain gang. She had great nerve, this girl, but she didn't like wasting her courage—not when the world required so much of it. Last Saturday, after they'd gone to the Corcoran and seen a boy hustled out because he was blocking someone's view, using too big an easel to copy the work of some second-rate master, Hugh had done a cartwheel through the last gallery to irritate the pompous guard. For his trouble, he had earned only Cynthia's anger. "You *fool*," she'd said, and meant it.

Prompted by this memory of the art gallery, he reached into his coat to withdraw a carefully wrapped pastel, done at his own request by Trouvelot, the sketch artist who was often around the Observatory to make pictures of phenomena like the Horseshoe Nebula, or Saturn sporting Professor Hall's white spot.

On the paper that Hugh unrolled Cynthia saw her own face and pastel streaks of her own hair, some of them gray, swirling like constellations toward the edge of the sheet.

He laughed at her disbelief. "You didn't know I had him watching you the other day, did you? You thought he was doing Venus, for Harkness, didn't you?"

"Is this for me?" she asked.

"It is not," he replied. "It goes on my wall. Next to the Gauss sketches."

•   •   •

"No one is safe!" cried Louis Manley, five days later in Mrs. O'Toole's parlor.

"You don't need to tell *me*," said Joan Park. "They're discharging Mr. Croggon, who's worked in the bond vaults for *twelve years*. It would seem that the honest supervision of four hundred million dollars is less important than someone's complaint about his owing his position to his brother."

"And can you imagine, Miss Park, if these new 'nepotism' standards were also applied to the Army and Navy?"

She and Mr. Manley shook their heads and clucked until this smug display prompted a cry of disgust from Fanny Christian: "I don't know how you can talk of *that* when there are mobs in the streets ready to tear up the rail tracks!"

"This sudden interest in public affairs, Miss Christian!" Dan Farricker nodded in mock admiration, and Fanny flounced from the room. As Dan well knew, Fanny couldn't tell a Knight of Labor from an Odd Fellow, but she did understand that this horrid railroad strike would likely keep her from showing off the new pair of shoes she'd bought for a wedding in Philadelphia this weekend. By now Baltimore was full of General Hancock's troops, charged by the President with preventing another convulsion like the one five nights earlier, when the local militia had shot into a crowd and killed nine people.

"You're not going to find *me* defending the government's property," declared Louis Manley, once the rustle of Fanny's skirts had receded. "I don't care what these Cabinet secretaries order us to do. They don't pay me enough for that!" The other lodgers didn't know that his savings had never recovered from the $300 depletion they'd undergone when he bought his way out of the war.

Mrs. O'Toole, who tonight had put out only half as many cookies as usual, sighed that if the unrest kept up bread would soon go to ten cents a loaf and bringing in coal would get even more expensive than

usual. Meanwhile, they sweltered in the late-July heat, and Dan Farricker reminded the landlady that ice was a local manufacture.

"*Locally*," said Harry O'Toole, "things may soon get quite a bit
worse. There's talk of those Baltimore mobs marching on the District."

His mother enacted a terrible shudder. The *Plymouth* and the
Essex had arrived this afternoon, with more than five hundred marines,
to defend Washington. It was all too reminiscent of the war, though
this time Mrs. O'Toole actually hoped the capital would prevail against
the threats to it.

"Oh, calm down, Harry." Dan Farricker was laughing again.
"You'll need an electric belt for your nerves."

The glass pane rattled in the vestibule door.

"It's our intrepid Mrs. May," said Dan.

"You *walked* home?" asked Mrs. O'Toole, unable to believe that
Cynthia, at a time of such disturbance, would continue doing without
the Pennsylvania Avenue streetcar. She handed her lodger a letter,
without saying anything more. The whole parlor already knew about
the foreign postmark.

"Paris," said Cynthia, regarding the blue envelope. "You've seen
views of it in your stereograph."

If she wasn't careful, she would get herself thrown out of here. She
might not end up in the District jail, but she'd be in a shabbier place
with an even worse landlady. What compelled her to be insulting? Was
it the emboldening effect of the florid penmanship on the envelope?
The certainty of whom the violet ink was from? Or was it—the most
astonishing fact—her realization that she didn't fear having the letter in
her hand?

She refrained from opening it until she'd shampooed her hair, and
even after reading it through to the bit about Conkling's wanting to see
the Observatory, she felt no great alarm. Since the extra funds for the
Transit arrived, she'd felt almost in league with him. It was their little
secret, and sitting with this odd piece of knowledge each day in the

Observatory, a place that always made her feel how *little* she knew, was strangely fortifying. And now, thanks to Hugh Allison's sentiments, however peculiarly expressed, she could stand by the window and read this letter without jumping out of her skin. Yes, she *was* more confident than she'd been that day in May when the last of Conkling's missives had arrived.

She slipped the letter back into her dress pocket and put up her not-quite-dry but progressively-less-hennaed hair. She trotted back downstairs, hoping, and failing, to escape the parlor without exciting comment.

"Going out again?" asked Louis Manley. "It's nearly eight o'clock. And quite dangerous, I should say."

"She's got a beau to protect her," said Dan Farricker.

"Oh?" was all Mrs. O'Toole added to that. The failure of Mr. Allison, that charming South Carolinian, to reappear here at 203 F Street was a sore point with the landlady, and ascribed to the selfish dictates of the dried-up Mrs. May.

A moment later the same Mrs. May was listening to the sparrows and on her way, with a fast, light step, to the corner of Third and D. She looked forward to Mary Costello's merriment, as well as her assistance with a quite sublunary matter. She found the astrologer in the little room at the back of the house, finished with the dinner Charles had brought and preparing what she announced would be her last dispatch to Conkling while he was still on the Continent. "Mr. Sharpe and Mr. Arthur have been in the city, negotiatin' with Mr. McCormick—at the insistence of the President himself," she said, with a slight uncertainty as to whether she had all the names right.

"I've read all that," said Cynthia, as if she were still a customer who deserved better. Perhaps one reason she couldn't take Conkling's letter too seriously was the silliness of the political atmosphere in which he fumed. Mr. McCormick, the assistant Treasury Secretary, had just been hoist on the petard of the administration's reforms: while he was ordering Sharpe and Arthur to clean out the Custom House, somebody had gotten around to reminding *him* that he now had to resign his post on the party's national committee.

"Have you told Senator Conkling that our local Lucy Webb Hayes Temperance Society has proclaimed its opposition to the railroad strike?" Cynthia laughed at the folly of it all, but Madam Costello, after a moment's consideration, shook her head: "No, he has a liking for Mrs. Hayes. A respectfulness, I should say. He's a complicated one, our War God is."

"Suit yourself," said Cynthia. She wished her companion believed a little more in fresh air. The room was dark, and it smelled of cabbage and cat.

"I'll tell you what I also don't tell the man," said Mary Costello.

"And what's that?"

"I don't tell him that Mrs. Sprague has rented out her Edgewood mansion for the summer—to no less than Mr. Schurz and the Postmaster General!"

Cynthia smiled. She was sure that Kate Chase Sprague, wherever she might be in Europe, hadn't informed Conkling she was providing a cool summertime perch to two members of the detested Cabinet.

"Come, Mary, let's take a walk."

The astrologer made a face, but Cynthia insisted, and as the older woman put on her hat, the younger one said, "Before we go I want to give you this." She handed Madam Costello a slim printed pamphlet, just struck off at the G.P.O., titled "Orbital Calculations of D'Arrest's Periodical Comet, 1877." Its authorship was identified only as "United States Naval Observatory," but the astrologer, quite aware of what Cynthia's little gift meant, got suddenly teary. "Oh, sweetheart" was all she said, knowing full well that Mrs. May would not actually be able to admit or discuss how this inscrutable, number-filled quarto embodied a friendship with Mr. Allison that four months ago had been just a flight of mortified fancy. The pamphlet was scientific proof of their connection, or at least its beginnings, and to Mary Costello it was practically a baby.

The two women walked to the Mall, across which ran a set of railroad tracks. On each side some blue-coated soldiers kept a listless watch.

"The Army must be feedin' these fellers regular," said Mary. "Else the brass would have to worry about the boys ripping up those wooden ties themselves."

"I suspect somebody's doing just that farther up the line," said Cynthia, who then confided: "That's why Mr. Allison and I will be taking our excursion on the water next week."

"Are you lookin' to know a propitious hour for that?" The planet reader wanted to repay the gift of the pamphlet.

"No," said Cynthia, avoiding Mary Costello's gaze and looking westward down the Mall. "It's something distinctly material I need. The name of someone who can fashion a device to prevent conception."

"Sweet Jaysus!"

"Oh, don't get *modest* with me, Mary. And don't tell me what-was-her-name in Chicago didn't—"

"Iris Cummings."

"Didn't acquaint you with such things."

"But you're talkin' about Chicago."

"The same people exist in every place, and you know them all. Mary."

"Well, I suppose—"

"Good. And later on, after you've gotten me this device, you can tell me the most propitious time to *stop* using it."

• • •

During these early days of his administration, Admiral Rodgers continued to conduct much of his business with the astronomers in the late evening hours, when they were on the scene making observations. Between appointments at his desk he could wander over to the

Great Equatorial or the 9.6-inch or the Transit Circle and keep learning what their real activities entailed.

Thus it was already growing dark on Monday, July 30, when Hugh
entered the gates for his meeting with the superintendent. Atypically
enough, he was early, and so he strolled to a point on the grounds
where, in sight of the river, he positioned himself under a lamp to give
a second reading to his mother's latest, and somewhat alarming, letter
from Charleston. *The losses at piquet were once sustainable. But what
he has whirled away at the roulette wheel (whose discovery behind Dr.
Brown's surgery has brought quite justifiable shame to your father and
his reckless friends)—well, I cannot remember how I began constructing
this sentence, but suffice it to say that it beggars all description. His losses
are infinitely worse than those incurred during what he still cheerfully
calls the "panics" of '59 and '66—whose full dreadfulness I shielded you
from in your youth. Except for the house (and my soul shakes to think
what secret liens may attach to it), we are quite nearly ruined . . .*

Because his mother's alarm and father's cheer galloped in a close
race, Hugh found it difficult, even on a second reading, to tell just how
dire these current reverses really were. He skipped the letter's last part,
remembering its implication that he really ought to be home, and that
even less honor attached to his continuing absence at this federal institution than to his sister's marriage to "that Philadelphia banker," sure
to be of no help during the current crisis.

He looked out upon the *Plymouth* and *Essex*—poised, one might
think, to fire upon the Observatory as if it were Fort Sumter, a shelling
he had actually witnessed as a boy. Because of Cynthia, he had given
the war more thought in the last four weeks than he had during its own
four years. The other day, in a supply room upstairs, Mr. Harrison had
pointed out a windowpane scratched with the nickname of Matthew
Maury's daughter and the initials of her playmates, and Hugh had
actually been able to follow the clerk's long, poignant story of how the
Observatory's last antebellum superintendent had had to resign his
post and go home and serve his native Virginia.

He felt light-headed going into the building. Pressing the back of his hand to his forehead, he thought of Cynthia's coolness to the touch, the invigorating chill she had not lost even in their moment of excitement in his rooms. Outside the admiral's office he found Lieutenant Sturdy—much better, thank you—chatting with Captain Piggonan and Henry Paul. "Going in to see the old man?" asked the latter.

"Yes," said Hugh, as the juice of Sturdy's tobacco struck the inside of the spittoon they stood near.

"Well, give him what he wants," advised Hugh's youngest colleague.

Admiral Rodgers did not look up from the book he held in front of his face, a Royal Astronomical Society publication, from 1857: "Report on the Observatories of His Highness the Rajah of Travancore," by John Allan Brown, F.R.S. "One of my opposite numbers," said the admiral, finally putting the monograph down. "Who worked on a smaller but even more difficult stage. I read these things to cheer myself up. Sit down."

A fly buzzed through the unscreened window and Hugh nodded, knowing he had nothing to say.

"Have you seen your friend Commodore Sands?" asked Rodgers.

"Not for a while, sir. He's in the country."

"To which he still removes his family every summer. He told me he nearly died the one time he lingered here."

Hugh expressed a wish for the commodore's long life.

"Look at this," said Rodgers, handing a letter across his desk. "Not as good as a death certificate, but useful nonetheless." Dr. Alexander Garrett, a physician at the Observatory around the time Hugh was born, pronounced himself ready to say that Professor James Ferguson—who back in the 1850s had seen a number of new asteroids through the 9.6-inch—had died, like so many of his colleagues, "due to malarial agencies."

Rodgers got up from his desk and went over to the window. With most of his back to Hugh, he continued speaking. Half his musings

seemed intended for whatever spirit of place might be hovering outside in the evening haze. "These constant eruptions requiring the
Army," he said softly. "They want my brother-in-law dispatching
troops against railway ruffians, against Indians in the Dakota, against
bandits down in Mexico. They want the *Navy* to stop these mobs in
California from terrifying all the poor Chinamen looking for work." He
paused for a second or two. "Mr. Hall tells me Mars is now approaching closer to us than it's been since the time of Antietam. Maybe that
accounts for our current bellicosity. It almost makes one believe in
astrology, doesn't it?"

Hugh was about to say no, it didn't, an opinion that Cynthia's
recently confessed acquaintance with the Irish planet reader had done
nothing to change. But the sight of Rodgers, at a low ebb and still not
arrived at his point, kept him silent.

"And with all this going on," the admiral finally concluded, "I'm
supposed to gain us the government's attention."

"I'm afraid I have nothing new to propose," said Hugh, relieved to
be out with it.

"I didn't think you did," the superintendent said, coming back to
his desk. "I felt sure that if you had something, you'd have been in to
see me before now. I suppose you *could* be in here proffering some list
of excuses, and I do thank you for not doing that. But the fact of your
relative uselessness remains. I must, I'm afraid, tell you that in my current state of mind, and in our current state of affairs, 'Orbital Calculations of D'Arrest's Periodical Comet, 1877' interests me rather less than
'Report on the Observatories of His Highness the Rajah of Travancore.'"

Hugh suppressed a smile, which was altogether quashed by the
admiral's sudden directive: "I'm putting you on a sunspot watch with
Mr. Todd. What we can do in that realm may not be much, but it seems
to interest the meteorologically minded chief of the Signal Corps, and
I'd rather have him in my debt than fighting me, the way I'm fighting
with Lieutenant Hoxie and the Corps of Engineers. I don't *care* if they

built that wall on the northern perimeter. It was the District that ordered it—trying to cut us off even further, I suppose—and it's the District that's damn well going to pay for it. But as I say, I'll take allies wherever I can find them. If the Signal Corps wants its sunspots, that's good enough for me. But it's not good enough for you, meaning for the talents I've been led to believe you possess. I suppose I should ask how goes your *letter-writing*." He gave the term an extended, feminine trill, and Hugh took the insult. What else could he do? Talk about Gauss's notebooks?

"The letters go well enough, sir. The ones relative to next year's transit of Mercury—"

"They don't take special skill, do they?"

"No, sir."

"Which is why, Mr. Allison, I'll be recommending to Professor Pickering that he find a place for you back in Cambridge. I've already written him a letter—and dated it September the fifteenth. I'll keep it in my drawer until then. And not one day longer."

"Yes, sir."

With no word of good-bye, Rodgers took up his book, transporting himself back to Travancore and someone's even harsher lot of astronomical administration. Hugh was left to show himself out and then, aimlessly, up to the Great Equatorial, where he saw Asaph Hall switching his intense gaze between the eyepiece and his notes and back again.

Hugh approached George Anderson, a Scottish jack-of-all-trades around the Observatory, possessed of as much motherwit as the rest of them had training, and whose assistance Hall preferred above all others'. The two of them were a respectful, odd pair—the Scotsman so peppery and the Yankee so grave—as unlikely in their way as Hugh Allison and Cynthia May.

"He's still excited about his white spot, isn't he, Anderson?"

"But of course, Mister Ally. Do you know he's knocked a whole quarter-hour off the length of Saturn's day? Every book you'll find down in that library is *fifteen whole minutes* off, because they never had something so noticeable as that white spot to fix on every time she comes round."

"Yes," said Hugh, not much interested. "I suppose that's so."

"Now don't it, Mr. Ally, make you wonder what else those books might be wrong about?"

Hugh watched Anderson hurry back to Asaph Hall.

•   •   •

"And you're certain you still want to go?""

"Yes," Cynthia insisted, despite the tearing wind and rain. "We're here, aren't we? And it's *marvelously* cool."

She held Hugh's umbrella while he handed a dollar, the cost of two tickets, to the *Mary Washington*'s paymaster. The crowd at the Seventh Street wharf was smaller than usual for a weeknight excursion, but the boat hadn't canceled its run. For all the tree branches and litter blowing across the city, the atmosphere was calmer than it had been a few nights before. The riots in Pittsburgh and Baltimore were said to have subsided, and meetings to settle the strikers' demands were reported to be in progress. It looked as if Mrs. O'Toole would keep getting her seven-cent bread, after all. "Fourteen loaves for what you just spent," Cynthia now told Hugh, in the only manner she could comfortably use to convey her thanks.

The two of them marched arm in arm between garlanded banisters to the upper-deck's grand saloon. The sofas and chairs that awaited them there were less plush and preposterous than what furnished Hugh's rooms on High Street, but still fancy enough to make Cynthia think of her landlady's parlor with renewed contempt. While a piano player warmed up for a vocal concert by Professor Piscorio, the couple lowered themselves into a small love seat and regarded their multiple reflections on the saloon's mirrored walls.

"I hope this doesn't turn out to be a preacher's Sabbath," she said, pointing to the glass. "I'd hate to have you pondering angles of refraction while you're supposed to be having an evening's holiday."

Hugh pointed to the smooth brimming head on the mug of beer he'd just been handed by the steward. "There are those who say you'd have a telescope of limitless strength if, instead of using a mirror, you spun a parabola of mercury with a uniform motion. Of course, the difficulty with that is you'd be able to look only at things directly above." He tilted back his head and started to balance the glass of lager on his brow. *"Please,"* said Cynthia, anxious to avoid looking foolish, even as she remembered this trick as a particular skill of her brother's.

"Is this mercury telescope what you talked about with Admiral Rodgers?"

"Goodness, no," said Hugh. "They can barely find ways to maintain the equipment they've got."

"Then what *did* you talk about?"

"Sunspots! That and my, what shall we call them, clerical duties. You're more the scientist than I am these days, Mrs. May." This might be putting it strongly, he thought, but it was better than telling her about the admiral's September deadline. He rose to his feet, took her hand, and led her to the rain-lashed window. "There's not a star in the sky," he said.

"So it's not a preacher's Sabbath after all."

"No, it's even sadder. Under all those clouds the moment is lost."

"Muffled, perhaps," she said, seeing no reason the weather should disqualify the moment from romance.

"No, lost. Blacked out and gone forever. Instead of going forth, as light, at 185,000 miles per second. This patch of Earth can't be seen, and so this moment is eternally obliterated. Remember the green bolts of your aurora?"

"Of course."

"Well, *they're* still flashing. That moment still lives."

"And this moment doesn't?"

"It might as well never have happened."

"The poor moment. I was hoping you were pondering its romance, but here you are denying its very existence."

"And even your aurora is just random flashes. One night of it looks like any other night of it. There's no method in it. No proof of personality."

"Except for God's."

"Really? Do you believe in Him, Mrs. May?"

"I certainly do. I strongly dislike Him, but I believe in Him."

He was, she understood, talking about the Gauss business, and she still had no idea whether it would be wise to draw him out on this confusing (perhaps mad?) matter. To add to her vexation, Professor Piscorio had just started his *bel canto*. The first syllables of Italian gave her the awful sensation she always experienced from the sound of a foreign language, a feeling that she'd been struck deaf and blind. She couldn't bear not knowing what the words *meant;* the lack of sense horrified her, as if random integers had been substituted for the sequence of pi.

"Come on," said Hugh. "Let's go."

"Out there?"

"Yes, *out there.*" He pulled her through the French doors and onto the deck. She shrieked like a girl, but in the rain the sound was not loud enough to deflect anyone's attention from Professor Piscorio's piercing tenor. The two of them raced under a little canopy. Only as they caught their breath did she feel the touch of his hand.

"You're burning up," she said.

"With passion."

No, she thought, trying to steady her nerves. *It can't be. If he were truly sick, if it were malaria, he'd be in a delirium.* "We should go back inside."

"No," he said. "If we've come out here, then we ought to get drenched."

"No!" she cried, as he pulled her out from under the awning and into the smack and splash of the rain upon the deck, a torrent of little silver globes and spangles that soon had them soaked to the skin.

The boat was passing Mount Vernon, which she had not seen since before the war, and which she had no desire to see now, not while she was in his arms and laughing. He was her boy magician; he had liquefied the hail of her girlhood into these magic, harmless, licking plops.

She looked up at the sky. "It's as I'm always saying, Mr. Allison. Washington, D.C., has the most divine climate."

"Cynthia," he answered, looking into her eyes. "I have immortal longings."

•   •   •

It was past 5 A.M. and the streetlamps were already doused, but the Pennsylvania Avenue trolley had another hour to go before its first run of the day. Cynthia knew her dress would be saturated, yet again, by the warm wet wind as she walked home in the dawn light.

They had returned to the Seventh Street wharf a half hour after midnight, and managed to find a carriage that took the two of them back to Hugh's rooms in Georgetown, where they changed out of their clothes and dried each other in the glow of the gaslight. His body was more slender and beautiful than either her brother's or John May's had been. It seemed to belong to some angel in the ether. She recalled it now, her eyes closed against the sight of a truck clattering its load of night soil to the Seventeenth Street docks.

The device she'd requested of Madam Costello had not yet been obtained from whatever party the astrologer had approached, and even so, Cynthia could hardly have expected to need it so soon as last night. In the event, she had *not* needed it. After a surprisingly long time, Hugh had expertly withdrawn from her, confirming—both to her relief and worry—his familiarity with women. Afterward, his passion safely spent, he had lain on top of her, his forehead still burning and his eyes still open, glazed and unblinking, like the dead soldier in an idealized engraving.

The weight of her drenched dress slowed her gait, and it was past six-thirty when she reached Mrs. O'Toole's and let herself in, quietly enough, she hoped, not to be heard by Daisy, who was clinking the breakfast dishes and silver onto the table. Upstairs, she dried off with a worn hand towel and reached into the bottom drawer for a flannel nightgown to guard against chill. As soon as she had it on, she sat down at the small secretary to the left of her window and extracted some stationery from the drawer.

She looked at the violet ink to which she would now respond and, before deciding upon the salutation, wrote out an envelope to the Utica address she had memorized off the letter before this one.

If you are on the ocean, she wrote, in a hand not half so fancy as the War God's, *I hope your skies are fairer than they have been over the District. The railroad siege has lifted—for a day or two it felt quite like '61—but not the clouds.*

I should have thanked you before now for your quiet munificence in assisting Venus on her exceedingly slow transit across the Sun. (I assure you there was no sign of her in last night's gloomy heavens.)

He would picture her, in her lonely room, looking vainly for that planet in the sky. Rereading the two short paragraphs she had composed thus far, she marveled at their sickening affectation. She had not known she possessed the talent.

I look forward to seeing you when you are next in Washington. You of course already know where to find me.

She could smell Hugh Allison on her hands, could feel his flushed brow. And she could still see his open eyes, barely holding in whatever wanted to escape from behind them at the speed of light. She shivered with fear inside the nightgown. But her instincts now told her that the moment might come when she required Roscoe Conkling. And in order to use him, she would have to be, as duplicitously as she could, *Most Sincerely* his, *Cynthia May.*

SIX

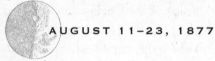

The second baseman caught a fly ball. "Only Neptune is missing," said Cynthia.

"Oh, lordy," replied Hugh, pulling his straw hat low against the hot sun. "Another's preacher's Sabbath."

"Well, surely it's occurred to you," said Cynthia, gesturing toward the ball field on the Astoria Grounds. "It all revolves around the pitcher, so he's the Sun, and the infielders are the four small inner planets. Jupiter, Saturn, and Uranus are way out there beyond them."

"Darling, it occurs to *every* astronomer. That's why they're tiresome company here—and why I thought to bring you along instead of Henry Paul." He put his head on her shoulder and was soon dozing off, even though she was the one most worn out by their recreations of the last two, sweltering weeks: picnics in the Seventh Street park; horse races at Brightwood; shooting contests at the Schuetzen Festival. Hugh acted as if frantic indolence might substitute for meaningful work, or at least distract her from pressing the issue of his idleness at the Observatory. Their traipsing from one amusement to another appealed to her with its appearance of ordinary courtship, but upset her Yankee thrift of money and time.

All the rented velocipedes and bags of butterscotch candy could not really sustain the illusion that they were two young lovers with nothing to do but lark, or that Hugh wasn't in serious trouble with the admiral. She had never learned the details of his meeting with Rodgers, but at the Observatory she'd begun to notice shrugging shoulders and pursed lips whenever Hugh Allison's name was mentioned in the industrious presence of someone like Professor Harkness. It was folly to continue this romantic pantomime, so unconvincing even to herself, but she lacked the courage to ask questions that might make him tell her his days in Washington were numbered.

She looked away from his long, sleeping lashes and back to the baseball diamond. In the celestial analogy, what was the batter? And perhaps more to the point, what was the ball? Was it the light Hugh talked about dispatching into the heavens? A loud, sudden crack sent the little sphere disappearing into the late-afternoon light over center field, and for a second she thought of jabbing him in the ribs, of waking him and demanding that he explain, right now and comprehensibly, his preoccupation with those drawings on his wall. But in turning to him, her eyes were caught by the glinting chain of his gold watch. When extracted from his pocket, it showed a quarter to six.

There wasn't time. She would ask him later, or next week.

"Wake up," she whispered, barely able to make herself disturb his nap, let alone hector him over his life's work and purpose. He only murmured, and nestled his head against her breast.

"Get up, you infant. You need to be at work."

"Mmhn," he groaned, rubbing his eyes. "My august responsibilities."

He had been assigned to record, from the Observatory's vantage, the time and position of some flares to be shot later this evening by the Army Signal Service. The Secretary of War and President Hayes, now said to be packing for his New Hampshire vacation, had attended the first round of these demonstrations last night on a road near the Soldiers' Home. Stations inside the District and along the coast were watching for the lights sent up by rocket and mortar. At the Observatory, this vigil could easily be performed by the watchmen making their rounds of the barometers, but the menial task provided Rodgers with another chance to try humiliating Professor Allison into renewed productivity.

Hugh and Cynthia began the long walk back across town in sleepy silence. She wished the Army signals involved some calculations necessitating her presence, or that another collaborative comet were available until he finally came up with some bold but within-the-pale project, one he'd start in order to impress her, but end up truly interested in. She had a fantasy of him rushing to her desk one morning, ablaze with a eureka he'd experienced during his clerical labors over the next year's eclipse, some exciting new scheme for doing those observations that would banish his self-disgust and make him a hero to the admiral.

"Be on the lookout for a red cow," he said, as the two of them crossed Eleventh Street.

She curled her lip against this latest piece of whimsy.

"No, really," he went on. "One's escaped from Gonzaga College. I have this from my barber. It could be anywhere."

She clapped her ears and raced ahead.

"All right," he said, struggling to keep up. "Then be on the lookout for your chariot instead." She was supposed to take the Georgetown horsecar that left from the Treasury building. They would have a late supper at the Union Hotel once the last flares had been launched and he came home from Foggy Bottom. "While you're at it," he added, "see if you can't find me a carriage."

No one could ever keep up with her nervous pace, especially the kind she was setting now, but since leaving the Astoria Grounds she'd noticed that he was a step behind his usual step behind; and now he had stopped altogether.

"Wait here a moment." He veered toward Milburn's drugstore—for a bottle of whiskey, she suspected. She made a face.

"Tomorrow is Sunday," he explained. "We have rather strict laws about such sales in quiet Georgetown."

"Yes," she said. "But today is Saturday."

"Which will be followed by long, lingering, endless Sunday. Don't move."

He came out of Milburn's with a bottle that he asked her to take to his rooms. They parted in front of the Treasury, and as her horsecar made its way up Pennsylvania and then High Street, she tried to look forward to the evening, reminding herself of all the reasons she liked Georgetown more than her own neighborhood near the Capitol. The alley dwellers weren't so thick on the ground, and sitting in the Peabody Library had a way of calming her, of making her feel less like the interloper she always imagined herself in public places. The trees were fuller, too. Alighting from the streetcar, she admired the little colonnade of them leading to Hugh's door, and took note of an advertisement tacked to one maple for a WHITE WOMAN TO DO GENERAL HOUSEWORK.

There was no chance it was Hugh who'd posted this bill. Letting herself in, she saw that his seraglio was even messier than usual, the pillows, cups, and newspapers a whirling agglomeration of debris, just like, he continued to assure her, the average comet.

She couldn't bear sinking into Mrs. Allison's pillows, so she settled into the chair behind the desk, the only hard one in the room, and looked around. Within an hour she could make this lair as orderly and right-angled as her own shabby precinct of Mrs. O'Toole's. But would she? What was the point of prolonging the fancy that she and this young man would soon become respectable dwellers on these leafy heights, with Hugh going contentedly off each day for thirty years to work on a successor to Professor Yarnall's star catalogue? This was not going to happen, and in any case, it wasn't the daydream that had drawn her to him. But what *had* attracted her, besides the eyelashes and mischief? Was it, inscrutably, whatever had made him tack those sketches to the wall?

Or was she drawn to his apparent determination to throw himself away? Did she love this stubborn profligacy, and hope it would drag her worried, frugal self down with him—into some lovely oblivion, where the waters could finally close over her head? She took the bottle from its wrapper and poured herself a glass of whiskey. But a moment later she began straightening up the desktop. No, she was not cut out to be a voluptuary.

And he, poor boy, was not cut out for this. She opened his sunspots notebook, the dull record he was charged with making by himself while young Mr. Todd remained on vacation in New Jersey.

AUGUST 5	10 A.M.	NO SPOTS
6	6 P.M.	THE SAME
8	10 A.M.	NO SPOTS
	6 P.M.	THE SAME

The sight of this stupid table caused her to throw back half the whiskey in the unclean glass. But before the sting had left her throat, her eyes widened and her hands began to tremble. He had not even been *near* the Observatory on the 8th, neither at 10 A.M. nor six in the evening. When she'd gone looking for him that morning, Mr. Harrison had said he was nowhere around; and that night they'd had an early supper at the Irving House.

So, she thought, negligence wasn't good enough; he needed actively to disgrace himself. Closing the little notebook, she began to weep, soundlessly, the way she'd taught herself between the thin walls of all her rooming houses. She took a last sip of the whiskey and set the glass down on two unopened envelopes from Hugh's mother—no doubt containing more shrill complaint of debts and darkies. They made her recall the sealed letters, a packet of ten, that John May had written her just before Chickamauga, one to be opened on each of her ensuing birthdays, if he didn't survive. He'd marked the corner of each envelope, 1864 through 1874, and she had read all of them at first light on the day she was supposed to. They became, as the years went by, shorter and somehow less audible, embarrassed by their own repetitions and the ruse they were attempting against fate, until they ceased altogether, John having run out of time to write, or just the ability to imagine her in the world more than ten years later.

In the ones he did write, he had always pictured her in New Hampshire, never here, and certainly not in August. The sun at the ball field had made her tired, she now realized, and as soon as the whiskey muffled her agitation over the sunspots fakery, she gave up the wooden desk chair for one of the couches, kicking away some of the pillows and falling into a dream of Rutherford B. Hayes, with whom she sat on a porch, watching the sun fall into Lake Winnipesaukee.

Hours later, she awoke to see Hugh drinking from the same glass she had used. He smiled as she came to.

"A little fizzle. Barely bigger than D'Arrest's."

She rubbed her eyes and looked at him.

"The Army rockets," he explained.

"Of course," she said, wondering if he'd even gone to the Observatory. Was there room for the sunspots notebook on the agenda of things she couldn't bring herself to ask him about?

At the Union Hotel they were shown to their table at a quarter past ten by Riley Shinn himself, the proprietor who took such pride in the "Pocket Tuileries" he had created on a corner of Bridge Street. They ate their supper, while at the bar several men drunkenly argued the recent railroad strike, each a loud parrot of what he'd read in the papers or heard on the streetcar. "No innocent man ever gets killed in a riot!" declared the loudest of them.

"Hall was there until things fogged over," said Hugh. "Just him and George Anderson. He gave up about an hour ago, and he did the strangest thing before he left."

"What was that?"

"He locked his observer's book in a desk drawer. I've never seen anyone do that before."

Cynthia dismissed the behavior with a shrug, relieved to have at least some evidence that Hugh had actually been on the premises tonight. Lucid with coffee, she was now determined to force him on to another subject: "You have to tell me the exact state of things between you and Admiral Rodgers."

"Things between us are perfectly fine," said Hugh, signaling the waiter for their bill.

"They're obviously not."

"If you don't change the subject, I shall sing. Or order another whiskey."

"Tell me what he—"

"*In the gloaming* . . ." He lilted loudly enough that two of the drunkards at the bar ceased their argument and made ready to join in.

Mortified, she seized his hand. "All right, all right. Fanny Christian had a scandalous letter from a friend who's on her honeymoon."

"That's better," he said, subsiding.

"Now take me out of here."

It was unspoken, not unclear, that they would end up in his rooms, but for a while they walked with no set destination. Two blocks' movement north brought them to Gay Street, and by way of apology, Hugh finally put his arm around her waist. Too weary to refuse the gesture, Cynthia leaned closer to him, and they turned the corner in silence, the whitewashed planting boxes at the foot of the trees helping to guide their steps through the dark.

She was the first to see several people, a whole family, kneeling beneath a cherry tree in the front garden of no. 18. She squeezed Hugh's arm, and the two of them halted, uncertain what to do next, having intruded on a scene that ought to be taking place indoors. Cynthia looked for a light inside, shifting her eyes from the crouched, murmuring figures toward the bay windows. But the house's interior was entirely dark, the people in the garden visible only from a lamp in the hand of Angeline Hall, who was leading her family in prayer. The wavering light flared against the cheekbones of her gaunt face, which looked up at the sky as her free hand urged little Angelo to look up with her. She seemed to be both surveying and beseeching the heavens, as if they were on the verge of revealing something spectacular for the first time. Her husband, Asaph, stole just a single glance upward, concentrating on whatever course of prayer his wife was directing.

"What could have brought them out here?" Cynthia whispered to Hugh. But he was already creeping comically away, his steps as high and stilted as an insect's. With a finger to her lips, she implored him not to make her laugh and give them away. Only after he'd disappeared around the corner, did she start after him, desperate to be away from the Halls' miserable worship, and irrationally frightened that Hugh was somehow gone forever.

She ran through the dark, clutching her reticule, which contained the device Madam Costello had finally procured. She knew that tonight she would not use it, that she would press on the small of his beautiful back and hold him inside her, make him give her a child, as if his sex were the center of the universe and she the god of all creation.

•　　•　　•

"They're cheering for you, Father."

"Yes, my darling," said Roscoe Conkling to his daughter, Bessie. He smiled modestly, and did not look up from the pile of mail and newspapers she had brought to his usual suite at Bagg's Hotel here in Utica, in time for his arrival a half hour before. When she'd gone into the other room for a moment, he had raised the window just high enough that he might hear the crowd swell and chant. Still smiling over her discovery of this action, she was nonetheless impatient for him to take his place on the balcony and make the appearance the crowd had been ordered to come out and cheer. But he continued to feign indifference. Looking through the serials that had piled up in his two months' absence, as if the latest number of *Appleton's* compared in importance to the full-throated electorate outside, he asked her for a second time whether she was truly pleased with Malone's edition of Shakespeare, the present he'd brought her from England.

"It delights me, Father. It will be the only Shakespeare in the house you haven't underlined for bits of rhetorical weaponry. Unless, of course, you marked it aboard ship while preparing something for tonight."

Without looking up, he smiled, trying to convey gratitude at her having spared him the sight of her fiancé this evening. "Have you looked through some of these papers you've brought me, my dear? It seems the Norfolk and New Orleans collectors have been getting the same scrutiny as our Mr. Arthur."

"Yes, Father, I've kept up with everything. You'll see that the same men in the Administration who couldn't understand why you went away are now wondering what's made you come back so early."

Conkling chuckled, and inclined his head toward the window. The crowd had begun a triumphalist rendition of "What a Friend We Have in Jesus."

"Sir?" said Lewis Herbert, chairman of the welcoming committee. He, too, was eager to get Conkling before the crowd, but feared disrupting the War God's anticipatory savor. "I'm sure they'll be keen to hear you prognosticate about the President's message to Congress."

"Oh, yes," laughed Conkling. "Tell me: Do you, too, believe he'll propose setting up a commission to arbitrate the next big labor strike?"

"Yes, sir."

"One could hardly expect different from an Administration *invented* by a commission."

Mr. Herbert threw his head back twice, indicating not only that this was a very good piece of wit indeed, but that, no, he had not forgotten who'd created the electoral commission *ex nihilo*.

Conkling still seemed in no hurry. This noisy welcome, smoothly churned out by the machine's local gears, would be the fourth one accorded him since Friday evening, when the *Neckar* had sailed past Governors Island and been greeted by trumpets, cannon fire, and the hoarse roar of every Custom House man aboard the *Thomas Collyer*, which had been chartered to run alongside Conkling's vessel. An observer on shore would have thought the machine had its own navy. Conkling had taken salutes from two other steamers in the harbor, and resisted being so unmanly or ungrateful as to stopper his ears against the thirty tugboats all blowing their whistles at once. He'd just clenched his teeth and tipped his hat, provoking another round of huzzahs and the comic tootling of "Hail to the Chief" by a pipe organ he never succeeded in locating through the salt spray and darkening sky.

The men from the *Collyer* had not let him disembark from the *Neckar* before boarding it themselves. They would have transferred him to the ferry on their shoulders had his formidable dignity not interfered. As it was, the crush of congratulation—about exactly what, no one seemed certain—delayed the party's arrival at the Fifth Avenue Hotel until past 11 P.M. But the hundreds waiting in Madison Square with torches and banners and an urgent need for encouragement from their returning chieftain stayed fixed to the pavements until he arrived to excoriate their blue-nosed enemies.

It had been the same in Albany and Schenectady, and it would be the same here in Utica, too, thought Lewis Herbert, but only if he could get Conkling out on the balcony. A plaintive look toward Miss Bessie produced a quiet nod and her movement through the French doors, where with a long taper she lit four Chinese lanterns tied to the balcony's railing. The gesture produced the new level of delirium the crowd understood was now required of it. Finally, even the will of Roscoe Conkling could not resist such a tumult. He rose from his chair, and Lewis Herbert, gathering up the scrolled proclamation with its eight hundred signatures welcoming the senator home, preceded him onto the little stone platform.

"Sir!" Herbert shouted into the summer night. "We welcome you home to the heart of New York. We welcome you as neighbors, and we pray that, whatever station you may ever adorn, the choicest blessings of heaven will attend you!" At this mention of Conkling's unknown prospects, two great laureled placards—GRANT IN '80 and CONKLING IN

'84—began waving and did not rest until the senator stepped forward and ordered the crowd's silence.

"My friends," he said, in a quieter voice than they'd expected, "I come back to you a stronger, if not better, American. Comparisons may be invidious, but I have had the chance to make intercontinental ones all summer, and I can tell you I have never been so proud of my country or so content with my countrymen."

A dozen grateful flags waved their thirty-eight stars, and a voice at the back, eager to test the universality of Conkling's compliment to his fellow Americans, cried: "What about Hayes?" The throng erupted in laughter and rhythmic applause, hoping to make the senator pour it on. Before Conkling could answer, two brave voices at the crowd's center posed another loud question: "What about reform?" They were shouted down by renewed agitation for an answer to the first interrogative. The crowd knew the two questions were really the same, but the first had a better chance of making Conkling dive to the *ad hominem* depths that might make August 14, 1877, a night to remember. Since Mr. Cornell had just once more refused to resign either his party post or his perch at the Custom House, this could be the moment that Conkling opened a frontal assault upon the Administration.

But the senator would do things in his own good time. Looking out over all their heads, he declared, in a quite unstentorian voice: "England may have her farflung empire, and her eight centuries of parliamentary rule, but every fair wind of progress and liberty blows more strongly at this country's back than hers." Cheers, somewhat less lusty than they might have been, greeted the remark; perhaps the parliamentary reference was the prelude to a first full salvo against the President?

No. More like Cook than Conkling, the senator went casually on with his travelogue: "English hotels would seem sadly behind the times here. Indeed, they would not be endured by anyone accustomed to the comforts of Bagg's." Local pride swelled the roar for this particular observation, but could not banish the confusion and disappointment that were starting to define the crowd's mood. Was it for *this* they'd been summoned from every post office and courthouse in four counties? "Telegraphic service in general," Conkling went on, "is inferior to ours. Railway travel is destitute of comforts and conveniences which here are matters of course."

One of the reformist handful worked up the courage to taunt the speaker with a shout of "Hail to the War God!", daring him to act like the bully he was supposed to be. The faithful, instead of tearing the mocker limb from limb, fell silent, secretly glad for the insult, which might provoke the sort of speech they'd come to hear.

Stung at last, Conkling snapped off a rejoinder. "Remember it was *Vulcan* who gave Jove his thunderbolts!" The crowd burst into a bedlam of delight over this allusion to the Electoral Commission. But the senator retracted his artillery as soon as he'd brought it out, returning to his dull memorandum about the severity of the European depression relative to America's; the undeniable greatness of French paintings; and the magnanimity of the Germans (a nationality well represented on the Utica voting rolls) who, in their conquest of Paris, had chosen to preserve the city's art instead of plunder it.

As things turned out, the crowd needn't have worried. Conkling had always known the moment at which to raise his voice, to take the sharp hook of his invective and yank the crowd up from the first inches of slumber into which it was sinking. "General Grant," he said, simply, letting the name hang in the air, a subject and predicate both.

The listeners, now silent and fully alert, prepared for the senator's verbal evocation of the former President.

"Honors wait upon him wherever he goes. Unlike myself, he may remain long abroad. But when he returns you will find that all the distinctions poured upon him have not washed out a jot of his Americanism or made him anything save the same upright, downright Republican without cant or palaver."

He spat out the last two nouns like bits of gristle, and the true believers roared their approval. The reformers would not dare raise another taunt.

"He remains a lion," said Conkling of the general. "Incapable of the flatulent self-righteousness with which these new times are furnished."

More roars; leonine ones, the roarers hoped.

"He would not recognize the politicians who have whined and crept in his wake these past six months. I suspect that they will creep and whine for another short time to come—until they turn around and see how the lion they thought was long gone is *charging up from behind!* Good night, ladies and gentlemen!"

He turned on his heel, the tail of his waistcoat slicing the air as he dashed back through the French doors. Bessie glimpsed his high color and sheer happiness. If his crescendo had been lacking in particulars, it hardly mattered. The crowd now knew the essential thing: the bloodlust of political combat was upon Roscoe Conkling. He was ready to push back the legions of change.

Within five minutes the senator was leading his own parade, marching with Mr. Herbert and other local worthies at the head of a lusty civic mob. Down Genesee Street and along Hopper, the torches daubed the night sky like paintbrushes. Snare drums and tubas heralded what could no longer be doubted: the War God was ready to unmake the President he had made. Block after block, Conkling literally set the pace, his army of favorites rushing to keep up on this opening charge against merit.

Upon reaching the house at Rutger Park, they saw its four chimneys hung with locomotive lamps. At the sight of them, the tubas gave their best imitation of a train whistle, and Conkling made a dramatic, solitary walk up his driveway to the open front door, where Julia stood, bathed in light.

"Mrs. Conkling," he said, with a nod so slight only she could detect this token of thanks for her usual forbearance. Both husband and wife knew that this—not the loudly applauded kiss that followed—would be their most intimate moment for the foreseeable future.

After what was more the suggestion of a bow than its actual execution, Conkling slipped inside and shut the door. Down at the end of the drive, Bessie sighed and smiled, knowing that her father, before another quarter hour went by, would slip out the back door and into a carriage for the discreet return to Bagg's.

Lewis Herbert, having been spared any eruptions of the Conkling temper, mopped his brow in relief over the evening's success. Turning to the senator's daughter, he fished for some small compliment: "It can't have seemed much after the New York and Albany welcomes, but I'm glad he wasn't too tired to enjoy our own small demonstration." Miss Conkling merely smiled. Hoping for something more, Mr. Herbert dipped his rod once again. "I meant to say, he seemed in just the right mood to indulge our little effort."

"Oh, yes," said Bessie, "his mood could not have been more lively." She did not tell Mr. Herbert its real source, which she felt certain lay near the top of the mail stack she'd brought to the hotel. She had taken note of her father's expression while he read the contents of a small envelope postmarked at Washington and addressed in a spiky, but recognizably feminine, hand.

·   ·   ·

"Look up, Mrs. May! There's a new moon in the sky!"

Young Angelo Hall was racing down High Street, thrilled to find an even slightly familiar face to whom he could shout his news.

It was Friday morning, August 17, six days since Cynthia had seen the boy kneeling in his front garden. It hardly mattered trying to disguise the fact that she was coming from Hugh's rooms. The boy was too excited by his tidings to notice such a thing, and she felt unable to justify the deception, in any case. This might be the first morning in the past five that she had awakened beside Hugh, but there was no getting past the fact that she *was* a fallen woman now.

"Tell me what you mean, Angelo."

"I'm not supposed to!" cried the boy, tugging the bow at the back of her dress, orbiting around her as if *she* were a planet. "My papa's done it! He's found the moon of Mars!" Saying the words only excited him further, and he was off on another dash, leaving Cynthia to continue alone on her walk to the Observatory.

She wondered if Angelo's proclamation could possibly be true, and whether she should go back and communicate such startling news to Hugh. No, she would keep on her way and let him sleep. The last thing she needed was to start showing up late to her desk. Quickening her step, she noticed how the murky weather of the last several days had finally burned off. Asaph Hall, she knew from Hugh, had been so eager for the skies to clear that two nights ago he had defied the usual prohibition against sleeping at the Observatory. Could it be a Martian moon that he'd been after? And could he actually have found it?

The mood at the Observatory offered nothing confirmatory. Indeed, everything was so normal—Mr. Harrison sharpening his pencils at 9:00 on the dot, Professor Harkness offering his usual shy good-morning nod—that one couldn't imagine any event out of the ordinary having occurred. Unless something *so* extraordinary had happened, an astronomical occurence of such moment, that it must, for now, be kept secret from peripheral employees like herself. As soon as she removed her bonnet, she reached into the top drawer of her desk for Thomas Dick's *Celestial Scenery,* published three years before her birth and passed along to her by a disappointed schoolmate at Miss Wilton's who'd received it as a prize.

Along with *Principles of Trigonometry,* the book had made the long odyssey of rooming houses with Cynthia, and sure enough it had something to say on the subject of the moment: "As Mars ranks among the smallest planets of the system, its satellite, if any exist, must be extremely small . . . it could scarcely be distinguishable by our telescopes, especially when we consider that such a satellite would never appear to recede to any considerable distance from the margin of Mars. . . . The long duration of winter in the polar regions of Mars seems to require a moon to cheer the inhabitants during the long absence of the sun; and if there be none, the people of those regions must be in a far more dreary condition than the Laplanders and Green-landers of our globe."

Thomas Dick made this moon sound like a flight of fancy, or at least wishful thinking, but she noticed that he did not rule out its existence—unlike Professor Hugh Allison, who had assured her that all serious astronomical thinkers felt certain any such moon, however small, would have been seen by now by *someone*. The subject had come up just a few weeks ago, when Professor Harkness dusted off some numbers from 1862, the year of Mars's last proximity, to send to old Commodore Sands, who intended using his spyglass during a weekend in the country for what he knew would be his last close-range glimpse of the planet.

The morning passed quickly. Thanks to Conkling's appropriation (one secret only she knew), Cynthia had made more uninterrupted progress on the Transit of Venus during the last few weeks than during all the stop-and-start months before; and she made a bit more now, even though she could not banish Angelo Hall's outburst—his own wishful thinking?—from her thoughts.

A little after noon, too curious to sit eating lunch at her desk, she wandered the building, chatting with Mr. Paul, looking at some old observer's notebooks in the library and, finally, passing by Professor Hall's office. He was eating lunch at his desk, and he politely smiled as she passed. When she saw Simon Newcomb approach, she decided to linger on the other side of the corridor, obliquely opposite Mr. Hall's open door. She pretended to study a portrait of John Quincy Adams, as did Mr. Harrison, who had just arrived at the same spot and also seemed to know that a bit of eavesdropping was in order.

"Now what's this you think you've seen?" Newcomb asked his dour colleague.

"Probably nothing at all," said Hall, who was handing Newcomb a piece of paper, if Cynthia's ears judged the situation right.

"Twelfth magnitude at its elongation!" exclaimed Newcomb. "Why, this looks very much like a satellite."

Hall murmured something, doubtfully. Newcomb continued to

hypothesize and, Cynthia realized, hope against hope. "Of course, it *is* more likely an asteroid," he said. Unless—you could almost hear him thinking it—the heavenly body really was an historic discovery made by someone other than Simon Newcomb? "Would you like me to try confirming it?" he asked Hall.

The New Englander politely declined the offer of help.

Newcomb's nervousness kept showing. "D'Arrest looked hard for a moon, fifteen years ago, in Copenhagen."

"Yes," agreed Hall, quietly. "Of course, the power of our new glass can turn up so many things these days."

"You seem rather casual about this object," Newcomb declared.

"Well, it's always best to be doubtful," said Hall, who by the sound of things was returning to his lunch.

Newcomb swept out into the corridor, ignoring Cynthia and Mr. Harrison. The computer and the clerk signaled each other with raised eyebrows and then returned to their work. Something was definitely afoot, and by the time she got back to her desk, Cynthia felt sure she'd figured it out. Asaph Hall had seen something special last night, and then excited his family with news of the discovery. But the first signs of the phenomenon had probably made themselves known last Saturday night—and upon hearing of them from her husband, the fervent, ambitious Mrs. Hall had hustled her brood into its outdoor petition of the heavens. Hall was now *feigning* calm in front of Newcomb: he had been too agitated not to let slip some news of his twelfth-magnitude observation, but smart enough not to set himself up for ridicule, should the object prove something humbler than a moon.

Later in the afternoon, Cynthia contrived another excuse to roam the building. In the library she found Newcomb dictating correspondence—no doubt more cover letters for more inscribed monographs—to his young dogsbody, Mr. Todd, just back from his New Jersey vacation. In the second or two she could stand nearby, she noticed Newcomb's difficulty keeping his mind on whatever lines he was dictating. He paced the length of the table, back and forth. Mr. Todd, infected with his mentor's agitation, had to apply his blotter to two different mistakes.

"I've got to extrapolate the thing's orbit," said Newcomb. "That's all there is to it. I should be doing that right now."

"It *could* be just an asteroid, sir."

"It's a damned moon, Todd. I guarantee you. I don't think Hall even knows what he has." His rival's possible success, not the suspense, was killing him.

Before the day finished, the whole Observatory had sensed the commotion. Admiral Rodgers himself came by Professor Harkness's desk to work off a flutter of nerves: "I don't know what Mr. Hall's engaged in, and I don't want to know. Not until we're sure it's something important." It mattered not to the superintendent whether the astronomer had seen green cheese or a half-dozen new Suns, so long as it was something *big*. "He'd better be looking for it again tonight," the admiral said, walking away before Harkness could reply.

Cynthia frowned. She would of course miss any excitement to be had this evening. It was being here in the daytime that kept her in the dark. But just before leaving, she heard Newcomb tell Harkness, "He'll have his only view of it immediately prior to dawn," and she realized that, by some peculiar, unspoken protocol, they would all be leaving Hall alone tonight. On her way out, she went into Mr. Harrison's office and left a note in Hugh's pigeonhole, knowing—or at least hoping—that he would arrive at 6 P.M. for the sunspot observations. "Stay late and be watchful," she wrote. "Mr. Hall may make history tonight." Perhaps *this* would shake her dear one loose from his lethargy.

•   •   •

Hugh read the injunction an hour or so later, and he did stay much later than he had intended, but only because he fell asleep at the little table near the 9.6-inch refractor. No one came in on him before or after the hour slipped past midnight and then 2 A.M. The high-pitched clamor of a mosquito, which hovered near his right ear before biting him on the wrist, roused him briefly, but it took a small, sudden clatter, coming shortly after four from the vicinity of the Great Equatorial, to wake him fully. He decided to investigate on his way out of the building.

"If that don't take the rag off the bush!" cried Asaph Hall's helper, George Anderson. Hugh found the two men taking turns looking into the giant telescope's eyepiece, which they had slid out as far as it could go, probably to diminish the blaze of a bright body obscuring something of greater interest in its vicinity. The pair were too busy to take any notice of Hugh in the doorway.

"It's a second one," declared Anderson. "That's for certain, Professor Hall!"

"Yes," said the astronomer. "Smaller and closer in." His quiet voice shook. "I had better make a fuller note." He hurried, with his observer's notebook, to a table at the far end of the room, but before he sat down, he dropped to his knees, thanking the heavens for their magnificent piece of self-revelation.

"Aw, now, Professor Hall," said Anderson, gently scolding. "There'll be time for that later." Anderson was embarrassed, but only in a protective way. He had just spotted Mr. Allison taking notice and did not want this young fellow making sport of Asaph Hall with his mates. Otherwise Allison's presence was no source of bother at all. What rivalrous problem could arise from such a rudderless lad's being on the scene?

"Come take a look," said Anderson, motioning him toward the eyepiece. "But you'll have to be quick about it."

As Hugh seated himself at the telescope, Anderson and Hall made plans for Professor Eastman and his assistants to measure this second Martian moon with the 9.6-inch during the coming week; the Great Equatorial would keep up the business of confirming the first one's existence. By tomorrow night, Hugh knew, the Observatory would be a changed place. Like the moons, it would be discovered, and briefly famous even to men who had never touched a sextant or binoculars. Every scientific here who got in on the act would be flattered and laureled.

Hugh found the smaller of the two specks and held it in his vision just long enough to see that it most definitely *moved,* like something alive, with respect to the glaring orange circle. Stunned in spite of himself, he felt his own light fizzling into darkness and inconsequence.

· · ·

"This great triumph, which will go down into history along with Herschel's discovery of Uranus and Leverrier's prediction of the existence of Neptune—is purely American." Commodore Sands put a flourish into his recitation of the last three words of this newspaper encomium from the stack of cuttings that had accumulated in the Observatory's library. On the afternoon of Wednesday, the 22nd, he had come to join the astronomers for a small celebration. They were catching their breath after five spectacular days.

"Here's a card from my friend Reeves in New York," said young Mr. Todd. "'Congratulations on those lunar appendages to Mars. But what am I to do with that astronomy they tried to teach me at Amherst?'"

Everyone but Simon Newcomb gave a chuckle. He had spent the past few nights confirming Martian observations and making measurements with Professor Harkness, and while he could hardly admit it here, certainly not in front of Admiral Rodgers, he had had quite enough of little Deimos and Phobos. That's what they were now called—Homer's names for Mars' attendants, rendered more aptly in translation to the current national scene: Panic and Fear. The Great Equatorial would be trained on the satellites through the middle of October, after which they would disappear from even that instrument's huge eye for another two years.

"I can remember when she was delivered," the commodore said

about the fantastic telescope that had made the find. Newcomb, too, could recall the November day in '73 when the clock-driven Cyclops had finally arrived—and could rue the day when he had relinquished its charge to Hall.

No one would ever again lord it over Asaph and his wife. Since Saturday night the rest of the scientifics had been asking *permission* to join Hall and Anderson in the dome, as if the 26-inch were the two men's personal plaything instead of United States government property. For all this glory, Hall was said to be hopping mad at Newcomb, since the first newspapermen coming around to hear about the discovery had asked to see the only astronomer they'd ever heard of, and Simon Newcomb had obliged them by saying that *he'd* realized the true nature of what Mr. Hall had stumbled upon before Mr. Hall himself did.

One could argue that they were everyone's moons now. Observatories from Missouri to the middle of Europe had been cabled or mailed an announcement that Rodgers had had run off at the Government Printing Office and gone to pick up in his own carriage. A special letter had been hand-delivered to the landlocked Secretary of the Navy.

Mrs. May's presence at a social gathering of the men was considered unsuitable, so she remained at her desk, regarding the sudden surfeit of numbers about Deimos and Phobos. The larger moon was 14,500 miles away from Mars, the smaller a mere 5,800, hardly the distance from here to London. Professor Eastman and Henry Paul, measuring Phobos with the 9.6-inch, thought it no more than seven miles across. Cynthia could imagine herself striding it from end to end in under three hours, though she supposed she'd collapse from motion sickness before finishing: the little satellite raced round Mars every seven hours and forty minutes, more than a thousand times every Earth-year. The other moon was a bit slower, but still quite a traveler.

All right, she said, rolling up her cuffs, where ρ is the distance of the planet from the earth, then

$$\Delta p = \frac{a}{\rho s} \cdot \left\{ f \cos p \cos (F + u) - g \sin p \cos (G + u) \right\} \cdot \Delta u$$

"Excellent, Mrs. May," said the admiral, who'd come up behind her.

"She never disappoints," added Professor Harkness, placing a piece of cake from the party beside her scratch pad.

"Thank you," said Cynthia.

"Wonderful to see every man pulling his weight in this affair," said Rodgers. "Every woman, too, Mrs. May, excuse me. No, there's no time for slacking. And tell me, if you will, Mrs. May, how is Mr. Allison feeling?"

Their friendship was an open secret, looked upon as one more peculiarity in Mr. Allison's feckless life. If he were properly robust and ambitious, he would have a comely young girl, not this scrawny widow. For a few moments, over the weekend, Cynthia had hoped the Observatory's sudden luster would take the admiral's pressure off Hugh, but something nearer the opposite now appeared more likely. Rodgers had had his breakthrough and would drive them all up from the swamp of Foggy Bottom if it was the last thing he did.

"Mr. Allison is only a bit under the weather, Admiral. I've promised to take him some broth, and I'll give him your good wishes when I do."

"Yes, Mrs. May, please do just that," said Rodgers, who now ran off to consult with Mr. Harrison about arranging some hours for the moons to be put on public view.

In truth, Hugh had insisted on fending for himself tonight. When the first signs of a fever had come upon him the day before, he'd acted as if another sweetheart had shown up, practically shoving Cynthia out the door on to High Street. "I can't have you seeing me unless I'm at my handsomest. Go. I'll send word when I'm presentable. Or at least not infectious." He'd blown her a kiss from several feet away.

So she would eat her dinner with Mary Costello, whom she found at the back of her parlor reading, with unusual intentness, *The Light of Egypt*.

"Listen to this, dearie. 'The true son of Mars is a genuine pugilist of the first water, and is never so happy as when thoroughly engaged in vanquishing his opponent.'"

"You must have had news of the War God. The *Star* reports prostration in Utica."

"'Without a spice of this planet,'" the astrologer went on, her finger following beneath the line in her book, "'all men would be shiftless, effeminate cowards.'"

"Why this burst of study, Mary?"

Madam Costello frowned. "I'm worried about me livelihood. Your scientific fellas are takin' all the mystery out of the heavens. Calculating how fast these little moons go and how many miles they are across—like they're some claim to be staked in Colorado!"

Cynthia laughed.

"Think I'm foolish, if you like," said the astrologer. "But you ought to be paying attention to the *real* importance of Mars, instead of totin' up all those figures. You know, in spite of his nickname, the War God's a Scorpion. Mars' chief sign is Aries. That's *you*, darlin', if you haven't forgotten."

"Well, Mary," said Cynthia. "It's too late to produce another Aries for 1878."

The subject of love and motherhood, even prevention of the latter, succeeded in distracting Madam Costello from her long-term business worries. She closed *The Light of Egypt*.

"It's as I promised," she said. "You don't have to worry about that, not if you're using what I gave you."

"I'm not using it. And I'm not worrying, either."

"Sweet Jaysus."

"There's nothing growing inside me, Mary. I can tell." Cynthia pressed on her womb through the pockets of her dress, faintly crackling a piece of paper as she did.

"Why would you want to do somethin' like—"

She could tell what the astrologer was thinking—that she had decided to use the oldest ruse of the sex to capture a younger man. But that was not it. Hugh Allison, her reason had been telling her, could only be a temporary phenomenon. His transit across her life would reach its conclusion when the admiral let him go, or some other unrealizable vision made him pick up one morning for a spot on the other side of the globe. She had no confidence that her love could long restrain him, and no desire that "honor"—the idea made her laugh—should keep him where he was. But a child would keep him alive to her, the way Sally was supposed to have continued John. If need be, she would go away to have it, and then raise it on her own, telling the boy—for so she imagined it would be—that she was his aunt or even his grandmother.

"Do you want to see the moons, Mary?"

"You're changing the subject, dearie. How can—" The astrologer's attention wheeled around, once she realized what Cynthia was offering. "You mean Demo and the other one? See them for *real?* Through the telescope?"

"Yes, and Mars itself," said Cynthia, who watched the planet reader bite her lip and consider. Going to the Observatory might mean surrendering to the power of her competition, but the chance actually to *see* one of the planets (she had never known how to spot them in the sky) was irresistible.

"Good," said Cynthia. "You can chaperone me." She extracted a telegram from her pocket and laid it before the astrologer. SHALL REQUIRE SPECIAL VIEWING, Conkling had wired her. EXPECT YOUR COMPANY NIGHT OF 6TH.

"I'm surprised you'd see him," said Madam Costello.

"I surprise myself," answered Cynthia.

•　　•　　•

"Once around the planet every seven hours."

Hugh groaned over Cynthia's report of Phobos' scurryings. "As bad as Miss Gray's goddamned little dog."

They were awaiting Dr. Kelly, who they both knew would be making a diagnosis of miasmatic fever. By Thursday evening, the 23rd, there could be little doubt. Cynthia had already done the mathematics: Hugh's malarial symptoms ran like a sine curve. When he'd shooed her away on Tuesday, he'd been fighting off the languor that typically precedes the paroxysms, which were coming every twenty-four hours. She could now remember him opening his jaw in great yawns while drinking coffee three mornings ago. She'd since stayed away, but today, alarmed that no one else at the Observatory had had word of him, she'd come up here to his rooms after lunch.

She was still asking for precise descriptions of his physical experience during the past three days and two nights. "It felt as if ice water were pouring down my back," he told her, obediently, about the chills. When she'd arrived this afternoon, his hair had been standing up like an angry cat's, his teeth chattering so hard she'd been afraid he'd crack one of them. All this had by now passed off. They were waiting for the hot stage, and then a delirious ocean voyage of sweating. In the current lucid interval, she tried to occupy him with routine matters, such as a slip of paper bearing Mr. Todd's observations from the previous afternoon: "A group of two sizeable spots, well surrounded by faculae, has appeared at the east limb of the Sun. I can define it into only two spots at present." Hugh regarded the paper with comprehension, but no interest.

"They have him writing out most of the announcements to the other observatories," Cynthia explained. "Or at least adding some custom touches to the typeset broadside."

"So they don't need me for even that. You know," he said, shutting his eyes, aware of the pain he was about to inflict, "they're going to let me go by the fifteenth of next month."

Cynthia listened without turning toward him, so he wouldn't see the tears that had welled. "I assumed as much" was all she said. "And, oh, I forgot to tell you. The old commodore sends you his good wishes. More sincere than those the admiral dispatched."

She sat down beside him with a freshly dipped washcloth. "Now tell me: when you looked into the mirror yesterday, did your lips appear purplish?"

"How do you know to ask all this?"

"I did some reading at the Peabody, an hour before I got here. I'd begun to have my suspicions."

"My darling, self-improving Cynthia. When Dr. Kelly arrives, please give yourself some relief. Go hear the lecturer at Forrest Hall."

"No. I'll want to stay. Besides, I dislike that place. What's now the auditorium was a gaggle of prison cells during the war."

Hugh moaned. "Oh, not the war again. *Always* the war. Don't you know we *all* die?"

"No one here is going to die," she said, briskly sponging his forehead. But as she looked into his eyes, she could see that he had not been remarking on his own sickness. He really had been speaking of the whole vale of tears. She made him drink another glass of Apollinaris water.

"Do you understand the problem of the glare?" he asked. "Why it is those two moons were always invisible?"

"Yes, of course."

"Then think by analogy. Think how, if bright planets have moons, bright stars must have planets."

His own eyes were shining now. She had the feeling he was at last prepared to explain his vision, and that she, knowing how little was left to lose, was prepared to listen. She knelt down beside him, and turned his face toward her. The skin was livid and would soon be flushed. "*Tell* me," she said. "This light you talk about sending forth into the universe. Who is supposed to see it? Is it the same as those patterns in the drawings?" She pointed to the pictures on the wall.

"Did you know there's supposed to be a total eclipse of the moon tonight?" he asked. He stared at her, and she realized that he was not changing the subject. "No one will see it for all the clouds," he said.

"Which means no one will see *us* for the clouds."

He looked at her and whispered "yes," knowing she was ready to understand him.

"Tell me what you want to do."

"Hand me the lamp," he said, softly. Once she brought it from the table, he sat up and held the glass cone just beneath his chin. "I want to stand inside a light that will travel for hundreds of years, and still be as young as I was when somebody finally spots it."

"Your 'immortal longings.'"

"Yes."

"You want to communicate with those faraway creatures."

"No," he said, sinking back onto the pillow. "I just don't want to die."

She could not let him lose the energy to tell her the rest. "Here," she said, pouring another glass of water. "You'll need this when the sweating starts. Now tell me, how would these creatures, supposing they were even to look at Earth, ever find *you*?"

He managed a smile. "I'd have to stand out, wouldn't I? Go get the newspaper. No, not today's, the one on the chair."

He wanted her to look at the *Evening Star* from August 4th, at an item he'd circled with a black crayon. "What would you think, as a stranger to this country and city, if you came upon that?"

This morning the President, accompanied by his son, Webb C. Hayes, visited the monument office at the City Hall, to examine the plan of Mr. Larkin G. Meade for the completion of the Washington monument. Mr. Meade's plan is to place on the column, as it now stands, a figure of Washington, 85 feet in height, of hammered bronze.

"I should think," said Cynthia, "that this must have been a great, unusual man."

"I wouldn't care about that. Only that he was still, in his way, conspicuous. Your eye would go right to him. Especially if he were lit up."

"What would it take to make this happen?" asked Cynthia.

"Are you talking about Mr. Meade's scheme, or mine?"

"Yours."

He laughed, and turned over on his side. "Equipment as expensive as it is unwieldy."

She said nothing for a time. Then she whispered, "You need to sleep." Unexpectedly, he obliged.

This could only be the fever talking. Whatever vision those drawings involved, it was surely not so lunatic as this. She would wait until the whole paroxysm was over. Then she would ask again, and find out what he really meant.

But when she reached down to feel his forehead, it was perfectly temperate.

SEVEN

SEPTEMBER 6–26, 1877

P lease, sir, there's no need for *you* to stand in line."

Lieutenant Sturdy had recognized Roscoe Conkling but not Mrs. May, who was on the senator's arm, closely cloaked and bonneted against the evening rain.

"Nonsense," said Conkling, glad to display his egalitarianism to the queue behind the telescope.

Visitors to the Great Equatorial were fewer but more choice than they had been a week ago. While encouraged by the great public interest, Admiral Rodgers had decided to restrict viewing to invited guests and those with specially requested passes; after a week of open doors, his temper had erupted over a smashed chronometer, three stolen library books, and all the grime tracked in on the boots of a thousand Washingtonians eager for diversion during the late-summer heat. Since the moons' discovery, the seasonal round of fevers had kept three astronomers and two of the watchmen away from the premises. Tonight, Lieutenant Sturdy, who had yet to make a full recovery from the attack he'd suffered in June, was on duty by himself to deal with callers.

Because the arrival of Conkling's carriage at Mrs. O'Toole's would have produced a bedlam of curiosity and comment, he had picked up Mrs. May at Madam Costello's, making it clear, as soon as he arrived, that both the trip to the Observatory and the dinner that followed would be *à deux*. Moving up the line now, he pointed out a wealthy spinster who'd set her cap for the widowed Vice President, and two rows ahead of her the unfortunate Mr. and Mrs. Henry Rathbone, whom Cynthia had recognized on her own. They had been sent passes by Professor Harkness, their neighbor in Lafayette Square, and were even now, a dozen years after accompanying the Lincolns to Ford's Theatre, exciting the whispers and nudges commanded by the freakish. Upon realizing who they were, young Mr. Todd stopped briefly in the tracks he was making to a temporarily installed five-inch equatorial, through which he had decided to find a trans-Neptunian planet and make a name for himself as great as Asaph Hall's. Hall himself, exhausted after three weeks of monitoring his discoveries, was unlikely to appear tonight, even if the skies should clear.

"This will be the first time you've ever held my hand beneath the light of *two* moons," said one young lady to her swain, repeating an already overused piece of popular wit. Cynthia wondered if the girl might be Miss Ellen Gray and, more alarmingly, whether Conkling might now be inspired to some amorous talk of his own.

In fact, he frowned, as if suddenly recalled to his serious involvement with the public purse strings. "Tell me exactly what I shall be seeing, Mrs. May."

"With what's left of the clouds, probably nothing but a splotch in the southeast sky. I'm afraid we've led you 'this way to the egress.'"

When they reached the instrument, he insisted she look first, and kept his hand on her back while she bent to the eyepiece. For all the rumors coming from Europe—tales of Italian astronomers seeing great channels, possibly even canals, on the nearer-than-ever planet—Cynthia saw no sign of either stripes or moons.

She straightened up until her gaze was level with the senator's. "The War God without his attendants, I fear. I'm sorry."

"I assure you, Mrs. May, I have all my troops in place." He flashed her his wild, white smile, unstained by tobacco, before leaning down to take a three-second look at Mars, which might have been an assembly district not worth carrying.

"Let me take you to *my* world," he said, coming back up.

Tonight that world was armed and roaring. Before leaving on a trip to Ohio and the South, the President had finally demanded the resignations of Arthur, Sharpe, and Cornell—and all three had refused to tender them. Still, in his carriage on their way to the Arlington Hotel, Conkling insisted on hearing more of Cynthia's own story, what she'd begun telling him on the ride out to Foggy Bottom. Passing the empty pedestal of Washington's Monument—and trying not to think of whatever strange illumination Hugh Allison imagined putting atop it—she recalled to Roscoe Conkling how, as an eleven-year-old girl in '53, she had seen a few of the last stones set into the base of the obelisk, before the money and national unity required for the work ran out.

"You precede me," said Conkling, his teeth still visible in the shuttered cab. "I did see them hoist some of the marble to the Capitol dome, but I can't claim an acquaintance with our history as long as yours."

"But I've been only an observer of history, not one of its makers." Good God, she was better at this—which was to say, worse—than she'd been writing that first note to him. She ought to be blushing with shame, but here in the dark what would be the point? There was nothing to do but laugh, which is what he began to do as well. They were on to each other, or so at least it would seem. But how could they be, when she wasn't on to herself, wasn't half certain of her plan, let alone whether this barrel-chested warrior with his glistening forelock could really, somehow, save Hugh from the admiral. But here she was, playing with fire, after six months of grasping at quicksilver.

"Now, Mrs. May, you *will* be a maker of history one day. You doubtless know it was I who presented the women's suffrage petition to the Senate before the end of its last session."

"Thank you," she said, laughing. "But no, thank you."

"You're indifferent to the franchise? To equality?"

"I'm indifferent to democracy, Senator Conkling. I've *seen* the mad shuffle of administrations—six different ones I can now recall myself. All the scrambling for someone else's place as soon as the election-night music stops. What good does it do anybody?"

"Ah," said Conkling, shimmering at the prospect of friction. "A reformer." What could be more exciting than to subdue this laughing, strong-minded woman? She was better than he'd let himself hope.

"No, sir," she replied. "I'm afraid I'm your ally, at least in opposition to what people call reform. But I should really prefer a king: no spoils *or* 'merit,' just one long, steady reign giving way to another, the clerks peacefully dying at their desks, the monarch doing the same on his throne."

"You're medieval, Mrs. May. Where would you put yourself in such a world? Inside a cloister?"

"No," she answered. "I too much prefer the company of men. And I don't generally like Papists. I suppose that's undemocratic of me, too. As a girl, I remember clapping with glee when they told us someone had stolen the Pope's gift of a stone from the monument back there and thrown it into the Potomac."

"You make me wish I were a Catholic *and* a reformer," whispered Conkling, leaning forward as if he might begin wrestling with her right here in the carriage.

The two of them laughed so heartily that a small bottle in her dress pocket banged against the armrest. She pulled it out to satisfy Conkling's curiosity. "Schenck's Pulmonic Syrup," she explained, since it was too dark for him to read the label. "For a friend."

"A queenly act of kindness," he said, warming back up to the medieval theme.

She just smiled, with teeth not so bright as his. She would let him assume that her errand of mercy was for someone at the boarding-house. In fact, she'd been carrying the bottle around all day, so nervous about tonight she'd forgotten to leave it in Hugh's mail slot inside Mr. Harrison's office. His paroxysms had stopped nine days after Dr. Kelly commenced treatment, and the great question now was how severe the recurrences, sure to take place every two or three weeks, would turn out to be.

"Malaria?" asked Conkling, to her surprise.

"Yes," she answered, evenly.

"Dreadful business. I had a touch of it myself last year."

She could feel his fears (Mary Costello had told her about the climacteric) and how immediately he wanted to be rid of the subject. Once the carriage reached the Arlington, he banished the topic with a practical gesture, ordering the driver to have someone in the hotel dispatch a large case of quinine to Mrs. May's address. "I don't care if it requires their getting Milburn's to open up at this hour. Tell them I want it done."

She gratefully tapped the back of his hand as he led her into the hotel dining room, where he was immediately approached by two partisans: a member of the Pennsylvania delegation and an undersecretary of state from Grant's last Cabinet. Cynthia withdrew a few steps to a point where only the War God's voice could be heard: "Meanwhile, we've succeeded in removing *him*." The hearty laughter of Conkling's auditors made her understand that they were speaking of Hayes and his trip.

The senator settled for broiled shad and seltzer, but delighted in Mrs. May's order of oyster soup, venison, and a blancmange dessert. She was happy to let him perceive her appetite as a kind of prestidigitation, instead of the poverty-instinct it actually was.

"Now add up the tariff." Conkling pointed her attention to the prices on the stiff cardboard bill. He knew of her numerical skills from Madam Costello, and her speed in performing this second stunt pleased him as much as her eating had.

"It isn't anything special," she said. "A bit like being double-jointed."

He reached across the plates and linen and took her fingers. "Are you double-jointed, too, Mrs. May?"

"No," she said, surprised at her ability to leave her hand in his. "Just slightly arthritic."

The remark pleased him more than her acquiescence would have. A scratch or slap, she realized, would have delighted him.

"Our special session doesn't begin until the fifteenth of next month," he explained briskly. "I shall be back a week or so beforehand. I usually stay here, but I'll be at Wormley's this year instead." Everything about the Arlington—its worn furniture, slow messengers, and clumsy bootblacks—had begun to irritate him. On the train down for this quick trip he had decided to have all his things, including the pulleys and punching bag, transferred to new quarters.

"How will you occupy yourself for the next five weeks?" she asked. "Can you obstruct the Administration from so great a distance?"

Charmed once more, he let his laughter peal. "Oh, there's much that can and will be done, Mrs. May. Our state convention begins in Rochester on the twenty-sixth—and how I wish you could be there! That would give you a taste for politics!"

"Will our friend be helping to tailor your rhetoric?"

At this reference to Mary Costello, Conkling's smile disappeared entirely. "Why do you consult her?" he asked, as if ordering Mrs. May to take on his own embarrassment over such a weakness.

"She amuses me," said Cynthia, who all at once despised herself for not saying, simply, that Mary was her friend. "I like to ponder the correspondences between her heavens and mine."

"Typology?" asked Conkling. "The Old Testament prefiguring the New?"

"Yes," said Cynthia. "Something like that."

The maitre d', having only now been made aware of Conkling's presence, scurried over to the table and interrupted: "Sir, how fine it is to see you! And Madame, a pleasure." So excited was he by Conkling's return—and on such a day of political swordsmanship—that he quite forgot himself and burbled over: "And shall we soon have the pleasure of seeing Mrs. Sprague again, too?"

Conkling looked at the man as if he might horsewhip him. "Mrs. Sprague will soon be home from Europe and in Rhode Island for a time. With the governor. Her husband."

On every occasion the maitre d' could recall, Conkling had gloried in inquiries like the one just made. Mortified to realize that this was not to be such an instance, the dining room manager beat the humblest of retreats.

Conkling turned back to his guest: "Are you ready for your carriage, Mrs. May?"

"Yes," said Cynthia, knowing that this time she was supposed to be; and that next time, when no carriage would be called, she would have to be prepared to stay.

•   •   •

A week and a half later, on Sunday, September 16, Hugh and Cynthia arrived in Annapolis an hour early for an appointment he'd made at the naval academy. He had hardly stopped talking on the train from Washington, and now, while they killed time strolling through the graveyard of Saint Anne's Church, he was still barely pausing to take a breath.

"Do you think I need spectacles from Alexander's? Of course, if this haziness is just some temporary effect of the fever, I don't want to be stuck with them. I couldn't count the number of pairs my father's gone through—never manages to hang on to them. Mother used to say he's lost as much at the optician's as at the gaming tables. Now, *your* eyes seem to me to be absolutely extraord—"

"We'll see about the glasses when we're back," she said as patiently as she could. She didn't know about his eyesight, but this nattering certainly *was* part of the disease, an aspect of the febrile excitement that rose from the sufferer in the interval between the clustered paroxysms. Hugh's gaze was darting and inattentive, and he couldn't keep his hands still. Otherwise, he seemed to feel fine. His spirits were high, and for the moment he was experiencing less physical discomfort than she. Four days after Conkling's visit, having saved up the money since June, she had had a wisdom tooth pulled by Dr. McFarlan.

Still, the throbbing in her jaw counted for nothing compared to a sudden upturn in their fortunes. For the third time today, as Hugh chattered on, she reminded herself of this, and tried truly to believe it. Deimos and Phobos, despite their names, had proved celestial boons. On Friday afternoon, everyone at the Observatory had gathered in the library for the admiral's announcement that Professor Newcomb, effective tomorrow, the 15th, would be leaving to assume the director-ship of the Nautical Almanac Office. "It is an unequaled opportunity for carrying on the work in mathematical astronomy I have most at heart," Newcomb himself told his astonished, and not altogether unhappy, audience. Later on, he came in to see Professor Harkness and put things a bit differently: "Over there they'll give my recommen-dations the respect that only comes with clear authority. Finally, Hark-ness, my hands will be untied. I've insisted, by the way, on a new office over in the Corcoran Building."

The real reason for his departure, Cynthia felt sure, was the unbearably bright light now shining upon Asaph Hall. In churning out the various publications of the Almanac Office, Newcomb might get the chance to conduct whatever research he chose; but nothing had ever much prevented him from doing that right where he was. The "annoyances" he complained about to Harkness were more truly the lustful itchings of his own pride, which suffered a fresh wound when the admiral, just a minute after announcing his departure, appeared pleased to get on to more momentous news, reading out a letter that would cover the report he was finally ready to send Secretary Thomp-son, a compendium of memoranda and death certificates "advocating the removal of the Observatory to a more healthful location, in which the services of the officers on duty at night will meet with no interrup-tions from malarial influences, and where the fogs arising from the river will not obscure the heavens." After a dramatic pause, Rodgers had

declared, "Toward this end, I am requesting a congressional appropriation of $100,000." While the astronomers marveled in silence at the
vastness of the sum, the admiral informed them that a copy of the
"removal report," as it would henceforth become known, was in Mr.
Harrison's office for their individual perusal.

Before the day was out, Simon Newcomb had asked Mrs. May if
she would consider joining him at the Almanac Office for a salary
equal to the one she was now paid, and with the opportunity, enjoyed
by all the Almanac's computers and copyists, of working at home.
"Thank you, Professor Newcomb," she'd responded to this man who
hadn't the slightest idea of how people like herself actually lived, "but
I can't think of any more awful privilege." His startled reply—"Very
well, then"—was no doubt the last set of words she would ever hear
from him.

Then Friday afternoon brought a second offer of employment, or
at least a reprieve. Admiral Rodgers, so occupied with trying to dispel
malaria's influence, suddenly realized he had to deal with the abrupt
lifting of Newcomb's. Aware of his shorthandedness, as well as how
unsympathetic it would look to remove a young malarial astronomer at
the very moment the Observatory was soliciting congressional pity, the
admiral informed Hugh that he could stay on for a while after all. "You
will continue working with Mr. Todd, not just on the sunspots, but on
his trans-Neptunian search." Though he took care not to say it, the
admiral hoped that pairing Allison and Todd might lead to the sort of
teamwork, or rivalry, that could in turn lead to another spectacular like
the moons. Rodgers's whole communication to Hugh had lasted less
than a minute, before he and Mr. Harrison were off to deal with one
more set of plumbers and plasterers proceeding with the peculiar task
of making the present Observatory look as spruce as possible for any
powerful visitors who might be able to help get it torn down.

Now, two days later, as Hugh and Cynthia approached the naval
academy's main gate via Hanover Street, she rehearsed all these events,
as well as her renewed fantasies, in the privacy of her imagination. She

would buy dress shirts for him at Thompson's; they would have an 8 percent interest account at the Riggs Savings Bank; each night their little son would wave good-bye to his papa as he went off to look at the stars from some new, "healthful location."

It was all nonsense, and she loathed herself for entertaining it. The academy's Lover's Lane, down which they now walked, with Hugh discoursing upon every tree and flagstone, was really still the thinnest of ice, cracked with the perils of further illness and renewed disapproval by the admiral. And yet, she could not stop herself from thinking that she might not need Conkling's help after all. What if, before she was in too deep, she just avoided another encounter, allowed him to go back to Mrs. Sprague or some other diversion as he brought forth political apocalypse?

They entered the old Government House library, where Hugh's meeting, arranged several days before Friday's events, was scheduled to take place. He had been maddeningly merry in withholding its purpose from her, teasing out the possibility it involved some new, sensible ambition, before hinting that, after all, it probably didn't. She had been, until they boarded the train this morning, fearful of watching him confide his "projection" scheme to another scientific, and after he started jabbering, she had begun to worry that he might not be able to sustain coherence on *any* subject, let alone his vision.

Hugh and the man he was here to see recognized each other by their conspicuous youth. It turned out, during their opening courtesies, that Mr. Albert Michelson, an instructor of physics at the academy, was even three years younger than Mr. Allison. A childhood emigré from eastern Europe, he had an accent more like the American West than Poland, the result of an upbringing in Virginia City, Nevada.

"Admiral Porter is up in Newport inspecting torpedo stations," Michelson explained. "This library is really his domain, but he's not around to see us trespassing over it."

"Ah, Newport," said Hugh. "Where you might all still be had things turned out differently." (He had learned only during today's train ride that the naval academy had relocated to Newport for the duration of what Cynthia still called, to his amusement, the "rebellion.")

"Yes," said Michelson, smiling at the possibility. "But I can tell by your voice that you would have been called home to join the other navy."

"Weren't we lucky to have been too young for it!"

Michelson might be more grave in his manner, but Cynthia observed a quick rapport between the two boys, and was relieved to see Hugh, even amidst the pleasantries, making an effort to concentrate.

"Mrs. May," said Michelson, once Hugh had introduced her, "that is my wife over there—Margaret."

Cynthia waved at the pretty young woman who sat across the room wearing a sweet expression and a frock that bespoke approaching maternity. The men's clear expectation was that Mrs. May would go off and join this other member of the sex, but Cynthia took a seat between the two of them.

"How are you feeling?" a now-awkward Michelson asked Hugh.

"Quite all right. A bit of late-summer languor. It was really nothing."

"They had me as a watch-officer on the *Constitution* for most of the last few months," said Michelson, who himself looked none too robust. "Nothing but dried apples to eat most of the time." After a pause, he asked, "So, did you learn of me from Professor Newcomb? I've heard that he's interested in the speed of light as well."

"Only in the hopes of outrunning it," said Hugh. "No, I learned of your interests through our friend Jack Cass."

"Oh," said Michelson, recognizing the name of Hugh's onetime Cambridge colleague. "Well, I thought we might as well come here instead of to my laboratory, because so far all I have is a drawing. As you can see," he added, holding up a pencil and managing to smile at Cynthia, "it's very portable." He began making a diagram in the margin of a newspaper:

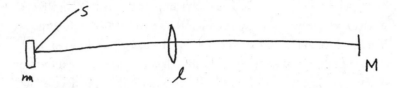

Hugh nodded as Michelson laid down each line. He knew, before the other man even said it, that *s* was meant to represent the light source; *m* a revolving mirror; *l* a long-focus lens; and *M* a plane mirror.

"Tell me," said Hugh. "If you're successful, how far off do you expect your results to be from Foucault's?"

"Oh, not much at all. He was very close, within a few thousand miles per second, I should think."

"That's good," said Hugh, with a peculiar delight that Cynthia and Michelson both noted, the latter with some perplexity.

Cynthia rose and excused herself and said she could not wait a moment longer to talk with Mr. Michelson's clearly charming wife. She'd been determined to monitor Hugh's demeanor, and she'd found it less erratic than she'd feared. But she didn't have the nerve to hear any more of what he might now say to Michelson. If he didn't start in on his vision, what else *would* he speak of?

Twenty minutes later, she and Hugh were back outside the academy's gates, walking down Annapolis's wavy brick sidewalks. He was now quite silent. With her palm gently brushing the telegraph poles they were passing, she wondered how anyone could imagine a need to project himself beyond the distances and speed these wires afforded. Strung under the sea, they could convey even Mary's Costello's words to England and France.

He slipped his arm around her waist. "Did Mrs. Michelson resent your lack of interest in her baby?"

"Oh," said Cynthia, laughing as gaily as she could. "Do you think it was so apparent?"

What would he say if he knew the truth? In the bed on High Street he had ceased withdrawing from her because he thought the press of her hands on his back a wordless reassurance that there was no risk of conception; that they needn't trouble themselves with anything but increasing their mutual pleasure. She had never used the device. But, however silently, she *was* troubled—by the thought that his misperception might, in a roundabout way, be true; that there was something wrong; that there *was* no risk of a baby.

"Tell me, *please*," she said, "that all this conversation with Mr. Michelson is applicable to finding a trans-Neptunian planet for the admiral."

He didn't hear her request. Once more, he had started talking with the rapidity of an engine. "Would you like to go to Philadelphia soon? We could stay with my hateful sister. A quick trip, just long enough for me to see about some equipment. Obtaining the machinery may be the hard part."

"I don't want to hear even the easy part," she said.

"Of course you don't," he replied, kissing her neck.

• • •

There was a new popular misconception in Washington that, if one held a mirror up to Mars, one would see Deimos and Phobos, no matter that they were invisible to the naked eye. It was a trick of optics, of course; a cheap mirror rendered multiple, diminishing images of the planet itself, an astral body that Cynthia, as she looked into her own mirror to brush her hair on Monday morning, the 24th, would be content never to see again. The new moons had made for so much work at a time when so many people had fallen sick that the healthy ones, like herself, were woefully tired. Professor Harkness had instructed her to take the day off, and she was obliging him. She had risen an hour later than usual, then brought a slice of bread and the newspaper back up to her room. Keeping one eye on the *Star* while brushing, she noticed

that the standoff between Conkling's men and the President continued. Mr. Arthur was meeting with Secretary Sherman at the Treasury
and, no doubt as Conkling wanted, resisting any compromise.

MADAME ROSS.

507 11TH ST.

THE CELEBRATED ASTROLOGIST

AND CLAIRVOYANT.

CURES ALL DISEASES INCIDENT

TO FEMALES.

CONSULTATIONS

STRICTLY CONFIDENTIAL.

LADIES $1, GENTLEMEN $1.50.

She spotted this advertisement for one of Mary Costello's rivals not
far from another promising "Happy Relief to Young Men from the
Effects of Errors and Abuses in Early Life. Manhood restored. Imped-
iments to marriage removed. New method of treatment. New and
remarkable remedies."

She tried counting the occasions of her intimacy with Hugh. She
wound up using her fingers, not from a sudden loss of mathematical
prowess, but because she kept pausing over some particular memory
of each night and losing track of the tally. The occasions were too few
in number to constitute a reliable scientific sampling, but something—
she felt more and more certain—was wrong, and it had nothing to do
with any "errors and abuses" of his. She had been cursed twice, as regularly as ever, since her first night in the bed on High Street. And yet, at
each monthly sign of her apparent fertility, she began hearing the voice
of her mother—in particular, the words Ellen Lawrence had said while
helping her stagger to a chamber pot the first time she'd bled after
Sally's delivery: *You will never again have to worry about that.* Her
mother had not been talking about the bleeding, but the nearly fatal
pain of the child's Cesarean birth. The reassurance had been echoed,

Cynthia could now recall with some effort, by the cluckings of Mrs. Sidney Robinson, a busybody neighbor who late in the war often foisted herself upon Mrs. Lawrence and who that day had sat in a corner of the room marveling over "modern miracles." At the time, Cynthia herself had been too weak and indifferent to think of anything but collapsing back into bed and cradling her undersized, too-quiet baby girl.

But this morning, thirteen years later, she could think of nothing but Mrs. Robinson's words, and when she completed dressing, she went immediately downstairs and out of the house. The morning was so hot, and her pace to Mary Costello's so fast, that she ought to have been carrying a fan, but waving one on the street always made her feel like an insect. She was perspiring heavily by the time she reached Third and D, where the astrologer was ushering out one embarrassed young gentleman, no doubt a troubled office-seeker, and showing in another—Conkling's lieutenant, who after taking a good look at Cynthia, went off with the latest portents to be telegraphed to his boss in upstate New York.

"Mary," she said, "please make me a cup of tea."

"Would coffee suit you as well?"

She thought of the grimy sugar spoon and the milk that would have gone off and asked again for tea, all by itself, if that would be all right. While the kettle boiled, she petted Ra and tried, against the fast beating of her pulse, to remember all she had once tried to forget: the unexpected rush to the Armory Square hospital; the bleeding and infection and delirium; the first sight of Sally, scarcely alive; and afterward, when she was conscious enough to hear them, the moans of wounded soldiers behind a door and down a corridor. She recalled the countenance of one of Miss Dix's nurses, a mixture of amazement and contempt that a girl could bring a new life into the world at such a time as this and take up a soldier's bed in order to do it. She had almost died, of course—that's what Dr. Malcolmson later told her, along with the news that Sally had been lifted out of her at the last possible moment like Caesar or Macduff, a fact that had interested her as a scientific curiosity and nothing more.

"Mary," she asked, as she was handed her tea. "Do you have a copy of Boyd's?"

"Over there, dearie. But it's two or three years old."

Cynthia put down her cup and went to get the city directory.

"What's eating at you?"

"He's not in it," said Cynthia, double-checking the page.

"Come sit back down and drink your tea."

"But old Mrs. Robinson's still around, I know it. I passed her in the street last year."

"*Who* ain't in the directory?"

"An old doctor named Malcolmson. He must have died without my noticing." Cynthia went on thumbing the directory, looking for where Mrs. Robinson resided—by now no doubt one more poor widow. She had left the Lawrences' street just after the war.

"Isn't it Dr. Kelly taking care of our boy up in Georgetown?"

"Dr. Malcolmson is the man who delivered my Sally—or who from my womb 'untimely ripped' her."

"You sound like Shakespeare. Did the War God teach you that?"

Cynthia put her bonnet back on. "I've found her."

"Now Mrs. May, what's this about?"

"Come with me, Mary. I have to see Mrs. Robinson."

"What's she supposed to tell you? I can't walk out of here, girlie. I've got one coming at half past twelve."

"It's only ten-thirty. Don't argue with me."

She required company, wordless support, if she was going to learn for a fact what she'd already deduced. As they walked to Mrs. Robinson's lodgings at Eleventh and E, the planet reader, sensing an urgency unusual even for Mrs. May, obliged with her silence.

The old woman who responded to the knocker was without a doubt Mrs. Robinson, even if she now lacked two of the teeth that Cynthia had seen in her mouth a year ago on Pennsylvania Avenue.

"Mrs. Robinson, do you remember me?"

"Of course I remember you," said the old lady, with more suspicion than friendliness. "You're Ellen Lawrence's girl."

"May I speak with you?"

"You already are."

Cynthia brought Mary Costello with her into the parlor. "May my friend wait out here while we go in there?" She pointed to the old lady's minuscule bedroom, which had a door they could close.

Left by herself, Madam Costello pitied the old woman's threadbare surroundings and puzzled over some distant bells and shouts that had begun to make themselves heard through the parlor's closed window. Ten minutes later, Cynthia emerged and said, "Let's go." The astrologer knew not to ask anything until they were outside and walking.

"What is it, darlin'?"

"Let's just say that I'll never have need of that device I asked you to procure for me. I'm sorry I put you to the trouble."

"I don't understand, dearie. What could she tell you that you didn't already know?"

Without slackening her speed down E Street, Cynthia answered: "That after Dr. Malcolmson took Sally out of me, he knotted up my tubes. He reasoned that a second lying-in would kill me, so he left nothing to chance. And saw no need to tell a half-dead widow. He told my mother and her friend Mrs. Robinson instead, and if they told me, it was in terms too vague to be grasped by a convalescent. Mrs. Robinson doesn't recall that part exactly, but she remembers every word Dr. Malcolmson spoke to her and my mother."

Mary Costello, out of breath, tried asking another question as carefully as she could: "I'm sorry, dearie. But why would you be wanting—"

"Exactly right, Mary. Why would I be wanting?" Cynthia took another dozen steps before her glance was drawn to a crowd gathering at the intersection of Ninth and F, a block away. "Look," she said to Mary, relieved by a chance to change the subject. She dragged the astrologer west to investigate the clamor.

The Patent Building, her former place of work, was crowned with flames. The greenhouse over the Ninth Street portico puffed great plumes of black smoke while broken glass crashed onto the sidewalk below. Burning papers rode the air, scintillating into wisps before disappearing altogether. As a team of fire horses rounded the corner, Cynthia recognized, across the street, two girls with whom she'd worked at Interior. She struggled to hear the rumors snaking from one part of the crowd to the next. The Wright and Thompson buildings, over on G, somebody said, were also ablaze. The records of the Indian office were burning just as Red Cloud and Spotted Tail rode the rails to Washington for a peace conference.

At a quarter past noon, the pine roof of the Patent Building's western wing collapsed, exposing its iron supports like tree trunks during a brutal winter. "There go all the models," said a sad old-timer, realizing that the room set aside to house so much Yankee ingenuity—a bit of it patented, most of it rejected—was now gone.

"They're going to need Baltimore!" cried one madly excited clerk a few feet from Cynthia. "They've already called out Alexandria!" Without a doubt, the District's hose carriages, which could barely get through the crowd, were never going to put out the fire by themselves.

"Get back!" cried a policeman. Mary Costello and Cynthia complied as quickly as they could, but not before a tiny, scorched contraption of balsa wood, hinges, and cotton completed its flying journey from the Model Room and landed at Cynthia's feet. What, had it ever been built, was this invention meant to print or weave or bake? She picked it up and let it cool in her hands.

"Mary," said Cynthia, "go back to D Street. You can still be there in time for your customer."

"I can't leave you here," the planet reader said. "You've got the hysterics." They both realized that Cynthia had some calm, preternatural variety of them. "What are you going to do?" Madam Costello shouted above the din of horses, clerks, and water.

"I'm going to watch," said Cynthia. "And think."

• • •

Two Dutchess County delegates regarded Roscoe Conkling on the dais. His forelock seemed more sharply twisted than ever, a perfect corkscrew, and his waistcoat an even brighter shade of blue than he sometimes favored.

"If Schurz thinks he got roasted on Monday . . ." said the first delegate to the second.

They laughed in anticipation of what the senator might dish out to the Interior Secretary as soon as he rose to address the state convention here in Rochester. Down in Washington, in response to the Patent Office blaze, the Cabinet was meeting without Hayes to discuss fire safety in federal buildings. The President was still off on his travels, and the odds were Conkling would raise a storm over a report that the other day, during his appearance in Atlanta, Hayes had tolerated a display of the Confederate flag.

"I see Cornell," said the first delegate, pointing the other's attention to the huge, stone-faced arbiter of the Custom House sitting two chairs away from Conkling. He was in double defiance of the President: having refused to resign his office, he was, by appearing here, also violating the June executive order against political activity.

"But where's Arthur?" the second delegate wondered.

"They say Sherman's offering him the Paris consulship if he'll resign."

The second delegate just laughed. "Conkling will never let him take it."

The two men now watched the gentleman approaching the podium, George William Curtis, Jr. "*He'll* have to take it a few minutes from now," said the first delegate. The *Harper's* editor, sure to be another victim of Conkling's rhetoric this afternoon, had not long ago turned down the British ambassadorship for something like the opposite of Arthur's reasons to refuse the French post. As head of the National Civil Service Reform Association, Curtis preferred to remain at home, waging war against the machine at gatherings like these and in the pages of his magazine. *Harper's,* along with its cries for the merit system, had of late also been running illustrated articles about women's fall fashions, providing Conkling's men the chance to make jokes they considered especially delicious.

Actually, Conkling liked the full-bosomed drawings better than anything Curtis had ever published, but his contempt for their pur- veyor was undiminished. As he watched him take the lectern now, he knew the business ahead would be almost too easy. Curtis would go down like some hapless redcoat, marching stiffly to annihilation.

"Fellow Republicans," said the editor, his softness of tone an advertisement of reasonableness. "I ask this convention to resolve that the lawful title of Rutherford B. Hayes to the presidency is as clear and perfect as that of George Washington, and that his efforts toward the correction of evils and abuses in the Civil Service have justified the promises this party made in its platform last year."

As the catcalls of the Custom House smothered any applause for reform, Conkling sat impassively, considering Curtis's strategy, which assumed that the senator could not repudiate the results of his own Electoral Commission without repudiating himself. It was a pitiful underestimation of Conkling's ability to maneuver, a failure to recog- nize his now complete lack of interest in compromise. Under the bright blue sleeves of his coat, the War God invisibly flexed the mus- cles of his forearms, thinking, as he got ready to rise, about the mes- sage he'd had from Kate, who wanted him near her, secreted in some Newport hotel until Congress convened next month. He had already told her it was impossible; he would never again let her sap his strength.

Curtis sat down in the front row of the auditorium, next to Chauncey Depew of the New York Central. Conkling strode to the podium and nodded down at the two of them.

"This is a state convention," he began, evenly. "Its business is to nominate candidates for state offices. The national Administration is not a candidate or in question here." Loud cheers from the machine's men; but Conkling stopped them with a sharp outward thrust of his hand. "Who has the right to say it wishes to influence our proceedings or disturb our harmony? I won't assume that any man has been entrusted to introduce matters foreign to our duties and calculated to foment discord."

The Irishwoman had said that the first blows against the Libra Hayes were best struck from the side and behind. And so he would attempt to make Curtis's resolution seem less reprehensible than unnecessary. He would have chosen this route by his own dead reckoning, but he was nonetheless comforted, to his small secret shame, to be navigating by the stars. The astrologer's most interesting report had been the news, telegraphed last night, that Mrs. May was slightly under the weather—a female complaint, but nothing of any consequence. Even at this moment, hearing the always inspiring sound of his own voice, his mind drifted south to her. He had to force himself to concentrate, to glare at Curtis, whose damp rhetorical life consisted mostly of eulogies and Phi Beta Kappa orations, phrases crocheted over a corpse or some banquet table of beardless students. Conkling would fire *his* words into Curtis's own ears, the way he did at whoever stood opposing him on the floor of the Senate. "The reformers' vocation and ministry," he proclaimed, "is to lament the sins of other people. Their stock in trade is rancid, canting self-righteousness. They are wolves in sheep's clothing. Their real object is office and plunder. When Dr. Johnson defined patriotism as the last refuge of a scoundrel, he was unconscious of the then undeveloped capabilities and uses of the word 'reform.'"

Curtis, still in the senator's sights, shook his head in apparent sadness, a gesture that infuriated Conkling. The War God now allowed the machine's men to let loose a deafening, discordant chorus, in which howls against the reformers seemed to contradict the allied cheers for Conkling himself. The speaker patiently allowed it all to subside, and while he never took his eyes off Curtis, he could glimpse the slender form of Cynthia May darting across the floor of his mind. He tried to ignore it, opening his mouth to declaim the next portion of his text, which contained the one insult that would put paid to Curtis, that would drown the editor in the glee of his enemies.

And yet, as he began to speak, he knew that he was also speaking to her. The same words he flung at Curtis were ones, at a much lower volume, he should like Mrs. May to hear after the two of them had wrestled over politics. They were words he would have her understand, for all their brimstone, as the truest definition of Roscoe Conkling. He *believed*, didn't he, the sentences he was now firing at the editor of *Harper's:* "For the last twenty-two years I have labored for the Republican party and stood by its flag; and never in twenty-two years have I been false to its principles, its cause, or its candidates. Who are these men, in newspapers and elsewhere, cracking their whips over the Republican party and its conscience and convictions? They are of various sorts and conditions—*the man-milliners, the dilettanti, and carpet knights of politics,* men whose efforts have been expended in denouncing and ridiculing and accusing honest men who, in storm and in sun, in war and peace, have clung to the Republican flag and defended it against those who have tried to trail and trample it in the dust!"

The senator's men now clapped as if they really were a machine, in great crisp waves. Conkling felt a surge of carnal excitement, which he quickly sublimated into fealty: "Gentlemen! President Grant and all who stood by that upright, fearless magistrate have been objects of the bitter, truthless aspersions of these 'reformers.' They forget that parties are not built up by deportment, or by ladies' magazines, or by *gush.*" He minced a half step or two away from the podium. The regulars bellowed their approval; the newspaper reporters added another inch to the Spanish moss of Pitman shorthand on their pads; Curtis whispered a few words to Chauncey Depew; and Bessie, from the wings, shot her father a cautionary glance, which he would ignore—her penalty for bringing Walter Oakman around the other night.

"Yes, gentlemen, there are about three hundred persons in New York who believe themselves to 'occupy the solar walk and Milky Way,' and even up there they lift their skirts very carefully for fear heaven itself might stain them. They would have people fill appointive office by nothing less than divine selection!"

The "solar walk" and "Milky Way" were for Mrs. May. Would she realize that when she saw the phrases in the Washington papers?

"I conclude with what a great Crusader told Richard of England and Leopold of Austria when they disputed the preliminaries of a battle." The regulars would think it Shakespeare and feel a stirring of sentiment at their chieftain's customary invocation of the Bard: "'Let the future decide between you, and let it declare for him who carries furthest into the ranks of the enemy the sword of the cross!'"

The nays soon had it, 295 to 109. Conkling stepped down from the dais and strode the center aisle of the auditorium, unblinking in his triumph. He passed Curtis and Depew without a handshake.

"Senator! Senator!" cried the reporters.

He ignored them too, on his way to the telegraph office that had been set up outside the hall.

A RAIN OF METEORS UPON MY FOES. A SHOWER OF KISSES UPON YOU. I RETURN WITHIN A WEEK. GO TONIGHT TO 3RD AND D. A PRESENT AWAITS YOU.

The key operator, shaking with the fear he would make an error transmitting what the senator had scribbled on a slip of paper, looked up in relief when Conkling was gone, replaced by the man from the New York *Herald,* whose dispatch reported that the War God, having just denied the President's right to hold office, had "acted the part of a blind and infuriate Samson, crushing himself beneath the edifice against whose pillars he leaned his mighty shoulders."

•　　•　　•

"Interior says no one new will be taken on just to deal with the fire damage," Louis Manley informed the other boarders.

"I should hope not!" replied Miss Park, who had spent her afternoon doing the paperwork for a taxpayer's anonymous $7,500 contribution to the Treasury's conscience fund. "We've *lost* thirty clerks under the new budget."

"Mrs. O'Toole," asked Dan Farricker, "are you disappointed the Sioux will be staying at the Continental instead of here?" Only Fanny Christian laughed at his suggestion. The landlady herself shuddered over the thought of the Indian peace delegation, now on their way by train to the capital, bringing their savage paints and smells into her parlor.

Dan patted his hand against his open mouth, silently imitating a war cry for the benefit of Fanny, who pulled an ostrich feather from a vase and stuck it behind her head.

"Miss Christian, please," scolded Mrs. O'Toole.

Fanny replaced the feather and sighed. "Buffalo Bill says Little Big Man's a bad egg, even though he's the one got stabbed by Crazy Horse and not the other way around."

Cynthia, passing through while putting on her hat, wondered how Conkling had kept himself from stabbing Curtis when the bloodlust was on him. She'd received his telegram upon arriving home. This afternoon she'd dispatched her own note, from the Observatory, asking Hugh to meet her, briefly, downtown at 8:00; she couldn't soon risk another early-morning return to Mrs. O'Toole's. Now, when the landlady asked where she might be on her way to, she replied, "A friend who lives on D Street. I'll be home before nine-thirty."

Glances exchanged by Joan Park and Louis Manley expressed doubt that Mrs. May would fulfill this pledge, but Cynthia ignored them on her way out. A few minutes later she was at her real destination, not Madam Costello's block but the steps of the badly singed Patent Building. She climbed them almost up to the columns, looking for a space between puddles of water and soggy wads of paper. When she found one, she gathered her skirts against her ankles and sat down, becoming as much an object of curiosity as the boarded-up windows to the occasional evening passerby.

Hugh did not arrive until 8:15, and he climbed the steps slowly, looking more gaunt than slender. But she could tell that he was calm. The nervous chatter had stopped a day or two ago, which meant, if she had her reading at the Peabody right, that the intermission of symptoms was ending. Another attack could come any day.

"The toasted Parthenon," he said. "An inspired location for our rendezvous." It was almost chilly tonight, and as soon as he sat down, he put his arm around her. She closed her eyes for a moment, grateful to be warmed this way instead of by Conkling's present—an expensive shawl with an appliqué of small silver stars, which he'd had sent from New York City. Mary Costello had excitedly forwarded the parcel to the boardinghouse, in time to arrive almost simultaneously with the War God's telegram. But it had gone straight into a drawer. As far as Cynthia knew, Hugh was still unaware of Conkling's existence—probably even as a public figure.

"What do you suppose this is?" she asked. From her reticule she withdrew the small damaged contraption that had flown through Monday morning's fire.

Hugh turned it over in his hand, twice, smiling with a sort of gay reverence toward the object's inscrutable ingenuity. "I haven't the slightest idea," he said, setting it down on the step below them.

"It came from in there." She pointed up toward the damaged Model Room.

"Someone's unpatented dream," said Hugh. "Someone's failure." She said nothing, and he looked back at her with concern. "You're not yourself, Mrs. May. Now, most people are so awful it comes as a relief when they're not themselves. But in your case it's a shame."

"Will you be going back to work with Todd tonight?"

"Yes," said Hugh. "It's becoming fun. He may be crazier than I am."

"You're not crazy," said Cynthia.

"You're right. I just have hidden depths."

"Why do you stay?" she asked. "Forget for a moment the admiral's reprieve: why do you *choose* to stay?"

"My dear, it's not as if the Allison family has any money to spare right now. I do more or less have to make my living."

"But there are other observatories. Ones whose telescopes aren't always cloaked with fog."

"Yes," he said, "that's true. And can you imagine how eager they'd be to have me after the record I've achieved here?"

"Those other places wouldn't make you sick."

"No," he said, smiling. "They wouldn't."

She couldn't bear it any longer—the feckless, merry fatalism. She put her head between her hands.

"Don't you worry about me," said Hugh. "Next summer I'm going to avoid the fever season altogether. I'll be out west, high and dry and healthy with one of the eclipse-observing parties. I ought to know, right? I wrote all those letters starting to organize them, remember?"

Next summer was too far away to imagine. Between now and then they both had to make a whole trip around the Sun. She wasn't sure she had the strength for even that automatic journey.

"I'll go out to Colorado and stay straight through August." He sucked in a great lungful of air and pounded his chest in imitation of the rude health they knew he would never enjoy. She closed her eyes, refusing to laugh.

"Cynthia," he whispered. "I stay because you're here."

She looked up at him.

"And you," he said, "are here for the duration."

He was right. She would never leave this city, any more than he would make a success or find some sensible home elsewhere. They were both incapable of reversing the eccentric courses they were on. They weren't traveling around the Sun at all. They were unperiodic comets, on their way to nowhere and never to return. They would leave no traces, no child to outlast them on Earth, from which he would be, she felt certain, the first to depart.

She grasped his right hand with her left. "I want to stand with you."

"You've already done that," he said. "You've taken good care of me."

"No, I want to stand with you in the light. It's all I want to do." She hoped he heard the echo of his own phrase, the words he'd used when she first sat in the room on High Street, beside the drawings.

He said nothing, just looked at the damaged contraption sitting on the step below them.

"Tell me," she said, "exactly what's in Philadelphia."

"A man who knows just the machine I require. An aplanatic-mirror projector."

"And this is the hard part?"

"Impossible, actually. It's built in France, and has so far been used only by the army over there. If I exceeded even my father's capacity for borrowing, I might afford the projector itself. But no one's going to lend me the import duty—probably half as much again—to get it through a Custom House."

She picked up the contraption and tossed it down the wet stone steps. "Order the machine," she said.

EIGHT

Cynthia helped Madam Costello put the supper dishes back into the tin box Charles would pick up tomorrow morning. She wished the astrologer might scrape the mashed potatoes off them a bit more thoroughly; despite the presence of Ra, there had been more than one mouse in evidence tonight. But they were in a hurry. She'd not gotten here until nearly seven, after checking on Hugh in Georgetown, and the sun was now long gone.

"All right, Mary, let's get going. Tonight's the last one I can get you in, and by Saturday the moons will have become invisible for two years."

"I'm just sorry I won't get to meet our boy," said the planet reader. "Poor thing. After all this time, I can't tell you how I was lookin' forward to it."

"He's doing much better," insisted Cynthia. "But it will be a while before he's recovered enough strength from this last spell to go back there."

He was a *bit* better: the most recent siege had consisted of four paroxysms, fewer than the last time, each only five hours long and further apart from one another than the last set. But even now, during one of the fever's intermissions, he looked sallow and lacked appetite. Cynthia would not tell Mary what the worst of it had been like—the hoarse cries for ice water, the blue fingertips and confused mind. When pressed, she would give up only one or two playful, less intimate, details—such as the way Hugh smiled when his ears began buzzing, a sign that the quinine had started to work.

She nudged the older woman out the front door and told her she could fuss with her bonnet on the way. Right now they needed to raise their umbrellas and get going. It was the wettest, warmest October anyone could remember. Gnats were still in the air, flying between the raindrops. Even at this hour the horsecar Cynthia flagged down was crowded with passengers too damp and uncomfortable to go about on foot. She put nickels into the box for herself and Mary, and then managed to find two seats near the glass rear doors. The car's population could also be attributed to the impending return of Congress, which had remustered an army of lobbyists to another season's residence in the District. Mrs. O'Toole, aware of how much more she could be getting for her rooms—perhaps even renting one of them to a congressman—gave her regulars a severe look if they tried to take so much as an extra pat of butter at breakfast.

The War God had informed both Cynthia and Madam Costello—not to mention the general public, through an announcement in the press—that he did not intend returning to the capital until Sunday, the fourteenth, just one night before the Special Session would open.

"I forgot to show you this," said Cynthia, reaching into her pocket for a newspaper cutting. "Or maybe he sent you one, too." A cartoon from one of the New York dailies showed Conkling as a colossus, one foot upon the Senate, the other on the Custom House: "The New Official Doorkeeper."

"He's proud of himself," said Cynthia.

"He ought to have picked on someone his own size," replied Madam Costello, reflecting the by-now conventional view that Conkling's ferocity had been greatly in excess against the dainty Mr. Curtis, whose reform partisans had just staged a polite rally of rebuttal in New York City. Was the senator really intent on destroying the rest of his own party? Wasn't it, some wondered, as if General Sherman had burned half the Union on his way to Georgia? To judge from his almost daily letters to Cynthia, Conkling remained convinced that he had triumphed in Rochester, and that his appearance there was only a foretaste of final victory in the Senate. "It was said of Burke that he did not always adapt his style to the capacity of his hearers," he wrote her in defense of himself. "Is not this a habit of men of genius?"

The two women got off the streetcar near Virginia Avenue, and entered the Observatory grounds at Twenty-third Street. Early fall was the worst time of year for both fever and fog, and the mist was rising thickly off the grass and mud. "It's a fearful-looking place," said Madam Costello, who had never been to this part of town. "Like the moors in one of those novels."

Inside, things were more cheerful. Captain Piggonan was up and around once more, and he greeted the ladies at the door. Despite atmospheric conditions, several astronomers had come out tonight: Professors Yarnall and Eastman were at the Transit Circle, and Henry Paul had left word that he might be over later, if the skies showed any shred of promise when he emerged from the National Theatre; Lydia Thompson and Her British Blondes were on the bill.

The admiral himself was bustling about, pleased to see so much activity. The moons, though fading from the sky, were still radiating energy into his scientifics. In fact, he was secretly disappointed that a few more of them weren't sidelined with miasmatic influence: it wouldn't hurt for there to be a lot of sickness about when Senator Sargent, an acquaintance from Rodgers's California days, introduced the removal bill, with its request for $100,000, to the reconvening Congress. This thought soon shamed him, and he decided, while passing the spittoon outside Mr. Harrison's office, to tell Captain Piggonan not to let people stay too late tonight. "We're leeward of the wind," he noted, "and that makes things worse."

"Yes, sir," said the captain, who resumed leading the visitors toward the Great Equatorial.

"Mrs. May," said the admiral, nodding politely to his computer and her companion.

"He's a handsome old gent," the astrologer whispered to Cynthia.

A voice rang out behind them—"This must be Mary Costello!"—a voice too young and emphatic to belong to Professor Harkness, who had arranged for the planet reader's pass. No, Cynthia realized; the voice belonged to Hugh.

"How can you possibly be up?" she asked, getting the whole question out before she'd finished wheeling around.

"For God's sake!" cried Madam Costello. "It's the boy himself!"

"I'm a miracle of modern medicine," he explained, with a big smile. "And the product of excellent nursing," he added, bowing to Cynthia, who three hours before had been soothing him with a cold sponge. "This way, ladies. I can take over from here, Captain Piggonan."

So light on his feet he appeared to be gliding, Hugh led them into the dome. Forgetting all about the admiral, Mary Costello confidentially pronounced Cynthia's fellow "as beautiful as a painting."

"An engraving from one of your novels," said Cynthia, who was truly distressed. "The ghost striding those moors."

Madam Costello registered awe at the sight of the telescope, and accepted Hugh's offer of his arm. "Let me introduce you to Mr. Todd," he said. "Beginning next month, the two of us will be using this behemoth to search for that trans-Neptunian planet. Isn't that right, David? Until then, Mr. Paul will be looking through it for Venusian satellites."

"Allison," said Todd, who looked to Cynthia for some explanation, "are you sure you ought to be here tonight? I mean, are you quite up to—"

"Mr. Todd and I," said Hugh, talking right over him, "have been having our preliminary looks through the nine-inch telescope. I'll show you that one later, Mary. He's been reading great stacks of stuff on Uranus when he's not been reading fairy tales to Mrs. Newcomb's children and Catholic theology to Mrs. Newcomb herself. He's a good and faithful servant, our young Mr. Todd, and we're all in a fright we'll lose him to the Almanac Office."

Todd, who had been hedging his bets—proofreading the great man's latest lunar manuscript each morning before he came to the Observatory—looked perplexed at the teasing. Cynthia, craving one moment of merriment without a hardship or emergency to avert, smiled for the first time.

"Here you are!" said Hugh, placing Madam Costello at the end of a short line behind the telescope. The current visitors were mostly legislators and their wives, back in the capital a few days early and sought out by the admiral to come see the Observatory-produced marvels they'd been missing while home. By next week, once the moons were gone, he would no longer be able to bribe their eyes with celestial delight, and the hard work of daytime buttonholing on Capitol Hill would begin. Rodgers wondered how he would secure even the small fraction of attention needed to get his bill passed, what with the competing claims of the Custom House battle and the bill to resume silver coinage—a bonanza for the western mining interests, represented here tonight by Mrs. Senator Jones from Nevada, who wore great quantities of the semiprecious metal and loudly extolled "the dollar of our daddies."

When Madam Costello's turn to look through the eyepiece finally arrived, she crossed herself before leaning into it. Cynthia and Hugh watched her take a long look, discerning heaven-knew-what patterns and truths, until the astrologer bounced away from the giant tube, laughing with such delight that she'd be bursting her stays, if she were wearing any.

"Now, Mary, admit it," said Hugh, "how can all your sorcery compete with our reality?"

She actually pushed him, gave the boy a playful shove in the ribs, and said: "You've got me, Mr. Hugh! You win hands down. It's better than the stereopticon!"

Cynthia watched the two of them laughing to beat the band. They had that quality so praised everywhere you went, that grace and ease she had never felt able to manifest herself. It was "charm," whose display by others always left her feeling defeated. She felt her own face hardening with impatience and envy.

The three of them moved away to let the remaining solons and their consorts have a turn. While Hugh and Madam Costello continued their flirtation, Cynthia watched the lawmakers and understood that their chief thought looking upward through the telescope was of dominion. News of Chief Joseph's surrender had come today; the West was won, and someday the red planet might have to give up just as the red man had. The silver jewelry clattering against the bosom of Mrs. Senator Jones seemed a kind of war cry, a signal that the momentarily strapped Republic was still irreversibly on the march, and quite unwilling to stop at fifty-four forty, at least without a fight.

Hugh offered to walk Madam Costello back to the line for a second look. "Only if you let me do a whole chart for you, Mr. Hugh! Not just these wisps and hints I attach to our girl's."

"Ah, Mary! There's no need for it," he said. "You'd see nothing but sunny skies!"

They were *giggling*.

"Would you excuse us for a moment?" Cynthia asked the astrologer. "I need to speak with him." Hugh shrugged in surrender, and kissed Mary Costello's hand before allowing Cynthia to lead him out of the dome and off to the library.

"Why are you here?" she asked.

"Just putting my shoulder to the cosmic wheel. Looking for that trans-Neptunian planet."

"You've got to leave. You're sick."

"Soon. I promise. It's already ten o'clock and the fog has pretty much put paid to the rest of the evening. But I should help little Toddy with a few things before I go."

"It's only nine o'clock, Hugh." She had reset his watch, as well as the two clocks in his rooms, just as the books at the Peabody advised: if a miasmatic patient thought it was later than it actually was, the mind could sometimes speed up the paroxysms.

He smiled as he adjusted the timepiece. "I'm on to you, my dear. That trick won't work again. Now let yourself relax a bit, and let me get out of your hair for a while. If I'm feeling all right on Friday, I'm heading to Philadelphia."

"You're not up to that."

"Yes, I am. The last paroxysms were five hours apart, according to your splendid record-keeping; and the last of those was more than a day ago. I'm entering a long interval. You said it yourself, just before you went off to Mary's this evening."

"Yes, I said it—while I was sponging your dehydrated limbs."

"Which will soon be dancing. Come, Mrs. May, it's time to get on with things. I'm going to inquire into the Frenchman's projector. To think I once imagined using a ring of Brush lamps and a double-sided mirror! The arrangement almost makes me laugh now. With this new machine, if I can get it, my little scheme will seem practically, well, practical."

She pursed her lips. "I don't want you going up there alone. You need someone to look after you, and I can't get away from here. Mr. Harkness wants to finish the Venus measurements by Christmas, because the admiral wants another accomplishment—a whole impressive, mystifying book of photographs and figures—to set in front of the senators before they vote. He's driving me relentlessly. And you're driving me crazy."

"I'll be fine, my sweetheart." He put his arm over her shoulder. "And have you forgotten? *You* want to do this, too. We're going to stand in the light together. A great flashing shaft of it two miles high."

"All right," she said, knowing she couldn't change his mind. "But promise me you'll leave here soon, not more than a half hour from now. You'll catch your death."

"I promise," he replied, kissing her, and not confiding his certainty that he already had.

THOMAS MALLON

. . .

The Sketch Club
Carmac Street
Philadelphia

Saturday morning, October 13, 1877

Dearest Urania,

I'm here as the guest of my old painter friend, Willie Dietrich, who's a member. This was all arranged at the last minute, so that I don't have to stay with my hateful sister in her mansion on South Third. Even so, last evening I did sit out on one of its cast-iron balconies with her and the brother-in-law. As I looked at Sister's black curls—stiffer than the wooden shutters behind them—I asked her husband (more Yankee than thou) how much 26,000 francs really is.

You do not want to know.

But you do want to know everything else about M. Mangin's aplanatic-mirror projector, version no. three.

My friend Davidson (this one not a pansy like Willie) has unimaginably exact diagrams of its every component down to the smallest bolt. We took the schematics outside onto the steps of the Franklin and sat between the columns under the flag, and I don't think I said anything for a full five minutes, some sort of record for me. After that I never stopped. I had a hundred questions and Davidson answered every one. Not only did he know Mangin; he even got to know some of Foucault's *confrères* during his three years in Paris. (This, my darling, is why you should have gone to college. The experience itself gives you nothing, but your fellow alumni can provide you with Mangin's projector, Gauss's drawings and rooms at the Sketch Club.)

Numéro trois—that's number three to you—is so small that

everything can sit on a single four-wheeled wagon: the projector (just 40 cm. in diameter); the dynamo-electric machine; a steam engine with its own tiny boiler! The projector itself detaches from the cart and can be *carried by two people.* Yes, carried up to where we'll be going. The rest of what's on the cart can stay below, regulated by someone else, sending up its energy through a cable attached to the projector. To accomplish our little plan we shall need no more than one strong-backed confederate (if I may use that word).

I must be in touch with a Frenchman in New York, an acquaintance of Davidson's who's Mangin's close friend. Only this gentleman can arrange the projector's sale—and its shipment across the Atlantic. (To think that this *machine merveilleuse*—fewer than a dozen exist, all in the hands of French generals—was designed to spotlight an advancing enemy and flash command signals upon the clouds. An "optical telegraph," Davidson calls it. Well, clouds are the *last* thing you and I will want its light to hit.)

Do you see how you've emboldened me? You're more persuasive than Mother. You've told me not to worry about the import tariff, and for the present, I shan't. This morning I am so excited I would be willing to steal whatever's required to pay it—notwithstanding Dr. Wills's "Sermon on the 8th Commandment," which printed pamphlet lies on the nighttable here. As for buying the machine itself: there should be enough money—if I empty the bank account I've still got in Cambridge and if my brother-in-law comes through with the sum that he promised last night. He wondered why the government isn't financing the purchase of equipment for its own experimenters, so I gave him a manly nudge and a wink, telling him my enterprise was being conducted after hours, and that the results of my light-projecting investigations were bound to have commercial possibilities. Once he thought my purpose was money instead of knowledge—let alone what it really is—both he and his purse strings relaxed.

As I have never been known to hunger for money (or to manage it), my sister appeared suspicious, but she remained more inattentive than anything else, preferring to discuss the sway she hopes to gain over Mother when Mr. Newsmith—my brother-in-law—extracts our father from his current embarrassment. Her only other topic of conversation involved General Butler, the martial flower of our home state, he of the silver whip and missing foot, and whether he will be allowed to take his seat in the Senate after having killed so many of your sectional partisans during the late war. Senator Conkling says anyone entering the chamber "with his hands and face dripping with the blood of murder, should be inquired into"—at the very least, I should suppose. Sister handed me the newspaper containing this rhetorical flourish, and kept on about it for the rest of the evening. (A discouraging thought: do you suppose a species that concerns itself with such things is *worth* projecting through time and space?)

What a paradise of invention I've been wandering through! Last night, once I left my sister and Newsmith, I walked over to Wanamaker's and looked at the blue-moon arc lamps (Brush's latest) now lighting up the store. I wanted to place you in their glow—and that's just what I did, in my mind's feverish eye. (Do not be alarmed. The "feverish" is a figure of speech.) Our proposed endeavor makes me wonder: am I at heart an artist, like poor little Dietrich? A philosopher? I'm surely *not* an astronomer. The admiral is right about that, and I can hardly blame him for thinking it. In fact, at some time I'll have to tell him all I've found out about the Mangin: if he's going to serve on the government's lighthouse board, he really ought to know!

I shall be home on Tuesday. Will you have this by then? It's not yet noon, and I can still rush it to the post office. Of course,

I could wait to tell you all that's in it face to face—in one of my great, teeth-chattering rushes—but I've decided you must have at least one letter from me if we're to call this a romance. It's unfair that, up to now, our proximity has denied you one.

I burn for you—though not, again I swear, with fever. I am fine.

H.

"Mrs. May, you must try it. It leaves you glowing."

Cynthia stopped rereading Hugh's letter when Fanny Christian burst in, carrying a brand-new brand-name jar of enamel. Fanny *was* glowing: a patch of her pretty skin, above the dainty hollow near her collarbone, caught the Monday-morning light.

"I'll try some on my hands, Fanny. They're aging even faster than the rest of me." Fanny eagerly rubbed in the heavy cream; she herself shone as much with commercial faith as with her own pulchritude.

"You do look even lovelier than usual," said Cynthia. "Careful, or Dan will lunge at you."

"Aw," said Fanny. "He isn't so bad. Did you know he's taking book-keeping classes down at Saint Matthew's Institute?"

Fanny's ensign had long since disappeared, and Cynthia gathered that Dan Farricker had crossed over into some new column of eligibility on the girl's ledger of marital prospects, relocated there more, she supposed, by some new anxiety in Fanny herself (had she just had a birthday?) than his own efforts at self-improvement.

"As long as he doesn't start going to gospel meetings at Lincoln Hall," Fanny declared.

"You're right. We wouldn't want him *too* respectable."

Fanny flashed a complicitous smile, as if to say that, when it came to a little disrespectability, well, these days Mrs. May ought to know. The older woman blushed and looked back down at her hands, pretending to concentrate on Fanny's cosmetic efforts. What business was

it of this girl, or of anyone else in this house, to speculate on her comings and goings? "I think that's enough, Fanny." She pulled away her
slippery fingers, and Fanny, disappointed over how little Mrs. May had
praised the magic jar, said all right and retreated from the room.

Cynthia closed her eyes. It had always been this way: she could
tease anyone, but never bear being teased herself. Was it any wonder
that Mary Costello—whose uncorseted nature took such pity on the
shackled, self-torturing Mrs. May—remained her only friend? What
other woman could bear me? thought Cynthia, opening her eyes and
looking into the mirror over her vanity.

It reflected not just her face, but the handwriting on Hugh's
Philadelphia letter. He *was* sick: in places the penmanship shook to the
point of illegibility. And if that wasn't enough to worry about, there
was this reference to Conkling! She tried turning it into a reassurance:
if the War God was now so famous that his public utterances had
begun to register with even Hugh Allison, then Hugh would never be
likely to believe that she knew the senator personally.

Would Conkling remark upon Butler today? Surely any fight over
seating the South's version of Sherman had to take place on the first
day of the session. She checked again to see she had her ticket to the
ladies' gallery; it had come last night by messenger from Wormley's.
Within the hour, she might see parliamentary war not only over Butler
but the Custom House as well: the Administration had just nominated
its three replacements for the machine's top men.

Her enameled hands shook. Hugh, still in Pennsylvania, believed
she would be at the Observatory, not on Capitol Hill, this afternoon.
But Professor Harkness—rewarding her for the extra time she'd put in
on Venus and, more tacitly, the nursing she'd provided their poor,
hopeless colleague—had granted her request for the day off. She had
lied to Conkling, too. He had asked for her company this evening, and
agreed to settle for an appearance in the gallery and at afternoon tea,
after she'd told *him* she was required at the Observatory for night work.

It could not succeed. Her life would catch fire like the Patent Building.

• • •

At one minute before noon, he began his march down the corridor, the oxblood shoes he'd bought in Bond Street tapping out a precise beat on the black-and-white marble. Conkling looked straight ahead, avoiding the lobbyist's salute and the newsman's cry, but he did cast a sidelong greeting to the seller of photographs (yes, his own was still at the front of the bin). Then he looked straight up, to Constantino Brumidi—still on the scaffold at the age of seventy-five, as he'd been for a quarter century, painting his frescoes on the Capitol ceiling—and Brumidi waved.

Conkling passed the Supreme Court room and entered the Senate chamber, taking his place and appraising the vase of fresh flowers on his newly varnished desktop. By his quick count, another dozen of the seventy-six desks were also so adorned, including Blaine's, which to his annoyance sported a much larger bouquet. He nodded to two of his colleagues, Burnside and Stanley Matthews, and signed a fast autograph for the page who'd been dispatched to acquire it by some partisan in the galleries. Favor-seekers and retired senators milled about the floor for the last minute or two before the Vice President picked up his gavel.

While the chaplain made his invocation and called upon God's mercy toward the absent and gravely ill Senator Morton of Indiana, Conkling's lip curled in disapproval of the mess so many of these lawmakers had already made of their places in the chamber. Newspapers lay crumpled under their chairs, and eraser shavings dotted the blotters. As the chaplain went on, Conkling quietly extracted the card from his bouquet. "Once more unto the breach . . ." From Kate, of course, her good wishes for the combat to come, and her rebuke for his not taking her to *Henry V* as soon as he'd arrived in town. She had returned to Edgewood, fleeing Rhode Island and Sprague earlier than usual.

"My little man," said Conkling to a nearby page—they all worshiped him, and he did his best to keep it that way—"will you do this kindness for me?" He indicated a desire to have the flowers removed.

"To your office, sir?" the boy whispered, as the chaplain yet continued.

"To your mother," said Conkling.

Kate was not in the ladies' gallery, but once he dared to look up, he could spot Mrs. May, in just the place he'd picked out for her. She made a stiff, charming wave, unable to hide her amusement over something.

She had not been in the Senate since Pierce's time, and while she watched the War God's comical housekeeping, she also tried to remember the name of the Vice President who would have been presiding in the old chamber on that long-ago day when her father had smuggled her in (twelve years old and already five foot three). She looked around at the female spectators and realized that Conkling had hidden her in plain sight. Dozens of eyes were on the companion he had provided her, the dazzling Mrs. Bruce, perhaps the best-looking politician's wife in the city and, to the mortification of its Southern women (and more than a few of its northern ones), a Negress. Married to the Mississippi senator whom Conkling had championed during the man's first, most difficult days here, she had told Cynthia, within minutes of meeting her at the appointed spot near the staircase, that she and Senator Bruce intended to name their firstborn son after the War God. Right now she sat serenely oblivious to the looks she was attracting, her eyes gazing up toward the light coming through the frosted glass of the ceiling.

Cynthia looked at Conkling's shiny hair and broad shoulders and wondered if he used glycerine lotion, like Fanny, to fight down dandruff. Even seated, he was a magnificent specimen, and for a moment, to her relief and secret disappointment, she thought: he cannot possibly desire *me* for *that*. It had to be some peculiar mental electricity she suggested. She had finally come to believe that Hugh's physical ardor for her was real; and yet she knew that her mothering aroused (in him as well as her) an odd, additional thrill. What sort of charge did Conkling imagine drawing from her?

Conkling listened to Vice President Wheeler murmur the senators toward the first day's business. A year and a half ago, Hayes hadn't even known the old hypochondriac's name. This dull burgher out of the House, so in love with his own rectitude he wouldn't accept a new post office for Malone, New York—let alone a pay raise or some railroad stock. Now, like Blaine, he had moved to the other side of the Capitol, and Conkling would have to look at him, day in and day out, as the session wore on, just as last year he'd had to read his reformist campaign speeches in all the newspapers. Since Wheeler lost his wife, the Hayeses had attached him, like Schurz, to the family hearth, creating the ridiculous spectacle of a President in near-constant touch with his Vice President.

The new senators, the ones filling sudden vacancies, took their oaths and were presented to the body by senior homestate colleagues; especially sentimental flourishes attended the younger Cameron's replacement of his retiring father. Two chairs remained conspicuously empty, but there would be no action today on Butler and Kellogg. The Republicans would not even caucus until tomorrow, a delay upon which Conkling had insisted; and when that meeting finally occurred, it just might have to continue through the reading of the President's message.

Hayes. Conkling twisted his forelock and thought about His Fraudulency down at the other end of the Avenue. The way the man humbly claimed not to "fill" his office but to "occupy" it: he hardly did *that,* just took up a few cubic feet of space, a paperweight, keeping things in place until a breathing man once more seized the premises.

But with all that was happening—Colonel Shafter raiding Mexico; the aggrieved Sioux leaving town; the aggrieved Ponca arriving; silver to be remonetized; the labor unions to be subdued—nothing mattered but the Custom House nominations, which Roscoe Conkling would strangle. Replacing Chet Arthur with *Roosevelt,* that detestable do-gooding businessman with his wheezing Harvard son! (The effrontery of little pince-nezed junior, wanting last year to talk *boxing* with

Roscoe Conkling, while the senator suffered through the last evening of Union League speeches he would ever endure.) Then young Mr. Prince, this "constitutional scholar" with his *book,* to be put in place of Cornell. And they said his Rochester speech was insulting!

They all thought Conkling would never fill *or* occupy the White House. Last year in Cincinnati, Roosevelt Senior had been with those who'd done their best to derail any movement by the convention toward that possibility. Well, after Grant came back in '80, the reformers would die off—perhaps for real, from the shock of it—and Roscoe Conkling would have his own reward four years later, when he would still be only fifty-five, and have safely outrun the climacteric.

This current battle would be fought subtly, slowly. He would bleed Hayes's pigs instead of butchering them.

"Mr. President," he said, rising during a short lull in the mutual admiration and torch-passing. "I move that we adjourn for the day."

His Republican colleagues fell silent, then seconded, and then said aye. Wheeler, confused, brought his gavel down.

Conkling nodded up at Mrs. May. A moment later she was safely delivered to the foot of the staircase by Mrs. Bruce, to whom the senator bid a grateful good-bye.

On their walk to Wormley's, Cynthia handed him the slender volume she'd bought at Morrison's: *Is Our Republic a Failure?* It was her attempt at humor, meant to continue last month's royalist flirtations, but he didn't see the joke.

"Hardly, Mrs. May. Only a mechanism misunderstood and falsely characterized. We are a government of laws *and* men, and must endeavor to remain so." He moved to illustrate his utterance, asking her, with his sharp-toothed debater's smile, if she knew that the supposedly reform-minded President intended to appoint an old friend, a regimental chum from Civil War days, to the consulship in Melbourne.

"I had no idea," she said, wondering if she was supposed to laugh or appear shocked.

"And the President's Democratic friends will vote the fellow in. We have a unique situation, Mrs. May: a Republican President whose incumbency is swelling the ranks of the Democracy." She started to tell him that it would be all right for him to shave off a few syllables, the way she and Professor Harkness sometimes did one or two decimal places, but he hurried on with his explanation. "This is how it happens: Republican officeholders, postmen, and tax collectors, even up in your native New Hampshire, are afraid of losing their positions for looking too 'political'; so they enroll in the other party. Madness! All these disloyal clerks."

"Who should be your footsoldiery."

"Exactly."

Mr. Wormley, the ex-slave who had made himself rich running the best-appointed hotel in the District, showed the senator and his guest to their table.

"I've talked too much of myself," said Conkling, as they waited for their tea—just lemon, no milk, he insisted to the waiter. "You must tell me how Deimos and Phobos have been."

"They're gone. They won't swim back into view until late in '79."

About when the General would. Conkling reached into his waistcoat for a small box. "To remind you of them in the meantime."

Opening the velvet-covered case to find a pair of earrings, she was amused at the thought of some jeweler at Galt's turning them out by the dozen to keep up with the senator's seasonal demand. But then she noticed the stones: each was red, like the planet, but one was larger than the other, in mimicry of the moons. She could no longer pretend that the War God's attentions weren't serious, or at least customized. Please, she thought, let these be garnets and not rubies. How much pressure could she bear? (But if they *were* rubies—her mind quickly began working—think how much they could fetch at the District Commissioner's pawnshop, a new depression-relief effort designed to provide the genteelly impoverished with some cash for their heirlooms. Enough to get the Mangin projector through the Custom House?)

"You're blushing redder than the stones," said Conkling.

"Yes," said Cynthia, "I am." She shut the little case and said, as demurely as she could, "I'll put them on later."

"Ah—*later.*" He made it sound like a place instead of a time, some perfumed Xanadu inside his mind or, more likely, a red-velvet lair behind one of the doors here at Wormley's.

"Yes, much later," she replied. "When I'm home after pushing Venus another few miles across the Sun. It will practically be dawn."

"Is this what comes from my supplemental appropriation? Are they working you that hard? Not to mention denying me your company?"

"Oh, yes," she said. "Every evening you can think of. It's the busiest time I've seen there yet." This work of hers, however falsely she described its schedule, was not just her best alibi; she could see, from the look he had, how much it excited him, the spectacle of a woman earning her bread with her brains, performing a task that even his supple mind couldn't manage. Did he also think she was *devoted* to this work, and extended those long hours out of zealous vocation? If he did, might it not be all right to ask his help for a deserving young man, equally passionate about the skies, a visionary who needed some equipment his superiors were too blinkered to requisition?

No, she could not ask for that; if she did, this young man would become personal to him—a *man,* in short; a rival different from Hayes and Evarts and Roosevelt, but meant to be crushed even flatter.

"You must *keep* working hard, Mrs. May, so that Senator Sargent's bill carries the day." He sounded like the admiral, until he pointed straight up, toward what she understood were his rooms, and said, "We must succeed in moving you to all *sorts* of higher ground." Pleased with his joke, he laughed, and glared, and said: "The health of us both depends on it."

• • •

Miss Clara Morris was "the greatest emotional actress living"—the placards outside the National said so—but from the third row Cynthia found the woman, so tiny and so tragic and so acclaimed for this impersonation of "Miss Multon," a bit hard on the ears. She'd rather have waited for Jefferson to come back in *Rip Van Winkle,* or even for Lydia Thompson to return with her British Blondes, than be seeing this, but once *Henry V* left, Hugh—madly Francophilic since discovering the Mangin machine—had insisted on their going to see these five long acts penned by two dull Frenchmen.

Loud as they might be, Miss Morris's emotings could not keep Cynthia's mind from wandering back to the time she had seen Salvini do *Othello.* If the War God knew she were here now—instead of, as she'd told him, making nightly use of his Transit appropriation with Professor Harkness—might he storm down the aisle and strangle her with his golden foulard? As her fingers drummed the armrest she shared with Hugh, she looked around the rebuilt theater, phoenixed from its ashes four years ago, and wondered how safe it was even now. The recent government inspection of the Observatory showed only what everyone there had known all along—it was a worse firetrap than the Patent Office—but the report's official stamp had somehow now allowed fire to crowd onto Cynthia's always long agenda of preoccupations. The jewels that dangled from the ears and bosoms of all the lobbyists' wives here in the audience were glinting even during this dimly lit moment of calamity for Miss Morris; with little effort, Cynthia could imagine the baubles' concentrated light igniting a velvet seat cover.

None of *these* jewels would end up in the District Commissioner's pawnshop, which entered her thoughts again. This laughable city! Until it learned to manufacture something other than laws and transcript, it would straggle behind the rest of the nation like an overage foundling. She'd realized the other day that the only reason Washington had avoided the summer's labor violence was an insufficiency of the workingmen needed to get a proper riot going.

She drummed her fingers more drowsily and wondered if they were watching the third or the fourth act.

On the other side of the armrest, however insistent Miss Morris might be for his attention, Hugh thought more about the stage's lighting than its passions. Did the suddenly bright backdrop for the actress's latest crisis of nerves derive its illumination from silvered glass or a lens? He wondered, too, when the day would come for the owners to replace the whole theater's gaslights with electricity.

Although she wore no necklace, Hugh still heard Cynthia's chin drop asleep upon her chest. He revived her with an immediate pinch: *"Allons, debout, ma chère."* The play *was,* he had to admit, pretty dreadful. The two of them squeezed their way out of the audience—*pardon, pardon, excusez-moi*—and into the street.

"You are not," he informed her, "delivered from the rest of the evening. Come."

"Where are we going?"

"Marini's. The season hasn't really begun, but he's giving a dance tonight—smaller than usual, but it's supposed to last late."

"I can't go like this."

In fact, though it might not be especially fancy, she had on her gayest dress, the bright green one she'd bought seven months ago, after being hired.

Hugh looked at her appraisingly—"One more touch, that's all you require"—and propelled her toward the tobacconist's on the corner.

"You're open late!" he cried out to the proprietor. "I'd like some hairpins for the lady."

Cynthia moved away, distressed by both the situation and the over-enthusiastic enunciation. It was symptomatic, and she would have to enter it into the fever notebook when she got home.

"I've got no hairpins," said the man behind the cash drawer. "But I can probably find something that would do you."

"You're a hero, my good man!"

Cynthia walked to the other side of the store and caught sight of Conkling's portrait above an open cigar box. An engraving of Hayes perched atop another. They formed a poll on the Custom House nominations: the patron was invited to purchase his cigar from the President's box if he thought Roosevelt and Co. would be confirmed, from the War God's if he felt they'd be defeated.

"Now, then," said Hugh, plucking two yellow flowers out of the corsage he'd given her to carry tonight. With one of the pipe cleaners he'd just bought, he fixed the blossoms to her hair. She felt mortified, like a goat being made to wear a bonnet, until he ran the backs of his fingers over her cheek, and told her, softly, without any sign of unnatural excitement, that she now looked even lovelier than before.

"Like a beacon," he said, holding up a hand-mirror that was on the counter. "Let's go."

At every point on their way to Marini's studio, she remained aware of just how many blocks she was from Mrs. Robinson's, and of that small box of a bedroom in which she'd learned what she went to find out. It seemed as much a coffin for her and Hugh's unconceived child as the small oak chest in which Sally had long ago been confided to the ground.

Hamilton Fish, Jr., the bachelor congressman from New York and one of Marini's social impresarios, greeted them at the door. "Come in!" he cried, gesturing toward the scene within. "Magnificent, isn't it?"

"Actually, less grand than I've seen it," Hugh whispered to Cynthia. The two of them entered a ballroom festooned with silk swag and lilies. Mounds of ice cream sat atop a table at the far end, not far from a magnificent *cheval-de-frise,* left over from the famous night that Sir Edward and Lady Thornton had appeared. This trellis of silver spears circled the musicians. Two young diplomats, one with a Spanish accent, the other speaking the purest Hoosier, passed by Cynthia, discussing whether or not Robert Lincoln would take an offer to become a Third Assistant Secretary of State. A cluster of naval officers, their dates mostly in pink and showing more bare bosom than ever, had just come from the circus, which would depart Washington two nights hence. If only, thought Cynthia, Hugh had taken her there instead of to the National, or here.

"What a relief from nights with Mr. Todd," he said, surveying the scene. He began mimicking the squirrelly movements of his trans-Neptunian colleague, whispering his excited surmises that made every nighttime speck a potential planet and promotion: "'What's that?'" "'Don't you see it?'" "'At the top of the arc!'"

Cynthia did not laugh. She would rather be around Mr. Todd than all the hearties and belles parading by her. She could now even recognize Miss Ellen Gray across the room.

"My rival," she told Hugh, pointing toward her.

"Oh, Lord," he groaned. "Let's find the dog and put him on the ice block." Actually, much to Miss Gray's disappointment, Marini did not permit even animals as small as Buster to get underfoot. He was serious about the dancing, and had several midshipmen here to display the skills he was known for teaching them at Annapolis. The dance floor itself was the last place Cynthia wanted to be, and after filling a silver bowl much past the rim with ice cream, she made a beeline for two empty chairs against the wall.

"I want to dance," Hugh protested.

"Then dance with her," Cynthia replied, nodding toward the *décolleté* Miss Gray.

He sat down, sighing. "All right. Let's talk about her still-prospective brother-in-law instead."

"You mean Henry Paul?"

"Yes. Can we trust him? If our projector makes it across the ocean and then through Customs and then down here, we shall still need a third person to run its little engine while we go aloft with the light."

Cynthia shook her head, forcefully. "You can't yet think of help from anyone else, least of all someone at the Observatory. There's too much danger the wrong people will find out." *Anyone* would be wrong; could there be a more repellent prospect than Hugh's sharing their intimate madness, their production of a cosmic imprint instead of a child, with a third party? She changed the subject. "You haven't told me the latest news from New York."

"Mangin's *ami* wants me there when it arrives, and you should come with me. I'm sure you can arrange two days off with Harkness and Harrison. You've put in so much extra time."

Henry Paul, catching sight of the two of them, crossed the room. "Mrs. May!" he exclaimed, not unwelcomingly, but with great surprise. She knew what he was thinking: a peculiar friendship was one thing, but for Allison to bring her *here*, like a girl you were courting?

"Watch out for Ellen," Henry warned Hugh, smiling as he spoke of his future sister-in-law. "She still hasn't forgiven you that night at the commodore's. She'll breathe fire if she spots you."

"My guess," said Hugh, turning to Cynthia, "is that she can put out five hundred carcels. We'll strap her to the apparatus."

Looking at the floor, Cynthia pressed the back of her cold spoon quite hard against his hand. Henry Paul, with a still-friendly but puzzled look, decided to leave these two odd ducks to themselves. He made a little bow and went looking for some pretty girl who could be counted on to simper over his impending removal from the marriage market.

Cynthia now struck Hugh's knuckles, much harder, with the edge of the spoon. "Don't tell anyone *anything*. Don't even make an obscure joke like that. It will get them asking questions."

"Why can't I jaw on about my project the way they always do about theirs?" He offered his hand to be kissed, and when she declined, he soothed his knuckles, babyishly, with his own lips, a gesture that irritated and then aroused her—and thereby irritated her all over again.

"Yours isn't a project. It's—I don't know, I suppose it's a vision."

"You're right. I really *am* a philosopher. I took the wrong diploma entirely. In fact," he said, his voice starting to rise, "I could—"

"You're more an addled poet," she said, sweetly, trying to calm him and herself.

"I sing the body electric—"

Afraid he would start singing for real, as at Riley Shinn's, she pointed to the wealth of ice cream dripping down the great block of ice. "I'd like some more."

"Tell me something. I must know: how *are* we going to get our miracle machine through Customs? My faith in you is complete, but I do find myself curious. I keep assuming it's through the good offices of someone your father once knew at the Treasury. Would that be right?"

Amazed that her facility for lying had blossomed so gaudily, she heard herself responding: "No, it's my brother-in-law. He can radically reduce the fee, and let you pay it in a few token installments over several years." All she had needed to answer was "yes." The useless lie and its embellishments had appeared like spontaneous growths in a laboratory dish. (To start with, John May had no brother.) Would she even remember the details of this duplicity? She wondered if she was developing powers of deception for further use with the War God, who no doubt imagined her, even now, toiling at the Observatory. "And that's the only brother-in-law I want to speak of," she added. "No more talk of requesting help from Henry Paul, not unless you want Miss Gray and perhaps even the admiral knowing what you intend to do. Now get me more ice cream."

She knew from his contented expression—he was probably back dreaming of the little Mangin—that he would never again bring up the import duty. But when he turned directly toward her, he insisted upon one thing: "Only after you've danced with me."

"Out of the question. Ice cream."

"No dessert for you until I've finished my dancing."

He pulled her on to the floor and into some complicated human geometry, whether a minuet or quadrille she hadn't the least idea. But, fearing the even greater embarrassment that fleeing the polished marble would bring, she began to move. She felt dozens of female eyes on her; they were agog that such a creature was *here,* and wondering, too, in their brief looks at Mr. Allison, if this young man was well enough to have come out himself. His fast, slender figure might be fetching from a distance, but close up it revealed itself as *too* slim, and his color looked decidedly suspect.

And yet, the more they watched, the more relaxed Cynthia became. The dance *was* geometry, nothing but, and Hugh Allison was an expert, describing its arches and angles and small circles with his extended arms and shining shoes. All she had to do was replicate the shapes, become the double-side of his glittering mirror. Within two minutes a dozen years had fallen from her face, and she cared no more about the cruel company and the waste, cared no more if the ice cream melted into a flood of gruel, so long as the violinists didn't stop.

"Tell me, Mrs. May," asked Hugh, when the pattern required that he hold her by the waist and sweep her twice around him, "how strong are *your* immortal longings?"

"Stronger and stronger," she replied, as the dance's next movement spun him off into a line of three males, each of whom faced his partner from a half-dozen feet away.

"And yours?" she called across the distance.

"Nearer and nearer fulfillment."

A moment arrived when the couples had to orbit an empty center, to swirl like a solar system without a sun. "Our" machine, he had called it. It was now her vision, too, a *folie à deux*, and she wanted it, as much as she still wanted him. Her hand in his, moving faster now, she asked: "How do we get inside?" How *would* they, after crossing the mud and debris at the site, get themselves and their machine into the absurd, abandoned plinth of the Monument?

"The same way," he said, while the music sped up and their feet followed, "that the light finds us. The same way," he said, as they reached maximum velocity, "that we make love." They spun and drove forward in a single movement, and the violin bows beat like wings. She trusted her feet and looked into his eyes.

"Breaking and entering," he explained, his voice flying on the music.

NINE

Cynthia stood outside the packing room, putting on her hat. The days remained as warm and wet as last month's, but they had grown short, and she hoped to be back at Mrs. O'Toole's before the sun was gone. She had just left a bag of oranges for Hugh in Mr. Harrison's office, where there was considerable activity for 4:45 P.M. Mr. Gardner, the instrument maker, had come bustling in, quite agitated, from the machine shop, unable to find some of the equipment on the admiral's latest list of items requiring service or superannuation. Mr. Harrison, "expecting an unexpected guest," had had no time or suggestions for him.

Now, though she had trouble believing her ears, she understood why. The nearby voice of the short-notice visitor, just arrived and braying for the superintendent, could belong only to the War God. A hairpin still between her lips, Cynthia leaned against the pier of the 9.6-inch and listened to the conversation coming from the doorway of Mr. Harrison's office on the other side.

"We were excited to get word of your coming," the flustered clerk was saying. "I've sent someone to bring back Admiral Rodgers. He's over at the Corcoran Building. As you may know, the Almanac Office just moved over there, and he and Mr. Newcomb are having to sort out some confusion over—"

"Yes," said Conkling, always bored with explanations of his inconvenience.

Cynthia made a fast, unseen flight back to her desk, her bonnet swishing in her right hand as she went. She did not want Conkling to find her, but knew she would be wise to let that happen—to make him think that she had just arrived for one of the long working nights she had said they required of her. Instead of putting her bonnet on the clothes tree, she threw it atop a pile of papers, to give the little room an appearance of her fresh arrival.

Conkling's visit, she realized, was in keeping with the strategy he had displayed throughout the whole first month of the Special Session. He had contrived to make the Custom House nominations look like the last thing on his mind—less important than the New York State bakers' complaints or gilding the statue atop the Capitol or, it now seemed, the future of the Observatory.

"Allow me to wander," she heard him saying to Mr. Harrison, who had stuck to the senator during a noisy passage toward the Chronometer Room.

"Yes, by all means," said the clerk. "You'll see just why the $28,909 has been requested in the interim, for repairs."

"Indeed," said Conkling. "Plus thirty-five cents. I've *read* the report to Secretary Thompson, my good man."

"It's not for me to say, of course," Mr. Harrison went right on. "But I'm sure the admiral will make the point that spending a hundred thousand dollars for removal instead would be the better bargain. So long, of course, as there's no factory nearby to shake the instruments and obscure them with smoke." Like some powerful ether whose effect varied with every person exposed to it, Conkling had turned the discreet, unflappable clerk into a chattering font of presumption.

Within another minute, the two men came upon Cynthia's little office, and the senator—all annoyance flooded out by delight—was crying "Aha!"

"Mrs. Cynthia May," said Mr. Harrison. "Our most exceptional computer."

"Charmed," said Conkling, taking her hand.

"Stunned," replied Cynthia.

"I shall let Mrs. May tell me about her work," said Conkling, dismissing the clerk with a definite glance. "She can guide me back to your office in time for the admiral's arrival."

"Certainly," said Mr. Harrison, who was subsiding back toward normality, except for a slight confusion about Conkling's familiarity toward Mrs. May.

"You have time for our esoteric affairs?" asked Cynthia, once she and the War God were alone.

"Oh, yes," said Conkling, who made a fast visual inventory of the space she inhabited every night. "The nominations are dying a slow death. I've just had the Commerce Committee draft a letter to Sherman asking the exact grounds on which my men have been dismissed. That should prolong the President's agony another week or two. I spent today on other matters entirely—in fact, I took to the floor to explain my latest interview. Did you read it? Everyone else did."

"Yes," said Cynthia. Friday's New York *Herald* had arrived by messenger at Mrs. O'Toole's this morning.

Conkling twirled a protractor on his right forefinger and laughed. "I did have to take back the bit about praising Tilden. That really was going too far, and I had to blame the newsman for making up exactly the words he'd heard from my mouth. But I did *not* retract what I said about the Republican party." He put down the little measuring device, and all at once seemed to glow before her eyes, as if attached to the engine of Hugh's magic machine. "There is one single bulwark, Mrs. May, against the old slavocracy, against German radicalism, against the silver-coining forces of inflation." She had begun to count, as if he were reciting the Seven Deadly Sins. "That bulwark is the Republican party," he went on. "And *that* is why I look upon these wealthy New York reformers as such fools. They are to be the worst sufferers if this nation passes back into the hands of the other party, controlled in the South by evil traditions and ruled in the North by its socialistic elements."

"You're quoting yourself."

"Good!" said Conkling. "Then you *did* read the interview." He closed the office door and took another look at the pile of photographic plates and charts beside her hat.

"I don't see the shawl I gave you."

"It's too warm."

"And I don't see the earrings."

"It's too ordinary a day for them."

He lunged forward and took her in his arms, crushing her against the well-tended muscles of his torso. For two or three seconds, before she began to struggle, she allowed herself, in the aroma of cologne and soap, to feel not the danger and caddishness of the moment, but a shameful sense of safety; if she chose, she could surrender to this man who helped control the forces that had always pressed down on her; that had sent her father packing and her husband to war; that appropriated and canceled all the little pots of money by which people like her rose in the world or fell into its alleys.

Suddenly, out in the corridor, the approaching sound of song:

"Oh, Susanna, oh, don't you cry for me—"

"Oh, sweet Jaysus!" Cynthia cried.

"An expression you learned from the Irishwoman?" whispered Conkling, as he pulled away from her. He picked up a chart and began to study it in the last seconds before Hugh Allison knocked at the door.

"*—with my banjo on my knee.* Hello!"

She glared at him. "You're here early, Mr. Allison."

"And you're here la—"

"What *brings* you here?" she quickly interrupted.

"Trans-Neptunian paperwork, Mrs. May. Until the Sun is fully down, we astronomers are just celestial clerks. You know that. But as soon as it's dark, Mr. Todd and I shall sweep between 8° 30' and 9°. Poor Toddy thought he saw his future a little above 9° last night, but it fizzled into another false alarm. Sir," he said, finally getting around to Conkling, "I don't believe we've met." He shook the man's hand, and without waiting for his name or giving his own, turned back toward Cynthia. "I've got something to show you. Find me when you're free. I'll be in the library with the old commodore."

Conkling, furious at being ignored, said, "Sands has come over to see *me*. To provide an historical perspective while Admiral Rodgers speaks from a future one."

"Well, it will be a pleasure for you," said Hugh. "And who would you *be,* sir?"

"Mr. Allison," said Cynthia, "this is Senator Conkling. Senator Conkling, Mr. Allison."

Hugh burst out laughing. "Senator *Roscoe* Conkling himself? Well, sir, you'll break my mama's heart if you don't give Matt Butler his seat! Anyway," Hugh said, his interest in politics already spent, "you're probably both here waiting for Harkness. I hear he's over with Mr. Newcomb and the admiral. Until they get back, Senator, I suggest you get the *present* perspective from Mrs. May. You could have no better guide to this place. Just don't keep me waiting *too* long," he said to Cynthia, waving good-bye as he vanished back into the corridor. The door's glass pane rattled, and Cynthia's heart thumped. At least, she told herself, he hadn't come in and grabbed her by the waist. At least he hadn't called her Urania.

Recovering her poise, she looked at Conkling and asked: "Why shouldn't I strike you?"

"Who," he replied, "is that preposterous person?"

"He's the most brilliant man here."

"He's an idiot. And he looks ill. I can't bear being around sickness."

"Then pass a law against it. But first answer my question: Why shouldn't I strike you?"

"You've answered it yourself. You had sufficient time to pull away from me, if that's what you wanted to do."

She slapped his face.

"Mrs. May," he said, forbearingly, as if looking at some hapless opponent who'd read only half the bill being debated. "That will only excite me further."

She hung her bonnet on the clothes tree and sat down behind her desk, as calmly as she could.

"I hadn't expected to find you here so early," said Conkling.

"When working this hard," she said, pointing to the Transit-of-Venus tables as if she really ought to be getting back to them, "one loses track of day and night."

"When do these long nights finally end?"

She calculated the lengthiest lie that she could get away with. "In a fortnight, I suppose. The whole project should be finished a few weeks after that."

"All right, then. Two weeks from tonight, a proper entertainment for the two of us. Write down the date."

"Do you really think *I* need to write such things down in order to remember them?" She pointed to the elegant tangle of trigonometry covering the sheets in front of her, then rose with whatever dignity she could manage. The War God was smiling, freshly aroused by her gumption and the thought of her breadwinning brain work.

"Let me take you to the superintendent's office," she said.

"I doubt the admiral's yet there."

"Good. Then you can sit outside it and wait, like an ordinary mortal." She could not take him to see Commodore Sands, not if it meant another encounter with Hugh, so she delivered him to Mr. Harrison, who would have to blither some more until Rodgers arrived. She herself went to the library.

"Is he as frightening as everyone says?" asked the twinkling commodore, rising unsteadily to greet her.

"He's a bogeyman," she said, while the old man kissed her hand. "He's about as scary as a Punch puppet." Wishing this were true, she urged Hugh, with her eyes, to spirit her away before Mr. Harrison thought to bring him in here.

The commodore laughed. "You two go off," he said, a little smile opening a hole in his long white beard. Alone of everyone at the Observatory, he seemed to accept the idea of an actual romance between Mr. Allison and the older woman. "I'll have one of my little dozes while I wait for the senator and the admiral. It will *fortify* me."

A moment later, Hugh was leading Cynthia down a flight of steps diagonally opposite the packing room. He lit a lantern and walked ahead of her through a dark, muddy tunnel. The two of them stepped gingerly, hoping no rats were about, until they reached the passage-way's bricked-up conclusion. Standing before a large puddle and a pair of abandoned brooms, Cynthia, who had had enough surprises for one late afternoon, asked Hugh: "What is this place?"

It was, he explained, the entrance to the old magnetic observatory, where thirty years before, the scientifics had studied the effects of earthly magnetism upon navigation. The underground annex had been built and buried too cheaply, soon becoming a flooded mess that had to be blocked off and abandoned.

"Why did you bring me down here?"

"Two reasons," he replied. "First, this one." He put his hands on her shoulders and kissed her deeply. She was afraid he might smell Conkling's various perfumes and pomades, but his own medicinal aromas—liniment and horehound lozenges—masked the War God's. His embrace was ardent but wholly different from the senator's ravenous assault. He came to her as if they were two children in a base-ment misbehaving on a rainy day. She could feel all the pure excitement of first love, and even as her pulse raced, she responded to his kiss with self-hatred for the subjugated safety she had let herself feel with Con-kling a few minutes before.

"Why?" she asked again.

"Why *here*? The illicit feel of it," he whispered, between kisses upon her neck. "Romance requires some of that, don't you think? As much as it requires the odd love letter."

"You said *two* reasons," she responded, the precisionist in her get-ting, as always, the upper hand.

"Ah, yes, the second reason." He picked up one of the brooms and pointed it at the bricked-up entryway. "A dramatic backdrop for the serious matter I'm about to bring up—we require one, just like Miss Clara Morris at the National. Now, do we know what's on the other side of this wall? What was left inside when they gave up this place?"

"We do not."

"Exactly. Any more than we know what was left inside the shaft of the Monument when they abandoned *it*. My point is simple: it's time for a reconnaissance mission."

"Already?" asked Cynthia, suddenly dreading the prospect. "The projector is still weeks away from arriving."

"It could be in New York as early as the thirtieth."

She said nothing, and wondered how she would keep her nerve when the time came.

"Thanks to your brother-in-law, it will *whoosh* through Customs," Hugh fairly shouted, swinging the broom like a baseball bat. "Then we'll get it down here, and it still won't even be Christmas! It's time to get ready, darling."

"All right," she said, taking hold of the second broom and squeezing its handle. "Some night soon."

•   •   •

Conkling watched her play with the larger earring, which dangled toward her freshly enameled neck. He was waiting for an answer.

"There is a good reason I can't be persuaded to go up there," she said, pointing to the upper floors of Wormley's.

"And what is that?" he asked, slamming his spoon against the dish of clear soup.

"You've just entered your forty-ninth year," she explained, crossing her fingers for luck beneath the tablecloth. "You're a Scorpio going through Scorpio's period on the calendar, and you're approaching one of the great battles of your life. Intimacy with an Aries would be folly until that battle is over. Do you want to know the exact alignments that proscribe it?"

"You've gotten this nonsense from the Irishwoman."

Cynthia measured the warring proportions of disappointment and fear in his eyes. Nonsense it was, and made up entirely by herself, but such nonsense was his vice, and she thought she could see it persuading him.

"I cannot speed up the battle," he said, pouting.

"I'm jealous," she replied. Her evasive mumbo-jumbo was going to work, and she felt giddy with relief. "You must prefer Chester Arthur to me."

"No," said Conkling, as he sank against the plush chair-back. He looked the way he did on those infrequent occasions when he allowed himself to compromise. He was trying to dwell on the essential fact: he had gotten her consent. It was a matter of when, not whether. It would be a slow conquest, like his undoing of Hayes. He reminded himself that the protractedness of *that* enterprise had afforded a great incidental pleasure, the spectacle of his enemies trying to second-guess and placate him. Perhaps it would be the same with this campaign.

"Did you see," he asked, "that Mr. Evarts is refusing to appoint any ex-rebels to ambassadorships?"

"Yes," she replied. "Mrs. O'Toole was decrying the injustice of it all at breakfast."

"That's *my* doing. He thinks I'll relent on the Custom House if I get my way in other matters. Well, he's going to be disappointed. And wait until your secesh landlady hears the speech I give against Butler tomorrow. I hope the mother of that idiot boy-astronomer hears it, too."

"Who?" asked Cynthia, feigning perplexity. "Oh, Mr. Allison."

"Yes, the one you say is so brilliant. What's your interest in him? Entirely dispassionate, I hope."

She began to play with the other, smaller earring. "Entirely passionate, I'm afraid. As to an idea that he has." Now that she had won a reprieve, she had to risk discussion of Hugh, had to gamble that the

War God could be made to believe she had only an intellectual affinity for the skinny, high-strung rebel.

"And what would this 'idea' be?"

"A piece of astronomical investigation you wouldn't comprehend any more than I can grasp your parliamentary strategy."

He glowed again, the way he had at the Observatory, excited by her intellect, this competing force that he would break against the rhythms of his will.

All at once, she declared: "I have a favor to request. A gift I would have asked for instead of the shawl and the earrings you bestowed."

"Simply name it, Mrs. May."

"It involves corruption." Before he could lose his sudden, thrilled expression, she launched into an account of the Mangin projector's current voyage from Le Havre to New York; of how it traveled fully paid for; of how Mr. Allison could not get financial backing from an Observatory that lacked his breadth of vision; of how American science would be noting his accomplishments long after the name of Asaph Hall had been forgotten.

"Does this concern his 'trans-Neptunian planet'?" Conkling pronounced the hypothetical body as if it were some cherished project of Evarts and Hayes.

"Yes," said Cynthia, hoping he understood as little of astronomy as he did Madam Costello's malleable art.

"What exactly do *you* hope to gain from this?" he asked.

"My own small bit of immortality." Let him think she meant a footnote in the history of science, not the mad gesture toward eternity that she and Hugh intended to make.

Conkling's eyes lit up further. Her ambition appealed to the same part of him that had been excited into accepting an invitation to address the Women's Suffrage Association after the New Year. He took out a small pencil and thick, gilt-edged notecard. "I *do* have to write myself reminders," he said. "Now when is this French machine supposed to arrive?"

• • •

A half hour later she was telling the carriage driver Conkling had summoned for her to head for the Mall, specifically the north-side entrance of the Agriculture Department.

She spotted Hugh standing there, just as he'd promised. She had selected this night for their scouting mission because a late rendezvous with him had ensured her resistance to Conkling: she could not have surrendered without Hugh's being stood up and herself found out.

"What ever made you pick such a pair of shoes?" Hugh asked, pointing to her feet as they walked west across the Mall's soft ground.

"Oh," she said, starting on one more lie. "It was Fanny's birthday and we were all being a little fancy. I should have thought to change them." She quickly changed the subject instead: "I see the cows are gone." The cattle sheds she could remember ringing the truncated Monument during the war had given way to a handful of what looked like miners' shacks: construction sheds for the Corps of Engineers. Thanks to the last Congress's centennial spirit, the Corps had been asked to inspect the Monument's foundations and see whether it was worth resuming work on the site after more than twenty years. Ground had been carved out around the steps at the base, exposing the old underpinnings.

Looking at the hundred-and-fifty-foot shaft, Cynthia had the impression of something being driven *into* the earth instead of raised above it. The fog was nearly as bad here as it would be at the Observatory, a short distance west and a few feet lower into the mud of the Potomac. She did not want to go any farther, but Hugh was scampering merrily ahead, pulling her by her right arm. As they raced to the eastern front of the obelisk, its massive door looking ever larger, she could hear her lunar earrings click inside her pocket.

"Make some noise," Hugh ordered, once they reached the steps.

"Why?"

"To excite a watchman. There must be one here."

"I can't think—"

"On the count of three. One, two, three: *In the gloaming*—" He bellowed the song until a sharp "Who goes there?" cut him off.

"See?" he whispered, as a uniformed man approached the pair of them. "And what cheer from you, sir?" cried Hugh, who pumped the guard's hand and offered a big smile along with his greeting. She could see that charm would be tonight's burglary tool.

He told Officer Shea who he was; and that the lady was Mrs. May, who worked with numbers over at the Observatory. The officer had a female cousin good with figures? Well, fancy that. And he'd really been at this post for fourteen years, ever since Gettysburg itself? Hugh kept sending the watchman's words right back to him, in a honeyed, lilting version that cheered their original speaker and made him think he was a much more clever fellow than he'd realized out here night after night, year after year.

"Oh, it's been dispiriting as can be, Mr. Allison. For a long time I thought they'd tear the thing down rather than finish it. And I don't mind telling you, I've had more than one bout of marsh fever sitting out here every fall."

"Have you tried Schenck's Pulmonic Syrup? It's marvelous, isn't it, Mrs. May?"

"The best remedy you can find," she assured Officer Shea, who nodded his thanks and went on to declare that matters had been more cheerful since the engineers arrived with their shovels and plumb lines. Their investigations of the ground had shown it surprisingly sturdy for a patch so near a swamp. If Congress and the Monument Society continued to provide the money, the shaft might yet rise to its full five hundred and fifty feet.

The watchman revealed himself as a frustrated guide who would rather be showing visitors around a finished memorial than guarding this sodden site of interruption and uncertainty. As it was, he could name every item that had gone into the cornerstone in 1848. "We've got something from your outfit, you know," he told Hugh, explaining that the *Astronomical Observations for 1845*, presented by Superintendent Maury, were right inside the stone, along with the *Farmers' Almanac* and every coin they'd minted to that day.

"The dollar of our daddies," said Cynthia.

"Perfectly phrased, ma'am," said Shea, a bit shyly, who embarked on a vigorous explanation of how resuming the coinage of silver might give help to debtors like himself. "Why should the banking interests get all—"

"Might we have a look inside?" asked Hugh, who said he hated to miss any of the officer's argument, but felt he must point out the lateness of the hour. He really ought to be seeing Mrs. May home, and they would so enjoy getting a glimpse of the interior first.

"Well," said Shea, pulling on his beard and giving it some thought. "It's against regulations, but I imagine the lady might like to see the New England granite on the inside walls. I wouldn't be surprised if some of it came from quarries she rode past growing up."

He said he'd fetch a key. Hugh accompanied him and made a note of where this crucial object hung. It was so massive it looked like a ceremonial joke, but it actually turned a lock, and with one push and a slight groan from both the hinges and Officer Shea himself, the giant eastern door gave way.

"Be careful in them shoes, ma'am."

Some squeaks indicated the presence of at least a few rats, attracted by remnants of the engineers' recent lunches.

"Even in this light you can tell the granite's blue," said Shea, holding his lantern up to one of the walls. Its stones turned out to be as heavily inscribed as an Egyptian tomb's.

Cynthia looked upward, calculating the rate at which the shaft tapered toward the night sky—one-quarter inch to the foot, she felt certain—while Hugh intently surveyed some rotten-looking scaffolds.

"How ever did they get up there?" Cynthia asked Shea. "The workmen, I mean."

"You've brought me to the most interesting thing of all," said the watchman. "There's going to be a steam elevator rising the whole five hundred and fifty feet! And two iron stairways, on the north and south sides. Fifty flights for the fellows who'll be doing the construction!"

"But in the earliest days?" asked Cynthia, whose lantern-lit expression, like Hugh's, was growing anxious.

Officer Shea walked behind one of the scaffolds and beckoned the couple to join him near the granite wall. "See there? Dangerous as all hell—you should pardon my language, ma'am. But there it is. Wooden steps on iron struts, winding around all four walls. The grade is nice and gentle, but I wouldn't trust those planks with *my* life. The air that seeps in here has made 'em soggier than my lungs."

Hugh knocked one or two of them with his hand. "At the very top, Officer. What caps the thing now?"

The watchman laughed. "Nothing but some wooden flats. You hear 'em banging up and down whenever there's a storm. The next big rain'll let in enough water to drown those rats, I promise you."

"But," Hugh asked, "one can still get all the way up—and out onto the top edge?"

"Well," said the watchman. "In theory."

•   •   •

Four nights after dining with Cynthia, Conkling sat in his rooms at Wormley's and let impatience get the better of him. Having her eventual consent meant nothing compared to her immediate absence. He wanted her here now, wanted the only numbers before him to be the grand exponential ones she dealt in, not these double-digit tallies, the yea-and-nay projections he'd been revising for weeks. Right now the nominations fight seemed less a thrilling strike at the king than a laborious effort to hoist his three overfed lieutenants above their own difficulties in New York.

Frustrated with ardor and suspicion, he reached for one of his gilt-edged note cards:

My dear Madam Costello—

This should be taken as a severe caution. Anytime you see
peril to a Scorpio from consorting with an Aries, you had better think to inform *him* and not her. I shall assume you were
telling Mrs. May the truth—at least as you see it from behind
your celestial counter—but I shall not have you informing her
of my worries and affairs. Where the three of us are concerned,
all intelligence is to travel in one direction only—from her,
through you, to me. Is that clear? I shall call on you tomorrow
evening, and when I do, you had better tell me everything there
is to be told about Mr. Hugh Allison. I do not trust Mrs. May
on the subject, and woe betide your little den of necromancy if
I cease to trust you.

Roscoe Conkling

•   •   •

When they got off the ferry from New Jersey, after the long nighttime train ride from Washington, Hugh and Cynthia headed straight to
the Battery. Each carried a Gladstone bag, but neither seemed tired
from the many hours of travel. The sunrise over the Hudson, this Friday, December 7, had appealed to both of them, but it stirred nothing
like the excitement they now displayed over the distant approach of
the *Juliette Marie*. The telegraph operator in Sandy Hook had com-
municated the first sight of the ship, and a revenue cutter carrying
inspectors from the Custom House was already setting out to meet her.
Cynthia imagined the mad salutes that had greeted Conkling's arrival
back in August, and felt certain they couldn't match the crowing gusto
with which Hugh Allison was waving his long white muffler at the precious cargo heading their way.

"Put it back on," she gently urged. She tucked the ends of the wool
into the lapels of his overcoat and reminded him: "We've got at least
six hours of traipsing ahead of us." By 4 P.M. the *Juliette Marie*'s cargo
would have undergone the required inspections, and the two of them

could claim the Mangin projector for its transfer to the ferry and a freight train south. Until then, with most of the day to kill, they wandered the many-leveled cornucopia of Stewart's department store and sat by the huge open hearth of a Bowery beer garden.

Even so, they arrived at the Custom House well in advance of four o'clock, and had to spend some time just gazing at the immensity of its facade. Its Ionic colonnade stretched a whole block, and its windowed dome, so much higher than the Observatory's, seemed to mock the tiny flag that flew from a pole on the roof below it.

She and Hugh made their way to an entrance on Hanover, or, as even the War God liked to joke, "Hand-over Street." They climbed to the Rotunda, where hundreds of desks looked like haystacks in some vast imperial barn. The place seemed an inverse of the pension office back in the District, where a similar profusion of clerks sat disbursing mites to survivors of the war. Here it was all a matter of intake, the huge dome sucking in money as if its windows were the sluice gates of a dam.

By now, if the dam had operated with its usual speed, the Appraiser's report to the Inspector would have made its way to the Surveyor and, at last, the office of the Collector, where it would be sitting on the desk of a Mr. Joseph Selden. He would report to Mrs. May and Mr. Allison that their projector had been cleared through the Port of New York with most of its fees paid and what little remained having been deferred to future installments. Cynthia looked forward to watching the professional smile that would appear on Mr. Selden's face in gratitude for the couple's contribution to the treasuries of both the United States and the New York Republican party. After handshakes all around, there would still be time to meet Mangin's *ami* at the bonded warehouse for an instructive glimpse at the mechanical marvel before it was recrated and sent off on the rest of its journey.

Instead of smiling, Mr. Selden, without raising his eyes from the paper on his desk, said, "One thousand and eight hundred and fifty dollars."

Hugh stood silent. "I don't understand," said Cynthia.

Mr. Selden looked up at her, his expression making it clear that, no, *he* was the one who didn't understand.

"I was told that the bulk of the fee had already been paid," said Cynthia, "and that what remained might be rendered—"

"One thousand eight hundred and fifty dollars. Payable immediately, or the item will be sold at auction thirty days from now." Mr. Selden was already looking past them to see who was next and ready with a bank draft. "Please move away," he said, putting the projector's certificate into one of his desk's lower drawers.

Hugh led Cynthia to a nearby bench. Even before sitting down, she realized what had occurred. Despite what he'd promised—*had* he promised? or merely indicated?—Conkling had decided not to work his will until *she* delivered the goods. To him, she was the same as the projector: a peculiar, desired commodity under embargo. Why keep his end of the bargain until she kept hers? She could picture him looking at the Senate calendar, counting the days until the nominations battle would be won or lost, and deciding not to play any card, in his public life or his hidden one, before it was absolutely necessary.

"Perhaps Mr. May tried and failed," said Hugh, soothingly. Not even at the height of his fevers had she permitted herself tears, but he saw her crying now.

The sound of "Mr. May" made her shake—over the ever-finer entanglement of her lies and the name's strange evocation of John himself, not the brother he had never had. "But he assured me—" she started to say, before guilty sobs overtook her.

"Come," said Hugh, more composed than she could have imagined. "We can't let the poor Frenchman just stand there."

They recognized Mangin's friend, waiting at the bonded warehouse, by the long ends of his mustache and a plaintive palms-out gesture indicating he had already learned of the difficulty.

"We have some apologizing to do," said Hugh.

Even Cynthia managed to express her hope that he hadn't been waiting too long.

"No, no," said Louis Hiver, "*un quart d'heure,* at the most. But such a shame!" He pointed to the projector, still uncrated from its inspection, but roped off to any but an official's touch. "And so easy to operate—it would be great pleasure to show you!" He leaned his head, insouciantly, to one side. "But if you like—maybe while you remain in the city and try to, how do you say, straighten this out—I will show you something else. I wish you could have been there this morning at the office!"

"What office is that?" Hugh knew almost nothing about him. Davidson had had him writing to Hiver at a rooming-house address.

"Of the *Scientific American.* I am the new 'European correspondent.' I am Scientific Frenchman!" He smiled and bounced, more like Cynthia's idea of an Italian.

"Come to the office tomorrow and you will have a pleasure."

She looked doubtfully at Hugh. However weary she might be, a lifetime of parsimony was urging her to start back for Washington tonight and avoid the price of the hotel. But she could tell from the sight of Hugh that he wasn't up to it. He had had to put down his bag several times during their walk here from Hanover Street. Right now it rested at his feet, and she worried that some over-zealous inspector might try to tax or confiscate it.

Hugh indicated to M. Hiver that their plans were up to the lady.

"We'll come round in the morning," said Cynthia, taking a card with the magazine's address.

When they'd set out yesterday, she had anticipated the delightful moment when they would register at the Astor House as Mr. and Mrs. Hugh Allison. Now nothing could dispel her dark mood. From the dining-room window, she could see the offices of the New York *Herald,* and while they ordered their meal she silently wished that that paper's reporter had vanquished the War God by inventing statements even beyond the ridiculous bombast he had actually uttered in his interview. She couldn't even stand that they were staying in a Republican establishment.

"Why didn't you arrange for us to lodge at the New York? Isn't that where Southerners stay when they come to the city?" The question came out like a fishwife's complaint, but she could hardly risk explaining her objection.

"Eat up, darling. We're on the American plan."

His equanimity was breaking her heart. Managing an expression that she hoped looked like a smile, she told him: "You know I'll end up filching every one of those rolls."

How wonderful this could have been. She looked around the room, guessing which diners were the excited transients and which the permanent boarders. She thought that she and Hugh, so subdued, must resemble the latter.

"Maybe tomorrow morning we can also have some fun riding the elevator up at the Fifth Avenue Hotel," he suggested. The Astor was too old and shallow to have one. This proposed lark, conceived sometime back, she was sure, when the Monument had begun looming large in their imaginations, threatened to make her cry again. She loved him *for* his fecklessness and failure, she decided. She wanted only those things, not the brute security of the War God's fleeting embrace.

Along the gaslit fourth-floor corridor, she steadied his exhausted frame. They were making their way toward a handsome double bed, another part of her earlier anticipations. It was covered by a beautiful white brocade, not the riot of pasha's pillows back in Georgetown. The key to the room had made her think of Officer Shea at the Monument, and the bedspread soon directed her mind to another, still unseen bed—the one upstairs at Wormley's.

While Hugh took off his shirt, and she laid her dress upon the hassock, she made a silent pledge to herself: *I shall yet make his dream happen. I shall free the machine.* Flushed, his forehead damp, he was soon asleep in her arms. With her eyes wide open, she thought: *what a small price it will be to pay!* Once the War God had his Senate victory and passed beyond the Zodiac prohibition she had fabricated—even sillier than Mary's actual divinations—she would let Roscoe Conkling have her tired form for whatever use he desired. And then she and Hugh would have the projector.

Stroking his wet hair and pondering the astrological lie she had added to so many others, she realized—amazed she hadn't thought of it sooner—that it was Mary who had given them up. Conkling had reneged on his promise because Madam Costello, in her infuriating brogue, must have told him about "that charming boy-o" Mrs. May was "so sweet on." There was no point to even cursing her in the bitter darkness of this hotel room. The planet reader's indiscretion about the War God's climacteric had, after all, been the basis for Cynthia's own lie. Mary Costello, the heavens' charlatan! She was more like the heavens themselves, directing all their destinies by who-knew-what proportions of shrewdness, stupidity, and sheer obliviousness.

•   •   •

The following day, Hugh and Cynthia did not make it to the *Scientific American*'s offices until past noon. Alone of all the editors and copyists, M. Hiver remained behind after the short weekend workday.

"Come in, come in," he said, looking up from the drawings of a contraption that appeared to Cynthia not so different from the one that had come flying out of the Patent Office in September. "Let me show you what the men from New Jersey brought in yesterday."

He led them into an adjoining room where on a table sat a small machine consisting chiefly of one brass rod, wrapped in tin foil, and a stylus. M. Hiver now cranked the rod into a fast rotation. "We write about it and make them rich," he said. He applied the stylus to the rod. "They soon go and build them by the hundred in Merlot Park."

"Mary had a little lamb . . ."

Hugh and Cynthia jumped back several inches.

"What is this little lamb?" asked Hiver. "I still do not understand."

The voice was feeble, but the ditty unmistakable, and it continued until M. Hiver ceased turning the crank and replaced the foil with a fresh piece. He then lifted the first stylus and set down a second one, which his visitors only now noticed near the other end of the brass rod.

"Hard to imagine, but a month ago they are experimenting with paper instead of the tin. Watch. We make music!" He grabbed a horn that stood in a corner of the room and, cranking the apparatus with his free hand, blew three loud notes. Then, as soon he cranked again and applied the first stylus instead of the second, the sounds came back out, not quite so loud as they'd gone in, but still, incredibly, alive.

He then quickly tore the foil from the machine and crumpled it. "We gave a promise not to make any more."

Hugh's amazement lasted for several minutes, but consciousness of the blow he'd suffered at the Custom House soon repossessed him. "M. Hiver," he asked, almost shyly, "have you got photographs of the Mangin projector? Davidson had only sketches, but he told me that you might—"

"Oh, yes, come. I'll show you."

They both looked at Cynthia, who wanly smiled and said that they should go ahead. "I'll browse here, like Mary's lamb," she said, gesturing at all the peculiar objects to be seen in the inner room. Hugh assumed she was too sad to look any more at the Mangin, and he only wished he could show the same resistance; as soon as he began examining the pictures with Hiver, he heard himself speak of the machine as something that belonged to the past, a lover who had died making the crossing.

Cynthia listened to his voice as she focused her energies in the other room. Carefully recalling each procedure she had seen M. Hiver perform, she took a new piece of foil from the small pile of sheets on the table. She would have to get Hugh to speak forcefully. As soon as she had the foil in place, she smashed an empty glass beaker and sliced her finger with one of the shards. After one loud shout, she bit her lip, swallowed the pain and applied the second stylus to the cylinder she was already cranking.

"Darling! I'm here!" shouted Hugh. He had run into the room with M. Hiver, and before either one of them could see what she had done—her body still blocked their view of the machine—she lifted the stylus.

"I'm all right," she said, apologizing for her clumsiness with a hapless, female glance at M. Hiver. "It's the smallest scratch, and I'm very embarrassed. Please go back to the photographs and let me clean up the glass."

"You're certain?" asked Hugh.

"Quite."

As soon as they were gone, she opened her Gladstone bag and laid the piece of tin foil, very carefully, between the sheets of Astor House stationery that she'd taken from their room. There it remained during the long trip back to Washington, during which Hugh, seeming to pass through several phases of disease all at once, rose into a febrile exaltation. The clock showed 11:45 P.M. when they arrived at the Baltimore & Potomac station. He was carried off the train by two porters, in a delirium, his teeth chattering so badly Cynthia feared he might swallow his madly merry tongue.

·   ·   ·

The bouquet on his desk measured twice the size of those still arriving for Butler, who had taken his seat the week before, despite the heavy guns of oratory that Conkling had fired to keep him off it. But the War God was about to win the only battle that counted.

"The clerk will call the roll," ordered Vice President Wheeler.

Conkling broke off a petal from one of the flowers and tore it with his fingers. He thought of the ladies who'd brought these blossoms yesterday, along with their twelve thousand signatures in search of a sixteenth amendment. Almost all senators had delivered the suffragists' petitions, more out of gallantry than conviction, but he had been rewarded with this great spray for the seriousness with which he'd ordered the scrolls be received by the Committee on Privileges and Elections. Did their twelve thousand signatures, he now wondered, exceed the number of letters the machine had churned out against the Custom House nominations?

They had been here in executive session for five hours, since 3:00 this afternoon, and under the rules of such a meeting there was no one in any of the balconies to look at him: no barely suppressed hisses and swoons, no encouraging notes from Kate, no serene looks of approbation from Mrs. Bruce. There was also, by custom, a rhetoric so free-wheeling that he had been reminded all day of his first term in the House, back in '59 at this very time of year, when he'd had to save the implacable Thad Stevens from a physical beating by six traitors coming across the aisle.

"Mr. Bayard!"

"Aye," said the Delaware Democrat, emphatically. Two hours ago, as the sky above the dome turned from deep red to black, Bayard had stood and recited long passages from the fifth Jay Commission report, trying to regale his colleagues into outrage over the New York machine's code names and tricks and strong-armings. "They have turned a fortress of protection into a den of thieves!" Conkling had listened, as he did now, playing with a newly struck sample silver dollar from the mint in Philadelphia, a jesting gift from Senator Jones of Nevada, who knew that the War God's only alliance with the Administration involved opposition to silver coinage.

"Mr. Blaine!"

"Nay."

Now what was his game? wondered Conkling, as he sent a barely perceptible nod of appreciation toward his enemy from Maine, who probably thought a defeat for Hayes would remove the President from the field in 1880, setting up a direct contest between Blaine's own forces and those of the General.

Along with the silver dollar, Conkling had an opal stone from Galt's jewelry store in his right pocket. The Irishwoman had made him carry it, just as she had advised him to release the Commerce Committee's report on the thirtieth and postpone this vote on the nominations until today, the twelfth. Discord and harmony, sorrow and joy: they all had their particular angles and solar rays, it seemed. Thirty and 120 (12, a division by 10, would do just as well) stood as beneficent numbers, and must be chosen to propitiate the heavens. Striking on a date that corresponded to the more malignant rays would be overdoing things, she'd assured him.

"Mr. Conkling!"

"Nay." Spoken as calmly as he could utter the word, just this side of boredom. There was no need for overdoing the theatrics now, not after pulling out every stop in the debate. It was time to let the alphabet continue its march toward Roscoe Conkling's victory.

When this triumph was had, he could concentrate on his next prize. The Irishwoman's recent intelligence in this regard should turn out to be at least as useful as her political portents. He had had to wring the information from her, threatening Mary Costello with everything from building-code violations to the District insane asylum before she admitted that Mrs. May "plumb adored" that idiot girl-boy. Even so, this astrologer was too much trouble, her trade too embarrassing. He didn't care what he derived from it: when these two campaigns were over, he would at last wean himself from her voodoo.

"Mr. Edmunds!"

"No!"

Conkling smiled. His Vermont colleague, at his direction, had mocked rumors that the War God would lift his opposition to the nominations if Evarts would resign. "I don't see Mr. Conkling playing checkers with this administration—no matter who's sitting on the squares."

Yesterday, in the cloakroom, he had been all gentle persuasion, working the divided Democrats with as soft a touch as George William Curtis himself might have applied, while Senator Matthews, Hayes's loyal fellow Buckeye, moved two steps behind him, hopelessly trying to shore up the other side.

"Mr. Kernan!"

"Aye!"

You couldn't blame old Fanny K., who by now had lost count of the defeats inflicted on his party by the machine back home.

As the tally lengthened, Conkling felt a moment's nostalgia for Kate. This could have been one of their victories, something to share; but she had gotten wind of his other campaign, and was for the moment too angry even to see him, let alone join in the crowing about to break loose.

He thought of that French apparatus, whatever it was, sitting in the bonded warehouse. A week from now, after Mrs. May had been good, kept her part of the bargain and forsworn the rebel pup, he would have Chet Arthur—a famous man now, thanks to all this—sign the item through personally. Surely she would get a charge out of that.

"Mr. Matthews!"

"Aye!" The President, Matthews had argued all afternoon, had a right to his own choices in matters of appointment. But what the President didn't have were the votes, and by the end of the roll, the nominations had been defeated 35–21, exactly the totals Conkling had predicted that morning. He had triumphed for the party, triumphed for the Union, and when the clerk announced the totals, the cheers and groans and cries of "Shame!" were louder than anything the galleries, had they been occupied, could have produced.

He raised his hand—he was calm even now—seeking recognition from Wheeler.

"Mr. Conkling."

He rose to his feet. His colleagues fell silent.

"'The heavens themselves,'" he began, making his fellow bardolators search their brains for the source of his trope, "'the planets, and this center / Observe degree, priority, and place. / Insisture, course, proportion, season, form, / Office, and custom, in all line of order.'"

He aimed the words at Wheeler himself, and ignored the roars of appreciation over their general aptness and the way he had hit "custom" with particular force. Plucking the tallest flower from the suffragists' bouquet, he strode out of the chamber, alone, and down the bronze staircase to the office where he would have a telegraph boy dispatch the news to Chet Arthur. In the near darkness of his descent, he had to feel his way along the frescoes, his right hand brushing first an eagle, then a Cupid, then a serpent.

•   •   •

A half hour later, as a case of champagne popped in the Custom House, Admiral Rodgers opened a single bottle of Möet & Chandon and poured out the tiniest portions, like a rum tot, to the large group he had assembled in the Observatory's library. Asaph Hall might not be present—he was home helping Angeline through one of her headaches, which newfound recognition had not permanently banished— but the company included Professors Eastman; old Yarnall and young Mr. Todd; Mr. Paul and Mr. Harrison; and the man and woman of the hour, Professor Harkness and Mrs. May.

"May this success," declared Rodgers, his glass held high, "prefigure others. I toast all of you who participated in the far-flung operations of the Transit of Venus back in 1874, and all who in the years since have brought the project to this point. We offer our special thanks, for their long labor, to Professor Harkness and our own sublunary Venus, Mrs. May."

"Hear! Hear!" the scientifics cried.

"Thank you," said Cynthia, who then nodded her apologies and left the library, as they'd all expected she would.

Mr. Harrison quietly followed and asked, as she put on her hat, if there wasn't something he could do to help.

"I'm fine, Mr. Harrison, I assure you."

"I daresay he's home by now," said the clerk. "Sleeping peacefully and gaining strength." After two nights in the Navy hospital, Hugh had been informed that he was suffering from nephritis. Captain Piggonan and Lieutenant Sturdy had this morning put him on the train to Charleston.

"Yes," said Cynthia. "I'm sure he's quite comfortable." She pictured him amidst whatever ridiculous furnishings the mother had now filled the house with; she wondered if he recognized anything on the walls, whether he was lucid enough to realize his circumstances or convinced he was somehow once again fourteen.

"It was probably high time for him to leave us," said Mr. Harrison, searching, not very successfully, for the right words. "This nephritis, he probably had it for months. The symptoms are so similar to malaria's."

"Yes," said Cynthia, quoting the naval physician, "'an allergic response to infection elsewhere in the body.' The one eventually caused the other."

"Prolonged bedrest," said Mr. Harrison. "That's the best medicine. The kind one can only get at home."

Yes, thought Cynthia, until his kidneys fail entirely.

"You gave him the very best care," said Mr. Harrison. "You couldn't have known it was anything other than it appeared. You were probably filling him up with water when you should have been denying it to him." He realized, hopelessly, that he was making things worse.

"I prefer the other name for nephritis," declared Cynthia. "Bright's disease."

"Yes," said Mr. Harrison, trying a smile. "Makes it sound more like a blessing than an affliction."

"Yes. As if the patient were sick with light. Drunk on it."

"Are you sure," he asked, "that I can't escort you home?"

"I'm sure," she said. "I'll see you tomorrow."

She walked past the Monument and toward the lights of Capitol Hill, down which news of the War God's triumph was already flowing. She carried with her two oranges that Hugh had left behind at the Observatory. She would eat them, alone, in her room.

TEN

Add some Pratt's, Harry."

Mrs. O'Toole gestured toward the kitchen, where her son would find a bottle of astral oil for the lamp that was running low. Four days before the solstice, a spirit of holiday profligacy—and the desire to display it—had taken hold of the landlady. The boarders nodded appreciatively. An hour after supper, Cynthia was still among them, reading the paper. She usually purchased her own copy from a newsboy two corners down, but he had been out of the *Star* as she arrived home, and it was considered bad manners to take the parlor copy up to one's room.

There was another reason she had so far declined going upstairs: a series of messengered letters, in creamy hotel envelopes, which had been coming from Wormley's, one each day since last Wednesday, and which the housemaid who received them in the afternoons had had the kindness to slide under Cynthia's own door rather than leave on the hall table with the always-much-picked-over post. Each of the War God's triumphant cries and pleadings to be sensible now lay, in small shreds, at the bottom of a wastebasket by her vanity.

Instead of facing another, she preferred to sit here yet awhile in the parlor, watching the ever-more-respectable Dan Farricker read *Baldwin's* monthly (perhaps even the poetry they set amidst the shirt-collar advertisements) and listening to the ever-more-sensible Fanny scold him with a new sort of proprietorship. If the announcement of an engagement had been made, Cynthia had missed it, but the way Fanny was complaining of Dan's trip to John Chamberlain's gambling house seemed to foreshadow a housewife with her eye on domestic economies.

Joan Park, who lately made much mention of her plans to work at the Children's Hospital on Christmas Day, now asked Cynthia if she had come to the paper's item about the new commissioner for the District almshouse. Sure that Miss Park's interest in the subject had less to do with concern for the poor than a fear—identical to Cynthia's—of ending her days in that very institution, she was about to reply that no, she hadn't, when Louis Manley, licking a postage stamp, observed that "Charity begins at home." He was sending five dollars to a sister back in Ohio.

"Make sure it sticks," said Cynthia, sufficiently disgusted by the sight of his tongue to retreat to her room, under whose door she found, sure enough, a letter, though not one from Roscoe Conkling. It had been postmarked four days ago in Charleston. The housemaid must have remembered that boy from South Carolina who'd come around a couple of times and decided, if this was from him, that it deserved the sort of privacy she'd given those envelopes from Wormley's.

But the letter was not from Hugh. It was from his mother, whose swirls of aquamarine ink informed Cynthia May that her Washington address had been found

amidst the hospital papers in the pocket of my son's greatcoat, the one I bought for him here in Charleston two, or perhaps three, winters ago. I am assuming that you are one of his assistants, and am writing to let you know that since his arrival yesterday evening he has been resting well and, by my own observation, rapidly improving. He fluctuates with fever but is already getting the very best medicine from our physician, Dr.

Berry, who succeeded in keeping my family supplied with potions during even the darkest days of the blockade; we were, I assure you, very glad to pay whatever the dangerous traffic might bear back then—and would have been, even if Mr. Allison, my husband, had not realized some unexpected gains during that dreadful period.

My son is now asleep in a room at the back of the house's third story, just behind a stretch of porch that has, I'm afraid, never been right since the great hurricane that preceded the war. (The storm also tore one of our box chimneys, since replaced, clean away from the house.) I am sitting in a Louis Quinze chair just two feet from the bed (same period) in which he now lies. As I've watched him, I have been knitting a ball of yarn that rests in a sweetgrass basket made by my downstairs colored girl, whose mother worked in the Petigru family, to which, as my son has no doubt told you, I am connected by my great-uncle.

If tomorrow is fine, we intend taking Hugh to the beach on Sullivan's Island. It was from there, near Fort Moultrie, that he watched the firing upon Fort Sumter when he was eleven years old. I remember seeing him, once fire was returned, count upon his fingers the interval of seconds between the cannon's flash and the roar of its sound. (He had always done this during a storm, after the lightning and before the thunder.) I'm sure his memory of the event is vivid enough to be with him even now. Perhaps an hour ago I heard him mutter something about "the battery," surely in a dream of that wonderful spectacle. The apparent rapidity of his mind, as he sleeps, convinces me of his waxing vitality. I have, as well, heard him say the words "cargo" and "shipment," and can only assume them to be portions of thoughts—escaping the arms of Morpheus!—about the shipping office on East Bay Street, where he repairs at this time of year to see his favorite Campbell cousin . . .

Cynthia could feel Hugh's consciousness, like one of the Observatory's telescopes in a fog, trying to poke through this mad letter. She could imagine the rolling eyes and laughter with which he would have greeted any glimpse of the screed unfurling beside that yarn basket. In its unstoppable egotism, the letter resembled the automatic writing of a medium, and for an idle second or two Cynthia wondered whether Mary Costello—should real astronomers ever put planet readers out of business—might switch over to that other black art and ruin a new set of lives by misdirecting their ethereal mail.

She stared at the envelope. She could not go to South Carolina. She had no money and, worse, no standing. If Hugh was as fevered as he appeared still to be—that "rapidly improving" was an empty piece of sociability—there would be no one to let her past the front door. She could not even *write* to Charleston: he now had less privacy than she did here at Mrs. O'Toole's. How could she put anything real, be it sentiment or news, onto a sheet that might be read aloud to him by that mother?

Still and all, his mind remained flickeringly alive. *She* knew what "cargo" still sailed upon his dreamy view—and she knew she had to bring that cargo here. To what practical purpose, she did not know. But *he* had never had a purpose for the Mangin projector that could remotely be called practical, and if getting him cryptic word of its arrival were to give him hope—assuming he ever regained sufficient lucidity to understand the news—then it would be worth it. She had to effect the machine's release and its shipment to Washington.

Five minutes ago, she had read an advertisement in the *Star*: "Wanted—By a Gentleman, two unfurnished rooms, communicating, on second floor, with or without Board, for a lady, where seclusion can be assured." One saw notices like that in the paper every day. The city was full of rooms stuffed with such ladies, who ate terrapin during the congressional session and dry toast once it was over. She would be luckier than they, as she would have to do what was required of her only a single time—if, that is, Roscoe Conkling would still accept her aging favors. She had abandoned the idea of submitting to him once Hugh went into the hospital, but now her determination flared back to what it had been two weeks ago, when she lay awake in the Astor House.

For days after the nomination fight, the papers had remained full of the War God's victory dancing: the champagne he had let himself drink at a dinner with Jay Gould; the duel he'd nearly fought with a Georgia senator who dared, during this period of triumph, to murmur disagreement over a parliamentary point. Lord Roscoe was at the opposite of his overdue climacteric; he was like some voracious rubber plant ready to reach out and strangle anything that crossed his path in the Senate chamber or at Wormley's. Her own ravishing, she decided, would happen so fast and completely as to escape her own notice.

She looked at the mingy sprig of holly attached to her window by Mrs. O'Toole, and a sudden anxiety overtook her. With Christmas eight days away, was the great man even still available? What if, after working herself back up toward surrender, she discovered that he'd just decamped for the chilly hearth in Utica?

She went quickly downstairs to scan the paper. "I'm looking for a bargain in gloves," she told the immediately curious boarders. Her eyes raced down the political columns for some assurance that Conkling remained in Washington. Yes, there it was, notice of a meeting, tomorrow morning, by his committee inquiring into the Mexican raids against Texas.

She put the *Star* back down on the table. "Have you found something you can afford?" asked Mrs. O'Toole.

"I'll *have* to afford it," said Cynthia, heading back upstairs toward her night's sleep.

She had never liked dreams—they made the mind a fun house, setting all the world's diameters loose from their circles, scattering them like tangents. Had she been aware of her own dreamlessness tonight, she would have been grateful. As it was, she didn't awaken until a half hour past her usual time, and even then she stayed in bed, with her eyes open, telling herself what she absolutely must do today. Looking through the sprig of holly and the windowpane, she regarded the Sun, whose light even forty years ago the author of *Celestial Scenery* had guessed to travel at 192,000 miles per second. Two decades before meeting Hugh Allison and Mr. Michelson, she had underlined the sentence that came just after the numerical estimate: "It follows that, if the sun was annihilated, we should see him for eight minutes afterward . . ."

She continued to lie beneath the counterpane, watching the Sun and wondering if somehow, so far from here, the planet Mercury had just gone dark; and then Venus; and soon, any minute, unaware it was about to be scuppered, Earth. She lay still, one eye on the Sun and the other on her clock, until eight minutes had passed, at which time she sighed and got up to dress.

•   •   •

The vendor was dozing when she asked for a bag of lemon drops. Along the Capitol's main corridor, both representatives and spectators had become thin on the ground. Tomorrow, the man told her once he'd awakened and apologized, he would close his stand until after the New Year. Cynthia noticed a similar lack of business for the photograph seller. Even the War God's picture went begging in the face of reduced holiday traffic. She looked at the forelock and wondered whether, since his recent triumph, Mary Costello had begun displaying this image of Conkling even more prominently in her parlor.

Admitted by one of the passes that had arrived inside each envelope from Wormley's, Cynthia took a seat in the ladies' gallery, only a minute or two ahead of Conkling himself, who strode past Captain Bassett, the doorkeeper, to take his seat on the floor. Senators with desks in the neighborhood of the War God's dared not light their cigars so close to his presence. The visual result, as seen from the galleries above, was a kind of smoke ring that swirled at a safe distance from Conkling's own clear, central atmosphere. So well known were his aversions that even nearby colleagues who chewed their tobacco made sure to expectorate a bit more carefully into the pink china spittoons by their desks.

She watched Gordon, the Georgia Democrat whose new enmity really stemmed from Conkling's attempt to impose a radical revenue collector on his territory. He glared at his foe from across the aisle. Conkling did not return the look, but Cynthia noticed old Hannibal Hamlin, Lincoln's Vice President, keeping an eye on both men; less than a week had passed since he and Senator Thurman had had to separate the potential duelists.

Conkling did not look up at her, but she knew he was aware of her presence. There was no possibility he had failed to receive her note by now—and sure enough, a page boy was soon kneeling beside her to whisper: "Mrs. May?"

He escorted her from the gallery to the basement floor beneath the chamber. A dull roar of running drains came from the baths on the House side and, even with its custom depleted, the restaurant's tabletops made a considerable noise beneath plates of oysters and tumblers of whiskey. The boy nodded greetings to a Capitol policeman and led her past a row of gas lamps to the small office Conkling maintained down here.

"He says he'll be with you as soon as he can, ma'am. Will you be all right here alone?"

"Yes," she said, perplexing the little fellow with her nervous laughter. "Much safer than I'll be otherwise."

As soon as he had closed the door and left, she busied herself with surveying the cartoons framed on the wall; even the ones from Nast paid tribute to Conkling's slim waist and broad shoulders. Then she went over to the letters on his desk. Up from the blotter came an exuberant rush of words from Chester Arthur in New York. "I appreciate how great the strain must have been upon you and hope you will now be able to get a little rest. For myself, personally, I thank you cordially for your vindication of my official character. We hope to see you here soon and to hear the details of the battle."

The Collector's gratitude lay beside a whole stack of letters from the Custom House. She supposed the pile of congratulations contained even the precious signature of Mr. Joseph Selden, which, if she accomplished what she was here to do, might yet appear on the Mangin projector's certificate of admission through the Port of New York.

She sat quietly on a horsehair sofa for the better part of an hour, her eyes closed, until, without any knock, the door opened, allowing in a gust of soap-scented air. The realization that Conkling had just emerged from a bath and changed his clothes repelled her more than filth would have.

"I've lately achieved one reconciliation," he declared. "Are you going to make it two, Mrs. May?" He extended both his hands toward her, smiling as gently as he could manage.

"Who was the first?" she asked, keeping her own hands in her lap. "Senator Gordon?"

"No," Conkling said, laughing as he sat down in a chair across from the sofa. "He still cowers every night at Willard's wondering if my aide will come by with a set of pistols. I was speaking of Blaine, actually. I still don't know what his game is, but I've thanked him for assisting in our victory. The other day I offered him the chairmanship of this Mexican committee—he *was*, after all, the one who first raised the alarm about those raids." He didn't tell her how disgusted he'd been when the newspapers' praise of Blaine's Fourth of July oration reached him in Paris. "But he's had to go out to Hot Springs for whatever's ailing him. That leaves me with the committee and a late start upon the holidays."

"What a shame," said Cynthia. "You could have gone to Utica already, perhaps via New York, in time to spend an evening with the Hayeses."

Conkling roared his delight. "And all the other Union Leaguers, licking their wounds at their big reformist dinner. By the way," he added, in a more subdued voice, while examining his fresh pink fingernails, "I hear that Roosevelt is dying."

"You'd like that, I suppose," said Cynthia. "It would mean you'd won a fight to the death."

"No," said Conkling, looking hurt that she should think such a thing. "I prefer a gentle submission." He paused and tried to read her expression. "I've missed you these last tumultuous weeks. Absence makes the heart grow fonder, you know."

"It does," said Cynthia. "When *do* you return to Utica?"

"Only when nothing is here to detain me."

"You mean the committee."

"No, my dear Cynthia. I mean you."

"Well, I should hate to keep you . . . embargoed."

He risked a quiet laugh. "Surely you've forgiven me by now. What happened in New York was only my way of keeping you tethered until the fight had reached its successful conclusion. My lovely reward, to be opened when the stars finally allowed."

"*Such* a lovely package. As shopworn as the jewels in the District Commissioner's pawnshop."

"You mustn't say such things."

"I'll say whatever I like!" Her shout surprised them both, but when she saw that her anger only further provoked his excitement, she retreated toward playfulness. "You're being rude, Senator. Offer me whiskey."

"I keep that for my colleagues," Conkling explained, his eyes traveling to the tray of decanters.

"Yes," said Cynthia. "Those unabstemious men, so much weaker than yourself."

He poured her a glass and sat down beside her on the couch. "Let us be friends again," he said, softly. "Just the two of us. No more Irishwoman in between, trafficking in our secrets."

"And no more Mr. Allison," said Cynthia.

"He's gone, too. Yes."

"You made it your business to find that out."

"Of course," said Conkling, without apology. He had inquired of the admiral himself.

"Mr. Allison may be gone," said Cynthia, "but I still want his machine."

"You do?" asked Conkling, much surprised.

"Yes," she replied. "For my own small glory. I know well enough what he wanted to do with it. I think I can do it on my own."

Conkling stroked her hand. "My *femme savante*." He rose from the sofa and went to his desk, extracting from its top drawer the same document Mr. Selden had consigned to his lower one eleven days ago in New York. "Come here and see," he instructed. She joined him behind the blotter while he dipped his pen into a bottle of violet ink and wrote across the top of the paper: "Let this through. R. C."

"Shall I have to claim it in New York myself?" asked Cynthia, knowing she would never have an advantage equal to the one she held right now.

"Where would you like it shipped?"

"Have them send it to the B&P station, to be held for as long as need be."

Cheerful and aroused, the War God asked if there were any further demands she had to make.

"I shall no doubt make some more when I'm ready to use the projector." Her feeling of success shrank to disappointment as soon as she spoke this small piece of bravado. Even if the machine's release from New York acted as a miracle potion and revived Hugh, the odds against his ever being well enough to use it seemed higher than even she could count.

Conkling took her in his arms. His eyes flared as he looked into hers. She dared not avert her own gaze.

"It is I who gild the dome," he said. "I who print the money and raise up the buildings, all from here. It is I who rein in the wayward men I've put on their little thrones." He kissed her neck.

"Your world moves too slowly for me," she declared, closing her eyes as she submitted to his touch. "And it disappears too fast."

"Riddles," he said, breathing hard and undoing the small bow at her collar. "How fast does *your* world move, Cynthia?"

"At one hundred and eighty-five thousand miles per second."

Flushed with ardor at the idea of her brain moving through territory where his could not follow, he ordered her: "Square the number."

Fewer than ten seconds passed before she said, "Thirty-four billion, two hundred and twenty-five million. Miles per second."

He flung her down on the couch, then removed his waistcoat and shirt, revealing his well-tended torso. In the dim light of the basement office, for all the fire in his eyes he looked to Cynthia like the painting of a lion, without a drop of sweat on him. She remembered Hugh, so different in the same sort of light, all damp and gleaming. At this moment, however, her mind filled up not with longing for him, or with fear of the War God, but a strange certainty of her own temporary power in the world, the force of her unlikely gravity this year upon these two moons who had revolved around Cynthia May as surely as Asaph Hall's discoveries made their race around Mars.

She undid her own hair. "I have one *immediate* demand."

"Tell me," said Conkling, hoarsely.

"Turn down the lamp," she ordered.

As he rose to comply, she thought of Hugh's words to her on the *Mary Washington* last July, while they had sailed down the Potomac in the rainstorm. *Under all those clouds the moment is lost.* He had assured her that any action taking place without light to carry it through the heavens simply died with itself. *It might as well never have happened.*

"Yes," she told Conkling, as he returned to the sofa. "I prefer being with you in the dark."

•   •   •

"I imagine you got sick of that disk crossing the Sun," said David Todd, referring to Venus.

"Yes," said Cynthia. Mr. Todd was the only other soul around the Observatory at 5 P.M. on Christmas Eve. "But it will be exciting if you find *your* disk." She knew that even tonight he hoped to see a trans-Neptunian planet streak across the nebula he'd begun concentrating on ten days ago.

"What are you working on now?" he asked, pointing to the still considerable piles of papers and photographic plates atop her desk.

"Just some last touches on the report," said Cynthia. "A very quiet conclusion to this part of the project. Certainly nothing like watching the actual Transit three years ago, I'm sure—though I must say, it's hard to imagine Professor Hall standing on a deck in Vladivostok with the Pacific crashing beyond him."

Mr. Todd smiled and leafed through a fair copy of what would soon go to the Government Printing Office. When he spoke again, he was too shy to look up. "I miss him," he said.

She couldn't bring herself to answer.

"I miss his amusing ways," said Mr. Todd. "The way he would josh me. The way he'd mimic the admiral, the way he'd mimic you."

She stared at Mr. Todd, sick for a moment with apprehension, until he looked straight at her, smiling. "It was reverent mimicry in your case, Mrs. May. He'd say, 'Be serious, Mr. Allison,' as if he wanted, that minute, to hear you scolding him. He'd laugh for a few seconds and then he'd *become* serious, or at least attentive to whatever he and I were supposed to be doing. I always knew it was you he was imitating, because when he did it he sounded like us."

Yankees, he meant.

"Are you not going home, Mr. Todd?" asked Cynthia.

"No," said the young man. "I'll be spending the holiday with the Newcombs."

"Well, I wish you a very merry Christmas."

"And I wish you the same, Mrs. May." He bowed slightly and made steps to leave the room, pausing at the threshold only when he heard her say "David?" and then—the most her emotions would permit—"Thank you."

Hard as it was to imagine Mr. Hall, another Yankee, on the eastern coast of Russia, Cynthia found it even more difficult to think of him making camp, seven months from now, near La Junta, Colorado, where he and Mrs. Hall would be, after a long trip on the Atchison, Topeka & Santa Fe, to observe the solar eclipse. Professor Harkness had taken over the preparations for the Observatory's next spectacular— a meticulously planned road show, unlike last summer's serendipitous- seeming lunar display. The admiral was hoping that Congress would grant his legislative wishes well before the observing parties set out, but either way, July 29, 1878, would find the Halls in Colorado, and Professor Harkness in Cheyenne along with Monsieur Trouvelot the illustrator and Mr. Alvan Clark, manufacturer of the Great Equatorial itself. Almost all the rest of the Observatory's staff would be at various points west. Harkness's desktop, which Cynthia was no shyer about inspecting than she had been Conkling's, revealed that Mr. Todd— who might not yet even know it—would be with a group in Texas. Deals for discount railroad fares to transport the scientists and ship the instruments were already being negotiated.

The Mangin projector, to be shipped from New York the day after tomorrow, would arrive in Washington late Wednesday night. Upon learning this three days ago, Cynthia had sent a telegram to Charleston, one that she hoped Hugh would comprehend and Mrs. Allison would fail to. Since then, she had heard nothing from either one, and had begun to wish for even a second letter from the mother, which might contain a gold nugget of information that she could pan from the babbling stream of self-regard.

It was soon past six o'clock, late enough that she had to think about leaving the premises and facing Christmas Eve with whoever remained at Mrs. O'Toole's. She bid Lieutenant Sturdy and Captain Piggonan good-bye and walked over the hardened mud toward Virginia Avenue. As she went, she looked up at the canvas telegraph ball lying unhoisted on the roof. She tried thinking about her first day here, but could not rid her mind of the War God's sofa, his well-oiled endearments and machine-like thrusts. Closing her eyes against these mental images sometimes had a helpful effect, so she practiced the trick right now, all the way to the edge of the grounds.

The sound of a familiar voice kept her from walking into the gatepost.

"I know you don't want to be seein' me, dearie, but please open your eyes. I can't deny you've got every right to turn and walk the other way. But, for the love of Jaysus, it *is* Christmas. Say you'll hear me out, for at least as long as it takes to walk to the streetcar."

Cynthia said nothing, and quickened her pace. She was determined to get away from the woman, but as she went even faster she could hear Mary Costello puffing, and see her pressing a hand against the stitch in her side. When the planet reader finally fell behind, Cynthia did not stop for her, and took this as proof of her own disinclination to forgive the stupid woman; she would have done with her mischief forever. But when she arrived at the stop for the streetcar, which she'd had no intention of taking—hoping that a walk would get her home as late as possible—she stood still and waited, as if it had been her plan to ride it all along.

"I've had me comeuppance!" Madam Costello cried out half a block from the stop. From there on, until she arrived out of breath at Cynthia's side, the volume and speed of her explanation never faltered. "He came and fired me the day after he won his vote. And he blamed me for spilling the beans about you and Mr. Hugh. Even though he forced me to! Said it caused all kinds of trouble I had no business making."

Cynthia's laughter stopped the astrologer's pleading narrative.

"Dearie, I don't know exactly what happened in New York. All's I know is—"

"*All you know*! That's your problem, Mary. You know everything, everyone's secrets, and you pass them around as if they're your own!"

"I can't stop meself." She was sniffling now. "I shouldn't have told him about Mr. Hugh, but I shouldn't have told you about the great man's climacteric, neither. I was just trying to give the spheres a nudge,

thinkin' that if I did, then maybe everyone would get what he wanted."
She wiped her nose and subsided a while, before asking, "How *is* the
boy? Any better?"

"So, you know that he's sick. And you got *that* from your War God.
Neither one of you can keep his mouth closed, it seems."

Madam Costello pushed out her lower lip a fraction of an inch,
adopting for the first time tonight the old, put-upon expression Cynthia had so often seen her deploy in the past. Surely, it seemed to be
saying, you can't be blaming *me* for the poor boy's illness. "Yes," the
Irishwoman finally said. "I heard about it from the great man." What
she could have said, genuinely, in her own defense, she did not—
namely, that she had never told Conkling, even when he threatened
her, that Mrs. May had *made up* that Scorpio-Aries prohibition. And
she would not embarrass the girl, even now, to let her know she had
such knowledge.

Cynthia recalled the way that Hugh and Mary had joked and
laughed and generally gotten on like a house on fire; and she remembered how shut out she'd felt. She wondered now whether Hugh—if
he knew the whole farcical truth and could see the two women on this
chilly corner waiting for a streetcar that showed no signs of coming—
would be laughing. There was no doubt, she had to admit, that *he*
would yield to the planet reader's entreaties. But how could *she,* whose
nature had never been forgiving, excuse this calamity-causing woman
yet again? Mary Costello had twice betrayed her to Roscoe Conkling:
first, by telling him her address and the ordinary details of her life;
then by telling him about Hugh. And yet, logic told Cynthia: if Mary
had not presented her to the War God like a bit of game stocked for a
weekend shoot, then the Mangin projector, however delayed, would
not soon be sitting a mile or so away at the Baltimore & Potomac station.

She took Mrs. Allison's letter from her reticule and handed it, without comment, to Madam Costello. The astrologer walked it a few feet
to the curb and read it by a lantern hanging from the side of a waiting

private carriage. "I can barely find the boy in it" was all she said when she returned with the sheets of paper.

Cynthia shrugged and put the letter back in her bag. After a long pause, she said: "It's his birthday, you know."

"Of course I know," replied Mary Costello. "Do you think planet readers forget such facts? You've *got* to forgive me, Cynthie! You got to be me friend again." She squeezed the younger woman's forearm.

"I have no friends," Cynthia replied, without any affectation. It was the simple truth.

"All the more reason to let *me* be one," said the astrologer. "I can redeem meself. I don't know how just yet, but I'll find a way. I'll make it me New Year's resolution."

"Another year!" cried Cynthia, bursting into tears as the streetcar came into view. Were another twelve months more than she could bear, or more than she should hope for?

"Let me feed you supper," said Mary, as they boarded the conveyance. "Charles is bringin' around something special tonight, a bit on the late side, just before he goes home to his family."

Before she could think it through, or again tote up the woman's treacheries, Cynthia let herself give in. She was soon eating two lamb chops off the clean portable plates that Charles set on the dirty table, and she let herself drink a quarter bottle of sherry while Madam Costello did justice to the rest, all the while telling stories of the famine and Chicago and Iris Cummings. The hours went by and Cynthia's own tongue loosened, but never to the point where she was in danger of telling Mary what had happened last week between herself and Conkling. As midnight, and Christmas, approached, it remained the one essential thing the astrologer did not know about her.

"Don't doze off, dearie. I want you to go to Mass with me."

"No," said Cynthia. "My head's too woozy already. I can't sit there amidst all your people's smells and bells."

Madam Costello took no offense—and Cynthia showed no real resistance. At ten minutes before twelve, the two women were at Fifteenth and H Streets, climbing the steps between Saint Matthew's red sandstone columns. They took seats in a pew near the back, but to the dismay of Cynthia's head and stomach, they were not allowed to *keep* the seats for very long. All the standing and kneeling and sitting down again seemed more complicated than the whirling movements at Marini's. But the Papists' Latin did, Cynthia had to admit, soothe her uncomprehending ears, and the olive-skinned children of the Catholic diplomats who filled the church were prettier than the native urchins one saw gamboling over the District. She looked at one girl for some resemblance to the eleven-year-old she'd been when she came to this city, and found none, though she did, among the congregants, discover approximations of both John May and her brother, Fred. All her life, it seemed, she had been seeking analogs of the dead or, more strangely, of herself, as if she were an afterimage instead of something real.

She would not, however, permit herself to look for any transposition of Hugh here in this church. When his face crossed her mind, she forced herself to imagine him for real, still alive, asleep, the blankets up to his chin in Charleston.

What was taking place up on the altar seemed no more a church service than the snowless ground outside had looked like the setting for Christmas. She pondered the host that Mary Costello, who could hardly be said to have fasted tonight, marched right up to receive. The idea of transubstantiation, that the bread could be the actual body of Christ, reincarnated after a fast flight through nineteen hundred years— and yet, to anyone's plain taste and touch, still bread—seemed not so much a miracle or fraud as a riddle. As Mary came back from her quick trip to the altar and presumably heaven, her head most piously bowed, Cynthia could not help but think of the farmer and the fox and the chicken and the corn—and of the superintendent's irritated letter, written just the other day, to a Mr. Sykes of Windsor Locks, Connecticut. Admiral Rodgers liked to respond personally to the simple scientific questions ordinary people often sent the Observatory; the task made him feel more akin to the astronomers under his authority. But

Mr. Sykes's inquiry, as to where light first appeared on Earth, had seemed unanswerable. Mr. Harrison, much amused, had shared with her a copy of the admiral's reply: "You ask of a circle, where does it begin? In a true circle, it is all alike, with neither beginning nor end. When light first appeared, then someone saw it on the horizon first. At the same moment, some one had it at midday; and at the same moment someone had the Sun setting—who saw it first? Your question is one that admits no answer—so it seems to me; and I do not care to ask the Greenwich Observatory about it."

She shared his lack of interest in conundrums. She didn't want theology to be the final end of astronomy, the way the author of *Celestial Scenery* seemed to think it could be, revealing God to man as never before. She believed in God, but wished she could make herself stop doing so. She didn't want yet another authority from whom she had to rent her life in the world. She didn't want Him in the sky; she wanted the specks of heaven that she and Hugh had seen together, like D'Arrest's comet, to belong to the two of them alone. The "experiment" that they would now never perform hadn't, of course, been an experiment at all. It had been meant as an act of pure self-assertion; not so much an inquiry into the heavens as an insult to them.

She looked at the gaudy golden sunburst of the chalice, not yet replaced behind its little set of curtains, and prayed to God, as politely as she could manage, that He cease to exist.

· · ·

A week later, on New Year's Eve, Cynthia sat before the mirror at her vanity and brushed her hair, which she now judged to be fully one-quarter gray. She had been home from the Observatory since the middle of the afternoon, after a shortened workday during which Mr. Harrison and nearly everyone available stuffed portfolios with dozens of reports—recent and obsolete, exciting and arcane—for the perusal of the Senate committee soon to debate the removal legislation. The rush of self-advertisement had turned them into a sort of collective Simon Newcomb, and one or two of the astronomers had been heard to wonder whether the admiral might not be overdoing it.

She had agreed to see Mary Costello tomorrow for a cup of tea and a New Year's trip to Center Market. No formal reconciliation had been achieved between them, but Cynthia's loneliness had effected a truce. In fact, she could use the planet reader's company tonight. She had come up here straight after dinner, avoiding the boarders who had declared their intention to stay awake in the parlor past midnight. Fanny was out with Dan Farricker, leaving behind a listless party presided over by Joan Park at the piano. Cynthia had even spirited a small plate of crackers from the kitchen, so that appetite wouldn't force her, any more during 1877, back into the lodgers' midst.

The day after tomorrow she would go to the station to see the projector, whose arrival had been delayed by holiday rail traffic until just yesterday. She would examine the machine carefully, and try to remember enough detail to prove its reality in the last-chance report she would make to Hugh.

Louis Manley and Harry O'Toole had been mildly drunk even before dinner concluded, and they'd come up and down the stairs two or three times already, singing to themselves in soft slurs. Cynthia thought she could hear the footsteps of one of them even now, and she began to bristle, until she realized that the singing voice in the hall belonged to neither Mr. Manley nor Harry:

> *While we seek mirth and beauty and music light and gay,*
> *There are frail forms fainting at the door . . .*

She gave a sharp cry and knocked over the plate of crackers. Racing to the threshold, she flung open the door and enfolded him in her arms. For a moment she would not even look into his flushed, ecstatic face; she merely held him as tight as she dared, and gathered him into the room.

He closed the door behind them and executed a deep bow. When he raised his head back up, too quickly, the blood drained from his face, leaving him wide-eyed and nearly translucent. He grabbed the bedpost so as not to fall over, and finally succeeded in his attempt to stand before her—in evening clothes and splendidly shined shoes.

"I snuck in as the cook was going out the back door. It's a good thing your Mrs. O'Toole didn't see me. She'd think Sherman was starving her countrymen even now."

He raised his hand as sternly as he could, to halt her questions and tears.

"I'm all right, Cynthia. I'm *not*, of course, but I'm obviously up and around. The fevers aren't so bad or so frequent as when I left here three weeks ago. I suppose the body has all it can do keeping my kidneys in torment; it can't be bothered with my once-flaming brow."

He walked over to her vanity, stepping on one of the crackers, and sat down.

"I've been trying to gain strength ever since I got your telegram. I got here yesterday—you might say I'm on the run—but I didn't want to scare you. I waited until I could appear a bit more robust." He began to laugh, but stopped himself, knowing jokes were sure to make her cry.

"It's here," she said. "It's at the B&P station."

He closed his eyes. "Great, great girl," he whispered.

"My brother-in-law was finally able to manage things." She looked at him as he sat sideways. He held the spools of the chairback as if he might otherwise fall off.

"You don't have the strength for this," she said.

"I have just enough. And I'll have more in a week. I'm learning how to trick Mr. Bright's little malady. We'll keep me a secret for a week or so, in my rooms, and send a rosy telegram to my mother and father. Once we've done what we're going to, I can collapse for a while. And then, old girl, I'm afraid you'll have to send me home for good."

A dozen objections and cautionary notes clamored in her mind, but she let none of them past her lips. What he now, and for the last time, required of life was a great burst of energy. She would help him kindle whatever he had left within himself.

"Why are you dressed like that?" For the moment it was all she could think to ask.

"It's New Year's Eve, darling, in case you haven't noticed. Put on your green dress, the one you wore to Marini's." From the pocket of his tailcoat he withdrew a loosely knotted handkerchief, out of which he extracted a single, mostly unhurt white rose.

As if there wasn't a moment to waste—knowing, in fact, that there never again would be—she went and got her coral comb in the vanity's bottom drawer. In a handful of fast movements, she knotted her hair and fixed the flower to her sudden coiffure. "Where are we going?" she asked.

"An anniversary party," he replied. "For an old Ohio couple."

She laughed. He was joking about the Hayeses' silver celebration taking place tonight at the White House. The subject of Miss Grundy's most recent dispatches and much of Fanny Christian's dinner conversation, it would be the grandest, least political, entertainment of the yearlong administration: only old friends from back home, and worthy Ohioans now living in the capital, had been sent invitations.

"Can you remember to call me Mr. Yarnall?" asked Hugh. "Or Mordecai, at more intimate moments?" From another pocket he pulled a stiff card with the presidential seal.

"The ancient star-cataloguer is a Buckeye, dear. Born in Urbana when dinosaurs roamed the earth. So he got an invitation, which he showed all around the dome one night, five or six weeks ago. Alas, he actually has to *be* in Ohio, for the holidays, so he can't go. But he made a great casual show of leaving the card out on his desk. It's been there since before Thanksgiving. I went in and retrieved it this morning."

She gave him a pinched, fearful look.

"Darling," he responded, "if we're going to travel a billion miles every hour and a half, we'd better be able to perform a little local trespassing." He stood up to undo the top button of the plain dress she had on. "There's another reason for us to go, but you won't know it until we get there. So, come. The green dress. Now."

His step was surprisingly quick, if not quite steady, across the dozen blocks to the Executive Mansion. He chattered on about his father's debts and mother's snobberies, asked for news of the Observatory and details of how Cynthia's brother-in-law had effected the Mangin projector's release from New York. She told him not to trouble himself with that, and made him take her arm for most of the way, until they spotted, near a score of other carriages, the Hayeses' new team of Virginia grayhorses, hitched up and ready for a midnight ride.

"Forgive me," said Hugh. "I'm going to be indelicate." He slipped behind the empty sentry box, a relic of Mr. Lincoln's day and soon to be dismantled. It took Cynthia a moment to realize that he was relieving himself, his kidneys having been tormented by the nephritis beyond another moment's endurance.

Mr. Loeffler, the German usher, let them into the main foyer and, once Hugh had flourished their invitation, announced them as Professor and Mrs. Yarnall.

There were flowers everywhere: smilax in the chandeliers; azalea on the tables and poinsettias against each mirror. Members of the President's old regiment, the Twenty-third Ohio Volunteers, by far the loudest and largest cluster of guests, admired the only gift that had been allowed by the honored couple: a silver tray engraved with the log cabin at Gawley Bridge, West Virginia—Hayes's headquarters for a long stretch of the war. Cynthia regarded the First Lady's schoolmates, most of them turned out in black velvet, while lawyers from Lima and Xenia who'd once practiced with the President consulted their fist-filling gold watches to get an idea of how much time remained until the Chief Magistrate and his wife descended the staircase. The lawyers' wives remarked upon whether the Ohioans living in Washington had acquired airs; their daughters ogled Webb Hayes, the President's handsomest son, who acted as his secretary and, on occasion, his bodyguard.

The Marine Band mixed Civil War marches with tunes like

"Grandfather's Clock." Hugh and Cynthia milled about, smiling at each other and their "fellow" Buckeyes, and avoiding Miss Grundy, otherwise known as Miss Austine Snead, lest the *Star*'s scribe—right over there, her white kid glove holding a small gold pencil—inquire too deeply into the history and current doings of Professor and Mrs. Mordecai Yarnall.

At 9:00, Dr. McCabe, the minister who had married the First Couple a quarter century before, was seen to put himself nervously into position at the foot of the staircase. The guests hushed and backed away as the Marine Band struck up the "Wedding March." The President and his wife, suddenly in view, began their descent. Mrs. Hayes, though decidedly plump, had elected to appear all in white, down to her slippers. A silver comb held her shiny black hair, and the President—a Grand Army button on his coat—squeezed her hand as it clutched his arm. They reached the bottom of the stairs just as the band finished its song; the crowd, unsure of what to do, broke into a great, spontaneous cheer.

As Dr. McCabe repeated the blessings he had urged the heavens to make so long ago upon the then-much-humbler couple, Hugh, standing with Cynthia at the back of the throng, reached into his pocket for a silver ring and placed it upon the third finger of her left hand.

"This is all I can manage for a ceremony," he whispered into her ear. "I'm sorry we didn't have more time together. But we'll take a wedding trip that lasts forever. Twenty-five years from now, *we'll* be beyond Aldebaran."

Cynthia said nothing. Her struggle to maintain composure succeeded only thanks to the sound of trumpets, which summoned the guests from the brief ceremony into the East Room, where they would be received by the remarried bride and groom.

Moving down the line in a daze, Cynthia was just enough conscious of the moment to be glad that, without a bustle, she had no need to attempt a "Grecian bend." When she came within earshot of the President, she could hear him talking to a banker from Toledo.

"In the language of the press," said Hayes, "'Senator Conkling has won a great victory over the Administration.' But the end is not yet. I am right, and I shall win in the long run."

The banker pumped the President's arm encouragingly, and Mr. Loeffler once more announced, "Professor and Mrs. Mordecai Yarnall."

Cynthia shook Lucy Hayes's hand and looked into her intelligent face—it was no wonder even the War God spoke well of her—while on her left, she could hear the President talking to Hugh: "It will be good if we can find a way to move you fellows, after all the fine work you've accomplished."

"Yes, indeed, sir," Hugh replied. "I'm looking forward to entirely new quarters."

The state dining room was filled with French foods and ices and pastries, but no wine of any kind. Cynthia and Hugh drank hot cider and sat amongst a gaggle of regimental wives, who teased Mr. Yarnall about his evident braininess, while his tall (and surely older?) wife made attempts—no doubt a nightly occurrence at home—to get him to eat a bit more. The two of them did not get up to dance, a concession to Hugh's frailty, though they told themselves it was to preserve the memory of their perfect moment on the floor of Marini's studio.

Just before midnight the entire company of guests went out to the south lawn to hear a volley of guns welcoming in the New Year. The old Ohio Volunteers joked about the greater safety they now enjoyed in proximity to this familiar noise, while Hugh cocked his head between each flash and boom.

"Sound is dreadful slow," he said, drawling a little and feeling pleased, as he held Cynthia's hand. "We'll travel much more quickly." She nodded her head, so that he could feel it, against his shoulder.

The Marine Band, knowing the Hayeses' preference for retiring early, struck up "Home, Sweet Home."

ELEVEN

*G*uide us on, thou great Jehovah!*"*

The wet spots on the upholstery—thanks to the Capitol's always leaky roof—had been discomfort enough to Cynthia. But now, while she continued to wait here in the ladies' gallery, there was this *singing* to put up with. The suffragists, having rallied for days at Lincoln Hall, had begun crowing in a nearby reception room, hoping their collective voice would carry down to the Senate floor.

Cynthia had passed them a minute ago, as Mrs. Crocker finished an attack upon a faction of the delegates she charged with being free-love advocates. A group of peacemakers had then tried smoothing things over with a recitation of the Lord's Prayer. At the present moment, across the way in the press gallery, Cynthia could see a beardless news-paperman picking up one of the just-installed telephones to see if it worked. The suffrage spectacle seemed wickedly trivial, but all its off-shoots had the city momentarily enthralled. The wives of Admiral Dahlgren and General Sherman had just assured the *Star* that they had not, no matter what anyone said, gone onto the Senate floor the other day to urge votes *against* the female franchise.

A cessation of song brought Cynthia only new irritation: leaving the reception room and crowding into the gallery, the singers pressed her wet dress into her skin. Down below, Senator Sargent asked that a representative of the ladies be permitted to address the body, a proposal sure to be rejected by his colleagues but only after it had earned him admiring glances from the sex. Known supporters of the cause found their entrances greeted with approving murmurs, none more so than Roscoe Conkling. He scanned the gallery's front row and made a gallant bow in its direction. Cynthia then saw him whisper to the page, and within a minute the boy arrived in the gallery to tell her the senator would be in his basement office twenty minutes from now.

She did not wish to watch his performance on the floor, so she made her way to the appointment well ahead of schedule and waited before the now-familiar cartoons. She avoided the horsehair sofa.

The War God swept in exactly on time. She sidestepped his embrace, and spoke the first words: "When did you get back?"

"Two days after the New Year," he said. "To convene my Mexican committee." He paused and glared. "As you surely know. I've sent three messages to your lodgings."

"The parlor maid is careless about getting such things to us."

"You're a liar, Cynthia."

"I'm preoccupied, Senator."

"It's well past time you called me Roscoe," he said, too pleased by her appearance this afternoon to risk scolding her any further. He sat down on the edge of the desk, gesturing for her to take the chair behind it. Once she did, he asked: "And what *is* the preoccupation? Your plans for fame?"

She smiled, approximating what she supposed, even now, might be his idea of flirtatiousness.

"Your machine," he inquired: "Is it safe? In good repair?"

He was looking, she could tell, for gratitude.

"It's in excellent order, though still at the B&P." One day last week, Hugh had had enough strength to go inspect it with her, but not enough to trundle it any closer to the Monument. She had begun doubting he would ever summon the energy required for what they still, through the pain-filled nights on High Street, referred to as the "experiment."

Conkling pointed to a letter from the Treasury atop his blotter. "Read it," he urged, as if offering a good occasion for laughter. "It announces the Secretary's intention to put my Custom House men into *uniforms*. They'll be more *professional* that way." With great delight, he let Mr. Sherman's words drip. "The only thing that matters, Cynthia, is Hayes's not sending the nominations back up. He won't do it even as a futile gesture. He's *scared* to." She remained quiet, wondering how she could get to her request and still flatter him into believing that she'd also come for his company.

"What refreshment may I get for you?" he asked, pointing to the decanters across the room, and leering a bit. They both knew, didn't they, how she required something to loosen her natural inclinations?

"Soda water," she said.

"I shall join you in that," replied Conkling. "And you will join me on the sofa. Come," he added, with a wave. While he poured the drinks, she sat down on the cushion closest the door.

"So what do you think of the women?" he asked. "Have you changed your mind about the suffrage?"

"No," answered Cynthia. "And from what little I've seen of the Senate, I haven't changed my mind about democracy, either."

Conkling scowled, genuinely hurt. "I suppose you'd like some Venetian doge or Bavarian king being the patron of your astronomic arts." He paused, then forced himself to resurrect his smile. "When are you going to *explain* this undertaking of yours?"

"Not until I've made a success of it."

Conkling took a sip of the soda water before replying: "That's one advantage you scientifics have over politicians. *Our* failures are forever documented"—he pointed to a pile of newspapers and the *Congressional Record*—"whereas only your triumphs need be."

"Your setbacks are triumphs, too. In their way." She indicated the cartoons on the wall. "There's more flattery than scorn in most of those."

"You wouldn't think so if you were the one being drawn—and quartered."

His look was so serious, so shamelessly in search of sympathy, that she had to resist laughing. Finally, she replied: "I should say I'm a very fit subject for caricature. There's the long neck to start with—"

Before she could proceed with a self-loathing inventory, Conkling took hold of her neck, lightly, between his hands, and used an index finger to twirl the hair at its nape. "Your height is an aspect of beauty."

"I need to be much taller," she declared, removing his hands, gently, taking care not to provoke him. "As high as a hundred fifty-six feet."

To her relief, he smiled. "Your experiment."

"Yes," she said. "Which leads me to ask a favor." She took an extra breath. "There's a guard, a federal watchman named John Shea, at the site of Washington's Monument. Can you get him reassigned, away from there, during the week of the twenty-first? The nights midweek, especially." The Observatory's Meteorology Department had pronounced them "promising" when Cynthia made a casual-sounding inquiry about the month's weather.

"Reassigned to another piece of government property?"

"Yes."

Conkling seemed caught between a desire to show how he could play with such minions like candies in a dish, and an inability to figure out just what he might do with this one of them named Shea. He twisted his forelock, then suddenly brightened: "We'll put him at Wormley's. The twenty-first? You're talking about the week of the Spanish minister's great party—to celebrate the marriage of Alfonso whatever-his-numeral to a cousin." He sniffed at the idea of such consanguinity, but soon resumed taking pleasure in his scheme. "There will be foreign eminences around the place all week, and I don't mean just the usual wastrels of the diplomatic corps. Important visitors. Evarts's department will jump at the chance to see them all better protected. And he won't question the particulars of any request from Senator Conkling—not this month, believe me! So, that's done. And at Wormley's I can keep an eye on this Shea while you perform your scientific mischief at the Monument."

Cynthia pointed to his desk. "Write it down. Put it on your list of things to do."

The War God, like Dan Farricker teasing Fanny, said, "Not until you give me a kiss."

She had been waiting for this moment, with but one poor card to play. "That's not possible right now." She rose from the sofa. "Do you recall how you needed to keep distance between us until *your* battle was won? Well, I need to keep away from you until I've accomplished what *I'm* trying to do."

He stood up and fumed: "You haven't been seeing the Irishwoman, have you? This sounds like her nonsense."

"No," said Cynthia, "it's my own nonsense. I can concentrate on only one great object at a time." She forced herself to stroke his whiskers. "Besides, I don't require astrology. I can make *real* contact with the heavens."

"Who's now helping you?"

"No one you know. Almost no one at all. I'm doing the important things myself," she said, and then thought to add, "now that Mr. Allison is no longer among us."

"Is he dead?" asked Conkling, so visibly encouraged he had to catch himself. "Or do you mean he's still so sick that he remains away?"

"I'm afraid he'll never be back."

Conkling took her in his arms, ignoring her prohibitions, though he permitted her to stand stiff and unresponsive in his embrace. "Cynthia, I don't want you for mere sport on the sofa. I want you to stimulate me in every sort of way. In return, I shall make *your* life exciting. You shall see how the next year, and especially the one after it, eighteen hundred and eighty, will—"

"I am amazed that we made it to *this* year." She withdrew, taking care to smile as she did, and to deny him his kiss as cheerfully as possible.

"By the time you've done your work," he mused, trying for a gentle *envoi,* "the sign of Aquarius will be underway."

"So you remember some of what our planet reader taught you." She was already on her way through the door, waving as gaily as she could. "Remember Officer Shea, too."

Her heart pounded as she strode the noisy basement corridor. She did not want to go out into the rain, and there was no point returning to the Observatory: by now they would have decided she was home sick for the day. But she could not face the real sickbed in Georgetown, either; not yet. So she walked the Capitol's corridors and climbed its staircases for a time, pausing to look up at the painted ceiling beneath the dome, on which Washington, ascending more quickly than his Monument, was assumed into the heavens.

•   •   •

"Will you really be ready by the twenty-third?" she asked. When she'd left this morning, sweat had been running down his back; now he was cold to the touch. His feet, which she could never get him to keep stockinged, were blue-veined blocks of ice.

"I shall *have* to be," he said, drawing the blanket tighter. "The only way to make this corpse of mine work will be to scare it. Let's have everything ready, one chance only, and then I'll know I have to do it. Do or die. Do *and* die."

She no longer let such remarks upset her, but the sight of the chamber pot, pitifully full of dark-colored urine, made her cringe. She went to the fireplace and with the tongs extracted the bricks she had warming. She put them near his feet and managed to get a pair of socks on him; they both smiled during the effort. Standing up, she ran her hands through his hair, which was bristled up like John Brown's. When the chills passed off, he would feel pleasant, perhaps even amorous, but soon after that he'd be burning up or doubled over with pains in his kidneys. She had ceased keeping precise charts of symptoms and medication. Neither one of them had time for the illness's details; the only tabulations and diagrams in the room pertained to the

Mangin and the Monument. The Gauss sketches remained on the wall, along with the pastel of her by Monsieur Trouvelot, though all the sheets had crinkled up like parchment during a year's alternations of humidity and cold.

"Now what about Mr. Todd?" she asked, as she placed his feet onto the warm bricks.

"No," said Hugh. "I remain opposed. He'll stand on the Mall looking up for his planet, and within a week he'll have reported the whole story to Mr. and Mrs. Newcomb."

"We need *someone*," she insisted, more gently than she would have if she weren't feeling the thinness of his ankles.

"We don't have many friends to choose from, do we?" he asked. "We should both have been more convivial all these years, darling."

She said nothing, and at last he made his own suggestion. "Well, what about your friend the astrologer? She's got a strong Hibernian back, I'd wager. She can help us wheel the machine, and then charm Officer Shea away from his post."

"You realize she has a looser tongue than Mr. Todd," said Cynthia.

"But we're the only ones she knows to talk to at the Observatory. Think about it."

She already had.

·   ·   ·

The train platform at the B&P station extended westward into the Mall. Cynthia stood near its end, looking toward the base of the Monument, unable to imagine herself at its top—even without the projector and a very sick lover. By Wednesday the 16th, Hugh was no more fit to proceed than he had been the week before, but she had decided she could no longer wait to get the Mangin out of the terminal's freight room and ready for its task. Several minutes ago she had asked Mary Costello to sit in the waiting room under the station's Gothic spires while she went to claim the machine. But so far she had just paced the concourse and the platform, doubting that she and the planet reader would succeed in their plan of getting the projector to a shed owned by a friend of Mary's, a farrier near Fourteenth and B. There they were supposed to find, already delivered, two hundred feet of cable, purchased with the last of Hugh's savings—"dipping into my burial money," he'd told her.

"You a magician?" asked the freight clerk, once the crate had finally been torn away from this object whose name and purpose he could scarcely guess at.

Cynthia was already too busy inspecting the machine to answer. She flipped open the metal blind that hid a 40 cm. lamp, and felt the outlines of the aplanatic mirror that would make the beam twenty times more powerful than any a cylindrical one could produce. She tested the trunnions on which the projector was mounted, moving the lamp vertically and around, making sure the light could be shined in the only direction that counted—straight up. The field wagon that supported the apparatus carried, as well, a tiny boiler, which drove a small steam engine, which in turn powered the little Gramme dynamo-electric machine. It was a sort of Lilliputian factory; but out on the street, with one woman pushing, the other pulling, and a tarpaulin on top, the whole assemblage would resemble nothing so much as a lunch cart.

The journey she and Mary took—avoiding the holes in the intersections and the missing planks of the B Street sidewalk—was less than the three kilometers the light beam was guaranteed to travel upward. The astrologer, aware that being helpful here was crucial to her redemption, took care to ask as few questions as possible. But there was one she couldn't refrain from posing.

"Once you take this *out* of the shed we're going to—on the night in question, is what I mean—ain't you worried about runnin' into a uniform? Maybe even an Army feller? After all, dearie, once you step on to the Mall you'll be on government property, and Lord knows, once you get to the needle itself—"

Cynthia said nothing. She kept pulling a trifle faster than Mary

Costello pushed. "I suppose you could drug him!" said the planet reader, with a laugh. "Just like Catherine Bailey did with that poor old gent from the Soldiers' Home. Knocked him out at the bar she keeps near Boundary. Took *fifty* dollars off him—can't imagine how he had that much—and when he woke up and found that she had it, she claimed—"

"—that he'd given it to her to buy a wedding dress." Cynthia read the *Star*'s crime columns, too, but ever since the War God had fired Mary from her political prognosticating, police items were the *only* thing the astrologer read, and repeated. "Your job," said Cynthia, as firmly as Miss Wilton had ever spoken to the girls back in Laconia, "will be to tend the fire." She tapped the boiler box beneath the tarp.

"I'm a quick study," Madam Costello assured her.

At the farrier's, Cynthia noticed the coiled cable—Hugh's purchase— resting on some straw in the corner. The wire, fortunately, was thinner than she'd expected, and with Mary's help she moved it to the single shelf on the bottom of the cart, then covered the whole conglomeration with a second tarpaulin: a glance above had revealed some damp rafters.

"We're allowed to come in and out of here at any hour, am I right?" she asked, nervously. "And how much does he want for us to keep it here?"

"Relax, dearie. He wants nothin' a'tall. He was me last beau."

•   •   •

That afternoon, back at her desk, Cynthia noticed how the astronomers who'd been to a reception given by the Smithsonian's Professor Baird talked with a new ease about their encounters with the Institution's worthies. There was a sudden air of confidence about the Observatory: the bill for its removal had just been voted out of committee, and some of the men had jokingly begun to call the place "Reservation No. 4," as did that portion of the legislation about selling the old site once a new one had been found. The bill now boldly called for an appropriation of *three* hundred thousand dollars, toward both land and construction, and no less sober a man than Professor Harkness was starting to imagine the rise of a modern wonder in the hills northwest of the city. "I mustn't let my fancy work more quickly than the Congress," he soon said, returning to the business of ordering special cameras for next summer's eclipse.

In the superintendent's office, however, utopian prospects remained the order of the day. Mr. Harrison was writing one letter to Professor Ormond Stone in Cincinnati, thanking him for all he'd done to support the removal bill; and then, without so much as stopping to re-dip his pen, writing another to Dr. Porter, the president of Yale, begging that he weigh in on the matter at this crucial moment.

At a quarter to five, while the first evening shadows crossed the tops of Cynthia's hands, Mr. Todd looked in on her. Having waited for Professor Harkness to step out, he asked, quite excitedly, if it were true that Mr. Allison was back. "Angelo Hall swears he saw him bundled up on a back porch on High Street. Oh, please tell me it's so, Mrs. May."

"Could we make it our secret?" she replied, after some hesitation. "Even if it means fibbing to little Angelo?"

"Yes," Mr. Todd assured her.

"He *has* come back," she said, "and he's gaining strength daily." She delighted in her own lie, stringing it out to delude herself as much as David Todd. "In fact, he's told me more than once that he hopes you're 'still looking'—not just for the trans-Neptunian planet, but also for new sunspots."

Mr. Todd clapped his hands. "You tell him that the other night I had a good look at this odd, elongated object I first spotted on the fifth. I suspect it's a nebula—probably Herschel G.C. 2776—but I'm not discouraged. And neither should he be! We'll find it yet."

"I'm glad you stopped in," said Cynthia. "I've made you more cheerful, I think—although you seemed rather lively to begin with."

"I'm cheerful and perplexed, all at once, Mrs. May. I'm taking Miss

Loomis to the opera tonight. *The Bohemian Girl.* That's the source of my cheer. But Professor Newcomb has finally asked me to transfer to the Almanac Office, as general superintendent of computations. That's the reason for my perplexity. He just dropped by to see the admiral and he made me the offer not ten minutes ago. I'm trying to make up my mind. You know," he added, as if afraid to think out loud about himself, "there's always a place for *you* there, Mrs. May."

She smiled.

"You can't stay here forever," he teased.

"No," she answered, glancing at the clock. "It's time for me to think of getting home."

"Will you be looking in on him?" asked Todd.

"Yes, David, and I'll give him your message."

On her way out, she passed Mr. Eastman and Mr. Hall, who these days was looking at Venus, not in transit across the Sun, but on her own bright rounds in the night sky. The two men nodded to Cynthia, and as she began her walk to Georgetown, she tried maintaining the false high spirits she had displayed to Mr. Todd. She returned to her old fantasy—less likely than Professor Harkness's—of a new, salubrious Observatory to which she'd send Hugh off each night, for years and years.

· · ·

At the same hour, two miles to the east, in the basement of the Capitol, Roscoe Conkling bore down on his gilt-edged note cards, composing a eulogy for Senator Morton, whose long fatal illness had preoccupied the upper body for much of the time since it reconvened last October. Mrs. Hayes was thought likely to attend tomorrow's orations in the chamber, and much as that possibility pleased him, he found himself more inspired by a fantasy of Cynthia May looking down on him from the ladies' gallery. "Death is nature's supreme abhorrence," he wrote, his violet ink beginning to flow. "The dark valley, with its weird and solemn shadows, illumined by the rays of Christianity, is still the ground which man shudders to approach." Yes, if she heard this, she would reflect upon it and seek his protection once and for all. "The grim portals of the narrow house seem, in the lapse of centuries, to have gained rather than lost in impressive and foreboding horror."

He looked up for a second, then reread what he had written. Morton, alas, was getting lost. So he turned to his bookshelf, as he had done composing so many other memorials, for the morocco-bound Bard. "Put out the light," he sighed, resolved to work through the evening. "And then put out the light."

•　　•　　•

At 9 P.M. on Wednesday, the 23rd, three senators stood near the front end of Wormley's canopy, continuing a debate they'd had on the floor that afternoon.

"My dear man," said Mr. Beck to Mr. Sargent, "the Treasury cannot write these men a check for three hundred thousand dollars before they've even found the spot they want to buy. With your bill, they will inevitably spend that much, even if some cheaper parcel were available. Money appropriated becomes money spent, as surely as night follows day."

Outside Wormley's, guests arriving for the Spanish minister's party would have been hard put to say which of its daily phases the world was passing through. Across the road, on the corner of Saint Matthew's, a calcium light had been set up to shine straight at the hotel's awning. Those coming to celebrate King Alfonso's marriage stepped out of their carriages into a bath of whiteness that was certainly not night, but not quite day, either, unless it were a sort of celestial day found in the afterlife. The glow was so pure that one expected to hear a seraphim choir instead of the mere stringed instruments whose sound floated out from the four hotel parlors that Wormley had combined into a huge single ballroom.

Senator Sargent, whose bill had been held over until tomorrow, used the opulence surrounding his colleagues as a retort to Senator Beck: "How much money do you think has been spent here tonight?"

"You stray from the point, my friend. I care nothing for the squanderings of the Spanish government. It's our own depleted Treasury—"

"Surely," said Senator Sargent, "a new temple of science—a permanent working display of the national genius—is better value for money than the fripperies of a single eve—"

"Beck is right," said Senator Edmunds, who had to squeeze left so that Mrs. Yoshida, wife of the Japanese ambassador, might gain entrance to the hotel. "This is going too fast. Have a commission select the site and report to Congress. *Then* we can appropriate the money."

"Consider the reports you've *already* seen," countered Sargent, now decidedly worried about his bill's fate. "Thurman was quoting from them this afternoon. We need to get those men out of there *now*. Do you want Admiral Rodgers to die the way his predecessors did?"

The wife of Senator Jones floated by, audibly, festooned with so much jangling silver she seemed a part of the orchestra.

"You should amend the bill," suggested Edmunds. "Make it say—"

"Come," said Senator Beck, tired of being jostled. "Let's get ourselves inside and settle things tomorrow."

•   •   •

"Easy, dearie, easy," said Madam Costello, less than a mile away at that same hour. Having left the farrier's, she and Cynthia were crossing B Street into the Mall, the latter pushing the wagon with such insistence she might soon lose her footing.

Hugh Allison, whose strength continued to ebb and whose kidneys remained ablaze night and day, was to meet them at the base of the Monument. As the two women trundled the projector across the hard ground toward the engineer's shack, Cynthia vainly tried to catch sight of him. The wind ripped through her plain coat, and she wondered how this obelisk, if it ever reached full height, would withstand such gusts—let alone how she and Hugh, if they succeeded in reaching its current summit, would keep themselves from falling off and sailing to the ground.

Perhaps they *would* have the strength, she decided all of a sudden, quite astonished, having discovered Hugh's silhouette in the distance. He was moving quickly, dragging a large plank to the stone steps of the Monument—a ramp for the projector.

"Hello!" he shouted into the night, actually running up to her and Mary Costello. He made a low bow to the astrologer, and took Cynthia in his arms. "No sign of Shea!" he cried. "I've already swiped his key from the hook and opened the place up."

"What if he yet comes?" asked Cynthia. She had no trouble counterfeiting worry over this point; her face showed real fear of all the work and risks they had ahead of them.

"An excellent choice," said Hugh, pointing to Madam Costello, who was already pushing the wagon toward the steps. "We can't keep up with you, Mary!"

"I can't speak for youse two, but I'm eager to get this boiler going. I'm *freezing,* children!"

•   •   •

Conkling did not see two waiters scrambling to extinguish the branch of evergreen that had just caught fire from a bronze candelabrum. Nor did he see the calcium light outside Wormley's, since he was coming down to the party, with Mrs. Sprague on his arm, from his own apartment in the hotel. Kate's *vert d'eau* gown, trimmed with roses and lily of the valley, was perfectly draped, and so were her pear-shaped pearls and diamonds, but she could not resist asking Roscoe to wait while she went to survey the enormous dressing room, where each lady had been promised the attentions of her own maid.

The War God told her to go satisfy her curiosity, but he frowned as soon as she was out of sight. Her boldness had begun to exasperate him. Coming up to his rooms just so they could make this entrance from the stairway! Half her attire was out of fashion, the other half a display of debt. He had succeeded in putting through tax relief for Edgewood—the late Chief Justice's mansion deserved no less, he had argued one day in the Senate, after persuading her not to sit in the ladies' gallery—but he hardly had the means Sprague had always had to dress her. Nor, in truth, did he any longer have the inclination. He would rather cloak Mrs. May's honest poverty, ornamenting the simple frocks she earned with her nimble brain.

He greeted Madame Mantilla, complimenting the evening's hostess on the roses that crowned her black hair. She tapped him with her fan—teasing this man whose eye for women the diplomatic corps knew as well as the Congress did. She suggested he turn around to admire the light streaming through the door.

"My!" said Conkling, startled by his first notice of the calcium display. The marvel immediately made him think of Cynthia's experiment, which she had damned well better complete this week. Once she had secured her triumph, he would fasten her to his life and the apartments upstairs, where dear Kate would henceforth be visiting no more.

"Will you excuse me?" he asked Madame Mantilla. "Senator Sargent seems to want my attention."

"Conkling," said his California colleague, "I should like to introduce Professor Simon Newcomb, one of the Observatory's chief eminences. We're talking about the bill for removal."

"Well," said Newcomb, delighted to add Conkling to his web of influential acquaintance, "I'm rather removed from the Observatory myself. These days I'm at—directing, I should say—the Nautical Almanac Office."

Conkling looked at him, unimpressed.

Newcomb went confidently on: "But I shall say this. Once the Observatory is up on safer ground, it will be time to think about reorganizing the whole place. We've been lucky with our naval commanders—lucky with them *individually*—but scientists need credit where credit is due, and there's no making sure the next superintendent will have the liberality of his predecessors. Having a scientific administer the place would—"

"Surely," said Conkling, "there's more danger of credit being grabbed by any fellow scientist put in there to run the show?"

"On the contrary," said Newcomb, in his best ladies'-club manner, unaware that Roscoe Conkling did not enjoy being disabused of ideas. "A navy man can know so little of astronomy that he'll keep men around the place who have no business being there. And that's the worst dispensing of credit there is—wasting equipment on someone who can't pull his weight. Why, they've got one young fellow over there now—I'm sure he looks, on paper, just like the rest of us to Admiral Rodgers—and he hasn't got any sort of investigation going. I couldn't tell you *what* he's been doing. And yet he's been allowed to remain on the staff for more than a year. He's sickly, and I thought that would take care of things—a shame, of course—but now I learn that he's back, still drawing his wages and still doing nothing that anyone can—"

"How do you *know* that he's back?" asked Conkling.

The question struck Newcomb as peculiar, but he answered it, untruthfully. "I heard one of the astronomers mention it." He couldn't very well say he'd overheard Asaph Hall's little boy jabbering to Mr. Todd.

Senator Sargent fidgeted, hoping they would get back to the important subject of his bill. Conkling said nothing more to Newcomb, didn't even nod. He just looked directly into the white light beyond the entrance. *She had lied to him.* That idiot rebel boy was still part of things. This experiment was still *theirs.*

He saw a guard cross in front of the doors. The uniformed figure cut into the light, and Conkling wondered if this might be the fellow she'd made him reassign from the Monument.

"Excuse me, gentlemen," he said.

"But—" pleaded Senator Sargent, to no avail. His colleague was already charging up the stairs to his apartments.

She had *deceived* him. Denying him was one thing—an obstacle, an incitement—but deception enraged him. Being laughed at was the only assault that could trump it in the host of life's assaults to which he was subject. He listened to the noise of the party come up the stairs. The fat, fleshy guests; the awful clinging of Kate: it all repelled his senses. He shut the door against it and struck the punching bag several times, until his hands, pleasantly stimulated, reached for his gloves and his pistol. He didn't arm himself as often as his critics claimed, but self-protection was only prudent when walking the District at this hour. He would find out just what was going on at the Monument this week, and he would give this overgrown girl—who had asked for favors, who had come halfway to heel, and who had now deceived him—the surprise of her unhappy life.

•　　•　　•

She feared each step up the wooden struts would be her last. Between them they carried the projector, dismounted from its wagon, like a giant loving cup. The attached cable rose from below like a snake being charmed. A fleet-footed person could make the whole corkscrew climb to the top of the Monument in two or three minutes, but she and Hugh had been at it for nearly twenty by the time they reached the last half-rotted steps. They finally sat down, putting the projector on the plank between them. Cynthia, breathing hard, at last dared to look down the hollow shaft. At the bottom she saw Mary Costello warming her hands over the little fire she'd got going in the boiler box.

Fearing the cable would soon be too taut, Cynthia shouted down for the astrologer to uncoil the rest of it.

"Right away, dearie!" came the response, flying upward through the granite-lined shell.

"Are you ready, darling?" asked Hugh, eerily less out of breath than she.

"Yes, I think so."

"Good," he said, rising from the top step. "Make sure your skirts are gathered up and tied."

She nodded, checking the knot she had made before leaving the farrier's.

He took a hammer from his waistcoat pocket and tapped on one of the wooden flats covering the obelisk's unfinished top. To their relief, it lifted easily—too easily, they soon realized, as the wind took it up and out like a kite. "Jaysus!" came Mary Costello's cry a moment later, when she heard it crash on the steps outside the Monument's open door. "Are you two all right up there?"

They were too occupied with the sight just revealed—a satin sky spattered with shining dimes—to answer. For a moment Cynthia wished they could stop now, right here, in this unexpected moment of perfection, but Hugh was already hoisting himself onto the stone edge. He sat down and held out his arms, reaching for the projector, urging her to lift it to the wooden step he had just vacated. She strained to raise it by herself, and for a moment, afraid she would fail, she frantically tried thinking of an alternative way. But then a surge of vitality allowed her to lift it in a single jerk. The lamp came down hard upon the already cracked step, threatening to fall clear through it, but the boards held, and once the projector ceased wobbling, she took Hugh's hand and joined him on the rim of stone. Seated with her legs dangling into the Monument, and her eyes on the stars, she felt as if they had climbed into the world's attic.

"It occurs to me," said Hugh, "that I've never asked if you're afraid of heights."

"I'm in love with them," she answered, truthfully, her words flying on the cold, rejuvenating wind. "I've climbed up from that swamp at last." She stopped herself from saying anything else, bitter or triumphant, lest it hurt the moment's majesty. Then she noticed he was shivering, and she began vigorously to rub his arms and back.

"*You're* shaking too, you know," he pointed out.

"But I'm shaking from excitement."

"Darling," he asked, "do you suppose I'm bored?"

Even now, in weather almost suited to a January night in New Hampshire, his brow looked damp. She went to mop it, but he shook his head, eager to get on with what he had come here to do. "Without any clouds to stop it," he explained, "the light will easily go three kilometers. You do understand that the beam breaks up after that? Even so, we'll travel out as spangles, like the top of a fountain's spray."

He took a length of string from his pocket, knotting one end of it to his left index finger and the other to the Mangin's metal blind. While he did this, she allowed herself a single look over her shoulder, down to the plainly visible river and Observatory. Farther north and west she could make out High Street and the Oak Hill cemetery, but she felt no desire to be on the opposite edge, able to gaze toward the Capitol and pick out Mrs. O'Toole's house from the little man-made stitchery below.

She heard the movement of a switch, the smallest scrape of metal, and then a buzzing sound. Just beneath her feet she saw a thin, amazingly intense ring of light, a circle no wider than a thread. It was the rim of the powerful beam, trapped behind the projector's blind.

"All right, girl," he said. "Get up. Carefully now." He had already stood up on the edge. She was ready to join him, except for one thing. "Wait," she said, taking off her coat and tossing it onto the step below the projector. "I suppose it's foolish, but I want to look my best."

She put her hands, and then her knees, onto the width of stone. He leaned down and with great, tender caution grabbed her waist. Slowly, in a wind they could hear agitating the pulleys on a flagpole far below, they rose to their full heights. Not letting go of her waist, he stepped behind her and to the outside, as if trying to protect her from horse traffic in the road, instead of the 156-foot drop to the Mall.

"Are you ready, darling?"

"Yes."

He shortened the string between himself and the projector, making one loop over his finger, and then another, until she could see it, straight and tense, transecting the imprisoned ring of light. As her heart raced, awaiting the pull and the beam's release, she became aware of a commotion far below, at the bottom of the shaft. Struck by the terrible thought that Officer Shea had found a reason to come back to his usual post, she said to Hugh, "Yes, dear. I'm ready. Let's do it now."

But he was prolonging the moment, oblivious to the noise below, and she could not bear to rush him, even while she thought of the mere minutes it would take for someone to race up the winding stair and stop them. The sound of voices was growing louder, but the noise of the wind prevented her from making out any of the sharp words being exchanged below.

"Get out of my way, you bog-trotting fool! I know who's up there!"

"Oh, do you now?" cried Mary Costello. "Well, I'm tellin' you to leave them be."

"You dare to give me orders?" He laughed. "Standing there at, what is this, your *tea wagon*?" He looked at the conveyance just long enough to spot the cable that was connected to it and—good Lord!— rising straight up. Realizing this was the crucial link to whatever they were doing, Roscoe Conkling strode toward the wire, until Mary Costello interposed herself.

"All right," she said. "I'll show you what it does. Give me your hand."

He'd done that when she'd added a bit of palmistry to their planet readings, but this time he extended his hand only to hear himself, a second later, screaming with pain, as she pressed it against the side of the boiler box.

Before he could even think to move, the astrologer reached around and removed a pistol from the pocket of his greatcoat. "I *knew* you was armed," she declared, with disgust. "You fellows always are when you're in a lather."

Conkling, holding his burned hand in his good one, stared at her in a tearful mixture of rage and humiliation.

"If you don't get away with yourself," warned Mary Costello, "I'll run for a watchman. One's bound to be down at the Ag'iculture building. *Then* you'll be in a fine fix for an explanation!"

She threw his pistol into a litter of boards and rags, and he took off into the night, not looking behind—or even up, to the unfinished pinnacle where Hugh Allison, at that moment, through the music of the wind, was telling Cynthia May: "Raise your arm!"

She kept her left hand tightly around his waist, but extended her right one up into the dark, until he nodded his approval and then, with his own free left hand, the one not encircling her, pulled hard on the string.

At their feet, the circular thread of illumination snapped open into a thick, blinding beam forty centimeters wide, a white shaft of light that flew a mile and a half up into the night sky. The beam rose twenty times higher than the Monument itself would ever rise; the man and woman, clasped into a single form, projected themselves upon it, unable to look down. As their lives depended on their balance, their eyesight would depend on Hugh's ability to close the Mangin's blind with another pull of the string.

But they gave no thought to that now. Awash in the light, feeling herself carried away on it, Cynthia, for the first time in twenty-five years, lacked the slightest sense of the city beneath her. Hugh's laughter and joy pealed into the heavens, and he let his right hand climb her back until it reached a silk hair ribbon. With one pull, he unfurled her gold-and-silver tresses upon the night. They waved like a pennant, a signal, eternally commending the two of them, and this moment, into the universe.

•   •   •

Mr. Harrison, the following afternoon, had charge of the Observatory's single copy of the *Star*. The astronomers kept making off with it during agitated discussion of what had happened just hours before in the Senate. Was it good news or bad?

Mr. Sargent, realizing the need to go more slowly, had agreed to Mr. Edmunds's amendment that a commission be appointed before the appropriation of any money. The bill that had passed instructed the commissioners to find a site that "shall possess relatively the advantages of healthfulness, clearness of atmosphere, and convenience of access from the city of Washington; and report to the present session of Congress."

Passing the newspaper from hand to hand, each professor asked the other if he thought they would be leaving Foggy Bottom sooner or later, or whether—the darkest possibility—their hopes for removal might end up forgotten, along with the Forty-fifth Congress, in two years' time.

Admiral Rodgers bustled out to Harrison's desk, dictating his next letter even before he reached the clerk, who had to start writing *in medias res:* "There are to be four domes for the Observatory: one for the twenty-six-inch telescope, and a smaller one over the room marked C, and two still smaller ones over rooms marked A and B . . ." Mr. Harrison didn't even know to whom these words were going, just that the superintendent had decided to continue on the assumption that transference to higher ground was still proceeding with all speed. "The floors," continued the admiral, "will be specially constructed to avoid vibration . . ."

Simon Newcomb now arrived, with Mr. Todd in tow, no doubt to discuss what influence he might have upon appointments to the new commission. Wary of him as always, Professor Harkness changed the subject to another item, much smaller, on the *Star*'s front page, about a "strange, powerful light, observed and reported last night by many residents of the District, shining straight up from a spot believed to be at the westernmost region of the Mall, for at least one and one-half minute's duration." Newcomb, who knew his optics and now had the chance to let everyone know of his presence at Señor Mantilla's ball, scoffed: "Absolute nonsense. People's spectacles playing tricks on them. They were only seeing the refractive movements of a big calcium

light the Spanish minister had playing outside Wormley's. I should
know, because—"

His social note was interrupted by the excited arrival of little
Angelo Hall, who earlier in the day had had a letter from his brother
Asaph up at Harvard. "He's going to teach me to box the next time he's
home! He's taking lessons from the best man in the college, in
exchange for teaching him geometry!"

"That's splendid, Angelo," said Newcomb, whose desire to be rid
of the boy was noted by David Todd.

"Come over here, Angie," said the younger man. "I've got a job for
you. And yes, there's a nickel in it." He hustled the boy into the corridor outside Harrison's office. "I know the weather's bad, but I want
you to go back up to High Street. Buy a copy of the *Star* along the way
and once you've got it, circle this item. Here's a pencil to use." He indicated the inches of newspaper type pertaining to the Observatory bill's
passage. "When you've done that, I want you to leave the paper face up
on the steps of the house where Mr. Allison used to live. Can you do
that?" he asked.

Angelo was perplexed—did Mr. Allison *still* live there, or not?

"For a *dime*?" Todd asked.

The boy nodded.

"Good," said Todd, who walked back into Harrison's office, telling
himself that Angelo's errand would give both Hugh Allison and
Cynthia—she was sure to be there with him—some needed encouragement: they'd realize that if Hugh could survive this siege of sickness,
he might spend the rest of a long career in a place fit for men instead of
marsh rats.

•   •   •

It was past sundown before Cynthia heard steps on the porch. She
moved to the window, parted the curtain and saw Asaph Hall's boy,
wet with rain, holding a newspaper and a penny whistle. She went

quickly down the stairs, acting automatically on the fear that Hugh's presence in this house had become known. She pulled open the door and said, sternly: "He isn't here, Angelo."

The boy gave her the same quizzical look he'd given David Todd a while ago. "No one told me he was. Mr. Todd just told me to leave this here." He handed her the newspaper, pointing to the item he'd circled with Mr. Todd's pencil.

She read it in an instant, and nodded her thanks. The boy waved good-bye and she closed the door behind him, setting the paper down on a table beside the unopened letter from Mrs. Allison in Charleston. She climbed back up the stairs and entered the bedroom. Taking off her shoes, then moving a pillow out of the way, she lay down next to Hugh.

He was fully dressed now. She had accomplished that for him, just before dawn, after she'd finished gathering his drawings and note-books into a single pile she could take with her. Around 3 A.M. she had heard him taking fast, shallow breaths and trying to rouse himself. As he'd struggled to get up, she'd taken him in her arms and felt him relax, as if he were remembering he had nothing left to do. Within the space of five minutes—sixty million miles—his breathing ceased altogether, at which moment she kissed his lips and looked out the window, fully certain, and trying to rejoice, that he was no longer in the room.

•   •   •

On Saturday morning the weather cleared and they buried his body in the Oak Hill cemetery. She stood at the freshly covered grave with Mary Costello, David Todd, and Commodore Sands, the only ones she had told. The old man appeared confused, but seemed to respond to the comforting pats of Mary's hand. When the astrologer eased him off for a stroll, David Todd nodded toward the mound of earth and made a frustrated admission to Cynthia: "I didn't really understand him."

"I did," she said, softly. "Even when he made no sense—or nothing the others would call sense—I understood him."

Fifty feet away, Mary Costello and the commodore made friends with the gravediggers, who had just made a place in the earth for Mr. Thomas Jackson, the eighty-nine-year-old currier from High Street, resident in the District since 1813. "Life ain't fair, is it?" Mary asked. "If that boy back there lived to a ripe age like that, we'd be where? All the way in nineteen-thirty-something," she guessed, removing her hand from the commodore's to do a quick count on her fingers.

After the funeral, it took the two women most of the afternoon to walk back to Third and D. Where Pennsylvania Avenue crossed Fourteenth Street, Mary Costello pointed south, toward the farrier's, and inquired as softly as she could about what Cynthia wanted done with the light machine, which Hugh had helped them wheel back onto its bed of straw just before midnight on Wednesday.

"Tell your friend to find an ironmonger who can chop it up and sell it for scrap," said Cynthia.

The astrologer couldn't help asking: "How can you sound so cross toward something that did such a bang-up job? It gave the boy his heart's desire."

"'Cross'?" replied Cynthia. "I'm nothing like that, Mary. I just don't want anyone else ever using it. Let it be scattered like the spray of a fountain."

She would sleep in Mary's back bedroom tonight, after Charles delivered them a meal in his metal box. She could not face going back to Mrs. O'Toole, who had probably given her room away for all the time she'd spent in it these last three weeks.

As they waited for Charles, she sat quietly on the window seat above the planet reader's sign and stroked a suspicious Ra. When Mary saw her staring through the glass and into the street, she asked, without thinking, "That's how you first saw him, ain't it?" It took Cynthia a moment to realize that she meant the figure of Roscoe Conkling, ten months ago, after he'd strode up the sidewalk for his reading.

"Well," said the astrologer, "I doubt he'll ever again be showin' his face here. *Or* his hand."

Cynthia said nothing for a minute or two, then looked back from the window toward Madam Costello. "Tell me the future, Mary."

It was a subject the astrologer would prefer to avoid. Thoughts of what would now happen to this girl, most of them discouraging, had dominated her mind all the way down Pennsylvania Avenue. She tried changing the subject. "What was the name of that feller at the grave today? Not the old boy; the young one."

"David Todd."

"That's right. He told me that he and Mr. Hugh were lookin' for a new planet."

"Yes, they were."

"Well, I hope he keeps lookin', and in the right place. Here's a piece of the future I *can* tell you." She got up from her chair to fetch *The Light of Egypt* from the kitchen table. "Here we go," she said, after locating the page:

"'To our esoteric system there are ten celestial bodies somewhere, namely, the Sun and nine planets. At present we have only nine in all. Where, then, is the lost one? The exacted adept alone can solve this problem. Suffice it to say that it symbolizes the missing soul within the human constitution. Pulled out of the line of march by disturbing forces, this orb becomes for a time the prey of disruptive action and ultimately lost form, and is now an array of fragments.'"

She stopped reading, noticing that Cynthia had closed her eyes.

"Go on, Mary. I'm listening."

"All right. 'The ring of planetoids lies between the orbits of Mars and Jupiter. The time will ultimately come when this orb will be recon- stituted.'" Stumbling over the long adverbs and hyphenates, Mary Costello wanted to quit, but she saw Cynthia's hand lift itself from Ra and urge, in an exhausted circular motion, that she finish reading what she'd started.

"'Until that time,'" Madam Costello concluded, "'the missing soul will seek its physical mate in vain, except in rare cases. When this day shall arrive, the Utopia of Neptune and the millennium of Saint John will begin upon Earth. May that time speedily arrive!'"

The planet reader looked up and saw that Cynthia had at last fallen asleep. She closed her book and gently took the cat from the younger woman's lap.

Across the city, in the last minutes of daylight, Mr. Todd, who *would* be looking for a new planet tonight, though in a different precinct of the heavens, made an entry in his notebook. At 1:00 P.M. this afternoon, through the Transit Circle, he had observed the disappearance of two sunspots.

EPILOGUE

MARCH 12, 1888

O utrageous!" cried Roscoe Conkling. "Forty dollars?"

The cabman tried to steady his horse; she was losing her footing in the deepening snow on lower Broadway, and he didn't care if this crazy swell became a fare or not.

"It's a real blizzard, sir," said William Sulzer, the young lawyer who came up alongside Conkling and tried calming him down while the cabman calmed his horse. "I heard a fellow at the next corner asking for fifty."

"Get along!" Conkling shouted up to the driver, before smacking the horse's rump.

"You may not find another," warned Sulzer. "I'll wager nearly every horsecar and coach in the city has stopped running." He struggled to keep a clear view of the older man, as the icy snow, more like needles than flakes, blew into his eyes.

"Damned near every *man* in the city has stopped running!" cried Conkling.

He had been furious for most of the day, ever since showing up this morning to defend an $80 million estate against some parasites trying to break the decedent's will. There he'd been in Superior Court at 9 A.M., ready to do battle for the shade of Mrs. A. T. Stewart, widow of the department store magnate, only to find that nobody else had braved the weather to get down to the courtroom. He'd spent the past eight hours at a desk in the Stewart Building, now almost invisible behind the swirling snow.

"I shall walk!" Conkling informed Sulzer.

"How far is your destination?" asked the younger man.

"Madison Square. The Hoffman House."

Sulzer attempted a low whistle, to signal discouragement, but it died in the freezing wind.

"You may accompany me, or you may wait for another thieving hack," said Conkling, whose expensively shod feet were already moving northward.

How could Sulzer say no? If he didn't freeze to death over the three-mile journey, he would be making conversation with Lord Roscoe himself, the most erect fallen politician any aspiring one could ever hope to meet.

The trick, he supposed, was to keep his head down and—except when he had to talk—his mouth closed against the icy buckshot of snow. "Fine week for the circus to be in town!" he managed to shout, before bringing his muffler back up over his lips.

No response from Conkling. Had the wind kept him from hearing? Or was the remark, in the blizzard's rage, too inane to produce any interest in a man who had for twenty years held every Congress and state convention spellbound by his flights of oratory and contempt?

It was best to stick to business. "Will you win the Stewart case, sir?"

"I should say so!" Conkling replied with a laugh, not breaking stride, his teeth glinting behind puffs of frozen breath. "If I can carry the day for Jay Gould, I can deliver justice to a widow's poor ghost."

Eighty million dollars must make the widow Stewart's poor ghost nearly as rich as the railroad baron, but who could count that high? thought Sulzer. Certainly not the thin, underclad Italian struggling, just ahead of them, to get his shovel one foot farther through the snow. He was the only other sign of life on the block in front of them. Ordinarily at this hour the lamps in the shops and offices would be multiplying themselves into a great chandelier; but today the few squares of visible light were twinkling off, one by one, the proprietors not wanting to lose another moment getting to their lodgings—which were surely, Sulzer thought, a lot closer than Madison Square.

He looked at the shuttered news kiosk, which had put on a hat of snow, and thought of the last rumors he'd heard before running into Conkling: the El switches had frozen and the sidewheelers had stopped running back and forth across the Hudson. The world was falling asleep, like Rip Van Winkle. Sulzer was so cold he could barely feel his feet, let alone the cobblestones buried inches beneath them. The whooshes of cold wind, carrying not just snow but ash from the sidewalk barrels, were pushing him into a sort of wakeful delirium. He plodded on, lifting one leg and then the other, beginning to wonder if he hadn't made Conkling up, conjured him like one of the spirits from the graveyard at Saint Paul's, which the two of them now were passing.

But Lord Roscoe was still very real and alive, setting a pace Sulzer knew he wouldn't be able to keep up for more than another hundred yards.

"Sir!" he cried toward Conkling's right shoulder, a foot ahead of his own left one. He gestured across the street to a saloon whose sign was big enough to be read through the riot of flakes and filth upon the air.

Conkling turned around, having caught the sound, though not the words. Seeing Sulzer motion toward the doors of the bar, which looked to be the only business open on the street, he yelled: "They should pour that poison into these horses!" He was managing to smile and walk backward as he bellowed toward the younger man: "It would get them moving, or put them out of their misery!" He pointed to two of the harnessed animals, confused and immobile at the curb. The effort to speak was now more than Sulzer could make, so he just struggled to catch up, wishing he'd never gotten out of bed today, let alone offered his company to this man twice his age and clearly twice his strength.

Conkling charged forward on the path he was breaking, fending off extraneous humans. He waved a beggar back into his doorway and, before she could fall on her drenched bustle, steadied a woman straining on tiptoe to catch sight of some still-distant rescuer. She didn't realize she was momentarily in the arms of the "War God of the Norsemen," but her expression of surrender showed Sulzer that Conkling still had his magnetism.

The younger man simply could not keep up, could not go another block with his face a frozen fire behind his sodden muffler. People were going to die out here tonight. This storm that had come out of nowhere was hungry for them. Escaping it, immediately, was more important than effecting contact with this other force of nature. "Mr. Conkling!" he shouted to the broad back in front of him. "Don't you think we should try for rooms here?" They had reached the Astor House, but as soon as Sulzer made the suggestion, the squinting doorman took a step out from under the canopy and shook his head from side to side. "'Haven't got a bed left, sirs. They've started renting space on the billiard tables, if you want to lie there for the night. I'm serious."

Conkling threw his head back. His loud laughter made itself heard, but he couldn't shake the icicles from his whiskers. He turned to Sulzer, whose name he had already forgotten. "Go get a spot for yourself, young man. No one's going to put *me* behind the eight ball!"

And with that, not stopping to wave, he was off, alone, block after block, for another hour, toward Union Square, the dirty needles of snow ever at him, no more interested in who he was, or used to be, than they were in the children struggling across the gutter with pails of milk and coal. "Don't touch it, you idiots!" shouted Conkling. The children had become entranced by a fallen, sizzling telegraph wire. They fell back from it at the sound of the stranger's voice—a good thing, too, for Conkling was now shaken to discover that the strength to roar another warning had suddenly left him. He was, he had to admit, exhausted, unsure how far he'd gone or how long he'd walked. He stopped at the corner, looking for a passable angle across the Square, trying to get the bearings he could never remember deserting him before. His coat was a heavy, wet ruin, his left arm sore from working to keep his hat upon his head during the long trudge. The hat was a ruin, too. He threw it into a snowbank and blinked a half dozen times, as if he might be able to wipe the maelstrom in front of his eyes into some sort of visibility.

He mustn't just stand here. He must do what he'd always done, bull ahead, ignoring all to his right and left, including a man who was staring at him, reconsidering him now that the hat was off. There had been a time when no one needed a second glance to know he was looking at the senator who kept his money sound and barred the doors of the Custom House to all the rebel-coddling reformers who thought their men could do the people's business better than the Conkling machine.

It was fine not being recognized; it was preferable, at such a moment as this, to all the fawning attentions of the past. As Conkling fought his way, much more slowly now, across the Square and into the Ladies' Mile, he tried to keep himself alert by remembering how a decade ago, in the city on his way to the state convention, he had walked this street on a hot summer day, craving anonymity. He had been shopping for a bracelet or a bottle of perfume, the kind of item he'd always made one of his clerks buy for the others, but which, that year, for her and only her, he had wanted to purchase himself, so that he could finger whatever object (a shawl, he finally decided) he would put into her hands.

Her. Even after ten years the anger could warm him in a flash; it propelled him into a quickened step for the next hundred yards—until the feeling became just one more element, like the wind and needles of snow, sapping his strength to a point where he feared he would never make it to his hotel. But he would. He would count off his steps, fifty at a time, and turn this killing journey, almost three hours long by now, into a series of smaller, possible ones, incremental ones that bit by bit would get him where he was going. Fifty steps and then fifty more and then fifty more.

By the time Madison Square appeared, like a great frozen plain, he could move with only a quarter the speed he'd had starting out. But Roscoe Conkling *would* make it across this last expanse and into the

Hoffman House, whose outline, behind the great swirlings of white and gray, he thought he could perceive. Steady on, he thought, struggling under the weight of his coat, wondering if he should rid himself of it, too. No, he would need it tomorrow morning, when all this would be a melting memory and he'd be setting off, at 8:00 sharp, for the courts.

He was falling, going down, and he braced himself for pain, but it never came: his form sank soundlessly into a cushioning drift. He was face down, and panicking, until he managed, with what felt like the last power in him, to roll over and see a band of gray sky above the two white walls he was caught between. But he could not raise himself, no matter how hard he struggled, and his shout, so much less loud than the one he'd made to the cabman three hours ago, died against the sides of this snowy coffin he had just dug for himself.

No. He would not die. He couldn't, not like this—not after a lifetime of exertions with his Indian clubs, of fanning away his colleagues' tobacco smoke, and fleeing the gluttonous mounds of chops and sauces they couldn't wait to wash down with port. He had the strength of three men, everyone had always said it, and that would see him through, even if his survival now seemed to depend on his right foot, which stuck out beyond the edge of the drift and which someone, even a dog, was bound to come along and notice. But there was no one coming, so he fought again to raise himself, reversing the struggle he had made all those years in the Senate, when it took every bit of his strength *not* to rise from his chair, not to interrupt or thrash whoever was speaking against him.

But he could not get up.

At all costs, he must keep himself warm. He tried imagining himself dry and splendid in one of his old velvet-collared cutaways. He brought his hands to his face and brushed away the beginnings of a new layer of snow that had already descended on the ice and frosted his forelock, no longer the golden one that had made the women swoon, but a good sturdy gray one that belonged to a man still only fifty-eight, and strong enough to see this through. He would be joking about it tomorrow in Superior Court.

But he was losing consciousness. He could feel it, could recognize the same delirious sensation he'd felt a half century before, when the horse had kicked up and broken his jaw. Just a little boy then. Broken his jaw. Broken it, just as he'd broken them, so many of them, Presidents even, and so many lesser breeds, so many political bodies you could tally them on that adding machine in the Stewart office.

But then he had lost his touch, failing to make the General a President once more, succeeding only in denying Blaine and Sherman the Mansion, and in putting Arthur—*Chet Arthur!*—on the ticket with Garfield. Who then went and did just as Hayes, nominating his own man instead of Roscoe Conkling's for Arthur's old job. So he had resigned from the Senate, creating the greatest storm ever, planning all the while to return in triumph once the state legislature insisted on his reappointment. But the little soldiers in Albany had had enough of him; they called his bluff and kept him out of office—until he glimpsed his redemption in fate's greatest joke of all: Garfield's killing and the ascension of Chet Arthur to the presidency of the United States. He'd gotten on the train to Washington and walked into the Mansion thinking he would now run the place as surely as he had the Custom House. And as soon as he asked Arthur to put one of their old men into the Collector's position, Chet Arthur, the President of the United States, showed him the door. In the seven years since, Roscoe Conkling had fired his rhetorical cannon in the courtrooms of New York, mastering a dozen jurors rather than six dozen senators, eyeing millions in damages instead of votes.

Twenty minutes more passed, and he could hear the whole parade of them drumming in his ears: Blaine and Kate and Evarts, and now, suddenly, again, *her,* walking down the Irishwoman's steps that other March day, clearing the humid stink that sat upon Washington like a curse.

Her. One day, at the end of the following winter, when it was all over and the boy long buried, he'd gone to her lodgings and told her that now, she must realize, was surely time for his protection and for their friendship to flourish. He had taken her in his arms, expecting, hoping, to have his face scratched before she submitted to his kisses. Instead, he'd heard only her laughter, a sound more final, and hateful, than that of any door he would ever hear slammed against him.

Her. The mere pronoun was sufficient to call up one last lucid surge in him, enough anger and strength for him to roll back over on his stomach and push his arms down into the snow and, by God, *get up,* which he did, up and out of the drift, to stagger the rest of the way across the Square, the snow still coming at him, the Sun unimaginably distant and forever gone, farther away than the moons she'd tried to show him through the telescope that night.

Hoffman House. Where was the sign? After all this, did he have the wrong building?

"Where am I?" he shouted to the bellman, who'd come out to the snow-covered steps.

"The New York Club, sir."

"Twenty-fifth Street?"

"Yes, sir."

"Well, I want the Hoffman House!"

"Where have you come from, sir?"

"From Wall Street. On foot."

"Good God!" cried the bellman, dragging in the form of Roscoe Conkling, which had just collapsed and was soon to breathe no more.

•   •   •

She watched the snow pile up on the windowsill. Looking out, she could almost imagine it was forty years ago in Laconia. Around herself she tightened her shawl—its appliquéd stars long ago plucked off.

Despite the weather, the Pension Building had refused to close early, and she had sat until day's end at her typewriter, addressing envelopes for checks and occasionally looking up to see the flakes come down outside. The new girl next to her marveled at the brain-

power of the men who in another part of the building actually calculated these disbursements, each number different from the next. As
always, when such a remark was made, she had nodded her agreement.

She had left the Observatory six months after he died, because she
could no longer stand to be around it, and because she realized that she
was getting sick herself. It had now been ages since she'd been west of
Lafayette Square, but the astronomers, twelve years later, were still
where they had always been. Some time ago she had read about the
purchase of a farm northwest of the city, off Tenallytown Road, and
had even lately heard rumors that construction of a new Observatory
was soon, at last, to commence there. Admiral Rodgers had died in '82,
of malaria that had turned into Bright's disease. She didn't know the
name of the current superintendent, but now, like everyone else, she
knew that malaria was borne by mosquitoes.

The Pension Building's ventilation was excellent—some of the
windows even had screens—and she was comfortable entering it each
morning, crossing under the frieze of tiny, endlessly tramping soldiers.
She felt at home with the superannuated and, especially, the dead—all
those names, more of them each year, crossed from the rolls. They
were easier company for her mind than the living. Mary Costello had
died two years ago, but she sometimes still enjoyed thinking of her.

Mr. Todd had sent Christmas letters for several years, telling her
such news as his marriage to Mabel Loomis and, eventually, his departure from the Observatory for Amherst College—in good health, he
assured her. She still saw Simon Newcomb, grayer and more stout,
engraved in the magazines. And she sometimes spotted Professor
Harkness and Mr. Harrison, from a distance, on the street, the first
quite straight and the latter by now badly stooped.

She opened the window several inches, wincing against the cold
air. Brushing snow from a length of the ledge, she located the wrapped
bit of cheese she had set out the other day. After undoing the paper,
she took out a box of crackers from beneath the bed. Eating upstairs
was strictly forbidden here at Mrs. Cleary's on Sixth Street, but she
had so far managed to stay out of trouble. Also from under the bed,

inside a hatbox, she pulled out two small bottles, one of rum, and the other Schenck's Pulmonic Syrup, which she knew she continued to buy more for its alcohol content than any prophylactic properties. She would drink from both tonight, but she never worried about waking up. It was rare that she could stay asleep past five.

She supposed she would like two more years, no more than that. D'Arrest's comet would be back for the second time before then. One night in '83, during hours of public viewing, she had gone to the Observatory, quite unrecognized, to see it through the Great Equatorial. She would see it once more, and that would be enough.

It was terribly cold tonight, and it took her several minutes to realize she hadn't closed the window after retrieving the cheese. She did that now, and then finished off the crackers with some rum. While she sipped, she argued with herself about whether to indulge a particular pleasure that up to now she had permitted herself only once or twice a year, most recently on his birthday. She mustn't overdo it, lest she wear out the pleasure and the little metal sheet, but she was especially lonely tonight, and the temptation was more than she could withstand.

So she crossed the room to her shelf of books, taking up the biography of Franklin Pierce that Mary Costello had returned to her once the War God was gone from both their lives. Pressed between the pages, she found his Harvard photograph; M. Trouvelot's drawing of herself; and the folded Gauss sketches, still bearing the tack-holes where they'd been fixed to the walls on High Street. What she wanted, however, was the piece of foil, even thinner than the sketches' paper. She extracted this latter item with great care and took it over to the apparatus Mr. Todd had managed to acquire, at her entreaty, a year before he left the District: a little machine nearing obsolescence even then and thought by now, by most, to be quite useless. Her fingers ached with the cold and her arthritis, but she managed, once she placed the metal wafer on the cylinder, to turn the crank. As soon as she placed the stylus onto the foil, she looked out the window and toward a star—which one, she did not know. She closed her eyes in time to hear him say: *Darling! I'm here!*

AUTHOR'S NOTE AND ACKNOWLEDGMENTS

For help and encouragement with this book I am especially grateful to Jan K. Herman, Historian of the navy's Bureau of Medicine and Surgery, which is today housed in the Old Naval Observatory in Washington. I thank Mr. Herman for his own history of the site *(A Hilltop in Foggy Bottom)* and for personally guiding me through the rooms and domes where Asaph Hall and Simon Newcomb and Admiral Rodgers once worked; and where Hugh Allison and Cynthia May never did.

I am also much indebted to Steve Dick of the U.S. Naval Observatory's Office of History and Public Affairs. I urge readers interested in the actual story of the Martian moons' discovery and the Observatory's removal from Foggy Bottom to keep an eye out for Mr. Dick's forthcoming history of the institution.

I would like to repeat, if I may, a cautionary word I gave in two previous novels of mine: "Nouns always trump adjectives, and in the phrase 'historical fiction' it is important to remember which of the two words is which." In *Two Moons,* even while attempting to get dozens of things right, I have deliberately gotten more than a few quite wrong—through distortion or outright invention. I have been largely faithful to Roscoe Conkling's public life, and to what I believe was the general tenor of his private one; for his particular adventure with the imaginary Cynthia May, only I, of course, can claim responsibility—and I confess to walking these days at a fast new clip past the War God's statue in Madison Square Park.

For archival help I would like to thank Frederick W. Bauman, Jr. (Library of Congress); Richard W. Peuser (National Archives); Brenda G. Corbin and Gregory A. Shelton (U.S. Naval Observatory Library); Richard Fraser (New-York Historical Society); Sam Streit and Mary-Jo Kline (Brown University Library); and William Massa (Yale University Library).

The staff of the General Society of Mechanics and Tradesmen's Library, on West Forty-fourth Street in New York City, always seem to be holding in reserve any arcane book I need, no matter how long it takes me to show up: the last "due date" on Commodore Sands's auto-biography, before I charged it out in 1996, was December 11, 1912. From the General Society's stacks came the basis for my version of the Mangin projector, illustrated in *The Electric Light: Its History, Production and Applications* (New York, 1884). I apologize to the librarians for having allowed Alfred R. Conkling's *Life and Letters* (1889) of his uncle Roscoe to fall apart in my hands.

Among the scores of contemporary books that have proved important to this one, I would like to make special mention of four: Thomas C. Reeves's *Gentleman Boss: The Life of Chester Alan Arthur* (Alfred A. Knopf, 1975); David M. Jordan's *Roscoe Conkling of New York* (Cornell University Press, 1971); Mary Mitchell's *Chronicles of Georgetown Life* (1986); and Mary Cable's *The Blizzard of '88* (Atheneum, 1988).

I'm grateful to Dr. Santina Siena for help with nineteenth-century obstetrics, and to Dr. Barry Goldstein for assistance with trigonometry.

•   •   •

I owe many thanks to Dan Frank, my editor, who has made the last five years of my writing life the most pleasurable I've known.

Andrea Barrett provided wisdom, books (including George B. Wood's 1855 *Treatise on the Practice of Medicine*), and chapter-by-chapter readings as shrewd as they were gentle; she has my thanks and love.

I'm grateful to my agent, Mary Evans, and her associate Tanya McKinnon; to my sharp-eyed, faithful readers Lucy Kaylin and Frances Kiernan; and to Gore Vidal, *il miglior fabbro,* for conversation about historical fiction.

I'm also grateful—more than ever—to Bill Bodenschatz.

Westport, Connecticut
June 17, 1999

ALSO BY
THOMAS MALLON

WATERGATE

For all the monumental documentation that Watergate gen-
erated—uncountable volumes of committee records, court
transcripts, and memoirs—it falls to a novelist to recon-
struct some of the scandal's greatest mysteries (who did
erase those eighteen-and-a-half minutes of tape?) and to
see this gaudy American catastrophe in its human entirety.
In *Watergate*, Thomas Mallon conveys the drama and high
comedy of the Nixon presidency through the urgent per-
spectives of seven characters we only thought we knew.
Mallon achieves with *Watergate* a scope and historical intimacy that surpasses even what he attained in his previous
novels, and turns a "third-rate burglary" into a tumultuous, first-rate entertainment.

Fiction/Literature

HENRY AND CLARA

On the evening of Good Friday, 1865, Henry Rathbone
and Clara Harris joined the Lincolns in the Presidential
box at Ford's Theater, becoming eyewitnesses to one of the
great tragedies of American history. In this riveting novel,
Thomas Mallon re-creates the unusual love story of this
young engaged couple whose fateful encounter with history
profoundly affects the remainder of their lives. Lincoln's
assassination is only one part of the remarkable life they
share, a dramatic tale of passion, scandal, heroism, murder, and madness, all based on Mallon's deep research
into the fascinating history of the Rathbone and Harris
families. *Henry and Clara* not only tells the astonishing
story of its title figures; it also illuminates the culture of
nineteenth-century Victorian America: a rigid society barely concealing the suppressed impulses and undercurrents
that only grew stronger as the century progressed.

Fiction/Literature

DEWEY DEFEATS TRUMAN

A masterful retelling of a legend and famous headline of modern American history—Harry Truman's upset victory over Thomas E. Dewey in the 1948 presidential election. Set in Dewey's hometown of Owosso, Michigan, this is the captivating story of a local love triangle that mirrors the national election contest. As the voters must decide between the candidates, so must Anne Macmurray choose between two suitors: an ardent United Auto Workers organizer and his polar opposite, a wealthy young Republican lawyer who's running for the state senate. Weaving a tapestry of small-town secrets, the people of Owosso ready themselves for the fame that is bound to shower down upon them after Dewey's "sure thing" victory. But as the novel—and history—move toward election night, we watch the townspeople, along with Anne and her suitors, have their fates rearranged in a climax filled with suspense, chagrin, and unexpected joy.

Fiction/Literature

YOURS EVER
People and Their Letters

A delightful investigation of the art of letter writing, *Yours Ever* explores masterpieces dispatched through the ages by messenger, postal service, and BlackBerry. Here are Madame de Sévigné's devastatingly sharp reports from the French court, F. Scott Fitzgerald's tormented advice to his young daughter, the casually brilliant musings of Flannery O'Connor, the lustful boastings of Lord Byron, and the prison cries of Sacco and Vanzetti, all accompanied by Thomas Mallon's own insightful commentary. From battlefield confessions to suicide notes, fan letters to hate mail, *Yours Ever* is an exuberant reintroduction to a vast and entertaining literature—a book that will help to revive, in the digital age, this glorious lost art.

Literary Collections